Acclaim for Cath[...]

'It's impossible not to fall in love with Cathy Bramley's **feel-good** stories'
Sunday Express

'Heartwarming and positive . . . **will leave you with a lovely cosy glow**'
My Weekly

'A **fun**, feel-good read'
Good Housekeeping

'A **gorgeous** story to lose yourself in'
Bookish Bits

'As **comforting** as hot tea and toast made on the Aga!'
Veronica Henry

'Thoroughly **enjoyable**'
U Magazine

'Such a **charming**, feel-good story'
Carole's Books

'This book **ticks all the boxes**'
Heat

'Reading a Cathy Bramley book for me is like coming home from a day out, closing the curtains, putting on your PJs and settling down with a huge sigh of relief! Her books are **full of warmth, love and compassion** and they are completely adorable'
Kim the Bookworm

'Cathy Bramley has quickly catapulted herself into my list of favourite authors . . . *Wickham Hall* is a **heartflutteringly lovely and laugh-out-loud** story wrapped up in a stunning package'
Page to Stage Reviews

'Do you know that feeling that you love a story and its characters and setting so much, **you just never want the book to end**? That's exactly what *Wickham Hall* did to me'
A Spoonful of Happy Endings

Cathy would love to hear from you! Find her on:

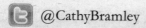 facebook.com/CathyBramleyAuthor

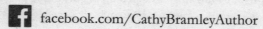 @CathyBramley

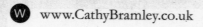 www.CathyBramley.co.uk

White Lies & Wishes

Cathy Bramley

CORGI BOOKS

TRANSWORLD PUBLISHERS
61–63 Uxbridge Road, London W5 5SA
www.penguin.co.uk

Transworld is part of the Penguin Random House group of companies whose
addresses can be found at global.penguinrandomhouse.com

First published in Great Britain in 2017 by Corgi Books
an imprint of Transworld Publishers

A CIP catalogue record for this book
is available from the British Library.

ISBN
9780552171557

Typeset in 11.5/13pt Garamond MT by Jouve (UK), Milton Keynes.
Printed and bound in Great Britain by Clays Ltd, Bungay, Suffolk.

Penguin Random House is committed to a sustainable future for our business, our readers
and our planet. This book is made from Forest Stewardship Council® certified paper.

1 3 5 7 9 10 8 6 4 2

I dedicate this book to my brother, Andy Turner,
for always playing the part of the slave in our shows

Chapter 1

It was the last Monday in January. 'Blue Monday', according to the newspapers. The most miserable day of the year. The sky was miserable, too: charcoal clouds scudded angrily over the rooftops and a mean wind rattled at window frames and snapped weak branches from trees.

How apt, thought Jo, rubbing her hands together for warmth.

Frédéric Lafleur's funeral had already cast a shadow over the day but now, at three o'clock, the thin light was fading from the afternoon and the little village of Woodby in rural Nottinghamshire was descending into gloom. Jo shuddered, dragged her gaze away from the steamed-up window of the village hall and blinked away tears that had been gathering since before the service.

Coffee. She needed coffee. It would warm her up and give her something to do. She pushed her way through the crowd towards the refreshments and was vaguely aware of a petite young woman with a cloud of pretty red curls hopping up and down, trying to hang a brightly coloured coat on a peg out of reach.

The room was muggy and Jo felt hot and restricted in her tight black skirt suit. She undid the button of her jacket and grimaced at the noise around her. The conversation, at first a respectful whisper, had risen to a more sociable hum as the mourners, with pinched faces and frozen fingers, thawed over tea and sandwiches.

A searing flash of fury gripped her and she had an urge to scream.

For God's sake, it's not a bloody party.

She took a deep breath and reminded herself that this was how people dealt with death in England; a nice cup of tea and a muted chuckle over shared memories. The hall was packed; tons of people had come to see him off, there was bound to be noise. Besides, Fréd had been a noisy bugger; he'd have hated a quiet wake.

She braced herself as Abi stumbled blindly into her arms.

'Hello, you,' said Jo, returning the hug.

Abi had lost so much weight this past year; Jo could feel every bone in her spine.

If anyone were to ask Jo how she was, she would probably smile through gritted teeth and reply that she was fine. She wasn't, though. Jo was angry. So furious, in fact, that she wanted to punch something or someone really hard. God, probably.

This was all wrong. Funerals were for old people. Abi and Fréd were still young. Or *was*, in Fréd's case. They should be popping out more babies left, right and centre, enjoying life, planning for their future. Fréd should be here, arm draped round his beautiful wife, knocking back the red wine and making jokes about English food.

Jo could feel her breath rattling against her ribcage, her throat burning with the effort of keeping her own emotions in check. She kissed Abi's hair and released her, dabbing the tears from her friend's face with a tissue that had seen better days. What do you say to your thirty-four-year-old friend who has just lost her husband to cancer?

'Thanks for doing the reading in French, Jo,' Abi murmured.

'Yeah, cheers for that,' said Jo, twisting her mouth into a smile. 'As if I wasn't stressed enough, you make me wheel out my rusty old French.'

At least now the service was over she could start to breathe normally again.

'It was brilliant; you still sound fluent.' Abi swallowed.

Jo shook her head. Abi was amazing, even now she managed to see beyond her own pain. 'Old Maman Lafleur didn't think so, she was giving me daggers.'

Abi winced. 'Sorry about my mother-in-law, I think she still blames you for introducing us at uni. If it's any consolation, she looks at me like that all the time.'

'Poor you.' Jo smiled in sympathy. Her eyes roamed the room until she located Fréd's parents queuing for food. 'Fréd's dad Henri is lovely, though. Handsome devil. Obviously where Fréd got his looks from.'

Abi's face crumpled.

Shit, wrong thing to say. Jo pulled her friend close again, cursing her own stupidity, as Abi cried softly into her neck. At the buffet table the French relatives were examining a pork pie as if it were a suspicious parcel, curiosity and distrust on their faces. Henri picked up a slice, sniffed it, then nibbled the edge. Showing every bit of his Gallic origins, he shrugged and pulled the corners of his mouth down. The others shook their heads and moved along.

Abi pulled away and rubbed her face dry with the back of her hands. 'Anyway, it meant a lot to me. You read at our wedding and Fréd would have liked the poem. I miss hearing his voice, hearing him swear in French.'

They looked at each other and shared a smile; Fréd had been bilingual but he always swore in French.

Jo nodded. A sudden longing for the day to end, to leave all this sadness behind, sent guilty shivers through her body. She ran a hand through her short, blonde hair distractedly. At times like these it was so much easier being single – no ties, none of this heartache.

Abi looked round the hall. 'I suppose I'd better go and mingle.'

Jo gripped her hands. 'Bugger them. You do exactly as

you like. People don't expect you to make polite conversation. Get yourself a coffee and let them come to you. And make sure you eat something.'

Abi nodded half-heartedly. 'What about you?'

Jo wrinkled her nose and pulled a single, slightly bent cigarette out of her bag. 'Not hungry. I'm going out for a fag.'

Abi frowned. 'Thought you'd given up?'

Jo shook her head, gave Abi a swift kiss and wiped away a smear of red lipstick on her cheek with her thumb. 'Not today.'

Carrie set down the heavy teapot, shook out her arm and wiped the sheen of perspiration from her brow. It was going well so far. Perhaps 'well' was the wrong word under the circumstances.

She bit her lip, flushing in case people could hear her thoughts. What she meant was that everyone had had a hot drink, and no one had asked for something she didn't have. In theory, they could help themselves from now on. She supposed she would have to come out from behind the table at some point. But not yet. She felt safer here, less conspicuous. Or at least as inconspicuous as someone of her size could ever be.

Still, she had been really good today. She'd only had one sausage roll all afternoon, even though her mouth was watering and her stomach wouldn't stop rumbling. Her eyes scanned the trestle table. There had been plenty of food in the end; she needn't have worried. Not very French, though, unless you counted vol-au-vents. And quiche, maybe. That sounded French. Doing the catering on her own had been hard work, but it had been the least she could do for poor Abi, plus, if she was honest with herself, she had enjoyed being busy, feeling useful for once. Was that really self-centred?

A blonde middle-aged woman in a long navy raincoat brought her teacup over for a refill.

'Lovely spread, Carrie.'

'Oh gosh, Linda. Thank you.' Carrie blushed and looked down shyly, noticing crumbs on her chest. *How did they get there?*

'Did you do the altar flowers too?'

She nodded. 'Not bad for supermarket flowers, are they?'

'Goodness!' Linda pulled the corners of her mouth down in surprise. 'No, not bad at all.'

Carrie could have kicked herself. Why did she always make a joke of things? Of course she had done the flowers. She had been to the wholesalers at five this morning to collect the blooms. Long-stemmed roses, masses of them: white for youth, red for courage and pink for love. Not chrysanthemums. She shuddered. She hated them: the symbol of death.

Linda leaned forward and lowered her voice to a whisper. 'I think you've got jam on your chin.'

'Oh? Thanks.'

How did that get there?

Carrie was still scrubbing at her face with a napkin as Fréd's mother approached the table and handed Carrie her paper plate.

'Thank you,' said the elegant Frenchwoman, ashen-faced and stooped under the weight of her grief.

Carrie's heart sank as she took in the barely touched food. Fréd's mum had hated it. She should have listened to Alex, perhaps she should never have offered to do this at all; her cooking wasn't up to catering standard.

'I'm so sorry. For your loss. And for the food,' she stammered.

Madame Lafleur didn't smile, but nodded and swept away to rejoin her husband.

Carrie regarded the remains of the buffet with dismay. It struck her as rather macabre now; chicken drumsticks, sandwiches, cake . . . like some sort of sick joke. It looked like the sort of food you'd do for a birthday party, or a wedding anniversary.

Strange how you had a wedding breakfast but a funeral tea. Or was it? If your whole life were to be crammed into one day, you'd want your wedding in the morning, save the funeral for the end of the day.

But some people didn't make it to the end of the day, did they? And some had their lives taken before they had even begun. A massive lump threatened to block her throat.

Today is not about you, Carrie Radley.

She shook her head to banish the memories, and without a thought of the calories she selected the largest slice of quiche and took a mouthful.

Oh my Lord! She had died and woken up in savoury pie heaven.

She took a second bite. The salty bacon, crumbly pastry and creamy custard disappeared in seconds.

She closed her eyes and then snapped them open, automatically checking to see where her husband was. He was easy to spot; Alex was one of the tallest men here. And the most handsome. As she brushed more crumbs from her bosom, he looked over and caught her eye.

'All right?' he mouthed.

She nodded. Damn. She felt guilty enough for eating without him catching her raiding the buffet. She couldn't stick to her diet today. Today she was too het up.

Patches of sweat prickled under her arms and her face felt hot, it would be as red as a beetroot, she just knew it. Her dark hair would be a mess too; the steam from the hot-water urn would have turned it to frizz. Fresh air was called for, perhaps with a snack. She grabbed a couple of chicken drumsticks and made for the door to the car park.

After eventually managing to hang her coat up on a peg that was ridiculously high, Sarah had stayed in the corner of the village hall waiting for her blushing face to return to a more normal colour. She pressed a hand to her cheek – still warm – and groaned inwardly. That was possibly one of her worst foot-in-mouth fiascos ever: 'I'd kill my husband if he did that,' Sarah had said, trying to make conversation with two women who were moaning about their other halves. Only to find Abi standing right beside her. Everyone had glared at her, Abi had burst into tears and run off and now Sarah felt like a social outcast, like a rabbit with MixyMcwhatsit.

She glanced at her nails for something to do and noticed that she had burst a button on her emerald-green blouse. *Great.* That would just about top it off if she flashed her boobs at Fréd's funeral. She was never going to make any friends in the village at this rate.

Had anyone seen? She whipped her head round to check. No, thank goodness. Shame Dave wasn't here to appreciate a peek at her bra. Not that it was a racy number; feeding bras, she had learned, were built for smooth operations, not to make the wearer feel the least bit alluring.

It was nerves; that was what she put her blabby mouth down to. She was normally quite comfortable in other people's company, but today she felt awkward and isolated and conscious that she really needed to be in two places at once.

Story of my life these days.

Supporting Abi and showing respect for Fréd was the 'good neighbour' thing to do, she told herself firmly, pushing aside the fact that she had inadvertently made Abi cry. But Sarah couldn't help remembering her boss Eleanor's sucked-in cheeks when she had asked for the time off. She'd only been back at the accountancy firm since the start of January. If Eleanor had had her way, she'd have come back in December. As it was she still felt like she'd cut her maternity leave short. Today was a massive day for the company — Sarah understood that — a big meeting with a potential new client. She sighed, twirled a lock of red hair round her finger and looked round for any familiar faces.

The funeral was just such bad timing.

NO! No, no! She didn't mean it! That made her sound like a monster! She almost gasped aloud with shame, took a deep breath and rearranged her thoughts. But try as she might she couldn't stop thinking about work.

Finch and Partners' new golden boy, Ben, would probably be given that client to manage now, even though Sarah had spent the last four weeks doing all the preliminary work. And she needed a biggie like that if she was going to make partner this year. At this rate Ben would be promoted before her, even though he had only been there five minutes and wasn't even thirty. But instead of furthering her career, she was standing in a village hall like a lemon, in a shirt that was still far too tight, with no one to talk to.

But she was doing the right thing. Definitely. Very neighbourly.

Food. That would give her something to do. Sarah approached the buffet table and picked up a paper plate. Her hand hovered over the cheese sandwiches as an idea occurred to her. She chewed on her lip and mulled it over. What if she jumped into the car now? She could make it back to the office before the new client left, and at least say hello. Stake her claim before Ben got in there first.

But what about Zac? Her stomach flipped. She had promised to get home early to feed him and when was the last time she had done that on a Monday? Time with her six-month-old baby was so precious, early finishes so rare. Her heart swelled with love for her darling little boy.

Sod the office for once. She'd stay here. She plonked a sandwich on her plate. Decision made.

There were about a hundred people here, she reckoned, as she slipped a slice of vegetable quiche on to her plate. Black, black, black. Why did everyone insist on wearing black at a funeral? Sarah didn't even own anything black. She liked happy colours. Her boss had once said that she would look more at home in the circus than in the boardroom. She'd thought it was a compliment at first until she had noticed two of the junior accountants sniggering.

She might as well try to meet people while she was here, assuming she could avoid any more social gaffes. She and Dave were still new to Woodby and with one thing and another – short winter days and dark nights, Zac arriving early and a new cottage needing a lot of attention – she hadn't made any proper friends yet. Except Abi.

Sarah felt the heat rise to her cheeks. How selfish to be worrying about her own trivial work issues with everything that poor Abi was going through.

There was no one manning the teapot so Sarah helped herself. She would drink this and then go and apologize to Abi for her faux pas earlier. She scanned the room but couldn't see where she was. She'd spotted her a few minutes ago hugging the elegant platinum-blonde woman who had done the French reading in church. Sarah recalled the woman's immaculate suit, endless slim legs and flat stomach and ran a hand through her own corkscrew curls and got a finger stuck in a knot. God, she was a scruff-bag, there never seemed to be enough time to see to her own appearance these days.

A group of women of about her age was gathered at the stage end of the hall. One of them had even brought her baby, for heaven's sake! She wouldn't dream of exposing Zac to such misery. He could be scarred for life. A few of the faces were familiar from the mother and baby group and her heart sank. She had only managed to go a couple of times and although they'd been friendly at first, they had all stared at her like she had two heads when she announced that she was going back to work full time even though Zac was only tiny. Still, no harm in trying again. She attempted her best friendly smile and began to cross the hall.

At that moment, the baby started to wail. Oh no! Sarah cringed and pressed an arm to her chest.

Too late. It was as if she had pulled the toggle on an

emergency life vest. She only had to hear a baby cry, even if it wasn't Zac, and her boobs inflated, ready for action. She felt warmth flood her bra and hardly dared glance down. The sensation was ten times worse than needing a wee. She normally expressed milk at lunchtime if she wasn't with Zac, but with the funeral service starting at one o'clock, somehow she had got out of sync.

Sarah abandoned her plate and hurried towards the ladies' toilets, praying that her painful personal problem wasn't visible.

She barged through the door feeling like she had two live hand grenades stuffed down her bra, but the only cubicle was taken and just as she contemplated expressing over the basin, an elderly lady entered. Sarah panicked and dashed from the toilets. The front of her blouse was definitely wet and the desire to relieve the pressure unbearable. With burning cheeks, she ran from the hall and into the car park. Heavy clouds dulled the sky and the wind took her breath away. She shivered but there was no time to go back for her coat; if she didn't do something about this in the next five seconds, she was going to explode.

She dived round the corner of the building, out of sight, to a narrow sheltered pathway bordered with shrubs. She yanked up her blouse, ripping off a button in the process, and then in a practised manoeuvre, unhooked the bra cups and squeezed both breasts.

'Ahhh!' *Thank God.* She let her head fall back, closed her eyes and exhaled deeply. Relief as two jets of warm milk squirted over the pyracantha.

It took Sarah a few seconds to detect the smell of cigarette smoke. A prickle of mortification crept across her scalp and down her back. She opened her eyes and looked over her right shoulder. Two women were staring at her, open-mouthed.

Sarah swallowed a groan. Well, that had to be a new personal best of total humiliation. They didn't tell you about

16

this in the baby manuals. The look on their faces. She didn't know whether to laugh or cry, but she certainly couldn't stop yet.

'Bloody hell,' said Abi's blonde friend, taking a long pull on her cigarette.

'Should I call an ambulance?' said the other woman, wiping her mouth with the back of her hand.

'No, no, I'm fine, nearly finished.'

That short burst had eased the pressure. It would do until she got home. Sarah swiftly tucked herself back in and turned to face her audience.

Jo flicked ash into the shrubbery. She should probably look away but she was transfixed. She had never really given much thought to the practicalities of motherhood. Does everyone have to do that ... that squeezing thing? A moment's peace to get herself together with a crafty ciggie, that was all she had needed, but she had already been joined by the pretty plump buffet girl with her hands full of chicken drumsticks. And now this – the tiny human milking machine. She wondered where the baby was. Her thoughts flashed briefly to Abi having to bring up little Tom on her own. Poor love. For the second time, Jo's commitment-free lifestyle looked quite appealing.

The woman tugged the lapels of her green velvet jacket across her chest, folded her arms and smiled. She reminded Jo of a curly-haired Kylie Minogue, only with bigger boobs. For someone who had just performed a full-frontal flash at strangers at a funeral wake, she seemed terribly calm.

'Any other party tricks?' said Jo with a grin, blowing smoke sharply out of the side of her mouth.

The woman shrugged. 'There's this thing I do with ping-pong balls, but not usually at funerals.'

Jo snorted with laughter. She dropped her cigarette to the floor, ground it out with the pointy toe of her shoe and picked it back up. She scouted round for a bin.

'Here.' The buffet girl stepped forward and held out her napkin. Jo dropped the butt on top of a pile of chicken bones.

'Thanks. I'm Jo, by the way.'

'Carrie.' She smiled shyly. 'Pleased to meet you.'

'Sarah Hudson,' said the one with the boobs, grimacing. 'Look, I'm really sorry about that; I thought I was on my own.'

'We all did,' said Carrie, tucking the napkin behind her back.

Even in this light Jo could see how embarrassed Carrie was. She wouldn't even meet their eyes.

'Sarah, you're shivering,' added Carrie. 'Let's go in and have a hot drink.'

Sarah nodded. 'Good plan.'

'No milk for me,' said Jo.

There were a few funny looks, Jo noticed, as the three women re-entered the hall together. Probably surprised at the sound of their laughter. The other two didn't seem aware of the attention: Sarah was occupied with preventing her cleavage from making another appearance and Carrie was busy foisting tea and cake on anyone who moved. According to Carrie, Jo needed fattening up a bit, and as Sarah was breastfeeding, she had to keep her strength up. Carrie wasn't the greatest advertisement for more cake, thought Jo, shaking her head to decline the offer of a slice of Battenberg.

Jo's gaze did a quick once-over of the room to check if Abi was OK and spotted her deep in conversation with a group of women. She seemed fine, considering. Jo accepted a cup of tea from Carrie and smirked at her blushing face as the rather delicious vicar joined their group.

'Are you friends of the family?' he asked, smiling round at them.

Jo watched with amusement as Carrie took his empty

18

cup and, with a shaky hand, poured a fresh one. Jo had heard about this new vicar from Abi. Apparently he held most of the village in thrall. He could only be in his thirties, he drove a Lotus and had brought a whole new congregation into church – predominantly female. He also had the most amazing eyelashes. What was the dating protocol with vicars, she wondered. She'd never had a vicar.

'Yeah, we're bosom buddies,' said Jo.

Sarah smothered a laugh, momentarily releasing the front of her blouse to cover her mouth. Jo noticed the vicar clap an eyeful of bra before looking Sarah in the eye. 'I've seen you in the village, but we haven't been introduced,' he said.

'Vicar, you naughty boy, she's married,' said Jo huskily.

Carrie's eyes widened. Jo wasn't bothered. A good-looking man was a good-looking man, man of the cloth or not.

The vicar choked on his tea and Carrie handed him a napkin.

'I'm Sarah Hudson,' replied Sarah, struggling to keep a straight face. 'A friend. I live in the village.'

'Ah yes, you're Dave's wife. You've got a baby boy, haven't you? Planning on having him christened?'

Sarah's eyes widened. 'Oh, you've met Dave? Um, we haven't really discussed it yet.'

'My favourite thing, christenings — more fun than weddings, even. Are you married?' he asked Jo.

'Good God, no!' Jo leaned in towards him with a wink. 'I prefer dirty weekends to dirty socks. Much more fun.'

The vicar opened his mouth to speak and then closed it again. Carrie made a faint high-pitched squeak and tried to refill his cup a second time. 'More tea?'

He shook his head and with darting eyes managed to make eye contact with someone across the room.

'I should, er . . . circulate. By the way, Mrs Radley, delicious food.'

He smiled bravely and moved away. The women watched him and shared a look of appreciation.

'Delicious *bum*,' muttered Jo, whistling under her breath.

'Did you do all this, then?' Sarah asked, pointing at the buffet table.

Carrie nodded. 'It was the least I could do. Poor Abi.'

'You're a caterer?' asked Jo, dragging her eyes away from the vicar's rear.

Carrie blushed. 'Goodness, no! I'm just – just a house-wife. And it's only a few sandwiches.'

If Jo had been in charge of the food, it would have been a job lot from Marks & Spencer. This amount of homemade stuff must have taken hours. Jo opened her mouth to object, but Carrie jumped back in.

'What do you both do?' she asked.

'Apart from being wife to Dave and mummy to Zac, I'm an accountant,' said Sarah. 'I work in the city centre, corporate mostly. Don't say it, I know – boring.'

Jo raised a perfectly arched eyebrow. 'After that floor show outside? I don't think so.'

'Not full-time, though, surely?' said Carrie. 'With a baby?'

'Yes, what's wrong with that?' Sarah glared at her. 'My job is very important to me and the company was desperate to have me back. Do you have children?'

Carrie's face flamed. 'No, I—' she stuttered.

'And I run a small family business,' said Jo, changing the subject rapidly as Carrie shrank under the force of Sarah's stare. 'Badly, most of the time. And I'm married to it; till death do us part.' She clenched her jaw, cross with herself for saying something so crass at a funeral. 'How do you both know Abi and Fréd?'

'We moved to Woodby last year, I didn't really know Fréd but I thought I should come to support Abi,' said Sarah.

'And my husband is the General Manager at Cavendish Hall, where Frédéric was head chef,' said Carrie.

'And *you* obviously have some French connection,' said Sarah. 'That reading you did was amazing.'

Jo shrugged and swallowed her tea. 'I did French as part of my degree. I spent a year in Paris, got to know Fréd. Abi came out to stay with me for a holiday and I introduced them. *Un coup de foudre,* as they say.'

Carrie shook her head slowly, her eyes looking moist. 'Such a lovely couple. So unfair. To have your life cut short like that. And that beautiful little boy.'

Jo's heart grew heavy again and she felt guilty for enjoying the last half-hour. 'I don't know how Abi's going to cope once the funeral's over. She's been focusing on that to get her through so far. I'll come over when I can, but I'm based in Northampton.'

'I've seen her a couple of times to sort out the arrangements,' said Carrie. 'But I haven't wanted to intrude. I can certainly pop in now and again.'

Jo smiled her thanks.

'I know it's a cliché,' said Sarah, with a sigh, 'but you've got to make each day count. Cherish every moment.'

'*Carpe diem,*' Carrie agreed.

Jo looked round at the hall; some of the mourners had gone now. Someone had brought Abi's son Tom along and he was sitting on his granddad's knee, bouncing up and down and giggling. With his dark wavy hair, he was the image of his father. Jo wondered what was going through Henri's mind. Probably looking at Tom and remembering Frédéric as a boy. It must be heartbreaking to lose a child, at any age, even if he was a grown man. *Another good reason not to have kids.* If she told herself this often enough, she might even start to believe it. She shuddered and tuned back into the conversation.

'A bucket list. A list of things you'd like to do before it's too late, like in that film with Jack Nicholson and Morgan Freeman? *The Bucket List,*' Carrie was saying to Sarah.

'I've seen that one,' said Jo. 'They're both terminally ill and decide to do a load of mad things before they die.'

'Exactly. Perhaps everyone should have a bucket list? So when you go, you'll at least have done *some* of the things you always wanted to do,' said Carrie ruefully.

Jo tried to read Carrie's expression; there was something behind that shy smile, as if she had a whole list of regrets. Mind you, that probably applied to everyone.

She picked a piece of fluff off her black wool jacket. 'Fréd's dream was to open his own restaurant. He was waiting for the right moment. And now . . .' She swallowed a lump in her throat.

'We could . . . Why don't we . . . ? Oh, nothing,' said Carrie, stirring her tea roughly. 'Ignore me.'

'Go on,' said Jo.

Carrie bit her lip. 'We could perhaps start doing the things we want to do. Make a list together. We can all add stuff to the list and tick them off when we've done them!'

'Together?' Jo gave a half-laugh. 'We've only just met.'

'And I've got a new baby, I can't start skydiving or jetting off to Timbuktu,' Sarah pointed out.

'It's probably a stupid idea. You're both right.' Carrie blushed and Jo felt sorry for her.

Her heart twisted suddenly. There was something in what Carrie said; perhaps she should start doing things she really wanted to do instead of spending nearly all her waking hours worrying about the business. No one knew how long they'd really got and she had to take something from losing Fréd so young. This could be the push she needed to live a little. She held Carrie's gaze.

'I might think this is crazy by tomorrow,' said Jo, 'but what the heck?' She winked at Carrie. 'I'm in.'

Carrie beamed but Sarah frowned. 'Don't you think it's a bit morbid? Thinking about your own death?'

'What about a wish list, then?' Carrie suggested, eager to get her on board. 'If a genie granted you three wishes, what would you wish for? I don't mean an endless pot of gold, or anything like that. Real things, attainable goals.'

'Oh God, that's easy,' Sarah said immediately, 'eight hours' continuous sleep, the ironing pile to have magically disappeared . . .' She tugged at her skirt. 'And my clothes to fit me again.'

The idea of a genie planted a seed of doubt in Jo's head; why on earth was she going along with this madness?

'Not a genie,' she said hurriedly. 'We have to make our wishes come true by ourselves.'

'With help from each other,' added Carrie.

Sarah shook her head in despair and her red curls bounced. 'I think you're both barmy, but go on then.' She caught sight of the village hall clock and gasped. 'Blimey, it's Zac's teatime. I need to get home.'

'Oh,' said Carrie, her face falling, 'we haven't chosen our wishes yet.'

'I need to get back too,' said Jo, checking her watch. 'Let's exchange email addresses and we can arrange to meet up again soon.'

'Um.' Carrie blushed. 'I don't do email.'

Sarah and Jo stared at her.

'How do you shop?'

'Or communicate with anyone?'

'Or do anything?'

Carrie shrugged and gave a small smile. 'Something for my wish list, I guess.'

Jo opened her slim black clutch bag. Nestled between her keys, iPhone and lipstick was a silver business card holder.

'Here's my card with my email and mobile number on it. Let's organize a date over the phone.'

Sarah tipped out the contents of her Mary Poppins-style handbag to reveal baby wipes, nappy sacks, two large cotton wool circles and a packet of baby breadsticks. She finally handed over a couple of rather dog-eared cards. 'Sorry, I'm normally really organized.'

Jo took in the gaping blouse, the crusty white stain on

23

her jacket and the patch of matted hair at the back of Sarah's head and said nothing.

'I don't have a card or even a pen,' said Carrie, 'so I'll phone you both. And thank you.' She lowered her voice. 'I hate social occasions like this, and meeting you two has made it infinitely more bearable.'

An awkward moment followed as Carrie leaned forward to hug Sarah and Sarah jabbed a hand out for her to shake.

'Sorry,' stammered Carrie, pumping Sarah's hand.

Jo strode over to say her goodbyes to Abi, wondering just what she had let herself in for.

Chapter 2

Jo slammed the car door against the wind with relief, fastened her seat belt and plugged her phone into the in-car charger. It was four o'clock and already dark. If the traffic was kind, she should be back in Northampton in ninety minutes. She manoeuvred the car out of the car park and headed out of the village, tooting the horn as she passed Sarah trotting down the road. A mile or so further along, her foot instinctively touched the brake.

'Shit! I should have given her a lift home,' Jo muttered under her breath, cross with herself. She was crap at this female solidarity thing. If it had been that divine vicar, she'd have screeched to a halt and gone out of her way to drop him off. Too late now. The idea of helping the other two women make their wishes come true already seemed faintly ludicrous; Jo had all the empathy of her mobile phone, which was currently refusing to pick up a signal.

As soon as she was able, she dialled the office.

'How did it go?' Her secretary Liz had been full of admiration for Jo when she'd heard the reading for the funeral was to be in French.

'Hellish. As expected.'

'Tragic,' sighed Liz.

'I'm on my way back now, so should be there for five thirty. If I miss you, can you leave any messages on my desk?'

'You'll do no such thing,' said Liz. 'There's nothing here that needs your urgent attention. You did have an email from Edward Shaw asking for more samples, but I've passed that on to Patrick to deal with.'

Jo tutted. 'More samples? He'll have more of our sample stock than us soon! What about the ShooStore order, has that gone out?'

There was a small hesitation on the line and Jo thought she'd lost the signal. 'Liz?'

'It did go out, but they called late morning and reduced the order by twenty-five per cent.'

'What?' Jo's fingers clenched the steering wheel and she frowned as she turned off the country lane on to the dual carriageway. The engine purred as it picked up speed.

'They've got Christmas stock left over, apparently, and so they're still in sale. The buyer was apologetic but her hands were tied, she said, she couldn't exceed maximum stock levels.'

Neither can we, thought Jo. The warehouse was already crammed with unsold stock and the summer range would be arriving soon. Only two weeks until Valentine's Day; she'd have to come up with a promotion to clear the decks.

'I can hear your brain whirring from here.' Liz laughed down the phone. 'Patrick's working on it now. Says he'll have something to show you in the morning. As in *tomorrow*. As in don't you dare show your face here again today.'

Jo grinned and shook her head. Thank God for Patrick. 'All right, boss.'

'Good, now go home or to the gym or something.'

Jo turned the radio on, then off. She wanted silence, just her and her thoughts, as she headed south on the motorway. It was sixteen years since she'd met Abi at university. God, she missed those days. The education side of it was almost secondary: an annoying interruption to a lifestyle otherwise dedicated to fun.

Not that everything about student life had been great:

the wet towels in the bathroom, the kitchen sink always full of dirty dishes, and the daily cry from someone of, 'Who's stolen my milk?' Jo smiled at the memories. On second thoughts, she wouldn't want to go back to that; she loved her own space and privacy. Most of the time.

Abi and Fréd had been the first of her friends to get married. But now the floodgates had opened. It was only January and she'd already had three *save the date* cards for the summer addressed to 'Jo plus one'. She sighed; the cards should read *find a date* in her case. A tiny voice in the back of Jo's head reminded her that if she dated commitment-shy men, what did she expect? She'd even been reduced to taking her mother with her to one wedding last year; she could still remember the look of pity on her old schoolfriends' faces as she and Mum took their seats at the table.

She lowered the window an inch and lit her second cigarette of the day; an icy draught filled the car and ruffled her hair. Sod the gym, she'd call in and see her parents.

Bob Gold opened the front door of the large split-level bungalow and beamed with obvious delight at his only child.

'It's my favourite daughter! Come here and let me give you a hug!'

Jo laughed and allowed herself to be enveloped by his strong arms.

He frowned suddenly and checked his watch.

'You're knocking off early. What's the matter?'

She stared at him; surely he can't have forgotten where she had been?

'Nothing's the matter,' she tutted. 'Except I'm freezing because you haven't invited me in.'

She followed him through the house into the kitchen.

'Once in a while won't hurt, I suppose,' he muttered, raking a hand through his thick silver hair. 'Coffee?'

'Please.'

He eyed the kitchen cabinets as if they were trying to catch him out.

Jo rolled her eyes behind his back. He *had* forgotten. Next he'd be giving her the 'Setting a good example to your staff' lecture.

'Where's Mum?'

'Upstairs getting herself dolled up. We're off out shortly to play bridge with the golf crowd.'

Her father opened several doors in an attempt to locate coffee and a mug. She leaned up against the Aga, relishing the warmth in the small of her back. It dominated the kitchen and had always been her favourite spot in the house. A place to share her news with her mum and pinch cakes straight from the cooling rack. Not that any of Teresa's domestic skills had rubbed off on her.

It was odd watching her father in the kitchen. She had barely seen him during term time when she was growing up; he had put in long hours at Gold's, struggling to keep up with demand during the eighties' boom. What a contrast to today's market.

'Summer stock in yet? What's the order book like?'

Jo groaned inwardly. He was off, firing his usual round of questions at her. *Hurry up, Mum.*

'Not yet and fine.'

'Sugar?'

'Of course she doesn't want sugar.'

Jo's mum stood in the doorway, hands on hips, elegant in a navy wrap dress and mid-heeled leather Gold's boots. They were from two seasons ago, Jo recalled. Available in tan, black and charcoal. Teresa held out her arms to her daughter.

'She gave it up for Lent when she was nine. Hello, darling, this is a nice surprise.'

Jo relaxed instantly, squeezed her mum tight and caught the familiar delicate scent of her perfume. 'Shalimar?' she said.

'I know, I'm boring but . . . Oh gosh!' Teresa took a step back, still holding Jo's hands and registered the black outfit. 'The funeral! How did it go? How's poor Abi?'

'Devastated. Lost. Overshadowed by a bossy mother-in-law.' Jo caught her father's expression and saw the light bulb going on in his brain.

'Ah, of course.' Bob cleared his throat sheepishly and set Jo's coffee down on the pine table. 'Better to have loved and lost, et cetera.'

Really? Jo flashed him a cynical look. That was not what he'd been drumming into her since boys started sniffing round when she was sixteen. His message had always been that business comes first. Once she allowed love to get in the way, he had warned, that would be it; her career would be over and where would that leave Gold's?

'Your father's right,' said Teresa, putting a coaster under the mug and pointing at a chair. Jo sat and her parents joined her. 'You work too hard.'

'Mum.' Jo tutted from behind her mug. Where had that come from? She thought they were talking about Abi.

Bob folded his arms and frowned. 'There's no such thing, Tess. I've every faith in Jo's ability to run the firm. But that comes at a price. Husbands, babies and business don't mix. Josephine understands that, don't you?'

Jo opened her mouth to speak but her mother got there first.

'Oh, Bob, shut up! Darling, you're all work and no play. It's not healthy. It's time to think about yourself.' Her mother's brow furrowed, full of concern. 'We're not getting any younger. Tell her, Bob.'

'Your mother's getting old.' Bob's lips twitched and Teresa swiped at him with a tea towel.

It was always the same with these two: Mum dropping two-tonne hints about wanting grandchildren and Dad warning her off. Jo couldn't win.

'Were there any nice men at the funeral?' asked Teresa.

Jo raised an eyebrow. 'Inappropriate, even for you.'

An image of the vicar popped into her head but she kept quiet; her mother would have a field day with that. She couldn't stay long and anyway they were on their way out, so she finished her coffee and her parents walked her to the door.

Bob took his daughter's face in his hands before kissing her cheek. 'Do you know how many small businesses have folded in the last ten years? Thousands.'

Jo looked into his vivid blue eyes and sighed. 'I know, but I can't see the light at the end of the tunnel.'

And it was a long, lonely tunnel.

'You're trading your way through it. Hang on in there and Gold's will survive. I'm proud of you.'

The magic words. Jo managed a half-smile.

'There you go, Mum,' she said, wrapping her arms round her mum for a hug. 'I haven't got time for a social life; I'm too busy saving the British economy.'

'Did I tell you Anna next door is having to have IVF?' said Teresa. 'She's worried she might have left it too late for a family. You can't ignore the ticking of your body clock, you know.'

Jo did know; she could hear it, loud and clear. She waved, climbed into the car and headed back to her empty flat.

Sarah bowed her head, shivered inside her coat and ran down the hill from the village hall. She raised a hand as a silver Lexus streaked past her, tooting its horn.

Nice car. She had a feeling Jo would be a very good contact to keep in touch with. Ambitious, successful . . . she might even be a potential client. But Carrie was an odd one. No job, no kids – what did she do all day? Sarah relished being financially independent, she was almost evangelical about it; she couldn't imagine being a housewife. She chided herself for being judgemental; who knew what Carrie's story was? She could be ill, or loaded, or anything.

The row of three little red-brick cottages, nestling between the church and the old schoolhouse, was already in sight. Despite the cold, the picture-postcard beauty of home gave her a warm glow and she hurried up the path towards the end cottage.

Last year Rose Cottage had cast a spell on her and Dave as soon as they set eyes on it. They had taken one look at its log-burning fire, stripped oak beams, stable door into a postage-stamp garden and withdrawn their offer on the three-bed semi closer to town that had been their first choice. Sarah had felt a bit bad about messing people around, but she was adamant that a village address had more prestige – important for when she made it on to the board at work. Besides, Woodby was an idyllic location in which to bring up a family.

Nearly a year on, Sarah loved it just as much, although she now wished the walls were made of elastic. The cottage had been quaint and cosy when they moved in. Since the arrival of Zac, it was perhaps a little too cosy. Her head was full of extension plans to build an extra room upstairs and down. But not yet. Not while money was such an issue between them.

She put her key into the lock and hesitated. *Please, please, please be tidy.*

Sarah chided herself: *Cherish every moment, remember? Think of Abi going home to an empty house.* She took a deep breath and pushed open the front door.

'Hello, boys!' she called, hanging her coat on the bulging coat hook. It was lovely to be home, all she had to do was close her eyes to the state of it and she'd be fine. She collected three large trainers from the floor and stacked them on to the overflowing shoe rack. One fell off and she booted it underneath.

'In here,' Dave shouted from the living room.

Sarah couldn't wait to get her hands on Zac and see his little face light up. She tried and failed to squeeze past the

31

pushchair blocking the hall and spent a tense couple of minutes stripping it of its bags and folding its bulk against the wall. *Sodding thing.* How could one small person need such a huge contraption?

At last she pushed open the living-room door. The fairy lights entwined around the mirror twinkled, two scented candles burned on the mantelpiece and flames danced in the fire.

It was magical and her heart flooded with warmth. It might be as messy as predicted, but it was home.

Dave was kneeling in front of the fireplace. Her big bear of a husband; kind, caring, a bit scruffy but very handsome. And full of life. She dropped a kiss on his head and then knelt down on Zac's activity mat. She picked up her son, covered his face in kisses and blew a raspberry on his tummy, breathing in his yeasty baby smell. Her heart twisted with love.

'Hello, my gorgeous boy. Mummy's missed you today.'

Zac kicked his legs and gurgled with delight.

'Oi! What about me? How come I only get one kiss?' said Dave. He poked the fire, carefully added more wood and closed the door of the log burner.

She settled Zac back down on his mat and crawled over to Dave. Reaching her arms round his neck, she cuddled him, feeling the rough wool of his jumper on her cheek.

'You can have more kisses later.'

'Is that a promise?'

He twisted round to face her and she smiled at the suspicion on his face. That was the thing with new babies: your partner suddenly took second place. They were both guilty of it. She was going to make more effort. Starting now.

She nodded and pressed a tender kiss to his lips. Dave wound one of her curls round his finger, released it and then tucked it behind her ear.

'I haven't started dinner.' He looked at her warily.

Two dirty mugs on the hearth caught her eye. She bit back

the retort that rose automatically to her lips and shrugged. In the grand scheme of things, what did it matter?

She smiled. 'That's OK, what do you want to do: bath or cook?'

He looked relieved and even more suspicious.

'Cook. Definitely. Boyo had a severe explosion after lunch and I'm still suffering flashbacks. He prefers it when you do his bath anyway.'

Sarah laughed. Dave had been really squeamish with Zac's nappies in the early days and even now occasionally went very pale. She could just imagine the look on his face while he sorted out a multi-layered leak.

'OK. But after I've had a cup of tea, I'm freezing.' She leaned across, handed Zac the teething ring that he was struggling to reach and stood up.

'Get a move on, then,' said Dave with a wink. 'I'm on a promise tonight.'

A couple of hours later, Sarah tucked a sleepy Zac into his cot and stroked his peachy skin.

'Night night, little one.' She wound up the musical mobile above the cot and closed the door softly.

Dave was in the kitchen pouring a beer.

'Ta-dah!' said Sarah, brandishing the silent baby monitor. She poured herself a glass of water and turned her back on the old butler sink full of lunchtime washing-up. *Ignore it, Sarah, he's doing his best.*

'So how was the funeral?'

What could she say? She shook her head, searching for the right words.

Abi and Fréd had been just like them: married, young family, just starting out in a new home. What must it have been like, living with cancer, knowing that his days were numbered? And now, Abi was left to bring up Tom alone, all their plans and dreams shattered.

'We're so lucky, Dave.' She wrapped her arms round his

waist and he turned to hug her. 'However tired I am, if I've had a bad day at work, or been up all night with Zac, I've still got you. We've still got each other.'

She closed her eyes, laid her head on his chest and reached a hand up to the back of his head. His hair reminded her of Action Man's. Soft and bristly.

'I missed you. At the funeral. I was lonely on my own.'

He kissed her and she inhaled the faint smell of his after-shave and tasted the beer on his lips. She wasn't telling the whole truth and a flush of shame niggled at her. In some ways she'd been glad he wasn't there. The 'What do you do for a living, Dave?' conversation still felt awkward.

He was getting used to being a stay-at-home dad and had a tendency to go a bit prickly when people asked questions. It was hard for him sometimes, she knew, but it wasn't that easy for her either.

In bed later on, Sarah put down her book and turned off her bedside lamp.

'Are you asleep?' She looked across at Dave. He had pulled the duvet up over his face to block the light and his breathing was slow. He found it tiring, looking after a baby all day. Bedtime was ten o'clock these days, in an attempt to get eight hours in before Zac woke at six. Every moment counted.

'Nearly.' He rolled towards her and opened one eye.

'I met two women at the funeral.'

'Yeah?' Dave didn't sound particularly interested. An image of their faces when she'd expressed milk over the shrubbery popped into her mind. She giggled; she'd been mortified. And she'd have to sew another button on that shirt.

'What?' he mumbled

'Oh nothing.' It was difficult enough to try to be sexy and feminine for her husband; she wasn't going to share that little episode. 'They were really nice. We're going to meet up again.'

'From Woodby?'

'One was. Carrie Radley.'

'I'm asleep now.'

Sarah snuggled down and reached for his hand, weaving her fingers through his. Despite her reservations, maybe Carrie was right, maybe she should start making a wish list because life was precious and she didn't want to waste a moment.

Balancing a crate of assorted crockery on her hip, Carrie let herself in to Fern House. She was exhausted. It had taken her over two hours to clear the hall once everyone had finally left. She could have asked for help, but Alex had popped back to work – Cavendish Hall was only in the next village – and everyone else was so busy that she didn't like to bother them.

The lamp was lit in the hall and Carrie's heart lifted at the golden glow of the daffodils she had piled into a vase earlier. New beginnings – that was what daffodils symbolized, which was very fitting given her meeting with Jo and Sarah. She felt a frisson of nervous excitement; her life had become more and more isolated over the last few years and today . . . well, today she felt a glimmer of hope.

The television was on low in the sitting room and her heart fluttered. What would Alex's verdict on the food at the funeral be? Impressed, hopefully, or at least not disappointed. As long as she hadn't embarrassed him, that was the main thing.

She plonked the crate on the kitchen table and stowed the milk in the fridge. Abi could have some of the leftovers; Carrie would pop round later once she'd seen to Alex. She hung her coat up in the cloakroom and caught her reflection in the tiny mirror. A tired pale face with a smudge of jam on one cheek stared back at her.

Urgh, it served her right for looking, she thought, brushing at her face.

Alex was in his favourite armchair, feet stretched out in front of the fire, his thick shock of dark hair, silver at the temples, just visible over the *Telegraph*. This was Carrie's favourite room; nice square proportions, French doors leading to her beloved garden and the lovely stone fireplace.

'Hello, petal.' Alex lowered the corner of his newspaper, smiled and looked pointedly at the clock. 'Thought you'd run off.'

As if. Who was she likely to run off with? She wasn't exactly much of a catch. If anyone was likely to run off in this relationship it was him; she was punching far above her weight.

'I had offers, of course,' said Carrie, plumping up a floral cushion and dropping gratefully on to the sofa. 'But then I remembered I'd still got the *Game of Thrones* boxset to watch so I decided to come home.'

'You looked like you were having fun with those two women,' he said, turning the page and flapping at the paper to make it lie flat.

Oh, how awful! Had everyone thought that? The shame of having fun at Fréd's funeral made her feel queasy. She shifted awkwardly. She had embarrassed him. Again. Why did he put up with her? She had so enjoyed meeting Jo and Sarah, though.

'It was a celebration of Frédéric's life,' she countered. 'He wouldn't have wanted everyone to be miserable.'

He didn't answer; his head was back in his newspaper. She watched him in silence for a few moments and willed him to compliment her on her cooking.

'What did you think of the buffet?' she said finally, unable to wait any longer.

Alex closed his paper, creased it in half and very deliberately laid it on the arm of his chair. *Oh dear.* He was pulling his schoolteacher face.

'Honestly? Cavendish Hall should have done the catering

as I'd suggested,' he said with a sigh. 'It would have been more appropriate for such a talented chef as Frédéric Lafleur.'

He was totally right, the food at Cavendish Hall was amazing. But Abi hadn't wanted – as she put it – 'poncy stuff'. She had wanted normal buffet food. Most importantly, Abi had wanted to stay in control of her own husband's funeral, not to have Cavendish Hall taking over. Carrie had been torn between helping her friend out and not upsetting her husband. But Abi had begged and Carrie hadn't had the heart to turn her down.

'As it was – no offence, Carrie . . .' He winced. 'Well, the food was a bit big and ungainly.'

He could be describing me, she thought wistfully.

'None taken,' she lied, swallowing her disappointment.

'The key to successful finger food is size. A mouthful, that's all it should be. That's important for presentation too. Small offerings look so much more attractive. People eat primarily with their eyes . . .'

At this point, Carrie's own eyes glazed over while Alex continued to educate his wife on the finer points of catering for a crowd. Again.

'You were deep in conversation yourself,' she said eventually, butting in.

'Well, that was another thing.' Alex checked his watch and sprang out of his chair. 'Gin and tonic?'

She shook her head and he strode through to the dining room and poured himself a drink, still talking. 'I hardly saw you all afternoon.'

'Hardly saw me? A big girl like me isn't hard to spot!'

'I've told you before. I like you being cuddly.' Alex frowned at her on his way back in. 'I mean that I missed having you at my side.'

Her heart leapt; he might be a bit of a snob where food was concerned, but for some unfathomable reason, he did really seem to love her. God knows why; she was so out of shape that no diet ever made a dent in her weight, she was at home all day so never had anything of interest to tell him and she had a habit of making jokes about herself that she knew he didn't like.

Carrie twirled her wedding ring round a few times before answering. 'I missed you too.'

They shared a smile.

Love was so complicated. She loved her husband, couldn't bear the thought of life without him, but somewhere along the line she had stopped loving herself and now accepting that someone else could still love her was hard.

'By the way,' said Alex matter-of-factly, 'I thought the pastry in your quiche was a bit heavy.'

'Like me, then.'

He pressed his lips together and exhaled wearily.

It had been a bit heavy. It was always the same with Carrie's pastry; she wasn't brave enough to roll it out thinly, just in case it gave way and split. He wasn't going to like what was coming next. She pushed herself up and walked to the doorway.

'Sorry, love, but that's what you've got for dinner. Leftovers. I'll serve it up as soon as I've had a bath.'

She scampered out to avoid seeing the disappointment on his face. Alex wouldn't eat the quiche. He'd rather starve than eat something he didn't like. Or make an excuse to go back into work.

She had barely trudged up the stairs, when Alex, jingling the keys in his pocket, shouted up, 'Just going to catch up on some paperwork at the office.'

She turned on the bath taps and lit her bluebell-scented candles. This was the closest smell to real flowers that Carrie had found and she inhaled happily. She loved flowers almost as much as she loved food. She waited until Alex's car had reversed off the drive before fetching herself a glass of chilled white wine. She ran back up the stairs, paused at the top, then raced back down to retrieve the bottle. He could be a pompous old fart sometimes, but he had excellent taste in wine.

Humming to herself, she left the bath to fill and went into her bedroom to undress. She unzipped her dress and unhooked her bra, letting everything fall to the floor. Tights next. Bending down to unhook her knickers from her ankle, she caught sight of herself in the mirrored wardrobe door.

Oh my Lord. Gravity was not kind to fat girls. She counted three rolls of blubber and then closed her eyes tight. She might be able to make jokes about her size to Alex, but it wasn't funny, was it? She hated looking at her own body with a passion.

Carrie lay in the bath with tears rolling down her face as the water went cold. That mirrored door was going to have to go.

Chapter 3

It was a cold February afternoon and Jo's teeth were chattering as she lugged her sample bag and briefcase across the cobbled street towards Shaw's in Nottingham's Lace Market. It was her first meeting with the new owner and she was already steeling herself for some tough negotiations. Ed Shaw had done nothing but make demands since taking over from his father, hinting that there would be a big order in it for Gold's at the end of it.

So today, buster, it was make-your-mind-up time; she'd had enough of the carrot-dangling. On the other hand, of course, she couldn't risk losing a customer.

She stopped short outside the Nottingham shoe shop and her breath caught in her throat. Bloody hell! It had changed beyond recognition. She checked the name above the door to be sure she had come to the right place. A stylish new black sign with Shaw's picked out in a white, capitalized fine font told her as much. But what a transformation.

The windows on either side of the doorway were stunning: feminine shoes displayed on Perspex plinths and oversized red props of gift boxes, hearts and flowers gave a playful twist to a Valentine's Day theme. Last time she was here, the windows had been shielded with a yellow plastic sun protector and crammed full of clumpy, frumpy shoes.

She couldn't wait to see what had been done to the interior. Her eyes widened as she pushed open the door. Gone were the 1950s wood panelling, the fluorescent overhead lighting and the two parallel rows of wooden chairs down the centre of the shop.

Now, glass shelves clung to the white walls displaying footwear by collection: heels, flats, boots and slippers. Small recesses, artfully lit, highlighted key styles. Stands displayed purses and handbags, adding splashes of colour. Jo's eyes followed the light wooden floorboards towards the end of the store where three squishy leather sofas were arranged around a low magazine-laden coffee table.

It was more Notting Hill than Nottingham and she loved it. This was a store that invited customers to browse, to sit and make their purchasing decisions in comfort. There was even a coffee machine in the corner.

A tall rangy man with trendy stubble joked with a member of staff at the till. Expensive brown brogues declared him to Jo as a man who knew shoes. Her sort of man. That had to be Edward Shaw. She approved; this was going to be fun.

Her earlier resolve to tell Shaw's that the size of their account with Gold's didn't warrant the concessions they were demanding waivered. The store looked fantastic; it was exactly the sort of retailer Jo longed to do business with. And as for the man himself . . . Jo couldn't wait to get to know him better.

He noticed Jo immediately, excused himself from his conversation and crossed the shop floor in three long strides to meet her, hand outstretched.

'Jo Gold? Ed Shaw. Good to meet you at last.'

He held her hand in both of his as he shook it. Jo smiled and a wave of attraction vibrated through her. There was humour behind his eyes and he had a confidence that she found extremely sexy.

'What do you think? Bit different to last time you came, I bet. Assuming you've been before, of course?' He grinned at her expectantly, hands on hips. He was like a big puppy; full of bounce and energy and looking for attention.

She smiled. 'I have been before. Several times. The refit is great, just what the store needed, and I approve of the rebranding too.'

No need to go over the top with the compliments. Jo wasn't one for gushing. Let's see what he was offering Gold's first.

He nodded. 'Don't know what Dad would have thought about it, though.' His face clouded over for a moment. 'He had very set ideas about what Shaw's stood for.'

He scrunched up his face and wagged his finger. 'It's all about the shoes, lad,' he said in a deep voice, mimicking his father, Jack. 'No gimmicks, no distractions.'

'I was very sorry to hear about your dad,' said Jo, feeling a pang of sadness. For all his domineering ways, she would be devastated if anything happened to her own father. 'He and my dad went back a long way.'

'Thanks.' Ed smiled grimly. 'It's had quite an impact on the family, as you can imagine.'

Jo nodded. 'Business was different in the seventies. Now it's all about the shopping experience, giving people a reason to leave their computer screens and buy face to face. I'm sure your dad knew that. He'd be proud of you.'

A couple of women nudged past them, loaded down with carrier bags.

Ed gestured towards the back of the shop. 'Come on through to the office and I'll get us some drinks.'

He held open the door for her and she brushed past him to enter his tiny office. He smelt divine. Limes. It suited him perfectly; exhilarating and lively. Her pulse quickened. *Focus, Jo*, she reminded herself, *this is business*.

She arranged her sales brochures and samples on the desk while Ed set two cups of coffee in front of them and met his eyes with a smile.

'I'm very impressed with the new look, Ed. Especially as you weren't in the business before your father died. How did you come up with the scheme?'

'I'm a designer by trade. Branding, corporate identity mostly, a bit of retail. So it wasn't too big a leap to join the family firm and hoick it into the twenty-first century.'

'And you find yourself running a chain of seven shoe shops. How's that going?'

Ed took a sip of coffee, apparently using the time to scrutinize her face. Jo hoped she wasn't blushing. An intimate moment passed between them as Ed seemed to be deciding whether to confide in her or not. He stood and closed the door. Jo took a deep breath and gazed brazenly into his blue eyes. He was gorgeous. This was ludicrous; her heart was pounding; she wondered whether he could sense her attraction and decided she didn't mind if he could.

He glanced at the door and lowered his voice. 'When Dad died, the plan was to put the business up for sale immediately – to take the money and run. But then I thought what if we rebranded first – created a chain of stores selling beautiful, stylish footwear that real women want to wear? That, I thought, would be a really viable business to sell. And with my design background, not impossible to achieve.'

'So the business is up for sale?'

Ed grinned. 'Nope. Seems like the shoe business is in my blood after all. Now I've got this far I want to see it through, see how far I can push the concept.'

'We seem to have quite a lot in common.' She flashed her eyes at him over the top of her coffee cup.

'So . . . Tell me about Gold's.' He sat back in his chair. 'In fact, tell me about you.'

'Like you, I'm a chip off the old block. I've got shoes running through me like the proverbial stick of rock. Started at the bottom in the warehouse, then time in admin, sales, buying . . . until Dad decided I was ready to fly solo. Then three years ago he buggered off to a life of golf, bridge and long-haul travel.'

Ed nodded sadly. 'That's my biggest regret. That Dad died before he could enjoy any retirement. My mum had been badgering him to sell up for the last five years so they could spend some quality time together.'

'I'm so sorry,' said Jo softly. She slid her hand across the desk between them to touch his fingertips. A beat passed between them before he withdrew his hand and picked up Jo's catalogue.

'Anyway,' said Ed, 'Gold's Footwear.'

Jo sat up tall, conscious she'd been brushed off. That was the worst thing about her short hair: her ears always turned red when she was embarrassed and they had nowhere to hide.

'That's our new summer range,' she said, pulling herself back together.

'How is business for you?' he asked, flicking through the pages.

He might have been open and candid with her, but she wasn't about to reciprocate. He seemed to be well on the way to turning his father's business around. Jo was still trying to figure out how to revive her dwindling order book.

'The Gold's brand is about comfort but it stands for quality too,' she recited. 'We're proud to manufacture in Britain with a reputation spanning forty years. We too focus on shoes that "real women" would choose to—'

Ed swallowed a mouthful of coffee and held up his hand. *Rude.*

'When we talk about "real women",' he drew apostrophes in the air, 'we're really targeting the thirty-five-year-old-plus market. It's a fictitious age bracket now, isn't it? A woman at thirty-five isn't ready to be palmed off with a stout pair of slip-ons with a cushioned sole, is she?'

Jo chewed the inside of her cheek. She'd never given it much thought. Comfort footwear was always aimed at the over-thirty-five market. But now that he mentioned it . . .

Ed peered over the desk at Jo's legs. Her buttery-tan leather boots had pointy toes and spiky heels.

'Not what I'd call comfortable.' He grinned boyishly at her.

'I'm not thirty-five.' Her eyes blazed back at him, making him throw his head back with laughter.

'Touché,' he said. 'But gone are the days when women stopped following fashion at thirty-five — or fifty-five, for that matter. I've brought Shaw's bang up to date. But our customer profile hasn't changed at all. We're still catering for a slightly older, less trend-driven market. And I need to fill the store with shoes that are going to send their hearts racing.'

He sat back, eyes dancing with excitement. 'Comfort footwear can still be sexy, can't it?'

He was sexy: his smile, his attitude, his eyes. She couldn't help but be infected by his energy.

'What about this range?' She took the catalogue out of his hand and pointed to Gold's new Athena collection.

He inclined his head to one side. 'Hmm.'

Jo's heart sank. *Not impressed, then?* Undeterred, she took the actual sandals out of her bag.

He picked one up, turning it round in his hand, examining the stitching, pressing his thumbs into the cushioned insole.

'Lovely quality, it's a pretty shoe, for sure.' He set the sandal down and sat back, bouncing against the back of the chair. 'Leaving summer to one side for a moment. Too late to do anything now but . . .'

Her stomach dropped a notch; this wasn't going as planned.

'Here's my dilemma.' Ed picked up a pencil and tapped his cheek with it. 'Gold's shoes cater for an older customer: someone looking for quality, comfort and durability. Perhaps at the expense of style? Is that fair?'

Jo narrowed her eyes. Athena *had* been designed with

style in mind, not just comfort. She had even considered wearing them herself. Ed had put her off now.

'Maybe. But those qualities are what made us such a good fit with Shaw's,' she said.

'But *we've* moved on. Your product is good and solid. But it hasn't got the X-factor.' He leaned forward in his seat and nudged the shoe towards her. 'It doesn't exactly scream, *Take me now or lose me for ever.*'

Take me now? As if she needed any encouragement. *Breathe, Jo.* She tried to meet his eyes, but he had picked up that bloody pencil again.

The dismissal of her new range hit home and she bristled.

He had been in the shoe trade all of five minutes and suddenly he was an expert. Jo had heard enough. After the run-around Ed had given them – requesting endless samples, querying colours and quibbling over costs – it was clear that he wasn't going to stock Gold's anyway. If there was one thing she hated it was time-wasters, even devilishly attractive ones.

She snatched up the samples and gave him a tight smile. 'Thank you for your feedback, Ed. I'll bear that in mind for our winter collection.'

'Wait.' Ed leaned forward and placed a hand on her arm. She stared at it, heart pounding – from attraction and frustration. 'I've offended you. Which means I haven't explained myself very well.'

'Not offended, no. You're not obliged to stock our brand. I'm disappointed after all the to-ing and fro-ing with samples.'

'Listen. I didn't ask you here under false pretences. Honest.' Ed released Jo's arm and started to sketch, continuing to talk as he did so.

'I'm looking for a manufacturer to partner with closely.'

Closely? That could work.

She relaxed back on her chair. 'I'm listening,' she said, perhaps a little too sharply.

'Someone who can help us to fill a gap in the market and

bring new shoppers into our stores. Having squishy sofas and coffee machines isn't enough on its own.'

Ed waved his pencil at her. She remained silent, still smarting from his X-factor comment.

'Look at the UK's best-sellers! Sheepskin boots are still huge and premium-priced.'

Jo exhaled and shook her head irritably. Surely he wasn't suggesting she join the flock and bring out a copy of the leading designer brand?

'And aimed at a younger market than both of our customers; kids with more money than sense,' she countered.

Ed looked up at her, seemingly amused by her reaction. 'You can't deny they're comfortable, though.'

He had a point but she wasn't about to admit it.

'What about designing something desirable, that you – when you eventually reach the ripe old age of thirty-five,' he grinned at her, 'would be proud to wear. I'm thinking quirky, sexy and irresistible.'

'Next birthday, then.' She smiled back. 'So we'd better get a move on.'

Everything he said was true. The so-called older market did need a shake-up. And the way business was at the moment, it was either do or die. Maybe Gold's could create something different, a new sub-brand, and launch it through Shaw's?

'Yes!' Ed punched the air. 'Does that mean you're on board?'

His eyes sparkled and he turned his notepad round to Jo. There were four rough sketches: two shoes and two boots. Totally off the wall, completely impractical. But gorgeous.

'Why Gold's?' said Jo suddenly, realizing that he could have been having this conversation with any one of her competitors.

Ed pushed his chair back and thumped his foot on to the desk in front of him.

'Recognize the brand?'

Jo nodded. Ed was wearing brogues from Loake's, one of the oldest footwear companies in England.

'They're from your neck of the woods, aren't they?' he said.

'Their showroom is thirty minutes from ours, yes.'

'Britain has got a world-class reputation for making shoes. I want to showcase the best the UK has to offer. Our fathers worked together and I'd like for us to carry on that tradition.'

Jo regarded Ed for a moment, taking in his boyish charm, his unruly brown hair and lean body. And he was in the footwear trade. If she had to describe her ideal man, it was quite possible that she was staring at him right now. Even her dad might approve of this one. There was absolutely nothing she would rather do than get to know Ed Shaw better.

'I'd be delighted to.' She smiled her sultry smile, not making too much effort to disguise her attraction for him.

'Here.' Ed picked up her folder as she re-packed her sample bag. The edge of it caught a photo frame and knocked it to the floor. Jo picked it up, glancing briefly at a family snapshot taken on a beach: Ed presumably with his wife and two children.

So he was married. Of course he was. They all were.

But that hasn't stood in your way before, a little voice nagged.

He showed her to the door.

'I'll put my designers straight on it and get back to you,' said Jo.

Liar. He was already looking at the entire design team. She shook his hand, lingering as long as she dared.

'Can't wait.' Ed smiled. 'And my mum sends her regards to your dad.'

Nottingham's shopping centre was quiet as she walked back to the car. A group of teenage girls walked by, giggling. Two of them wore a variation on the sheepskin-boot theme. One girl's had collapsed so that she was no longer walking on the sole, but on the side of the boot. Jo shuddered at the poor quality. Fifteen pounds from a supermarket, no doubt.

Prices for footwear were now so polarized that the mid-market had been left diminished and floundering. Ed was right. Gold's needed a point of difference if it was going to survive. If only she had someone to confide her fears in. She had Patrick, but even talking to him was difficult when he might be in line for redundancy by the end of the year. Being the boss was so lonely at times.

Jo thought of Sarah and Carrie. They were all going to meet up again tonight. Perhaps she should put *save Gold's shoes* on her wish list. She made her way back to the car park. Time to call in on Abi first, see how she and Tom were faring since the funeral. That would put her own problems into perspective.

Sarah was racing to leave the office. She swept her mobile phone off her desk straight into her bag, kicked the filing cabinet shut and jiggled her computer mouse. A message on screen informed her not to switch off her computer. She tutted and checked her watch. Why choose tonight to install one million software updates?

She would just have to leave it to do its thing. Traffic was a nightmare on Fridays and she was already later than planned. She lifted her coat from the back of the door, pulled one sleeve on and froze. There was the unmistakable sound of her boss's heels doing their rapid *scrape, scrape, scrape* march along the carpeted corridor outside her office.

Sarah groaned under her breath, she had thought Eleanor was still in the boardroom. She paused, leaving her coat dangling from one shoulder. How was she going to escape with the boss still prowling the corridors?

'Sarah?' Eleanor poked her head round the door and she jumped a mile.

'Eleanor!' she gasped, clutching her chest. 'You startled me. I was . . . I was . . . what can I do for you?'

Elegant as ever, with chunky beads, tailored trouser suit and elfin crop, Eleanor was the epitome of the professional woman. Why, oh why did she have to come in now? Technically, Sarah finished fifteen minutes ago and it was Friday. But all the ambitious types at Finch and Partners played a corporate point-scoring game of 'who could stay the latest'. Sarah always lost.

She quickly stuck her arms behind her back and jiggled her shoulder blades as discreetly as she could until her coat slid off. She kicked it behind the door. With any luck Eleanor wouldn't even have spotted it.

Sarah felt her mouth go dry as Eleanor lowered her gaze to the floor and then flexed her eyebrow a fraction.

'Looks like I just caught you,' said Eleanor icily. 'The other partners and I are meeting the Chamber of Commerce team for drinks later. I thought you'd like to join us?'

Wowzers! Sarah narrowly avoided a tell-tale gasp. *Play it cool*, she thought, as the significance of Eleanor's proposal began to sink in. This had to be a sign. Eleanor was singling her out for the board's attention, which could only mean one thing. She pulled herself up tall; partnership was almost within reach.

Reality snapped back at her with a jolt and her heart plummeted. She couldn't go. Not tonight. As it was, she would only have half an hour with Zac before she was due to meet Jo and Carrie at the pub. And it was too late to cancel. Jo would already have left Northampton and Carrie was so looking forward to it, she had been sending her daily text messages, it wouldn't be fair. But drinks! With the board!

Eleanor was regarding her curiously as if she couldn't comprehend why Sarah wasn't performing a celebratory conga round her desk. Her forehead was remarkably smooth for a woman of her age. *Botox*, thought Sarah uncharitably.

Her heart raced as she mentally wrote her own death sentence. 'I'm so sorry. Any other night, I'd love to. You know I would,' she said, smiling hopefully at Eleanor.

A blatant lie. After-hours entertaining these days was a no-no. Sarah had a nightly bath-time date with a baby boy and his Peppa Pig pirate ship. Dull clients and their tax avoidance ideas were no match for that.

'Shame.' Eleanor held her gaze for a second, shrugged and disappeared.

Sarah ran to her office door. 'But on the plus side, I am meeting with a potential client . . .' she called after her.

Eleanor wasn't listening; she was already poking her head into Ben's office. 'What are you doing after work?'

All the way home, Sarah muttered under her breath, persuading herself that she had done the right thing, then disagreeing and finally getting so cross that she turned the radio up loud and refused to listen to one more word about the matter. She was nearly home when she remembered Dave's text message from earlier with horror.

AM TAKING ZAC TO BARBERS. BOTH NEED TRIM. BIG DAY FOR THE LITTLE LAD! XX

Dave had been right; Zac had grown a mini Mohican: long and straggly on top and a bit bald at the back. He would have had his first haircut by now. The thought made her heart flip; she had wanted to be there for that.

She had a beautiful memento book at home that someone from the office had given her, with *Baby's First Year* embossed on the front cover. It was a place to record special occasions: his first tooth, his first crawl, his first word. But since she had gone back to work, it was Daddy not Mummy who got to witness those precious moments. Daddy who sent the text messages starting GUESS WHAT!

She had planned to keep a lock of Zac's hair from his first visit to the barbers. It was unlikely Dave would remember to ask, no disrespect to him, but those sort of small details were her forte not his. She had been about to text him to do so when her office phone rang. After that, she had been so busy she had forgotten all about it. Forgotten about her own son. She truly was a terrible mother.

A nervous Dave and a smartly trimmed baby met her at the door of Rose Cottage. A lump formed in her throat as she held out her arms to take a wriggling Zac. She examined his new haircut.

'He looks exactly like you.' She smiled at her husband, who was sporting an identical buzz cut.

'Is it OK?' said Dave, searching her face. 'It's the first time I've ever had to instruct a barber on behalf of someone else. I kept thinking that if I got it wrong, you'd go mad.'

Sarah swallowed. Was she really that much of an ogre? Apparently so. She was sure she hadn't used to be. Now she daren't ask whether he'd kept a lock of Zac's baby hair. It didn't matter, anyway. She could just as easily trim a bit off at bath time. No one would know it wasn't officially from his first haircut. Apart from her.

'Oh and look!' said Dave, plunging his fingers into his jeans pocket. 'The barber gave me this.'

He pulled out a small plastic bag and handed it to her. 'Apparently it's a tradition to keep a lock of baby hair from their first cut. I thought you'd like to stick it in that scrapbook of yours.'

Her heart swooped with joy and she flung an arm around his neck.

'Thank you, thank you, thank you.' She covered his face with kisses, kicking herself for ever doubting him. Zac grabbed at her hair and she kissed him too.

'He shoots, he scores!' said Dave, punching the air. 'And while I'm in your good books, do you mind if I nip over to Southwell tonight? I promised a bloke I'd quote him for some decorating.'

'Oh.' Sarah's heart sank. She had been looking forward

to a night out all week. Not to mention that she'd just blown her chances of promotion because of it.

'It'll be a weekend job,' said Dave, looking pleased with himself. 'It's an empty factory unit. Good money, too?'

Sarah weighed up the options and adjusted Zac on her hip. They did need the money. And it was good for Dave to keep his hand in with his old job. Plus, she definitely didn't want an argument.

She waved a hand. 'Of course. You go. It was my night out with the girls, that's all. But it'll keep.' She started to walk away to hide her disappointment. 'I'll go and phone Carrie.'

Dave groaned. 'I'm sorry. It totally slipped my mind. Wait!' He grabbed her round the waist. 'Why don't you invite the girls round here instead? Have a few drinks, let your hair down and I'll get up in the night with Zac if necessary. Plus, it's Saturday so you can have a lie-in in the morning; I'll give him some formula when he yells. How's that?'

Bless him, he was trying. As compromises went, it wasn't a bad one. And after making a complete idiot of herself in front of Eleanor, the idea of a couple of glasses of wine was particularly appealing. All she had to do was tidy up.

She grinned at her husband who was waiting with bated breath for her response. 'Deal.'

Carrie set the browned beef to one side and checked her mobile phone for messages. Nothing. Good. That meant they hadn't cancelled. It felt funny being so attached to the thing waiting for messages; she didn't use it much normally, seeing as she was at home all day. It was Alex's old one, very basic, no good for surfing the web or taking pictures, Sarah and Jo would probably laugh at it, but it was all she needed. She placed it back on to the granite worktop and immediately picked it up again. Perhaps they had forgotten? She debated sending them both a quick text to remind them about tonight. On second thoughts, maybe not. Sarah's responses had been getting shorter and shorter as the week had gone on.

Carrie scraped her shoulder-length hair into an unflattering pony tail, consulted the recipe book and tipped the shallots and garlic into the pan.

She was really nervous about tonight, but excited too, and for once it wasn't food-related excitement. Ever since she had suggested this crazy idea of the wish list she had been feeling all fluttery inside. This was it. A fresh start. A chance to lay the old demons to rest, make some new friends and let their busy, fulfilled and motivated lives drag her into the real world. What were they going to wish for? What was *she* going to wish for, more to the point?

Perhaps the other two were simply humouring her. But right now she felt a spark of determination that she hadn't felt in years and she was bloomin' well going to make the most of it.

Taking the cork out of a bottle of Burgundy, Carrie added about half the wine to the pan, popped the lid on her Le Creuset casserole and bundled it into the oven.

That was dinner taken care of. Now for the worst job of the day. She groaned and dragged her feet upstairs.

She spent the next two hours immersed in the clothing dilemma from hell, discarding outfit after outfit until she narrowed her choice down to the two things that made her look the least whale-like: black baggy dress or black baggy dress. Her wardrobe was arranged into what she referred to privately as 'nostalgia', 'inspirational' and 'reality'.

The nostalgia collection went way back. Goodness knows why she kept them; she had as much chance of ever fitting into those clothes as she had of donning a bikini, winning Miss World and finally achieving world peace. And talking of which . . . she pulled out the unworn two-piece that Alex had bought her as a surprise on their honeymoon. What had he been thinking? Ten years ago she had been much slimmer than she was now, but even so . . . she would have cleared the beach quicker than Jaws in that. She shuddered and dropped it back into the drawer.

The inspirational section contained all the clothes she couldn't wear but wasn't ready to part with just yet. Like her favourite ever navy silk shift dress. Things that she could get into, but then couldn't walk, move her arms or sit down in.

The largest section belonged to grim reality. It contained a minimum of 3 per cent Lycra, very little colour and even less shape. She plumped for one of her black dresses, added a sweep of mascara to her lashes and returned to the kitchen to put the finishing touches to dinner.

'Dinner nearly ready?' came a voice from the kitchen doorway.

She added a splash of cream to the mashed potato and nodded but Alex was leaning on the doorframe, flicking through the post.

I am invisible to him.

'Yes, go through.'

Alex picked a bottle of wine from the kitchen and followed her into the dining room. He sat down with an appreciative sigh as she set the casserole dish on the table and went back for the rest.

'You remember I'm going out tonight, don't you?' she said, placing a warmed plate in front of him.

'I do. And it's nice to see you getting out more.' He hesitated and then placed a hand over hers. 'With people your own age. Although I don't really understand why grown women would want to write a wish list.'

'Oh go on, don't tell me you never make a wish? Like "I wish I was married to Jennifer Aniston", for instance. Anyway, it's just a way of, I don't know, doing something for me, I suppose.' Carrie felt her cheeks flush as she ladled boeuf Bourguignon on to Alex's warmed plate. 'Mash?'

Her husband frowned. 'Mashed *potato*?'

'Of course, I thought you might turn your nose up at mashed banana.' Carrie held the spoon poised over the dish of potato, whipped with cream and horseradish.

'Yes please, it's just that we serve it with celeriac mash in the restaurant, that's all. Delicate flavour offsetting the richness of the beef.'

'I'll bear that in mind,' she said through gritted teeth. *Here endeth the lesson . . .*

They began eating, exchanging small details about their respective days. Carrie's news didn't take long and she didn't bother relating how depressing it was only to be able to fit into a tiny percentage of her clothes.

'I meant to tell you!' Alex jumped up and dashed to the hall, coming back with a thick cream card, his face lit up like Tiny Tim outside the butcher's. 'We've been invited to the opening of Jordan Lamb's new Nottingham restaurant. That will be some party; it will be his first outside of London!'

Alex was always receiving invitations to openings and launches, but Carrie had never seen him this excited. He leaned across the table and placed a smacking kiss on her cheek. 'I expect we'll get to meet him. What an honour!'

She could see his brain whirring, planning how he could make the most of this opportunity; perhaps he'd attempt to get the celebrity chef to visit Cavendish Hall. She smiled back weakly at his enthusiasm. All she could think of was, *How on earth can I get out of it?*

She had been to these restaurant launches before. Despite the fact that it was the food industry, all the women – the PR girls, the waitresses and even the management – looked like they survived on a diet of air. She would look like a rhinoceros. In a black baggy dress.

'Treat yourself to a new frock or something; we'll both need to scrub up for this one,' he said, patting her hand.

'No problem. It doesn't take much for me to look like a scrubber.'

She caught his eye and the look of disappointment he gave her sent shivers down her spine.

'You're my wife,' he said quietly. 'Not a scrubber.'

Her stomach trembled with fear. One day she'd push him too far and he'd start agreeing with her when she put herself down, or simply leave her for someone else. She couldn't help it, it was a defence mechanism, she recognized that, but she didn't seem to be able to do anything about it. Maybe he should leave her; he could do so much better, he deserved so much better.

'Anyway. About this wish list.' He sighed, poured them both a glass of red wine and cleared his throat. 'I'd give you anything, you only have to ask, you know that, don't you?'

Alex picked up his knife and fork, pausing briefly to meet her eye.

But I need to achieve it for myself . . .

Carrie stared at him and her heart fluttered. She did love him and she knew he loved her. But she wanted – needed – some independence. When they married he had taken on the role of protector, educator, even father figure, and gradually her world had become smaller and smaller until she had started to feel trapped and isolated by him and their home. After ten years of marriage, she mused with a sinking feeling, it was too late to change now.

'Did you make this?' asked Alex, poking at a shallot with his fork.

'Why, do you like it?' Carrie smiled hopefully. He had eaten most of it so she assumed it had passed muster.

'Can I suggest less salt and perhaps a touch more pepper? It tastes a bit like a ready-meal.'

Carrie's shoulders sagged. When had she ever served him a ready-meal?

In that second, she made up her mind. She knew exactly what was going on her wish list. And while she was at it, she changed her mind about that last thought, too. It was *never* too late to change.

Carrie jerked her chair back from the dining table and whisked his plate off him. 'Certainly.'

'I hadn't quite finished,' said Alex, open-mouthed.

'You can't possibly eat that,' said Carrie. 'With all that salt.'

She carried the plates into the kitchen. She heard Alex sighing as he shuffled placemats, replacing them in the drawer, the silver cruets clinking as he put them on the sideboard.

She tried so hard to impress him with her food, but it was pointless. She could never meet Cavendish Hall standards. She'd have to do it some other way. The problem was that he loved her like an old jumper, something you don't have to think about, shapeless, comfortable and always there at the back of the wardrobe. But deep down she wanted to dazzle him, like a daring dress, covered in sequins, impossible to ignore.

She wanted him to be proud of her, but most of all she wanted to be proud of herself.

As it was, dinner was ruined, she'd completely lost her appetite and her chest pounded with resentment. She stood on the pedal and flipped up the lid of the bin. Carrie's face glazed over as she shovelled forkful after forkful of food into her mouth.

Chapter 4

Sarah opened the door, looking pink-cheeked and vaguely surprised to see them. A cute chubby baby in Tigger-striped pyjamas sat on her hip. His fingers, Jo noticed, were down the neck of his mum's top.

'Sorry for the change of plan, hope you don't mind not going to the pub?' said Sarah, standing back to let them in.

The tiny hallway struggled to cope with the added burden of visitors and Jo stifled a giggle as she and Carrie ended up wedged between the wall and the staircase, both hurrying to get out of the cold.

'Of course not!' said Jo, not really meaning it.

She held out two bottles of wine, a red and a white, and hoped Sarah wouldn't be stingy with them. She could murder a drink tonight and had been banking on the ambience of the pub to help her relax. Did women even drink while they were breastfeeding? God knows. It wouldn't stop Jo either way.

Carrie bit her lip. 'I should have brought wine, sorry,' she said. 'But these are for you.' She handed Sarah a posy of tulips.

'How pretty!' Sarah held them at arm's length away from the baby's inquisitive fingers.

Carrie waved a hand. 'Just a few flowers from the garden, nothing special. And these to nibble on.' She held up a huge bag of crisps and shrugged. 'I didn't have much dinner, so . . .'

Sarah made a couple of trips to the kitchen, still carrying Zac, while Jo and Carrie tried to find space on the rack for their coats.

'Pretty cottage,' said Jo. *If you like that sort of thing.* She was more into open plan and clean lines herself.

'*Bijou*, I think is the estate agent's term,' said Sarah. 'Even the bath is miniature. Good job I'm small.'

'No good for me, then!' said Carrie, elbowing Jo in the ribs.

'I didn't mean . . .' Sarah floundered.

'Nor me; my head's not far off the ceiling,' said Jo quickly, reaching her hand up to touch a wooden beam.

'Er. Come on through.' Sarah led the way into the living room and stopped abruptly. 'Gosh! Pigsty alert! Two seconds, just needs a quick tidy. I got in late and there's never enough time. Um, could someone . . . ?' She held out the baby.

Me, me, me. Jo's breath caught in her throat and by the time she had recovered, Carrie had already stepped forward.

'Would you mind using the hand-sanitizer first?' Sarah nodded towards the kitchen, where a giant bottle of yellow liquid sat on the counter top. Surely she was kidding? Jo watched in amazement as Carrie, looking bemused, scurried to the kitchen to disinfect herself.

'You probably think I'm one of those totally neurotic mothers,' Sarah laughed.

Jo remained silent.

'Noooo!' said Carrie, taking hold of Zac with lemon-scented hands.

'Thanks. Sorry. I'm normally very organized,' said Sarah, scooping up a plethora of brightly coloured toys and balancing them on an already full wicker basket. 'Not easy with a cottage this size and a husband whose idea of tidying is just to hide stuff.'

She stood motionless for a moment as if she had forgotten what she was supposed to be doing. Jo, Carrie and Zac hovered in the doorway.

'Come in, come in,' Sarah said at last, waving them towards the sofa. 'Oops!' She darted forward to retrieve a nappy – thankfully an unused one – just as Jo was about to sit down. 'Right. Drinks. I've got tea, coffee, wine or . . . just wine, I think?'

Jo sat down gingerly, wondering what else was lurking under the sofa cushions. She watched as Carrie buried her nose in the soft crease of little Zac's neck. It was all she could do not to grab him from her.

'Wine. Definitely,' she replied. She would be needing a good couple of glasses if she was to get through this 'wish list' thing.

'And crisps,' said Carrie.

'And then we can all relax,' said Jo.

She looked at Sarah, who was leaping round the room like a demented salmon. *Hopefully.*

An hour later, Zac was fast asleep in his cot and the second bottle of wine was open. A couple of candles, some pretty fairy lights and the flicker of flames from the log burner provided the only light in the room and Jo felt very mellow. They were all a bit giggly and amazingly comfortable in each other's company and probably past the point at which common sense would prevail. Although Jo had drunk the most, she seemed the most sober, and lay with her feet stretched out across Carrie's lap.

'So who's going to go first, then?' said Jo, cocking an eyebrow. 'With this bucket list?'

'You,' chorused the other two.

'And let's call it a wish list,' said Carrie. The firelight gave her dark features an exotic glow and Jo saw a glimpse of her natural beauty. 'That sounds far more aspirational. It's not as if any of us are on our last legs.'

'Legless more like,' snorted Sarah, who was sitting cross-legged on the floor like a floppy pixie.

'You've only had one,' Jo laughed.

Strangely, she was really enjoying herself so far. Even Sarah was quite good company now she'd calmed down after that weird hand-sanitizer routine. What the hell had all that been about?

In truth, she wasn't really one for having girlfriends. Being with men was much less complicated and girlie chats had never been her thing. So far they had talked about themselves, learning about each other's lives. It was surprisingly therapeutic.

She felt a twinge of guilt for not trying hard enough to make Abi come along. But she had been adamant that she wasn't ready to socialize just yet. The poor girl had spent an hour on the phone to her sister in Australia earlier this evening, while Jo watched *Toy Story* with Tom. Abi's sister had just had a baby and had been too pregnant to fly over for the funeral. Jo had left Abi looking into flights to Australia online and hoped she would book something. Getting away for a while could help her take her mind off Fréd. Tom would start school in September; this would be their last chance for an extended visit.

But there was a part of Jo that was glad Abi hadn't come. They had been friends since they were eighteen and Jo would do anything for her. But right now, with Gold's on the brink of collapse, she needed someone to lean on, to confide in, and it didn't seem right moaning to Abi; she had enough problems of her own.

'I'll make notes,' said Sarah, rummaging on the shelf by the fireplace for a pen and some paper. 'Go ahead.'

A wish list. Where to start? A night with David Beckham? Bigger boobs? How about getting the Duchess of Cambridge to wear Gold's shoes? *Get real, Jo*, she chastised herself mentally. As willing as her new friends were, they didn't possess magic wands.

'Go on, I'm poised!' Sarah prodded her with the end of her pen.

'And nothing to do with the vicar, please. Something you

might regret not doing,' added Carrie, brushing a piece of crisp from her chest.

'Who says I won't regret not doing the vicar?' Jo laughed at Carrie's worried face. 'OK, here goes.'

She stopped. There was something she wanted to do. But was she really up for that sort of challenge? They were watching her; Sarah, pen in hand, chewing on her lip, Carrie, hand hovering over the crisp bowl. Oh what the hell! It wasn't as if any of this wish list stuff was actually going to happen. *Just say it.*

'I wish I could go right to the top of the Empire State Building.'

'New York!' gasped Carrie. 'Oh, I'd love to go there too!'

'Easy peasy,' said Sarah, writing it down in a very wobbly hand. 'But didn't you say you've been to New York before on business?'

Jo nodded and pushed herself upright. 'Every year in September. And every year I look at the Empire State Building from a distance and wonder what it must be like to stand up there and . . .' She sighed and shook her head impatiently. 'The thing is I'm scared witless of heights. I almost didn't buy my flat because it's on the first floor. I don't even like standing at the top of an escalator. I worry I'm going to throw myself down. As if I've got no control over my own body. I've been known to fall to my knees in a quivering heap. So ridiculous.'

'I can't imagine that of you,' said Carrie, wide-eyed.

'Oh yeah. It's entirely possible that I'll get to the edge and try to jump off.' She shuddered. 'Actually, I've changed my mind. Let me think of something else.'

'I'm sure there are safety barriers, Jo,' giggled Sarah, apparently too tipsy to take Jo's phobia seriously.

Carrie nodded. 'I get it. For your wish to come true you have to conquer your fears first. We can help with that, can't we, Sarah?'

Jo gave them a weak smile. She doubted it; she'd only told them half the story.

A scene from her favourite film – *Sleepless in Seattle* – flashed into her mind. She had told the truth, well, part of it; she was afraid of heights and she would love to stand at the top of the Empire State Building and look out across Manhattan, from Central Park right down to the Statue of Liberty. But the whole truth, the rest of her wish . . . to find the man of her dreams waiting for her there, to fall in love, get married, have a family . . . Well, she kept that to herself.

If life was a stage, to paraphrase Shakespeare, Jo's role was cast: she was the businesswoman, the one who didn't do romance, or cook for her man or have children. She had a career. That was just the way it was.

Anyway, the whole thing was futile. There was no way she could ever overcome her fear of heights and climb the Empire State Building, no matter how sincere the other two were with their promise of help. Which was fine, because then she could hold on to the fantasy that if she did make it to the most famous observation deck in the world, her hero might just be there to sweep her off her feet . . .

'All right, I'll do it. Write it down, Sarah.'

All of a sudden she needed a cigarette badly and cursed herself for giving up. She didn't even have her emergency one in her bag. She made do with a cheese-and-onion crisp and poked Carrie with her toe.

'You next.'

Carrie had thought about little else for the past forty-eight hours. Jo and Sarah must both expect her to say she wanted to lose weight. She was so fat, it was obvious. But after that last insult about her cooking from Alex, she had to do more than that. She'd stop making jokes about her size and admit how unhappy she was. Scary, though; if she didn't have food, she would have nothing. Her life revolved around planning the next meal, shopping for it, preparing it and finally serving it to Alex, who invariably had something nit-picky to say.

Both Jo and Sarah had figures Carrie could only dream of; Jo's long slender legs in her skinny jeans hadn't got an ounce of fat on them and petite Sarah in her off-the-shoulder jumper and leggings had a far trimmer body than Carrie had ever had, even after having a baby.

Her own stretchy black dress did nothing to hide the rolls of fat on her belly; she was kidding herself that it was flattering. Alex swore blind that he loved her the way she was, but how could he? She couldn't even bear to look at herself.

So much had happened since she dropped out of uni at twenty. She had been skinny then, before ... everything that happened ... And more importantly, she had been confident, ambitious and not afraid of anything.

A path stretched out in front of her, leading towards her future. The same path she had been following for the last ten years. It was time. To get a job, to be someone, to do something. She thought back to her wardrobe. If 'reality' was grim, it was only Carrie who could change it. She gulped as a sob rose up in her throat.

'Car-rie?' Jo waggled her feet on Carrie's lap to get her attention. 'Still with us?'

'Umm.' Carrie stood up and picked up her handbag. 'Just need the loo. Upstairs?'

Sarah nodded. 'It's the door on the end, next to Zac's bedroom.'

Carrie excused herself and made her way up the tiny winding staircase. At the top she faced three doors. Brightly coloured wooden letters spelt out Zac's name on the middle one. Carrie aimed for the open doorway and poked her head inside. It was Sarah and Dave's room. A chair in the corner was piled high with clothes, bunting in a vintage print hung across the curtain pole and a patchwork quilt covered the double bed. It looked tiny compared with her own king-sized version. There was something more intimate about a smaller bed, though, she thought wistfully. She crept out and headed towards the remaining door.

The bathroom was tiny, bottles of shampoo and shower gel competing for space with about two hundred bath toys. Carrie used the loo quickly and washed her hands. She didn't have much time before they would wonder what she was up to. If she was going to go through with this mad wish, she needed to do one more thing first. She took a bag of crisps from her handbag and ate them in large handfuls.

Looking in on Zac would buy her another minute, she could finish her crisps off in there. She gently turned the door handle to the baby's room and went inside.

Zac was lying on his back with his arms up in surrender. Carrie's throat contracted. He looked angelic; he was such a sweet little thing.

What would she have wanted, boy or girl, she wondered as she tipped the crisp crumbs straight into her mouth. She sighed; there was no point dwelling on what might have been. She stowed the empty packet in her bag and licked her fingers. As she turned to leave, she noticed a red glow in the corner of the room and froze. *Dammit! The baby monitor!* How loud had her crunching and rustling been?

With a lump in her throat, she tiptoed silently from the room and went to join the others.

'Here she is,' said Jo, topping up their glasses. 'We're expecting something deep and meaningful now, after keeping us in suspense for the last five minutes.'

'Was there any sound from Zac?' asked Sarah with a frown. 'We just heard the oddest crackling noise through the baby monitor.'

Oh crumbs, they'd heard her! Now she had gone bright red. Talking of crumbs . . . Carrie brushed a hand over her face. 'Sorry, that might have been me. I just peeped into his room. He's fast asleep.'

She picked up her wine glass and took a large sip. *Please*

let's change the subject. Jo and Sarah exchanged glances but nothing was said.

Carrie managed a shaky laugh. 'So my wish: I want to wear a bikini. In public. This summer.'

Her heart thumped as a few seconds of heavy silence hung between them until Jo clapped her hands.

'Whoo-hoo! Go Carrie!' Jo waved her arm in a circle above her head.

'Why does that need to go on the wish list? You can just do that, can't you? Mind you, you're a braver woman than me,' said Sarah, her pen still poised. 'My bikini days are well and truly behind me.'

'Rubbish,' said Jo. 'You're as dainty as a doll.'

'Seriously, under this jumper is a stomach like a deflated balloon. I'm a martyr to stretch m— Carrie, are you OK?'

Carrie looked from Sarah to Jo, her throat tight with emotion, and wondered whether either of them had ever felt taken for granted, worthless, invisible. Probably not.

'Sorry,' she said, pressing fingers under her eyelids to ward off tears. 'Ignore me, it's just the wine.'

Sarah put down her pen and patted Carrie's knee. 'You can choose another wish if you like. Look. I haven't written anything down yet.'

Alex had offered to give her anything she wished for. She only had to ask. But this was something she had to do for herself. She wondered whether Jo or Sarah would ever get it.

'It's not just about wearing a bikini,' said Carrie carefully. 'It's about being the sort of person who would wear one.'

Jo and Sarah exchanged looks. Sarah squeezed herself on the other end of the sofa and Jo put a comforting arm round Carrie's shoulders.

'I look at you two and I realize I'm just wasting my life. You're both so successful. You've achieved loads already. People look up to you. I thought that being a home-maker would be so rewarding, that the "Ladies who Lunch" lifestyle would be fantastic. But it's not. It's boring and it makes you fat.'

Carrie looked at her friends' faces, trying to work out whether their expressions were of concern or horror.

'You're not fat, Carrie. You're just big-boned, you – ouch!'

Sarah rubbed her arm where Jo had just pinched her. She turned back to Carrie and frowned. 'I don't mean to pry but why don't you work, Carrie? You're the same age as me, no children . . .'

'Don't go there,' said Carrie harshly. 'I'd be a terrible mother. And Alex is ten years older than me. It was something we both agreed on when we first met.'

She felt a stab of pain at the memory. He had made a throwaway comment about not being able to imagine being a parent and she had seized on it at the time, saying she didn't want to be either. It had become something of an elephant in the room.

'Oh.' Sarah shrank back from Carrie, looking stung.

'Is Alex wealthy?' asked Jo. 'Is that why you don't work? And if so has he got a brother?'

Carrie could tell them everything. The whole sordid truth. But then they might not want to know her at all. She was tempted. Maybe one day. But not tonight.

'I've never been the career type, you know, dropped out of uni. Not very confident. A bit shy. Alex didn't really like me working. I was in a dead-end job when I met him. He was doing more shift work then. We never saw each other.' She tried to read their expressions; Jo looked puzzled, Sarah looked a bit drunk. 'I know it's a bit old-fashioned. But it suited us. I wasn't earning much anyway. So I stopped.'

'And now?' asked Jo. 'What do you want now?'

That was a good question. Carrie wasn't quite sure yet. She was going to have to tackle one thing at a time.

'No idea.' She managed a shaky smile. 'Of course I know employers will be falling over themselves to have me – no experience, no qualifications and an extremely wide

68

backside. But first things first – my bikini. I'm going to have to lose at least three stone if I'm going to fit back into one of those.'

'Not that I agree with any of that nonsense,' said Sarah, moving back to the rug in front of the fire, 'but I'm writing it down. You are now officially on a bikini diet.'

'She can finish her wine first,' said Jo, topping up their glasses.

Sarah opened the log burner and added some more wood, waggling the poker around to coax flames from the embers. It always seemed to work when Dave did it. She was ready for the other two to leave now, to be honest. She could happily collapse into bed and sink into oblivion.

This wish list was a stupid idea. She had no idea how she could help cure Jo of her fear of heights or encourage Carrie to lose three stone. Even if she did have the time – which she blatantly didn't. And now it was her turn.

She felt all fidgety and nervous. They would hate her if they knew what she really wished for. She wanted her old life back: the one where she was a promising young accountant with a sharp pencil and an even sharper mind. Now her employer was lucky if she remembered to turn up for meetings, let alone stun them with her financial acumen. And as for this evening's ordeal with Eleanor . . . She shuddered. She would never live it down. She was an embarrassment. She bulged out of all her clothes and more often than not went to work with some sort of baby-related goo on her shoulders.

And what about her and Dave? Only a year ago they were madly in love and had had mutual respect for each other's career instead of this churning resentment that they both had to work so hard to keep at bay. He resented her for being the chief breadwinner; she resented him for getting the golden moments with Zac. And then there was living in Woodby. Popping to the shops used to mean vintage boutiques and the city centre, not the farm shop and Tesco. Village life wasn't all it was cracked up to be.

Yes. She wanted her old life back. The one before Zac.

A shudder of revulsion ricocheted through her; how could she even think that?

'You OK?' Jo asked.

Sarah glanced round to see two pairs of watchful eyes staring at her.

Right on cue an ember fell out of the stove and she fumbled with the tongs to pick it up. Ringlets of hair fell forward and hid the two bright spots on her cheeks.

Take it back. Take it back. I wouldn't change being a mother for all the world.

But sometimes she wished she didn't feel quite so torn.

Jo stood up and stretched. She picked up a picture of Sarah and Dave on their wedding day from the mantelpiece and whistled. 'Looks like you've got your Prince Charming. You both look gorgeous!'

Sarah's eyes softened. Happy times. 'Thanks. I think that was the one and only day my hair behaved itself.'

She closed the log burner and sat back on the armchair. The room span and she blinked her eyes a few times. She hadn't drunk this much wine for months. That was the reason she'd had such a terrible thought. It was just the wine talking. She didn't mean it. She was *so* going to regret this in the morning.

She picked up the wish list and doodled along the margin. She was fine, everything was fine. She was overreacting. And she did have a wish. It was the same wish she'd had since leaving university and in the absence of having anything better to say, where was the harm in spitting it out?

She dropped her pad on the floor, picked up her wine glass and drained the last drop. 'My wish is to be a partner in the firm where I work.'

'You go, girl,' Jo said, pinching her spot in front of the fire.

70

'It's not a new wish; it's always been my long-term goal. I hope that's not cheating? It's been on hold while I had Zac but I think I'm ready to go for it now. One of the partners in the practice is retiring this year and this could be my way in. Besides . . .' She felt her voice give way. 'I haven't mentioned this, but I'm the main breadwinner and the extra money wouldn't go amiss.'

She scanned their faces for a reaction; some people could be quite judgemental about men taking on a traditionally female role. Her dad would have had something to say about it, that's for sure. God rest his soul.

'I don't know how you do it, Sarah.' Carrie's hand stole towards the bowl of crisps and stopped.

Sarah pressed her lips together, silently pleased to see Carrie showing some self-restraint. Sarah pulled the bowl towards her. It was empty.

'Your career must be very important to you to want promotion,' Carrie went on. 'Especially with Zac still so little.'

Sarah felt the heat rise to her face again. 'Like it or not, people judge you on your job title. That's just the way it is.'

'Write it down, then, if that's what you want,' said Jo with a shrug.

There was an uncomfortable silence. Sarah's blush deepened and she hid her face behind her hair. Not everyone had Daddy's empire handed to them on a plate like Jo. Her father's empire had disappeared long ago when he and the other coalminers had ended up on the scrap heap, most of them never to work again. It had made him bitter and resentful of other people's success and made Sarah more determined than ever to educate herself and get on in life.

But Sarah had niggling doubts. Becoming a partner would inevitably mean longer hours, less time with Zac, more pressure on Dave. Oh God. Was this a bad idea? Was it the right timing?

She cleared her throat. 'Or alternatively, I could wish to feel more part of things in Woodby.'

Her new friends were happier with that; she could see it in their faces.

Carrie sat forward in her seat. 'Go on.'

'My old life in the city was so . . . I don't know . . . *me*,' she said. 'I don't feel like I fit in here.'

Carrie tucked her feet underneath her and set down her wine glass. 'It does take a while. Everyone's so busy with their own lives.'

'We moved to a village to start a family. We thought it would be a great place to bring up kids. And it is. But I feel . . . isolated.'

'It can be isolating,' murmured Carrie, reaching out to touch Sarah's arm reassuringly.

'Get involved more, then,' said Jo, checking her watch.

'There's the village show,' said Carrie. 'The whole village turns out for that. End of the summer. Competitions for jam-making, flower-arranging, that sort of thing.'

Jo put her hands up. 'I'd be no help with that. My skills lie outside of the kitchen and that's putting it mildly.'

'It's not my forte either,' said Sarah, pulling a face.

'We're all amateurs,' said Carrie, lifting her shoulders. 'It's the way to get involved. I promise you.'

'So. What are you going to put on the wish list?' said Jo.

Sarah opened her mouth and hesitated. For all their obvious disapproval, she knew what she had to do. 'I'm going for partner.' She winced. 'It's the thing I'd most regret not achieving. Sorry. And I've no idea how you can help me do that.' She busied herself with her pen and pad.

'It's your choice,' said Jo, standing up. 'I should go back to Abi now we've made our wishes.'

'Hold on!' said Sarah, peeling three sheets of paper off her pad. 'You both need to sign here.' She handed them each a handwritten contract. 'Sorry it's messy; I think I might be slightly drunk.' Maybe making them sign contracts was a bit bossy, but they might as well do things properly.

'I thought we should give ourselves a six-month

deadline, what do you think?' she said, handing Carrie a pen. 'That would make it September. OK with you?'

Carrie had gone a bit pale and Jo was looking at her like she had two heads.

'Whatever.' Jo shrugged. 'I usually have a research trip to New York in September. It works for me. Carrie?'

'Semi-naked. In public,' Carrie whispered hoarsely. 'What am I letting myself in for?'

'Sorted.' Sarah collected the sheets back. 'I'll make copies and circulate them at the next meeting.'

'Bloody hell, Sarah,' Jo said with a smirk. 'I thought this was meant to be a bit of fun?'

Sarah felt her cheeks flame.

'When I say meeting, I mean, you know, for a drink.' She shrugged self-consciously, feeling a bit silly.

It was the contracts that had done it; they thought she was a control freak.

Carrie came to the rescue and pulled them all close for a hug. 'OK. Let's make our wishes come true.'

Jo took one last lingering look at Sarah's wedding photograph. 'A girl's got to have dreams.'

Chapter 5

Sarah jumped up to hold the door for an unsteady old man who was trying to angle his Zimmer frame into the doctor's surgery, his sparse hair ruffling in the harsh March winds.

'I'm back for more Viagra,' he called to the receptionist, winking at Sarah.

The receptionist sighed wearily. 'Morning, Mr Prior.'

'Here to see the nurse. Ten o'clock. I hope it's that bossy one with the big—'

'Take a seat, thank you, Mr Prior.'

He shuffled into the waiting room and eased himself into the chair next to Sarah.

He nudged her arm. 'Nothing contagious, I trust?'

'Oh no,' said Sarah, hoping the same could be said of him, seeing as all the other seats in the room were vacant. He waited, presumably hoping for some interesting ailment story.

'Just a check-up with the nurse.' She certainly wasn't going to tell him that she wanted contraception. In view of his Viagra comment, it might be seen as tantamount to an invitation. She hoped the nurse hurried up, before she changed her mind.

'Don't tell me they're handing out Viagra to you youngsters as well?' Mr Prior guffawed, sparking off a mucusy cough.

'Sarah Hudson?'

'Yes!' Sarah jumped up with relief as a sturdy nurse appeared at the door.

The nurse ushered Sarah into a chair and sat down opposite her. 'What can I do for you?'

Deep breath.

'I'm going to stop breastfeeding, so I want to go back on the pill,' said Sarah, twisting her wedding ring round and round. The decision had taken her days to make. It was the only sensible solution, but the guilt was unbearable. She stared down at her lap.

'How old is baby now?'

'Eight months.'

'And is he doing well, thriving?'

'Oh yes.' Sarah's face softened into a smile.

'Any problems with feeding?'

'None at all. Zac eats everything we try him with, well, what doesn't go in his hair or down his bib.'

'I remember that stage with mine. Mind you, my eldest son could still do with wearing a bib and he's twenty-five.'

Sarah watched as the nurse untwisted the blood pressure monitor cuff and she dropped her gaze. Her eyes were hot and she felt a wave of emotion take hold.

'It's all getting too much: trying to feed him myself before work, then there's nowhere private in the office, so I have to try to express milk in the ladies' loo, surrounded by God knows how many millions of germs. I'm terrified of passing on germs. Half the time I'm in a meeting when my milk comes in and all I can think about is my aching boobs. And the looks I get . . . One of the men even got my expressed milk out of the office fridge the other day and started gagging. On top of that I'm not concentrating at work and I'm always in a rush at home.'

She took a deep breath and tried to swallow the lump in her throat. The nurse sat down in front of her and gently took her hand. She pushed Sarah's sleeve up and fitted the blood pressure cuff.

'Sounds like you're doing a fantastic job to me.'

Her chin wobbled.

'I'm not. I'm letting Zac down. Depriving him of precious antibodies. I had planned to carry on breastfeeding until he was one, but it's just not practical. And . . .' If she was going to get promoted, she needed to get herself under control and prove to Eleanor how focused she was. The nurse wouldn't understand that.

The nurse squeezed her hand, giving her the encouragement she needed to go on.

'And I can't take him to mother and baby group because I work. He won't learn to share or play with other children. He'll probably start school unable to make friends, completely lacking in social skills. And I don't meet other mums . . .'

She stopped. Where had all that come from? The nurse stared at her for a moment, patted her hand and turned away to jot down a few notes. *Damn!* Sarah's heart sank; the nurse probably thought she had post-natal depression. She hadn't got time to be depressed.

'First things first. I can sort you out a prescription for the pill now. You could cut right down and only feed baby yourself at night. That takes the pressure off a bit. And even if you did stop completely, he's had eight months to build up his immune system. You've done much better than many mums already.'

Sarah swallowed hard; she always felt like crying when someone was kind to her. She was a ridiculous, over-emotional wreck. The nurse smiled at her.

'As for the other stuff . . .' She leaned forward and whispered, 'I hated mother and baby group: two hours of talking about the contents of other babies' nappies.' The nurse shuddered. 'Spring is on its way, you'll be out and about more then. Take him to the park; you'll soon start meeting other mums.'

76

Sarah felt the cuff tighten as the nurse started to pump it up. 'And how about waiting until he can walk and talk first, before you start worrying about school.'

Sarah made a noise that was halfway between a laugh and a sob. 'I'm getting carried away, aren't I?'

'A bit.' The nurse stood up and went to the counter. 'What do you do for relaxation?'

'Yawn, mostly, then go to bed.'

The nurse laughed.

'You need to make time for you. Here.' She held out a small booklet. 'The village magazine. Tells you what's on. Try yoga.'

Make time for herself? As in, do what's right for herself? That must mean that the nurse thought it was OK to go for promotion. Sarah perked up immediately. *Wish list here we come.*

Email to: Jo Gold (work)
From: SarahDaveZac

Jo,

Can you make it over on Friday night? There's a yoga class in the village hall at seven. I know Carrie says she hates exercise, but she might enjoy something like this. Anyway, if we say we'll be there to keep her company, she's bound to agree.

Sarah x

Jo was at her desk with five minutes to spare before the staff meeting when an email from Sarah arrived. She opened it on her phone and read it through carefully, cringing as she did so. Yoga in a village hall. Women kidding themselves they were working out, whale music and fleecy blankets. *Give me strength.* Her idea of exercise was to push herself through the pain barrier, working her body until her lungs threatened to collapse and her leg muscles trembled. None of this 'My body is a temple' rubbish.

Jo leaned back in her chair and pulled this month's sales

report towards her. *Please let it not be as bad as I think it's going to be.* She flicked to the bottom of the page. Bugger. Ten per cent down on last year. Which in itself didn't sound too bad, except that last year they had hit an eight-year low.

The sound of her staff making their way to the warehouse made her stomach churn. She should get going; it was time to face the music. She could murder a cigarette.

Liz knocked on the door and pushed it open. 'All set?' she asked.

'Not really,' Jo replied. 'But thanks for asking.'

'I'll tell them you're on your way.' Jo's secretary smiled and pulled the door to behind her.

Liz had worked for the firm for over fifteen years and had been her father's secretary until he retired. And if Jo wasn't mistaken, he still tapped her up for information even now. God knows what he was going to think about today's news.

She rolled her shoulders back to release the stiffness, caused by hunching for hours over her laptop. Yoga was supposed to be good for relieving stress, wasn't it? She certainly had plenty of that. Besides, she had nothing better to do this Friday night. Maybe there would be some hot and flexible men. *In Woodby? Yeah, right.* She typed a quick reply to Sarah's email and left her office to join the rest of her staff.

Patrick McGregor, Gold's operations director, stood in the middle of the team, head and shoulders above the rest of them. He had assembled the staff by the warehouse doors. Despite her nerves, she suppressed a smile. He couldn't have picked a worse spot, the plonker; it was freezing there with the draught coming through the metal shutters. Patrick was sharing a joke with Len, the workroom manager, and grinned at her as she strode towards him and stood at his side. Nice to see someone was happy.

Her insides quivered as she smiled and took a deep breath.

'Morning, everyone.'

A loaded silence descended.

'I'll be as brief as I can,' she said, shooting Patrick a teasing look, 'seeing as Patrick has chosen the North Pole for our meeting.'

Patrick bit his lip comically and smiled back. His adoring fans in the sales team giggled. How did he do it? He managed to have the whole company eating out of his hand and still keep a professional distance. Whereas although they all seemed to respect her, at least she hoped they did, she didn't get the same warmth from them. Apart from Liz. She caught her secretary's eye and Liz gave her a reassuring half-nod.

'OK?' murmured Patrick. 'I've got all the figures here, if you need them.' He tapped a finger on his notepad. She gave him a sideways glance. Perhaps it was that soft Scottish lilt to his voice that they all loved; there was something musical about it even when he was being serious.

She nodded and tried to channel her father; he was always good at this sort of thing – putting a positive spin on even the most depressing results.

'It's been a mixed start to the New Year,' she began. 'We've launched the new collection and early signs are encouraging from some of our oldest customers. Sadly, this isn't translating into sales . . .'

Jo was maintaining a brave face but it broke her heart to watch her employees as she delivered the bad news. Most of the staff had been with Gold's for years. It wouldn't come as a shock to many that redundancies were now almost a certainty. They had seen the order book fall, the leather delivery dwindle, the courier collect ever smaller pallets of shoes to distribute to struggling footwear retailers.

Jo wanted to be honest with everyone; there was no use making promises she couldn't keep.

Gold's still retained the honour of being a British manufacturer. Just. The bulk of their stock arrived in container loads from the Far East, to be hand-finished and boxed in the Northampton factory. Only a tiny range was still made here. It would be more cost-effective to import these too, but Jo, like her father before her, was adamant that Gold's would make shoes in Northampton for as long as possible.

'It goes against all my principles to contemplate letting anyone go,' she said, making eye contact with as many people as she could. 'But if we can't trade profitably, the company will go under and we will all lose our jobs.'

She had her hands in the back pockets of her jeans. Today was set aside for stocktaking, getting ready for the end of the financial year. Jo would be shifting boxes with the rest of them.

'There is a glimmer of hope, though. Although it is a bit of a slow burner, I admit.'

She spotted Patrick's cheerful smile with gratitude; he wasn't fully sold on the idea yet, but she appreciated his public support.

'Shaw's, most of you will know, has seven stores around the Midlands and the new management are planning to open another six this autumn. The company has rebranded and looks amazing. Ed Shaw has offered us a lifeline.'

Jo paused in her speech and met Patrick's gaze. She had to make the next bit sound plausible. In his opinion Ed Shaw's idea was the long shot to end all long shots.

'It's a bit of a wild card but if we can come up with a new quirky collection, he'll stock every single style and promote us heavily.'

Murmurs of interest rippled round the room.

'There's one proviso, though.'

Jo paused and her angular face softened into a cheeky smile.

'It will have to be made here at Gold's. We are going to create a new *British* collection, designed and manufactured for the modern woman right here in our factory.'

'Awesome!' said Patrick, leading the rest of the team in a round of applause. The six-strong team of craftsmen and women even cheered. Liz caught her eye and gave her a dreamy look. Jo looked at her feet to hide her smile. Liz was a good twenty years older than Patrick, but she had a mammoth crush on him.

'It's early days, but yes, very good news,' Jo said, gesturing for them all to calm down. 'Patrick?'

As she stepped back to let him take over, he smiled at her, his dark eyes twinkling with such pride that she felt a warm glow light her from within. He was a good friend; it was a relief to know he was on her side.

He ruffled a hand through his fair hair and smiled at everyone.

'If anyone can get us through this sticky patch it's Jo. But we're a team, aren't we? We're like family.' He flicked both his hands like a compere at a comedy club and was rewarded with a small sea of smiling faces. Liz put her hand to her chest and made an 'ah' face.

'We welcome all your ideas for this new collection,' he continued. 'We're still designing for the same customer, but apart from that, anything goes. Please come forward with any suggestions, however off the wall you think they might be. That's it, everyone. Thanks very much.'

Liz gave them both the thumbs-up as people started to move away in small groups, murmuring to each other.

Probably all going back to print off their bloody CVs, thought Jo glumly.

'Post-match debrief?' said Patrick, jerking his head towards his office.

Patrick's office was next to hers and identical in size but whereas hers was devoid of clutter, his had stacks of paper on every surface. Jo sat at the table opposite him, chin in her hand, as he added the final details to the summer marketing plan. She was trying to focus on what he was saying but her thoughts kept drifting back to the staff meeting and what her employees would be saying behind her back.

'So it's between that promotion or the three-month magazine subscription with every purchase over fifty pounds, which is a good offer,' he said. 'I think that's quite tempting. Are you listening to me, Gold?'

'What? Oh sorry.' She shook herself from her reverie and sniggered.

Years ago, they had spent a brief spell working together in the warehouse at Gold's for an ex-army sergeant who insisted on calling everyone by their surname, including the boss's daughter. It never failed to raise a smile.

She and Patrick had started at the company together, fresh out of university, and had hit it off straight away. Then when she had taken over from her dad, Patrick had had to report to her. All a bit weird to start with but they had soon reverted to taking the mickey out of each other. The only thing that had really changed was that she couldn't always confide in him like a friend any more. With the threat of redundancies, it wasn't impossible that he might lose his job. Jo didn't even want to think about that. Sometimes having the top job was crap and very lonely.

A sigh escaped and she met Patrick's eye.

'Look, you were ace in that meeting,' he said, pointing a pen at her. 'Your dad couldn't have put it any better himself.' He leaned forward in his chair and smiled. 'After lunch, I'll go through the file of suppliers, see if I can find any freelance designers for Mr Shaw.'

'Do you really think we can design this new collection, Patrick?' She studied his face, willing him to share her hopes.

'Yup. Or at least die trying.' He grinned. He dropped his pen on the table and sat back, linking his fingers behind his head confidently.

Jo tried not to shiver. That was what she was afraid of.

There was a knock on the open door and they both looked up.

'Come in, Cesca,' said Patrick, waving her towards a seat on the other side of his desk.

Francesca, from the sales office, glanced at Jo and closed the door behind her. She had an artist's sketchpad clamped in front of her like a shield.

'I didn't mean to disturb you,' she said timidly. 'I can come back later if you like?'

'No, you're fine,' said Jo. 'Love the hair, by the way.'

The twenty-four-year-old was part Italian, with strong dark eyebrows and long thick hair. The bottom third was dip-dyed a striking cyan blue. Jo always felt boring by comparison. And old.

'Thanks.' Cesca flicked her hair back over her shoulders and laid her pad on the desk.

'Sales query?' asked Patrick.

'Um. No. It was just an idea I had about the new collection. For Shaw's.'

Jo poured herself and Patrick coffee from the cafetière and held up a mug for Cesca, who shook her head.

'All suggestions gratefully received.' Jo was intrigued. She looked at Patrick, who shrugged, apparently none the wiser.

'I wanted to show you some designs I've been working on.'

'Designs for shoes?' asked Patrick in surprise. 'Should I have known about this?'

Cesca's job involved collating orders sent in by the sales agents and taking replenishment orders over the phone from retailers. It was standard office stuff.

'It started as a hobby,' she explained. 'My dream has always been to be a shoe designer. Even more so since working here.' She smiled shyly at Jo. 'I'm doing a foundation course in art and design in my spare time.'

'Then what?' said Jo, unable to take her eyes off the sketchpad and itching to grab hold of it.

'The London College of Fashion to study footwear design. If I get in.'

Patrick nodded. 'Good for you.'

'Not that I want to leave Gold's. But ...' Cesca blushed and looked down at her lap.

Jo's heart sank. So she'd been right. She guessed that very little work was being done this morning, despite the Shaw's opportunity. Everyone must be too busy planning their next move. Except Cesca, evidently. The girl certainly had a flair for fashion. Jo felt a stirring of hope. Imagine if Gold's had its very own fledgling designer. She mentally crossed her fingers that Cesca had talent as well as fashion sense.

'You're right to have ambitions,' Jo said, seeing the young woman in a brand-new light. 'And you never know, your designs could be just what we need. So what's in the book?'

'I used my mother for inspiration. But it was when you said quirky; it made me think perhaps some of them could be useful for Gold's. I have to warn you first, though.' Cesca's mouth twitched. 'My mother is, er, quite flamboyant. Let's just say beige doesn't feature in her wardrobe.'

'Sounds interesting. I can't wait,' said Jo, and she meant it. Not quite the quintessentially British combination that would first spring to mind. But interesting certainly.

Cesca gave a nervous laugh and opened up her sketchpad.

Five minutes later, Jo had passed in and out of the speechless stage and was fizzing with ideas. Patrick looked impressed too. Cesca had drawn pages and pages of shoes; some were fully finished colour sketches, others were just rough out-lines. Most of them were way too over the top, but enough of them showed promise to get Jo excited.

'Cesca, you're a genius,' she murmured. 'Not to mention the darkest horse ever.'

Patrick was still flicking through the pages. 'There's some potential here, Jo, do you agree?'

She nodded, keen to make a start. 'Would you be happy for us to select, say, twelve styles and get Len to see if he can work them up into samples in the workshop?'

Cesca's olive skin had blushed an even darker shade. 'I can't believe it. I thought you'd laugh at them.'

'If we can make use of them, we'll sponsor you to go to uni,' said Jo spontaneously. Cesca's face lit up.

'But we will need to make them quirkily English.'

Jo didn't want to offend her, but the emphasis had to be on British heritage and not on Cesca's Italian roots.

This would be the first brand-new collection that Jo would have had anything to do with. Designed and made in Northampton, the heart of the British footwear industry. And it might just save their souls, thought Jo happily, or should that be *soles*.

Carrie hummed as she finished unpacking the supermarket shopping, amazed at where the morning had disappeared to. Usually she just raced along the aisles, thoughtlessly tossing food into the trolley. Today's trip had taken for ever; checking every label for calories and cross-referencing it with her menu sheet. This diet malarkey was a full-time job. It was a good thing she didn't work, or she wouldn't have time to lose weight. She paused, holding two digestive biscuits that didn't fit into the tin in her hand. Of course, if she had had a job she might not have got so big in the first place.

She set one biscuit aside to have with her morning coffee. She had been so good today, she reasoned, snapping the other in half, popping one piece in her mouth and the other in the bin. Now that was real progress; before going on this diet she would never have thrown good food away.

The post clattered through the letterbox on to the tiled floor. Carrie fetched it, set the boring stuff aside and opened the only interesting-looking item. A free sample of a new breakfast bar fell out of its packaging, fat free and packed with calcium, apparently. She turned it over in her hands and read the calorie content. The edge of the wrapper was slightly torn. It wouldn't take much to open it. If it was nice, she could swap it for tomorrow's breakfast of porridge made with water, which she wasn't looking forward to one bit. Maybe she should just try a mouthful now in case she didn't like it. She popped a piece in her mouth and chewed. Not bad.

Right. Food diary. She was religious when it came to recording her food intake. Carrie sat down at the desk in the little bedroom which until recently had been Alex's territory, and turned on the computer. While she waited for the program to load, she opened a packet of ready-salted low-fat crisps. Chosen because they had fewer calories – thirteen fewer, to be precise – than the cheese-and-onion ones. Every calorie mattered. Carrie was allowed three small meals a day and two snacks at one hundred calories each when she was feeling peckish. Which was most of the time.

She pulled up her spreadsheet and typed 'Coco Pops and skimmed milk' in the box for breakfast and apple for snack. Today was going so well; she marvelled at her own will-power.

Finding new ways to cut her calories and stick to her daily allowance was Carrie's new obsession. She took great delight in pulling a fast one on the plan. Why have two Ryvitas and a satsuma when you could tuck into a bag of low-fat crisps? And who would choose a boiled egg and a rice cracker over a two-finger KitKat?

She felt a brief pang of loss for that jar of peanut butter she'd had to throw away the day before. One hundred calories in only one measly teaspoon! That had been a real blow. She had rarely passed that cupboard without delving in for a scoop. She turned the computer off and glanced at her profile in the mirror. The weight hadn't really started to come off yet, but with all these sacrifices she was making, it wouldn't take long.

She began gnawing through the crisps like a beaver building a dam and went in search of suitable clothes to wear to yoga.

It was time to go and meet the others but no matter how much tugging and pulling she did, Carrie felt far too exposed in this outfit. The only T-shirt she could find that covered her bum was one of Alex's with the slogan *Hog's breath is better than no breath at all*, which had to be debatable, and her leggings didn't do her any favours either.

She would never in a million years attempt yoga on her own. But Sarah had been very persuasive. Apparently it was a great way to get in shape for beginners, it was gentle and relaxing and as none of them had ever done any yoga before, they would all be in the same boat. Until the teacher asked them to touch their toes, and then they would be in entirely different boats, thought Carrie, trying to brush away the mental image of a chubby tug boat. Anyway, she was too scared of Sarah to say no, so that was that.

Carrie slid a knife along the edge of the cardboard, stabbed the cellophane lid repeatedly and read the instructions on the box: *Microwave on full power for five minutes then leave to stand.* It was not what Alex normally sat down to on a Friday night, but she had had such a busy day, she hadn't had time to cook. It felt really naughty, though. She had better go and deliver the bad news.

Alex glanced up from his newspaper and she saw his eyes widen. Her hands flew to the hem of her T-shirt and she yanked it until the shoulder seams started to complain.

'You look very,' he hesitated, 'casual.'

'I'm off to make a fool of myself at yoga with Jo and Sarah. We might come back here afterwards. You can go out if you like.'

A bit of a white lie, they were definitely coming back here; she had made post-workout snacks and everything.

A cloud passed over Alex's face. 'Is that an order?'

'Of course not.' She gave him a peck on the cheek. 'Just didn't want to subject you to the intrusion of three sweaty women.'

Another white lie. Her budding friendship with Jo and

Sarah, the whole wish list project, was the first thing she'd done entirely without him for years. She was loath to let him in just yet.

'What about dinner?' asked Alex.

The microwave pinged right on cue.

'Sounds like it's ready.' She picked up her longest, most shapeless hoody and made for the front door. She pressed her lips together to suppress a giggle. 'Hope it's not too salty?' she called over her shoulder.

Diet, exercise and leaving her husband to fend for himself. She was getting more confident already. She could do this. She really could.

Chapter 6

At Rose Cottage, Sarah was having doubts about her outfit. Carrie and Jo seemed to be taking this seriously and were both dressed in Lycra. Sarah, on the other hand, was wearing black tights, her denim shorts and a Bambi T-shirt. Oh well, too late to change now.

Whooping and splashing noises were coming from upstairs. She was leaving Dave in charge of bath time this evening and it sounded like they were having great fun.

'Has everyone got a towel for the relaxation bit?' she said, remembering she still hadn't got one.

They had.

'Whose car shall we go in?' Carrie was peering at her rear view in the hall mirror and trying to stretch her hoody down as far as her knees.

'Carrie! It's a two-minute walk.'

'Someone might see us.'

'Yeah, that hot vicar, with a bit of luck,' said Jo, adjusting her cleavage. Even head to toe in Nike, she looked amazing.

'It's all right for you two; you're both skinny, everyone's going to look at me.'

'It's the village hall, not Muscle Beach.' Sarah laughed. She ran up the stairs, kissed her men goodbye, grabbed a towel and shooed Jo and Carrie out of the door.

A delicate Chinese woman with the poise of a ballerina sat in the lotus position on the stage, eyes closed and hands resting palms-upwards on her knees. She was wearing loose linen trousers and a tunic with a mandarin collar. Her black hair, threaded with a few strands of silver, was scraped back into a bun. A second, elderly Chinese woman, with a toothless smile, sat at a small table just inside the door of the hall and collected their money.

The hall's main fluorescent lighting was off and the spotlights created shadows across the stage. The only other light source came from the green emergency exit lights, casting a ghoulish glow on the bodies lying prostrate on the floor. Relaxing sounds of pan pipes, waves crashing and the occasional distant sound of birds emanated from a speaker, and Sarah felt as if she should walk on tiptoe and hold her breath.

'It's packed,' she hissed, as they laid down mats at the back in a row and placed their towels at the end, copying everyone else.

'And pitch black,' said Jo.

'Thank goodness,' said Carrie.

'Namaste,' said the teacher. She stood in one fluid motion, hands together, and bowed to the room.

'Ooh, we're off,' said Jo.

Following the teacher's moves took up all Sarah's concentration and for the next fifteen minutes, she focused solely on her posture and her breathing. It felt good to exercise again. Before giving birth she had been acutely aware of her body, her muscles and her joints. But since Zac had arrived she had been so wrapped up in his tiny form that she had ignored her own flabby figure. This was just what she needed.

She was sure she had read somewhere about a yoga class for babies. That would be amazing. But it would probably be in the daytime when she was at work, filling in time-ledgers and dealing with HMRC. Like every other parent and baby activity . . .

As the instructor talked them through their poses, Sarah

couldn't resist a smile. Friday night spent in the village hall – she was really living on the edge. Twelve months ago, she and Dave would have been heading off to a restaurant. Now she was going to yoga. Her social life had well and truly taken a nosedive. Still, this was village life. This was what she had wanted. The trendy unmarried set from work was going out for drinks in town tonight. They hadn't invited her, but that was fine, she wouldn't have gone anyway.

This was definitely what she wanted.

She bent forward and grasped hold of her ankles as instructed. She glanced sideways at Jo, who had her hands on Carrie's back, pressing her down to the floor. The poor thing was going red in the face, trying to reach her ankles.

A rough count told her there were about thirty others in the room, only two of them men. A shiny curtain of dark hair hid the face of the woman on the front row, but Sarah could tell straight away from the slender body it was Rebecca, from the mother and baby group. Sarah eyed her figure enviously; her little girl was only a few weeks older than Zac, but Rebecca's Lycra-clad body showed no signs of baby weight. She was tall, toned and gorgeous. Sarah sucked in her tummy and looked away.

She knelt down on all fours as the teacher instructed.

'Visualize yourself as a cat, arching and stretching your back, exhaling and inhaling.'

All around her people were hollowing and arching their backs to the rhythm of the gentle music and from the back of the hall, Sarah's field of vision was filled with row upon row of bums in all shapes and sizes. It all started to feel slightly surreal. A wave of hysteria lurked dangerously at the side of her consciousness. She pinched her lips together and tried to concentrate.

'Meow,' said Jo softly, pretending to lick one hand and rub it behind her ear. Sarah snorted.

'This isn't exercise,' Jo muttered, 'it reminds me of drama at school.'

'Shush,' panted Carrie, flicking her eyes nervously to the front, 'you'll get us thrown out.'

'Sit back on your heels, forehead to the floor, stretch your arms back towards your toes in the pose of the child.'

'I can either sit on my heels or rest my forehead on the floor. Not both at the same bloomin' time!' moaned Carrie.

Prrrufff.

Jo clapped both hands across her mouth and collapsed on to her face, shaking with laughter.

'What was that?' giggled Sarah, thinking that yoga might not be much of a night out but she hadn't had so much fun in ages.

'Sorry!' Carrie squeaked.

'Carrie just farted,' Jo sniggered breathlessly.

Sarah stuffed the corner of her towel in her mouth and rolled on to her side. Seconds later all three of them were writhing with illicit silent laughter.

It was like being back at school, Sarah thought. The more they tried to be sensible, the more hilarious everything seemed.

A pair of tiny bare feet appeared at the back row.

'I am very glad you are finding happiness in my class. But for the benefit of the rest of the group, please channel your positive energy into your postures.'

The teacher nodded her head once and turned back to the room. Jo poked her tongue out but Carrie looked mortified. Sarah's grin faded as she caught sight of Rebecca staring at her, stony faced. She felt her heart sink. Bang went any chance of making friends there. Still, her loss.

Sarah realized the rest of the class was on the move. She blinked and checked out what Jo was doing.

'From there we will push up, straight arms, straight legs and into downward-facing dog.'

Sarah closed her eyes, bit the side of her cheek and tried to block out Jo's voice murmuring, 'Woof woof.'

It was dark as Carrie led Jo and Sarah up the hill towards Fern House. They were helpless with laughter as they relived their yoga highlights. The three of them had really bonded in the last hour and Carrie was glowing with happiness. She put that mostly down to her unfortunate bout of wind. It was a good job the lights had been low; her face had been scarlet with embarrassment.

'I can't believe I fell asleep during the relaxation bit at the end,' groaned Sarah, rolling her eyes. 'Did anyone notice?'

'Not until you started snoring,' said Jo. 'How does Dave sleep with that racket?'

'Listen, when you've had a baby, nothing stands between you and sleep. We can both zonk out at the drop of a hat. As you have now witnessed.'

A security light came on as they reached the front door, dazzling Carrie's eyes and making her drop the door key. She bent down to retrieve it and Jo blew a raspberry.

'Pardon you, Carrie.'

'Very funny.' She put the key in the lock and gave the oak door a shove. 'Be grateful I didn't have Brussels sprouts for dinner. Anyway, I wouldn't be too smug. The rest of the group couldn't tell which one of us had done it. So, guilty by association, I'm afraid, girls.'

She held the door open and ushered them inside.

'This is a proper grown-up house, Carrie,' said Sarah. 'Huge compared to ours. Want to swap?'

Carrie beamed; this was her domain and she was proud of her home.

'Wow!' said Jo, wide-eyed, turning a full circle in the hall. 'Will you come and do my flat?'

'It's like something out of a glossy magazine,' breathed Sarah, wandering round like Alice in Wonderland, trailing a finger along the oak banisters, huge hall mirror and oak console table.

Country Homes and Interiors to be precise. Carrie tweaked a dead leaf from her vase of lilies, secretly thrilled with their reaction. Alex had come into some money after his mum died and had given her carte blanche to do up the house. She'd spent ages choosing all the furniture, getting the look just right.

Everyone's trainers squeaked on the flagstone floor in the hall. Alex was out, she was sure, or he'd have made an appearance by now.

'Come through to the kitchen, I've got healthy nibbles.'

Once inside, Sarah gasped. 'It's a Farrow-and-Ball-hued oasis of calm. And I love this table.' She pulled out a heavy wooden chair and sat down at the huge pale wood table and circled her hands on its surface. 'I think it's bigger than our whole kitchen.'

'Thank you,' murmured Carrie, pulling dishes of hummus and raw vegetables out of the fridge and arranging them on the table.

'I've got some serious kitchen envy,' Jo laughed, pulling open cupboards until she found the glasses. 'Water everyone?'

Carrie marvelled at Jo's confidence as she watched her pour them all some drinks. She would have dehydrated before helping herself in someone else's home.

'My kitchen walls are decorated with random tester-pot squares of paint and splattered baby food,' Sarah sighed, dipping into the dish of crudités. 'And look at your surfaces: where's the clutter, or fingerprints and grease-smears?'

'Sterile, you mean?' said Carrie, thinking that at least Sarah's cottage was full of life.

'Oh Carrie, what I wouldn't give for sterile,' groaned Sarah. She swirled a carrot stick through the dish of hummus. 'You have no idea!'

'I think we do,' said Jo with a snort. 'We've seen your hand-sanitizer habit.'

Sarah's face went pink. 'Just trying to keep my little boy safe.'

'Shall we talk about the wish list?' Carrie suggested, keen to keep the conversation light.

'Absolutely,' said Sarah. 'Can you take notes please, Carrie? I think we should keep a record of progress.'

Jo met Carrie's gaze and quirked an eyebrow mischievously.

'Have you lost any weight yet?' asked Sarah, once Carrie had sorted out paper and pen.

Sarah could be a little bossy, but Carrie couldn't help but be impressed by her dedication to the wish list, even if the directness of the question made her twitch anxiously.

'Getting there. I've weighed and measured myself,' said Carrie, not quite meeting Sarah's eye.

'And?' Sarah probed.

Jo tutted. 'You don't have to tell us your weight,' she said with a sideways glance at Sarah.

'I've stuck to my diet like glue,' said Carrie, widening her eyes, trying to convince herself as much as anything. 'But I've only lost a couple of pounds so far.'

'A few pounds is progress,' said Jo, giving her a round of applause. 'Don't be too hard on yourself.'

'It's a start,' Sarah agreed, patting her hand. 'Write that down.'

Carrie did as she was told. What she didn't tell them was that after standing on the scales and finding out what a pathetic result it was, she had spent the afternoon consoling herself with the top tray of a box of chocolates.

'This partnership wish of yours,' said Jo, pushing her chair back from the table and crossing her long legs. 'Tell us more.'

'Ah, well.' Sarah pulled out a scruffy square of paper from the pocket of her shorts. 'I found this in *Accountancy Times*. It's a job advertisement for a partner to join a practice. It's not for my firm, but it's a starting point. It says, "Must have business acumen, impeccable networking and people skills, a flexible approach to working hours and be highly organized". Which is good news, because I've got all of that.'

Carrie stayed silent. She didn't know Sarah all that

well, but highly organized? She couldn't say in all honesty that Sarah fitted into that category. And wasn't 'flexible working hours' another way of saying 'long'? And as for people skills . . . She bit her lip.

Sarah shifted awkwardly. 'Actually, I'm not sure I do have any business acumen. It's all about profit at our place. We're given a set number of hours to complete each job and I hate rushing, that's when mistakes are made. I'm not that flexible either, come to think of it.' She pushed a hand through her curls. 'I've got the rest of the skills down pat, though.'

'Good work. I'll put "research into required skills done", then.' Carrie made a note then stood up to put the kettle on. 'How about you, Jo?' she asked. 'Have you thought about when your fear of heights kicked in?'

Jo shuddered. 'I asked my parents about it the other night. Turns out I was a bit of a daredevil when I was young. I used to frighten my mum to death. She was quite over-protective towards me, which my dad says made me worse.'

Sarah smirked. 'I can imagine you being a bit of a handful.'

Jo pretended to look offended and helped herself to some grapes.

'And did something happen?' Carrie asked.

'Yeah, when I was seven in the Lake District. We were up a mountain and I was running ahead shouting "look at me, look at me" and pretending to fall off the edge, to wind my mum up. Then all of a sudden I let out a scream and disappeared. Then there was an eerie silence.'

Carrie pressed a hand to her mouth. 'Oh, Jo!'

'Had you fallen?' Sarah asked with a gasp.

Jo nodded.

'Apparently I'd spotted a dead sheep and had leaned out too far to have a better look. My parents found me clinging to a tiny rocky ledge, luckily just at arm's length from where they were. My dad yanked me up and my mum grabbed hold of me and forced me to look over the cliff edge again, screaming at me that I could have fallen to my death like that sheep. After that I was so traumatized that I couldn't put one foot in front of the other.'

'Your poor mother,' said Sarah. 'If anything ever happened to Zac . . .' She shuddered.

'And poor you,' said Carrie, putting a mug of coffee in front of her. 'Has it helped you, do you think, getting to the root of the problem?'

Jo shook her head. 'Nah. Other than raking up bad memories and making my mother feel guilty at being responsible for my phobia, it hasn't achieved anything. I don't know where I go from here.'

Carrie felt a surge of euphoria. She had bought a book about phobias and had come up with a plan to help Jo.

'Well, I've got an experiment I'd like to try with you one day, maybe next week?' she said, her eyes sparkling with hope. 'If you'll trust me, that is?'

'Sure,' replied Jo with a shrug. 'Hey, look!'

She nodded at Sarah whose eyes were closed and her head was lolling on her shoulders. Jo smirked. 'I think I'd better get Mrs Impeccable-People-Skills home before she starts snoring again, don't you?'

Chapter 7

The multi-storey car park was busy for a Monday morning. Carrie had chosen the tallest one in the city, nine floors in total, and she was struggling to find a space to park on the ground floor. It had to be the ground floor or else the plan might not work. Her four-wheel drive wasn't the easiest vehicle to park either in these narrow spaces. She'd wanted something small and nippy and easy to manoeuvre, but Alex had argued that a big car was more sensible for country living, especially in the winter. He was right, of course, as usual.

She spotted a space and saw Jo locking her car, looking effortlessly sexy in a short wool coat and heels. Damn. She was a little bit in awe of the glamorous Jo and would have liked to have made a good impression. Now she was going to have to reverse-park the beast with an audience. And to make matters worse, there was a car waiting to get past.

Two minutes later she took the keys out of the transmission with a pink face and aching arms. The alarms on both of the neighbouring cars were sounding angrily. The driver of the waiting car roared away, shaking his head.

She opened the door a few inches. Jo was standing at the front bumper, wiping tears from her eyes. Carrie's smile slipped a bit. If she was to have any chance of helping Jo overcome her fear of heights, she needed to give off an air of confidence. So far she was vastly underachieving.

'Oh, Carrie, sorry, I shouldn't laugh, but you did make a meal of that. I thought that man in the other car was going to hit you.'

'I can't get out,' said Carrie weakly, her heart sinking.

She'd parked too close to the car next to her. She couldn't face shunting the car backwards and forwards again. There was nothing else for it; she threw her leg over the handbrake and gingerly climbed across the gear stick to the passenger door. It took some effort and with Jo splitting her sides laughing, it was hard not to see the funny side herself.

'Very ladylike,' said Jo.

'If I wasn't so big this wouldn't be an issue,' Carrie said breathlessly.

'If your *car* wasn't so big, you mean. Don't worry, you haven't done any damage to the other cars. Yet.'

'Good. I'll just get my bag out of the boot. Oh no . . .'

Carrie didn't think her face could get any redder as Jo clapped a hand over her mouth. Carrie had reversed so close to the wall behind that she couldn't open the boot. This wasn't a good start. She was supposed to be in control of today's task, demonstrating to Jo that she was competent and capable. Instead, she was looking like a prize buffoon.

'Thanks for the distraction,' said Jo, after Carrie had inched the car forward enough to retrieve her bag. 'You made me totally forget the reason for being here for a few minutes. And much as I'm quaking in my boots, I really appreciate you doing this for me.'

Carrie was ridiculously flattered.

'I can't believe you agreed to come. I mean, with you being so busy at work.'

'I can't guarantee that I'll cooperate,' Jo said with a smirk. 'But I thought I'd show willing.'

Carrie took a deep breath, tried to remember everything she had read and put on her most authoritative voice. 'OK. We're starting on the ground floor and we're going to work our way up.'

'Actually,' Jo looked around her and pointed to the exit, 'I really fancy a coffee. Shall we go and find a café first and then—'

'No,' said Carrie firmly, recognizing a delay tactic when she saw one. 'We're starting now. You can earn the coffee.'

Jo was looking uncharacteristically nervous and kept flicking her eyes to the perimeter of the car park. The office blocks on the opposite side of the street were visible through the drizzle on all sides.

'Are you OK?' said Carrie more gently. 'We'll take it at your pace. I'll be led by you.'

Jo nodded and linked her arm through Carrie's.

This was surreal to Carrie, to have the super-confident, smart-talking Jo Gold leaning on her for support. Carrie directed her to the outside edge of the car park. She had read countless articles on the internet about overcoming a fear of heights – or acrophobia, to give it its proper title. No one could accuse Carrie Radley of not taking the wish list seriously.

Although . . . A pang of doubt stopped her in her tracks. What if she made Jo worse? She wasn't a trained psychologist; she was a well-meaning amateur. Could she cope if Jo had a panic attack and tried to do something crazy?

'What is it?' Jo's eyes narrowed.

'Just choosing a spot,' she said brightly. 'The theory is that you can desensitize yourself to your fear of heights by being exposed to mild situations and gradually increasing the height.'

Jo's arm tensed in hers as they approached the chest-high railings.

'We're at ground level. Hold on to the railings and look out at the pavement.'

'That's all?' Jo blinked nervously.

'Yep.'

She swallowed and gripped the railings tightly. The

building in front of them stretched up beyond their view, row upon row of smoked-glass windows.

'I couldn't work there.' Jo shuddered.

Carrie examined her friend's face. She looked fidgety and mildly nervous, but there was no sign of sweating or anxiety. So far so good.

'Feel OK?'

Jo nodded warily.

Carrie's stomach flip-flopped with relief. 'Good, let's try the first floor.'

They made their way up the concrete steps. Either Jo was extremely unfit, which Carrie doubted seeing as she had the physique of a whippet, or else she was getting very nervous. Carrie could hear her breathing as they approached the first-floor railings.

She stopped and forced Jo to face her, taking hold of both her hands. She couldn't help it. It was glorious to feel more confident than someone else for a change.

'Deep breathing.' Carrie inhaled slowly through her nose and exhaled sharply, nodding at Jo to copy her.

'Are you sure you read the right book?' said Jo between breaths. 'This is what I had to do with Abi when she was pregnant.'

'It's calming.'

'Is it hell.'

'Let's do it,' said Carrie.

The two of them stopped a couple of paces from the edge.

'You can't fall and you won't fall.' Carrie glanced at Jo; her face was all screwed up. 'You can easily take hold of these railings and look down. It's not far. You could even jump it from here.'

Jo looked at her in alarm.

Carrie laughed. 'You only have to look.'

Jo chewed on her bottom lip. 'How high up are we?'

She leaned over to check. Jo gasped and clutched at her arm.

'It's all right! I don't know, about five metres?' She mustn't freak Jo out. The book advised caution for the first session. 'You don't have to do it, Jo. It's up to you.'

Sliding one high heel in front of the other, Jo edged forward until she was within reach of the railings. She grabbed them with both hands.

'Keep breathing,' murmured Carrie.

'It reminds me of yoga when you say that,' said Jo in a shaky voice. 'You'll be breaking wind next.'

Carrie tutted. She would never live that down. But at least Jo was making jokes; humour was a good sign.

'Look at that huge umbrella with the poppy on. That's gorgeous!' said Carrie, pointing down to the pedestrians on the street below.

Jo poked her head over the railings and frowned. 'Where? I can't see it.'

'Made you look!' Carrie grinned. 'See, it wasn't so bad, was it? Do you think you can manage the second floor?'

'No,' said Jo defiantly.

'How about we just go up the stairs and see how you feel?'

'I'm seeing a new side to you, Carrie Radley,' Jo grumbled, but she allowed Carrie to lead her through the rows of cars towards the staircase.

Me too, Carrie mused proudly.

The cars had thinned out slightly on the second floor and, as they emerged from the stairwell, the line of sight to the car-park perimeter was clear.

'This is very high,' said Jo, tugging at the collar of her coat.

'High-*er*,' said Carrie, 'but no taller than, say . . . the roof of a house.'

She took Jo's arm again, but this time as they got closer to the edge Jo began shaking her head, using both hands to try to undo her top button.

'I'll fall.'

Carried looked at her sharply. She wasn't joking. She was

pale and a faint sheen of perspiration had appeared above her top lip.

'I'll slip and fall over the railings. I'm hot and I feel sick.'

Carrie started to feel panicky herself. She tried to remember what you were supposed to do when somebody fainted.

'No problem, you've done really well. Have you had enough?'

Jo nodded.

'Then let's call it a day,' Carrie replied gently, passing her a bottle of water from her handbag.

'I feel like such a wimp,' Jo mumbled when they reached the ground floor, her breathing still a bit ragged.

'Rubbish! You actually looked over the railings on the first floor. That's progress.'

Carrie felt a bit of a failure too, she hadn't expected Jo to have such physical reactions. She'd had a fantasy of talking Jo through her fears, getting her up to the ninth floor and Jo being eternally grateful. Never mind. 'Coffee?'

Carrie swallowed a mouthful of coffee and tried not to grimace. Jo had ordered a skinny cappuccino and she'd felt obliged to have the same. And the hot chocolate with whipped cream had looked so delicious.

Jo slipped her coat over the back of the chair and cast a cursory eye over the coffee shop.

'That barista was cute,' she whispered, nodding her head at the counter.

Jo had fully recovered. Carrie grinned. She still felt a bit star-struck in Jo's company. Her white-blonde hair and full red lips drew the attention of all the other customers; it was like being with a celebrity. She caught sight of their reflection in the window and baulked at her own drab outfit. The two of them looked like the town mouse and the country mouse. Her smile faded a bit.

'It'll be great if we both get our wishes to come true, won't it? I mean, I had no idea how bad your phobia was.

As for me, I don't know, I think I'll be a different person once I'm thinner,' said Carrie.

Jo shrugged. 'Sorry, Carrie, but Gold's shoes will still be teetering on the precipice of doom, whether I dangle myself off the Empire State Building or not.'

'Is that the most important thing in your life, then – work?'

Jo's expression clouded for a second before she gathered herself and smiled. 'Of course.'

Carrie took another sip of her disgusting drink. Jo was all things bright and beautiful, but there was something else. There was a flippancy and defiance to her answers that spoke volumes.

'Have you ever been in love, Jo?' she asked quietly.

'More times than you've had hot dinners,' Jo replied with a wink.

At this point Carrie would normally make a joke about that being quite a lot then. But she held her tongue and she didn't believe Jo for one minute.

She leaned forward, changing the subject. 'I feel a bit disloyal about saying this but Sarah's wish seems strange for a new mum.'

'I agree,' said Jo instantly. 'I wonder why it's so important to her to be a partner?'

'I know I'm old-fashioned,' Carrie admitted, 'but Zac is still little and if you ask me she's already struggling to cope.'

Jo nodded. 'If he was my baby, I'd put my career plans on hold and spend as much time with him as I could.'

Carrie could hardly believe her ears. 'But you said work was—'

'For me, yes. Sarah's different,' snapped Jo. 'She's living the dream, she's got the husband, the baby, she's probably even got roses round the door, I couldn't tell in the dark.'

A pink climbing rose, if Carrie remembered rightly. It would smell heavenly in summer. She shook her head and tried to make sense of what Jo was saying. *Sarah's living the dream.*

'Anyway,' said Jo briskly. She replaced her empty cup on its saucer and checked her watch.

Carrie's happy mood deflated. Of course, she'd have to rush off. She probably had some important meeting to get to. For Carrie it was back to the house. Maybe an hour doing some weeding if the rain cleared up. Whoopy-doo. She scrabbled around to think of something to say, to keep her a bit longer.

'The experts recommend gradual exposure to your fears, so shall we do this again?'

Jo was staring out of the window and didn't reply. Carrie tried a different tack.

'I was quite concerned for you at one point up there. Your pupils were so dilated—'

Jo looked back at Carrie and grinned. 'Are they dilated now?'

They were. Carrie was confused. Jo knocked on the window and then waved madly to a tall unshaven man in his thirties outside.

'Yes, why?'

'Sexual attraction,' said Jo, pulling her coat on. 'Carrie, you're a star. I love you. We must do this again.'

'But—'

Jo kissed her cheek and dashed out of the coffee shop.

'Ed? Ed? Wait up!'

Carrie sighed and watched Jo run away to her interesting life. She pushed her skinny cappuccino to one side. Still, looking on the bright side, at least she could order a hot chocolate now.

Chapter 8

Sarah did up Zac's straps and tucked a blanket over his legs. He looked like a little lamb in his white fleecy onesie. She pulled on a denim jacket over her dress; it was printed with cherry blossom, had a net underskirt and made her feel happy and spring-like.

'Come on, little man, let's go to the park.' She looped her bag across her body and opened the door. 'We might make some new friends.'

Zac kicked his legs eagerly. Sarah tucked a ringlet of hair behind her ear, manoeuvred the pushchair over the front step and set off towards the children's play area.

It was early April and the nicest Saturday that Sarah could remember so far this year. The sky was a triumphant shade of blue with wisps of white cloud too high to pose any threat to the warm spring sunshine. Sarah took the footpath through the village. The birds were tweeting and the grass verges were full of pretty little pale yellow wildflowers.

Zac babbled away happily and Sarah talked back as if it was the most normal conversation in the world.

It was wonderful to have him to herself for two whole days while Dave was out working. Although time with all three of them was precious, she always got a sneaky feeling Dave was hovering over her and checking she was doing things properly.

'I think you forgot to put on nappy cream,' he would say. Which was doubly annoying, because he was usually right.

She'd been back at work for over three months now and Dave was so much better at deciphering Zac's attempts at communication. It was the way it had to be, it had been her choice, after all, but that didn't make it any less heartbreaking to see the tight bond between them that she sometimes struggled to infiltrate.

A tabby cat tiptoed towards them, meowing insistently, and Sarah crouched down to stroke it. Zac pointed at the cat and squealed, 'Da, da!'

Sarah gasped. 'Clever boy! Did you just point? Point to the cat. Good boy.'

His first point. And Sarah was the one to see it. She beamed at him, took her phone out of her pocket and turned the camera on.

'Where's the cat? Point to the cat!'

Zac obliged and Sarah took a picture.

'Come on then. Bye bye. Wave, Zac.'

He didn't wave, which was fine. Pointing was perfectly adequate progress for one day.

Sarah resumed her walk, steering the pushchair uphill towards the park. This was lovely. Out in the fresh air, with her beautiful boy, enjoying the scenery. The gardens were full of daffodils and tulips and the trees were covered in blossom; the village looked picturesque and Sarah felt her spirits lift. This was what it was all about, this was why they had moved out of the city. She could almost feel the stresses of work draining from her body.

She gave an involuntary shiver.

She didn't want to think about work. This week had been hideous. She had spent most of it doing battle with HMRC on behalf of one of her clients, an organic bakery. Sarah had only been allocated twelve hours to do the bakery's account and it had already taken twenty-five. But what was she supposed to do? She couldn't just abandon the client and say, 'Sorry you have reached your allotted hours, sort it out yourselves.' The case had been problematic at every turn; she couldn't possibly have finished in less time. Even so, Eleanor was going to go ballistic when she found out.

So much for not thinking about work.

Wouldn't it be lovely to reduce her hours; maybe go down to working four days a week? Then she could enjoy more time with Zac. Dave might like that idea too; he could take on more regular painting jobs.

The gate to the park was a heavy metal affair and Sarah struggled to hold it open and wheel the pushchair through it at the same time. Her bag got caught in the gate latch and for a second she was stuck.

She yanked it free and groaned as a thought occurred to her. What was she thinking? She had set herself a career goal to achieve by September. Going part time did not fit in with that at all. The fresh air must be going to her head. Oh well, nice idea. Maybe one day.

Zac's legs began to kick excitedly as he realized where he was and Sarah's heart squeezed with love for him.

Life was so confusing; she loved her career, she had made a pact with herself long ago to aim for the top. But every so often, the temptation to give it all up for a lifestyle lived at less than one hundred miles an hour held huge appeal. She sighed and plodded onward.

The play area was directly ahead of her and through the bright spring sunshine, she could just about make out someone on the swing. That nurse had been right. Now spring was here she was sure to meet other mothers. Right now, with any luck.

'Shall we go and play on the swings, Zac?' She parked the pushchair by the fence surrounding the children's play area and lifted him out, catching a proper glimpse of the other person as she did so.

Her heart sank; it was Rebecca and her baby. Of all people. Dressed in a woollen miniskirt and tan leather boots, she looked like a supermodel doing a spring shoot for *Vogue*. Sarah hefted Zac on to her hip.

'Hi,' she called, opening the gate and kicking her way through the bark chippings.

'Oh, hello,' said Rebecca, not looking particularly pleased to have their solitude broken.

She stopped the swing and bent to lift out her daughter, a pretty little thing dressed in a furry lion outfit with ears on the hood.

'It's OK,' said Sarah hurriedly, 'we'll wait. No need to take Eva out.'

'*Ava.*' Rebecca's lips twitched.

'Oops. Sorry. Ava's such a lovely name,' Sarah stammered.

'I thought so. And it's fine. Anyway, Zac loves the swing, don't you, Zacky?' Rebecca tickled his chin.

Sarah bristled. *Zacky*? Loves the swing? How did she know?

'Well, if you're sure,' she said, plastering on a smile.

Rebecca took Ava over to the slide and without letting go of her, slid her down the bottom third.

Getting Zac's legs to bend so she could settle him safely into the baby swing wasn't as easy as it looked and Sarah was feeling the heat inside her denim jacket by the time he was swinging gently back and forward.

For the next couple of minutes Sarah watched Rebecca playing with her daughter and racked her brains for something to say. She had to make more of an effort to be friendly with her; Rebecca was her sort of age, with a baby of a similar age, and in a village this size, beggars couldn't be choosers.

'You're right; he does like the swing,' she called.

Rebecca smiled. 'I see Dave and Zac here a lot. It must be so hard for you, developing a close bond with him, when you spend so little time with him.'

'Not at all.' Sarah felt her face flush. This didn't feel much like the friendly yummy-mummy chat she'd been hoping for.

'I don't know how you do it.' Rebecca swooped Ava up from the swing and kissed her, making her squeal with delight. 'Going off to work every day. Leaving him with Dave. I admire you.'

It didn't sound like admiration to Sarah, it sounded a bit judgemental.

'Not all of us have a choice,' she replied, keeping her voice deliberately light.

'Oh, I think we all have a choice,' said Rebecca airily. 'I think the most important thing I could be doing right now is bringing up my daughter. That's my choice.'

'I am bringing up my son, Dave and I share it.' *How dare she?* Sarah busied herself taking Zac out of the swing so that Rebecca wouldn't see how rattled she was.

'Even so.' Rebecca pressed her lips together and inserted Ava back into the swing efficiently. 'Dave says he'll be going to nursery soon. That is going to be heartbreaking for you.'

Sarah's insides trembled; Dave hadn't mentioned anything about it. They'd viewed a nursery before Christmas as an alternative to him giving up work and decided against it.

'He'll love it,' said Sarah defiantly, marching to the round-about. 'The chance to socialize with their peers is priceless.'

'Oh, I wouldn't take him on there.' Rebecca winced as Sarah sat him on her knee and pushed off.

Sarah's blood pressure was going off the scale. This woman was insufferable. He was going on it now as a matter of principle. Rebecca could sod off. 'We'll only go slowly. Look, he's fine.'

Zac gave a little moan just before throwing up his break-fast of oaty surprise all over Sarah's dress. Which was no surprise to Rebecca, thought Sarah wryly, catching her know-it-all expression. She jumped off the roundabout and tucked Zac under one arm while she rummaged through her bag for a cloth.

'That's what he did last time, poor thing,' said Rebecca handing her a baby wipe. 'Bye bye.'

She wiggled her fingers at Zac and carried Ava out of the park.

Sarah fought the urge to fling the puke-soaked baby wipe at her back and concentrated on not bursting into tears instead.

'Thank you, Rebecca, for ruining our lovely day,' muttered Sarah under her breath as she made her way back towards home. *Bloody village.*

Further down the hill on the grass verge, moving at a snail's pace towards her, was a woman who, at first glance, appeared to be dragging a beige-coloured cushion along on a piece of string.

'Carrie!' Sarah waved merrily at her friend; never had she been so grateful to see a familiar face. 'New dog? Or old dog, I should say.'

She squatted down next to Zac and pointed out the dog to him. It was a mangy-looking thing. Sarah prayed that it didn't have fleas.

'I'm dog-walking Reuben for my neighbour,' said Carrie. 'I thought the exercise would do me good. Although I'm probably using more calories carrying him up hills than actually walking. You look frowny, what's the matter?'

Sarah groaned. 'Everyone in this village is mean and unfriendly. Except you.'

Carrie bit her lip and nodded over Sarah's shoulder. She turned to find Abi right behind her, her lips twisted in a half-smile.

'You heard that, didn't you?' Sarah cringed.

How did she always manage to put her foot in it where Abi was concerned? She still hadn't forgiven herself for her tactless comment at Fréd's funeral which had made Abi cry. 'I'm so sorry.'

111

Abi kissed first Carrie's cheek and then Sarah's. 'Don't worry, I felt a bit the same when we moved in. It takes a while to make friends.'

Sarah exhaled with relief and the two women smiled at each other. Sarah's heart went out to her. There was a brittleness to Abi's smile and she wanted to ask how she was, how she was coping. On the other hand, everyone probably asked that; Abi could be sick of having to repeat the same old lines.

'What are you up to this weekend?' she asked instead.

Abi smiled gratefully. 'I'm supposed to be doing some sorting out before we go to Australia, but I feel as energetic as this old dog.'

'Where's Tom?' Carrie asked.

Reuben flopped down on the grass at the women's feet much to Zac's delight, who kicked his legs.

Abi shook her head. 'Playdate with a friend. Gosh, Sarah, Zac is growing up. He looks just like his dad. Tom's the same.'

Her eyes glittered with tears suddenly and she bent down to say hello to Zac, who reached out to grab her finger and pull it towards his mouth.

'Someone's hungry,' Sarah said with a laugh. 'Do you two fancy coming back for a coffee?'

'I would,' said Carrie, stooping to lift Reuben to his feet. 'But one of us is incontinent. And for once, it's not *my* bowels we're talking about.'

Sarah kissed Carrie goodbye and she ambled off, tugging the reluctant dog behind her.

'Abi?' Sarah bit her lip. 'I could do with some adult company.'

'Oh, me too,' Abi groaned. 'Sod the packing, I'd love a coffee.'

They started walking again and chatted about the weather and Abi's travel plans and how old Tom had been when he said 'Mum' for the first time, and a couple of minutes later they arrived at Rose Cottage.

'I'm looking forward to seeing inside,' Abi said with a smile as Sarah unlocked the door.

'You've been here before, haven't you?' she said with a frown.

She distinctly remembered Abi calling round with a bag of clothes for Zac a couple of weeks after he'd been born.

Abi shook her head and grinned. 'I only made it as far as the doorstep, you said the place was a tip and didn't invite me in.'

'Did I? Oh God, I'm sorry.' Sarah squeezed her eyes shut. 'Seriously, it's no wonder I haven't made many friends in this village.'

How embarrassing. Thankfully, the cottage wasn't too untidy this time; she had had a quick tidy-up this morning on the off chance that she might strike lucky and bag herself a potential friend at the park. God, she sounded desperate.

Abi helped her lift the pushchair inside and laughed. 'That and the fact you're a busy working mum. Stop beating yourself up.'

Sarah sighed. 'You're right, thank you. Yes. Tea or coffee?'

'Coffee please. Shall I get Zac out of his coat?'

Sarah dithered. Her eyes flicked to the hand-sanitizer on the worktop. She was supposed to be reaching out to her neighbours. Making them feel unclean was hardly going to endear her to anyone.

Abi caught her looking and twinkled her eyes at her. 'Don't worry, I'm perfectly safe.'

'Of course,' said Sarah, darting into the kitchen before she noticed her furious blush. 'I'll get the kettle on.'

'So come on,' said Abi, once they had settled themselves in the living room with Zac playing happily on the floor. 'What brought on that outburst earlier about us all being unfriendly?'

Sarah sighed. 'I thought that moving to a village would mean being part of a tight-knit community.'

'And we'd all be part of some big happy family?' Abi added, raising a cynical eyebrow.

Sarah nodded. It felt a bit silly when she heard someone else say it. But that was exactly what she had imagined.

'Please don't take this the wrong way,' said Abi, 'but I think you've been watching too much TV.'

Sarah immediately thought of St Mary Mead, where Miss Marple was invited out to tea on a daily basis only to discover a dead body in the parlour. Maybe Abi was right.

'Dave and I wanted a change of tempo, to opt for a more peaceful life. And it is definitely quieter, because we haven't made any friends to socialize with!'

Abi took a sip of her tea before she spoke. 'The whole peaceful life thing . . . that's a myth. People's lives are just as busy here as they are in the suburbs. They just have a longer commute to work.'

That was certainly true for Sarah.

'You're right. I just need to establish my place in the social scene here, find a role for myself . . .'

'There's no conspiracy going on.' Abi laughed. 'There are no coffee mornings and church fêtes happening secretly while you're at work. Either people take part in village events or they don't. And many don't. But if you do, you'll meet plenty of people and you'll soon feel like you fit in.'

'I did try,' said Sarah flatly. 'I went to the mother and baby group but I didn't make any friends. Quite the opposite, in fact.'

She told Abi about her traumatic experience and how the other mothers had reacted when she'd said that she was cutting her maternity leave short.

'I remember being an emotional wreck when Tom was born.' Abi's eyes softened. 'The slightest thing made me cry and I was convinced that everybody was doing a better job of motherhood than me. And most women, at some time or another, feel the same.'

Sarah swallowed. Abi was so accurate it was untrue; that was exactly how she felt.

Abi stood up and held out a hand. 'Come on, stand up.'
She pulled her in front of the mirror above the fireplace.
'Now what do you see?'

Sarah pulled a face at her reflection. 'One knackered
mother.'

'Ha, we're all in that club.' Abi laughed. 'Go on. What
else?'

'Frizzy hair in need of a trim, bags under the eyes,
smudged mascara, wobbly belly.'

'Weird,' said Abi, narrowing her eyes. 'Because I see a
beautiful girl, with lovely hair, a figure to die for, a delightful son, living in one of the prettiest cottages in the village
with . . .' she picked up their wedding photograph off the
mantelpiece ' . . . a gorgeous husband.'

They smiled at each other in the mirror, Sarah's throat
burned with the effort of trying to keep her tears in check.
Abi's eyes were misting up too.

'I'm very lucky,' Sarah said quietly. She hesitated, wondering whether to mention Fréd.

'And that's what everyone else will see too. And coupled
with the fact that you have a really good job – so good that
they couldn't do without you for long – do you know what I
think?'

Sarah shook her head.

'The other mums are probably a tiny bit jealous.'

'Jealous of me? I'm jealous of them.' Sarah's cheeks coloured, realizing for the first time how true this was. 'With
their playdates and their precious bonding time and their
choice to embrace motherhood as the most important job a
woman can do.'

Abi sat back down and cradled her mug. 'I gave up my
career when Tom was born. It seemed the best thing to do.
Fréd works . . .' Her voice faltered. 'Fréd worked crazy
hours at Cavendish Hall. If I hadn't have stopped work
we'd never have seen each other. But was it the right thing
to do?' She shrugged. 'It seemed like it at the time. But I

bet you enjoy the adult company, the chance to be a professional woman, rather than simply Mummy, for a few hours a day.'

'That's true,' Sarah acknowledged.

As much as she loved her time with Zac, she relished the challenges that she faced on a daily basis at the office. Apart from her encounters with HMRC.

Sarah looked down at Zac clutching a soft rabbit to his chest, his eyes starting to droop. She got the best of him really: first thing in the morning when he was full of energy and bath time, which they both loved, followed by a story and a goodnight kiss.

'I feel like I'm missing out, though,' she said quietly, 'and I can never get that time back.'

'Sometimes,' said Abi carefully, 'going back to work can be the easier option. If I hadn't stopped working, I'd have something else in my life to focus on now instead of just seeing the space that Fréd has left behind.'

Her bottom lip wobbled and Sarah quickly set her mug down and sat beside Abi, drawing her into a hug.

'I'm sorry, Abi. What am I like going on about my own problems, when you're grieving for Fréd?'

'Don't apologize.' She sat up and managed a smile, brushing the tears from her eyes. 'You're a breath of fresh air, actually,' she said half-laughing. 'I'm fed up of people tiptoeing round me. And don't be afraid to be proud of your career. There is no one way to bring up a child. Just do it your way, do what feels right.'

Sarah knelt down in front of the now dozing Zac, held her hand to his forehead and loosened his clothing.

Abi was right. There was nothing to be ashamed of about wanting to do well, to be the best you could be. And she was a good – no, make that an excellent – accountant. As much as she adored her son, she couldn't simply give it all up for motherhood. She just couldn't.

Chapter 9

Jo propped the three mood boards up against the wall in her office and took a step back. A tingling sensation shot up the length of her spine until even her scalp felt excited.

They looked fantastic.

Each of the large pieces of card was covered with catwalk photographs, swatches of leather and fabrics, ribbons, buttons, colour squares and, of course, Cesca's design sketches.

They had taken Jo hours of research, snipping, rearranging and general fiddling, but they were done. Her stomach felt like she was on a roller coaster; the new collection was ready. She had promised Ed Shaw that she'd have something ready to present to him by mid-April and they had made it. Just.

Jo turned to her desk and picked up a shoebox. The new box design was a work of art in itself. All Patrick's idea. He had suggested making the box look like a luxury suitcase with the new Josephine Gold logo printed on to a luggage label. It was a great concept and it worked. No woman was going to throw away one of these shoeboxes.

It had been Karen from Payroll who came up with the name: 'Call it Josephine, Jo's Sunday name,' she had said. 'It's all about a new generation of Gold's Footwear and that's what she is. Simple.'

Jo resisted for about five seconds. Seeing her name on

the logo gave her a tiny thrill every time she saw it. For the first time since taking over from her dad, she felt as if she was truly putting her stamp on the company.

Jo had gone over and over Cesca's sketchpad and had eventually settled on the most commercial styles. They had then worked like demons to refine and modify them, creating shoes and boots that suited the Gold's brand but had the quirkiness that Shaw's was looking for.

There were to be three collections: English Rose, Carnaby and Bond. Each had six styles and was available in three colourways. It wasn't a huge range, but it was a starting point and as Patrick pointed out, it was big enough until they got the go-ahead from Shaw's.

Jo turned to her desk where three piles of boxes were stacked and ready. She opened one from the English Rose range and took out a mink nubuck leather court shoe. Square-heel and round-toe, a row of tiny suede roses edged the front. Not really Jo's thing, but it was absolutely gorgeous.

Gold's had never had anything so delicate in its range before. She tucked the shoe back into its box and carefully wrapped it in tissue paper.

It was Carrie, she realized with a jolt, glancing back at the mood board, English Rose reminded her of Carrie. The colours were muted and discreet, just the way she dressed. And each one was embellished with three-dimensional flowers, from huge suede roses to small leather daisies. She seemed to have a thing about flowers. Plus, the styles were feminine and understated, and that was just like Carrie too.

She took the lid off a Carnaby style shoebox and it screamed Sarah at her. Jo couldn't believe that she hadn't noticed this before. The collection had a kookiness to it that Jo knew Ed was going to go mad for. Primary colours, contrasting fabrics and even floral soles, Carnaby was slightly off the wall. Sarah would look fantastic in these with her vintage style of dressing. Jo smiled to herself; she had never met a less stereotypical accountant.

So was Bond her collection, then, she thought wryly, lifting a box from the final pile. She traced a finger around her name on the logo. It was more edgy than the other two; monochrome and metallic, harder textures, spiky heels. She shrugged. No use soft-soaping it. That definitely was Jo's nature.

She could see herself ordering every style in Bond and possibly in more than one colour. She couldn't wait to have production samples. She couldn't remember ever feeling this excited about Gold's Footwear. It was a million miles from anything they'd done before.

Jo felt a shiver of apprehension. What would her dad think about this new direction? Every new addition in the past had been simply a modification to the existing range. And God knows what he would say when he saw the budget to develop her new collection.

She gave herself a shake. Get a grip; she was in charge now and it was up to her to turn the business round. Ed Shaw was the one she had to impress, not Bob Gold.

She was ready.

Tomorrow she and Patrick would present the collection to Shaw's in Nottingham. But today was the staff meeting, time to show the whole team the finished product. Jo picked up the boards and the prototypes and set off for the warehouse, praying for a positive reception.

The following morning, while Patrick stowed all the samples in the boot, Jo diligently brushed what looked like flapjack crumbs off the passenger seat. If she got chocolate on the seat of these skin-tight trousers, they were going to have words.

'If I'd known your car was such a skip, we would have gone in mine.'

She gave Patrick a stern look and climbed in.

'Sorry, ma'am,' said Patrick, not looking very sorry. 'Holly had to eat in the car last night on the way to swimming practice. I apologize on her behalf.'

'Hmm,' said Jo, unable to stay cross at her god-daughter for long. Holly was a total bundle of fun and Jo adored her. Also the thought of Patrick valiantly trying to feed his eleven-year-old on the run and get her to her after-school activities gave her a funny feeling in her stomach which she couldn't quite put her finger on. She shook them away and gave him a sideways glance.

'Glad to see you've made an effort in the fashion department anyway, McGregor. Ed Shaw is into his designer brands; we don't want to let the side down.'

Patrick rolled his eyes. 'So he's – how do you normally put it – hot, then?'

'Might be.' Jo pressed her lips together and focused her gaze out of the window as Patrick started the engine and pulled out of Gold's car park.

'Single?'

'Er . . . no.'

Patrick sighed and shook his head.

'Oh, give it a rest.'

He was like a big brother sometimes. Annoying and judgemental. And, she suspected, a big romantic at heart; he couldn't resist the odd dig about her casual approach to relationships. It was all right for him; he hadn't had Bob Gold drumming it into him for the last sixteen years about the dangers of 'settling down'.

She examined him out of the corner of her eye. His dress sense wasn't in the same league as Ed Shaw but it was a major improvement on yesterday. Then, his trousers had been so short they had appeared to be having an argument with his shoes. His hair looked nice today too – tamed into submission. He had thick, wavy hair; in the hands of a good woman, he could be quite attractive.

Since his divorce last year Patrick had gradually become

more mismatched and, she didn't like to say unkempt, but . . . well, unkempt. She had been contemplating having a subtle word with him, but had so far put it off, not quite able to find the right words or the right moment, aware that there was a line between them now that shouldn't be crossed. And of course, she knew he had a lot on his plate: working, looking after Holly, moving into a smaller house. Thankfully, the subtle word might not be necessary any more. He looked really good.

She changed the subject to break the silence. 'So how is my delightful god-daughter? Coping without her mum?'

Jo had quite liked Melissa, Patrick's ex; she was clever, good fun and had a wicked sense of humour. The two of them used to stand outside with a cigarette and have a laugh together at work parties. For some strange reason, over the last couple of years, Melissa had grown less chatty, hostile even on some occasions. Nevertheless, it had been quite a shock when Patrick had announced they were getting a divorce and sharing custody of their daughter.

Jo remembered when Holly was born and they had asked her to be godmother. She had accepted, of course. How could she refuse? But really? Couldn't they have found a more suitable woman than a workaholic smoker with no idea about kids and debatable moral standards?

'She's great.' Patrick's face softened into a gooey smile. 'She does miss her mum, but they FaceTime each other when Melissa can get Wi-Fi, or speak on the phone. God knows what it costs to call Nepal. Holly seems to think that I'm the one in need of parenting half the time and that she's in charge. She made me go clothes shopping last weekend.' He tutted and shook his head, but Jo could see the pride on his face.

So she had Holly to thank for today's improvement. At least she wouldn't be presenting the Josephine Gold collection to the impeccably dressed, pulse-racingly attractive Ed Shaw with a scarecrow as her side-kick.

They entered Nottingham's one-way traffic system and

she felt a knot of tension ball in her stomach; Ed literally held the key to Gold's' survival in his hands. She was glad Patrick had come with her; he'd be a good calming presence. Even if it did make orchestrating a date with Ed more tricky.

It was a filthy morning and the world and his wife had decided to drive into Nottingham instead of hang about in bus queues. Patrick spotted a parking space outside Shaw's, but Jo waved him on.

'You'll have to park in a side street, around the corner,' she said.

'Why?'

She shot him a cheeky smile. 'I don't want to be seen getting out of this heap.'

The shop was looking fantastic; even Patrick whistled under his breath with admiration as they walked through to Ed's office.

Jo allowed herself a little smile, remembering the last time she had seen Ed outside the coffee shop. He'd been late for an appointment and hadn't had time to linger, but there was definitely a spark of interest there. Were her pupils dilated today, she wondered. In her all-black suit, she was aiming for sexy seductress; she hoped he picked up on the signs. Her stomach fluttered with nerves and she tried to put her personal feelings to one side. For now, it was on with the show.

'The original muse for the designs was a quirky Italian woman in her late forties,' said Patrick, 'but we worked with our own designer to put a British spin on the collection.'

Jo kicked him under the desk. What was he saying, for goodness' sake? She had wanted to give the impression that the collection was inspired by Kate Middleton or someone. What did he have to bring Italy into it for?

'An, um, quintessentially English twist,' said Patrick, rubbing his ankle, 'which you can see reflected in the choice of style names.'

Ed nodded appreciatively, turning a dove-grey court

shoe round in his hand. He set it on the desk and bent down to examine the shoe in profile. Jo's heart was thumping. With his thick black hair and navy eyes, he was looking dangerously sexy in a tight-fitting grey suit, black shirt and another pair of expensive black brogues.

'The balance of the heel at the back and the delicate flower on the instep is magical.' He stared at Jo. 'And sexy.'

She stared back.

'That's exactly the effect I was hoping to create,' she said huskily.

Patrick cleared his throat and picked up a tan knee-length boot.

'We also want to remain practical. The Gold's customer needs to know that her boots are going to withstand British winters. That's why we've made sure that on all our boots, any fabric panels are placed higher up the leg, to protect the wearer from the rain.'

'I'm speechless.' Ed rocked back in his chair and then went on to say in detail how excited and impressed he was with the collection. Patrick snorted faintly under his breath and Jo treated him to a sour stare.

'I asked Gold's for something fresh, British designed and quirky. Footwear to generate shoe envy amongst women,' he continued. 'You've delivered it in spades.'

'Thank you,' said Jo. 'I've played our conversation over and over in my head during the past few weeks. I tried to imagine what you'd really want from me.'

She ran the tip of her tongue lightly over her top lip.

A shoebox fell off the desk and the corner of it hit Jo's ankle.

'Ouch!'

'Sorry. That might have been my fault,' said Patrick, bending to pick up the box.

She couldn't prove it but she had a suspicion that he'd done that on purpose and that Ed was holding his mug up to his face to hide a laugh.

'I'll have to take a few days over my formal decision,' said Ed, nodding and smiling confidently from Patrick to Jo. 'But I think we can safely say that Josephine Gold will take centre stage at Shaw's from September.'

Yes! Jo's face was wreathed in smiles. She contemplated kissing both men, but settled for clapping her hands together instead. It was as if a heavy weight had been lifted off her shoulders. They had done it! She forgave Patrick for the Italian thing. They made a great team. This was going to make a massive difference to the future of the company.

'This is great news for Gold's and I personally look forward to developing our relationship further over the next few months.' She gave Ed a lingering look. He gave her a friendly smile in return and swallowed the rest of his coffee down in one.

'Me too.'

She chewed the inside of her lip, wondering how she could get a moment alone with him.

'Patrick,' she said with a flash of inspiration, 'did you want to take a look round the shop while we're here, before we go?'

'Saw it on the way in, thanks.' He stood up and started jingling the change in the pockets of his new trousers. 'We need to get back really.'

It was no use; she'd just have to go for it with him in the room. She took a deep breath.

'Well, I don't know about you, Ed, but I feel like celebrating. How about we put a date in the diary to get together over dinner? Somewhere special. My treat.'

Patrick stopped jingling. Ed appeared to think about it, and then his face broke out into a lazy smile.

'Great idea,' said Ed. 'I'll bring my wife, Lisa, along if you don't mind. Don't want to sit between you two like a gooseberry.'

'No need,' Jo blurted out a little too loudly.

Ed and Patrick both stared at her and she flushed.

'I mean, you wouldn't be a gooseberry. Patrick and I aren't . . . But of course Lisa is very welcome.'

What was she saying? Jo had to stop herself from gnashing her teeth together; she was mortified. 'I'll just pop to the little girls' room before we leave.'

Five minutes later she pushed the door of Ed's office open and paused. The air between the two men was thick with tension. They were squared up to each other, chests puffed out like a couple of peacocks. What the hell had they been talking about? Jo stared at them both and prayed that Patrick hadn't cocked up the deal as soon as her back was turned.

Ed broke the silence.

'So,' he said, clapping a hand on Patrick's back. 'I was just saying to Pat, I'm looking for a new General Manager, someone to help with the day-to-day running of the business, to allow me to carry on expanding and rebranding the other shops. Must have footwear and managerial experience. Can you think of anyone?'

Patrick's jaw was rigid. Jo's mouth twitched; he hated being called Pat.

She sucked in sharply. 'No one comes to mind immediately. Patrick, any ideas?'

Ed was looking at Patrick and raising one eyebrow, James Bond style.

Patrick shifted his weight awkwardly from foot to foot. 'Nope.'

'If I come up with anyone,' she said, breathing in Ed's lime aftershave one last time as she air-kissed him, 'I'll let you know.'

Patrick shook Ed's hand and said a curt goodbye.

The rain was pelting down outside and Jo regretted making Patrick park so far away.

'What the hell was all that about between you two?' she asked when they finally made it into the car.

Patrick's nostrils flared as he threw all the samples into the boot and refused to meet her eye. 'Let's just say he and I have differing opinions about working for a woman.'

'What is that supposed to mean?'

'It means the man's an arse,' said Patrick. He pressed his lips together, closing down the conversation, and drove too fast all the way back to the office.

Chapter 10

Carrie should have tried harder to come up with an irrefutable reason not to accompany Alex tonight, she mused, as they made their way towards the party huddled together under an umbrella. Jordan Lamb's new restaurant was up ahead and the pavement outside its doors was alive with stilt walkers, fire eaters and semi-naked exotic dancers. Jordan was clearly doing his utmost to get his guests in the party spirit despite the April showers that had pummelled the streets all day.

'I'm looking forward to tonight,' said Alex, putting an arm around Carrie's waist.

'Me too,' said Carrie, mentally adding 'being over' to the end of Alex's sentence.

'You look pretty, darling.' He gave her an appraising look. 'I'd have happily bought you something new, although that is nice and colourful.'

'You can't fail to see me in this.'

She already regretted allowing Sarah to choose her outfit. Not only was it bright and bold, and Carrie didn't feel bold, but it was right at the end of the Inspirational spectrum, i.e. uncomfortably tight.

Sarah had been adamant that the dress was a winner: it showed off Carrie's slim calves and the lightweight silk fabric would be both comfortable and glamorous. Carrie had only managed to get it on with the help of reinforcements: magic knickers and extra-brave control tights. If she got hit by a bus tonight she wasn't altogether sure who would come off worse.

Alex shot her a wounded look. 'Carrie, why do you put yourself down?'

She was saved from responding by a man wearing a bowler hat and gold lamé leggings. He ticked them off the guest list and ushered them inside. Carrie clung to Alex's arm and tried to make herself invisible.

Let the torture commence.

The restaurant was pulsating with people and noise: a saxophonist and pianist were struggling to be heard over the chink of glasses, the chatter and laughter. Carrie could just make out leather banquette seating with tiny bistro tables along one side and a huge bar taking centre stage on the other. Mismatched lampshades on long cables hung in clusters from the ceiling and stainless-steel ducting hinted at the building's previous industrial life.

A beaming waitress held out a tray of flute glasses. 'Bellini, madam?'

It was fizzy and fruity and didn't taste at all alcoholic. Carrie tipped her head back and swallowed. Just what she needed. She had no intention of getting drunk but it would be nice to feel a bit more carefree, just loosen up a bit. Her jaw for starters. If she didn't relax soon, it would lock completely and she wouldn't be able to speak.

'Let's head to the bar,' said Alex. 'I want a proper drink, G and T, I think, before seeing the man of the moment.' He nudged her in the ribs playfully and his elbow bounced off, courtesy of her magic knickers. 'Talk of the devil, look!'

Jordan Lamb was holding court at the far end of the room, signing autographs underneath a huge photograph of himself dressed in chef's whites with his piercing blue eyes watching over his new restaurant. Carrie shuddered, hoping she'd get away without having to meet him.

'I'll collar him later,' Alex said. 'Come on, stay close.'

Carrie swapped her empty glass for a full one and

grabbed his hand. She would just have to pray that they would be standing up all night. The car journey here had been quite painful by the end. She had felt all trussed up and breathing had only been possible through tiny in-and-out puffs. Now she was feeling dizzy with lack of oxygen.

God knows how women in the olden days managed with those corsets that gave them their wasp-like waists. Her undies were tight enough and had only managed to give her the silhouette of a bumblebee.

They made slow progress to the bar; Alex kept stopping to greet people, sharing a joke with some, touching the arm of others. He was so confident, so at home at this sort of do, and he seemed to know everyone. She felt a flutter of pride for her handsome husband, which was swiftly followed by a pang of regret that she didn't provide the arm candy he deserved.

She lost his hand as he slipped through the throng at the bar. She stood out of the way and sipped her Bellini while she people-watched. Thin women flitted past her like tropical fish with their unblinking fake eyelashes and iridescent sequinned dresses. She felt done up like a . . . a kipper.

Her glass was empty again.

She squeezed in beside Alex and tugged his jacket to get his attention. He stepped back from the bar to bring Carrie into the conversation.

'And this is my wife, Carrie.'

She put on her sociable smile and leaned forward to see who Alex was talking to. A shot of adrenalin coursed through her.

It couldn't be. It was. It was him.

Receding hairline, crinkles around narrow eyes, and square jaw slackened with age – even with these changes, Carrie instantly recognized the student he had been twelve years ago. When he had charmed her into bed. One night of indifferent sex that had changed her life for ever.

The shock produced sparkles in front of her eyeballs and she blinked ferociously to clear her vision. Her entire being plummeted downwards through space as if someone had cut the cable on a lift.

His eyes flickered, there was a hint of a frown but then the smile came back.

'Carrie, pleased to meet you,' said Ryan Cunningham.

Her hand was shaking so much that it took two attempts to make contact with his.

'Hi,' she croaked. She had goosebumps over every inch of her body, even her mouth felt odd.

He knew. He recognized her but couldn't believe how different she looked.

'This is Ryan,' said Alex, exuberantly, oblivious to Carrie's rising panic. 'He's a Member of Parliament.'

Ryan took his hand away and pulled a blonde woman with an impossibly angelic face into his side. 'This is my wife, Anna.'

Anna appeared to be wearing a dress made out of the same shimmery material as the top of Carrie's maximum-security tights and looked stunning. Ryan placed a kiss on his wife's temple. 'She's Swedish.'

'Pleased to meet you.' *She would be*, thought Carrie. *Smug git.*

Whether it was the magic knickers, the two gulped Bellinis, seeing the man who had abandoned her in her hour of need or just the whole bloody nightmare, Carrie couldn't be sure, but she felt hot and nauseous and on the verge of a panic attack. She mumbled to Alex about needing the Ladies and escaped.

Ten minutes had passed since Carrie had locked herself in the loo and she knew she should really get back to Alex. Struggling back into her tights reminded her of the time she'd made her own sausages; trying to stuff soft flesh into tiny gossamer tubes. One false move and it was game over. She pulled the waistband up high until it met with her bra to give herself a smooth line. But where had the excess flesh gone? It had to be somewhere. Maybe it was billowing

130

out of her bra strap at the back. She stretched her hand round to see whether she had back boobs to match her front ones but couldn't reach. Never mind, she would check in the mirror.

She opened the cubicle door and found Anna waiting for her.

'Oh, hello.'

'Alex sent me,' Anna said. 'You've been gone so long; he was worried about you.'

Carrie's eyeballs burned with embarrassment under the weight of Anna's worried gaze. 'Oh, I'm fine,' she said, dipping her head while she washed her hands. 'I've been constipated for ages and then you know how it is, like buses; you wait all day for one then three come along at once.'

What the hell was she saying? Even Anna blushed. *Please leave me alone.*

Carrie dried her hands. Anna was still there. 'No need to wait for me, honestly.'

Anna opened her mouth then closed it again and inched closer. 'I'll be honest, I hate these parties, I was glad of an excuse to get away. You wouldn't believe how many events like this I have to go to.'

She took a lipstick from her purse and reapplied it.

Carrie smiled. 'I would believe it actually, I'm in the same boat.'

Anna was nice; far too good for Ryan. She looked in the mirror trying to catch a glimpse of her back view but she couldn't see anything. Maybe if she stretched her right arm across her body on the pretext of taking a paper towel it wouldn't be too obvious.

There was a horrifying sound of tearing silk. Anna's hand flew to her mouth. Carrie stared at the crescent of pale skin which had appeared behind her armpit.

'Oh my God,' she gasped.

'Oh, darling, you poor thing!' Anna seemed genuinely upset. She took hold of the flap of sleeve and tried tucking it in. 'It's not too bad, actually. Have you got a needle and thread?'

Carrie blinked at her. 'Not on me, no.'

She could feel the hysteria beginning to mount. Anna was being kind; it *was* bad and they both knew it. This was the icing on the cake. She wasn't sure whether to laugh or cry.

'You could perhaps tear both sleeves off?' Anna chewed the side of her cheek.

The idea of ripping the sleeves off her dress and then swanning back into a party full of Nottingham's elite was ludicrous. She wished Jo or Sarah were here to tell her what to do. She covered her face with her hands and started to shake, tears of laughter mixed with shame slid down her face. Anna hugged her but didn't join in.

Two minutes later, Anna had dried Carrie's tears and was patching her face up with concealer.

'There,' she said, flashing Carrie a smile. 'You look fab. Now, get back to the party and style it out.'

'Thanks,' said Carrie. 'I'll keep my arm pinned to my side and no one will even notice.'

Back out in the restaurant, Anna pointed at Alex talking to Jordan Lamb at the far end. Carrie's nerve wavered. Trust him. The thought of re-joining her husband with her ripped dress while he was talking to a celebrity filled her with horror. Anna gave Carrie a hug and went back to find Ryan at the bar. *Keep calm, Carrie.* Besides, the worst had already happened. The evening could only get better.

Carrie hovered at Alex's elbow, listening while he did his best to interest Jordan in paying a visit to Cavendish Hall. He wasn't having much luck by the sound of it.

'Oh, and this is my wife, Carrie,' said Alex, finally noticing her. Jordan inclined his head politely and held out a hand.

He turned his blue eyes to Carrie and it was as if there was no one else but him and her in the room. She felt her pulse thump in her ears. There was such an aura about him.

His face was so familiar from the TV, but at the same time she was struck by his masculinity. *Sex on legs*, she thought, imagining what Jo would say.

Jordan still had his hand extended.

If she shook it, she would reveal her bare armpit, unless . . . Carrie stepped right up to him, keeping her elbow in to her waist and shook his hand. They were only inches apart. Jordan looked down into the space between them.

'And you're expecting a baby! Congratulations!' In one swift move he pulled Carrie in closer and kissed her cheek. Carrie looked down. The top of her tights were pulled up so high that they had created a waist just under her bust. Her stomach billowed out like a balloon.

'No, no, I'm not pregnant!' she exclaimed far too loudly. The colour drained from Jordan's tan and his eyes widened.

OK, so maybe the worst hadn't already happened.

'The only baby in there is the one I had for lunch.' And then she laughed, a high-pitched, open-mouthed laugh. Jordan, looking mightily relieved, joined in, giving her arm a playful punch. Behind her she heard Alex groan.

Only she, Carrie Radley, could say something so inane to one of most recognized celebrity chefs in the world. What sort of person says they've eaten a baby? She wiped a non-existent tear from her face and flattened her right arm to her side. Inside she was dying. She couldn't keep this façade up for long. She wasn't pregnant, she was fat and everybody knew it. What she wouldn't give now to disappear. For ever.

Alex was wearing a blank expression that she recognized as embarrassment. The evening had been a disaster and it was all her fault.

'I'm not feeling well, Alex,' she said quietly. 'Please could you take me home?'

Alex was at once solicitous. 'Of course,' he said, throwing Jordan a look of apology. Jordan was still grinning. He would be dining out on this one for weeks: the day I thought a fat woman was pregnant.

133

Carrie cringed.

'Oh dear, nothing you've eaten here, I hope?' asked Jordan.

'I'm, er, I've got, er . . .' Carrie looked up at the huge photograph of Jordan on the wall behind them. For God's sake, as if it wasn't bad enough having the real Lamb staring at her, the unblinking eyes in the picture appeared to be waiting for an answer too. 'Conjunctivitis,' she blurted out.

Jordan nodded goodbye to Alex, wiped his hand on his trousers with barely contained disgust and turned to the next group of eager fans.

That was it, Carrie promised herself during the drive home. She was going to diet properly from now on. No more cheating, no more kidding herself. She would get her wish. She would have a bikini body by September.

Alex pulled on to the drive in front of Fern House and stopped the car. They sat in silence in the dark for a moment before he reached for her hand.

'What happened back there, Carrie? You seemed fine and then—'

'Ryan Cunningham happened.' She turned to him, the golden glow from the security lights highlighted the concern in his deep brown eyes. 'Remember the Ryan I told you about from uni? That was him.'

'Oh, darling.'

Alex moved towards her as if he was going to take her in his arms, but she flung her door open and jumped out. She disgusted herself, she didn't deserve a hug.

Chapter 11

It was May by the time Jo managed to meet Carrie and Sarah again and she was the first to arrive at the Pear Tree in Woodby. There were no other women in the pub, just several ancient men. Jo strode up to the bar and ordered a glass of wine.

God knows why she had come tonight. She was in a foul mood. Work was crap. Her love life was crap and she had just said goodbye to Abi and Tom who were flying off to Australia in the morning for the whole summer. Sometimes she wished she could do that, just fly off and escape her life for a while. Come back when someone else had sorted everything out. She checked her watch. Sarah and Carrie should be here any minute. She had got the time right, hadn't she? She scrolled through her emails until she found the three-way conversation they had had last week. A reluctant smile tweaked the corners of her mouth.

Email to: Jo Gold (work); SarahDaveZac
From: Carriebikinibod@gmail.com

Dear Jo and Sarah,
   Just wanted you to know that my diet is going really well and I've actually lost weight!! Hope you are both having success with your wishes too. How about meeting in the Pear Tree for a drink next week (diet coke for me!)? It would be lovely to catch up.
   Carrie xx

Seeing Carrie's email address never failed to raise Jo's spirits. It seemed to radiate hope. She was happy for her. If Jo was honest, Carrie's was the only wish that she really had any interest in making happen. She always had a suspicion there was more to Carrie under that jokey exterior than met the eye; that there was something she was not telling them, like a flower that was afraid to blossom.

She took her change and the glass from the barman and chose a table in the corner.

That husband, Alex, could be the root of the problem. Jo hadn't met him yet, but everything that Carrie had told her about him led her to think that he might be a bit domineering. What Carrie needed was a job. Something to give her a bit of confidence and independence outside of the house. Then maybe if she wanted to, she would have the courage and means to leave him.

Jo felt a twinge of guilt; she hadn't even met the man and she was plotting to split them up. Just because she wasn't the marrying kind, didn't mean she had the right to pass judgement on other people's lives.

The door opened and Carrie and Sarah appeared. She told herself to be sociable and gave them a wave.

Half an hour later, the little pub was packed. Two glasses of water sat in the centre of the table holding the pretty bunches of bluebells Carrie had given them both from her garden. Jo was making her way through a stack of beer mats; peeling the top layer off and shredding them into tiny pieces.

'It's times like this that I really miss smoking,' she said, her eyes trained on a group of young men – too young for her, really – who were laughing and joking at the bar. 'A nice glass of wine, a chilled-out evening . . . my hands don't know what to do with themselves. I've completely ruined my nails.'

This village had no suitable talent whatsoever. She

abandoned her manhunt and swept the scraps of cardboard into a pile.

'Your nails are immaculate,' argued Carrie, pulling Jo's fingers towards her.

'Compare them to mine,' said Sarah, holding hers out. 'All dry skin and blunt nails.'

'Two words,' said Jo, who was in no mood to soft-soap anyone this evening. 'Hand-sanitizer. It's terrible for your nails. I bet you've got some in your bag, haven't you?'

Sarah looked taken aback. 'Well, yes, but you can't be too careful with germs, especially with a child in the house.'

Jo tutted loudly. Abi had never been that precious over Tom and he had never picked up any dreadful diseases. 'I don't understand how you can be so paranoid about Zac when you're out at work all day.'

Sarah's jaw fell open. 'It's precisely because I'm out all day that I'm *paranoid* about germs. It's one of the few things I can do to minimize risk. I feel like I'm short-changing him by not being there, but what can I do?'

'Let's not argue,' said Carrie, shifting uncomfortably in her seat.

'Surely if you were that bothered, you'd stay at home with him?' said Jo flippantly.

'I realize that the perfect mother should sacrifice everything for her child,' Sarah replied tartly, 'but I'm obviously not a perfect mother and Dave staying at home with our baby works for us.'

She folded her arms and looked the other way and a frosty silence descended between them.

Jo mentally kicked herself. What did she really know about motherhood? 'I shouldn't have said that. Ignore me. I apologize.'

Sarah gave her a tight smile and nodded, but Jo wasn't convinced that she'd been forgiven. She turned her attention to Carrie, who was swirling the ice round in her glass and making a bad job of not staring at the table next to them, where the waitress had just set down two large plates of steak and chips. Carrie looked good; her hair was pulled back into a pony tail and Jo could see the beginnings of a fine set of cheekbones.

'Is temptation striking, Carrie?'

Carrie scooped out an ice cube and crunched on it. 'Yep. Bloody starving.'

She sighed and dragged her eyes away from a chip that had been dropped on the floor. 'I keep telling myself that a craving is just a thought conjured up by my imagination. If I repeat it in my head often enough my imagination might give up and start craving iced water.'

'You're looking really thin, Carrie,' said Sarah.

'Do you think so?' Carrie blushed and sat up a bit taller.

Jo bit her tongue, glad that Sarah was at least still talking. It was good that she was being positive, but there was no reason to exaggerate quite so much. Carrie was doing well, but she was some way off 'thin'.

Sarah took her notebook out of her bag and rifled through the dog-eared pages until she came to a blank one. 'I suppose we ought to take notes for the wish list. Although I don't feel as if I've made any progress.'

Neither did Jo. In fact, she realized, she couldn't give a stuff about her wish. It had been a stupid idea in the first place and nothing was further from her mind than curing her pathetic fear of heights. She opened her mouth to admit how she was feeling and then caught sight of Carrie's face glowing with pride. Her heart sank. She couldn't do it; Carrie would be so disappointed.

'Who wants another drink first?' she asked instead.

Sarah was talking about work when Jo got back with the drinks.

'Sometimes I question the ethics of my profession,' she said, fiddling with the hem of her polka-dot skirt. 'I mean, the job's great. I love totting up figures and making the balance sheet work and I love seeing clients' faces when I've saved them loads of money by doing things with their capital asset register.'

'You make it sound quite naughty.' Jo arched an eyebrow at her as she handed her a second glass of wine.

'You think everything sounds naughty,' scoffed Sarah. 'But it's the endless pursuit of profit that gets me down.'

'That's business, Sarah,' said Carrie. 'You'll have to get used to that if you want to be a partner. Not that I know anything about it.'

Oh, for God's sake . . . Something in Jo snapped and she felt her heart speed up with stress. What was she doing in this village pub with these two women, who she barely knew and who definitely didn't know her? They were nice enough people, but Sarah pretty much had it all and Carrie, the cosseted housewife, didn't have a care in the world except how many calories were in a Diet Coke versus a lemonade. Meanwhile back in the real world, Jo had thirty-odd livelihoods to worry about, a factory to keep going and nobody – *nobody* – to love her.

'It's a nice position to be in,' said Jo, trying to rein in her frustration, 'not being bothered about profit. But the reality is that if *I* don't make a profit, I make a loss. Correction – I *am* making a loss. That means that I can't just sit there tutting and shaking my head sadly. I have to plan for redundancies. I have to decide which members of my staff I can do without, and which ones I will be telling that they have lost their jobs, that they won't be able to pay their mortgages next month.'

She sat back in her seat, heart racing, and took a sip from her glass. The frosty silence was back. Sarah looked like she'd been punched in the face, her eyes wide with shock, and Carrie was squirming in her seat.

'Well, when you put it like that,' Sarah muttered meekly, 'I can see that the pursuit of profit is quite important.'

They all stared into their drinks.

Well, this was fun. Jo cast about for a safe topic of conversation.

'Here's the vicar,' said Carrie with relief as the door opened and he walked in accompanied by a group of middle-aged women. There was something about that man; it was as if the mood lightened when he was around. Jo watched him share a joke with some of the other customers and then wait in line at the bar.

'Such a waste.' She sighed. 'To be that good-looking and choose a life of holiness. I'd quite like to be sinful with him.'

'Is that the type you go for?' Sarah pushed a ringlet of hair off her face and looked at her defiantly.

'Eyelashes like that? Don't we all?' said Jo, relieved to get the conversation back on to a lighter note.

'I think Sarah means the unattainable type,' said Carrie, earning a nod from Sarah. 'Married to his job.'

'Married men are totally . . .' Jo paused.

She stopped herself from adding 'attainable'. Her standard procedure of casually dating married men because they were so undemanding and not interested in commitment might not go down too well in present company.

'Story of my life,' she said, changing tack. 'All the men I ever meet are married to someone, or something. And unfortunately I don't think I'm the marrying kind.'

'Rubbish,' said Carrie, 'you just need to meet the one.'

'Like you did with Alex?' asked Jo.

'Exactly. Now have you been trying those visualization exercises I sent you to lower your fear levels?' Carrie asked. 'Our New York trip is getting closer, you know.'

Jo narrowed her eyes, but decided to let Carrie's change of subject go. In truth, she was regretting having agreed to even attempt to cure her heights phobia; in the grand scheme of things, it was the least of her problems. She was regretting inviting them both to come to New York with her too. She would be far better off on her own in September, trawling Manhattan streets for inspiration for Gold's.

'It's not a priority at the moment,' she said. 'To be honest, I'm not really sure I want to carry on with this wish list.'

'Really?' said Carrie, disappointed. 'That trip is the high-light of my year.'

Oh God, now she felt like a total cow.

'So what did you come tonight for, then, other than to have a go at my parenting skills?' said Sarah, two pink spots forming on her cheeks. She shoved her notebook back in her handbag. 'You made a deal, signed a contract and if I remember rightly, you were more up for it than me.'

Sarah looked furious and Carrie was chewing her lip. Jo's heart sank. It wasn't their fault that she was consumed with getting the Josephine Gold collection off the ground, that that was the only spark that was keeping her going. They weren't to know that Patrick had been subdued since the meeting with Shaw's and that even he seemed to be losing hope.

She groaned and ran a hand through her hair. 'Look, I'm sorry. Again. I'm not on great form tonight. I'll be honest, the main reason I came tonight is that Abi flies to Australia tomorrow. She's renting her house out for the summer. She'll be back in September for Tom starting school. I had to come to Woodby to say goodbye, we both shed a tear. Daft as it sounds, it felt like we were saying goodbye to Fréd all over again,' said Jo quietly.

The tension between them hung in the air, the noise of the pub fading away until Jo felt as if the three of them were inside their own little vacuum.

Carrie shifted forward to the edge of her seat and grasped both of their hands.

'Come on! Remember how this started? Fréd's funeral? We can do this, can't we? Besides . . .' she eyed up the plates on the next table. There were still a few chips left and the waitress was on her way over to collect them. 'If you don't hold me back I might have to rub my face in those chips.'

Carrie's stomach gave an almighty rumble, breaking the spell, and they all giggled.

'OK, OK, you've persuaded me.' Jo took a deep breath and resigned herself to continuing with the wish list. Carrie was right: she was still that workaholic person she had been at the funeral. She hadn't changed a bit. If she didn't lift her head up from her computer every now and then, she'd be a spinster for the rest of her life. She couldn't bear that.

'Now then, lady.' Sarah nudged Carrie's arm. 'Tell us about the diet. Last time we saw you you'd only lost a couple of pounds. Now you look like you've lost loads?'

Carrie shifted awkwardly, opened her mouth and instantly shut it again.

'Come on, spill!' said Jo.

Carrie shrugged. 'I'm trying to cut out sugar and keep busy, so I don't have time to eat. I've been gardening, going to yoga . . .'

Jo stared at her thoughtfully; she still got the impression that Carrie was keeping something back.

'Well done you,' said Sarah. 'Do you mind if I write that down?' The scruffy notebook came back out of hiding.

Carrie caught Jo's eye. 'That probably doesn't sound very busy to you,' she stammered. 'If I'm totally honest, I want to work again. But it's been such a long time that I don't think anyone would employ me.'

'What would you like to do?' asked Sarah. 'What's your dream job?'

'Caterer!' suggested Jo. 'You're an amazing cook.'

Carrie shook her head. 'I don't want a job where I'm surrounded by food all day long, the temptation would be too much. Besides, Alex is already in catering and I think one of us in the industry is enough. I've been dog-walking for a couple of people, not for money, and I've quite enjoyed it actually.'

Jo bit her tongue. Dog-walker? Carrie could do so much more. What a waste of potential.

Sarah looked doubtful. 'I'm not sure you could make a career out of dog-walking in Woodby. Everyone around here seems to love walking their own pets. Oh!' She sat up straight. 'I've got it – child-minding!'

Carrie's face darkened, but Sarah continued undaunted, counting off the benefits on her fingers. 'You're great with Zac, your house is definitely big enough, it would keep you busy and active . . .'

Carrie shook her head.

'Why not?' said Jo. 'Self-employed, independent, hours to suit . . . It could work.'

Sarah nodded. 'Honestly, Carrie, you should think about it. There are loads of preschool children in the village and it would be good to have an alternative to nursery.'

'No!' Carrie yelled, slamming her palms down on the table. She stood up roughly, knocking over one of the glasses of bluebells. Sarah gasped and Jo quickly fished her mobile phone out of the pool of water.

'I'd be a terrible mother and I'd be a terrible childminder. You know nothing about me!' The diners at the next table swivelled their heads round. Carrie flushed bright red and lowered her voice. 'I can't look after children. Not my own, not other people's. So just drop it, will you?'

Without another word, Carrie grabbed her bag and fled.

'That was a bit intense,' whispered Sarah. 'What do you think's behind it?'

'I don't know,' said Jo thoughtfully, 'but I think there's more to the meek and mild Carrie Radley than meets the eye.'

Chapter 12

Sarah unwound her long hand-knitted scarf that she'd got from the Fairtrade stall in town and stuffed it up the sleeve of her coat. Home at last. She gave a little shiver of relief; she couldn't wait to give Zac a cuddle.

She had spent all day at work counting down the hours until she could leave with Jo's hurtful words circling round in her head.

If you were that bothered, you'd stay at home.

The whole evening at the pub last night had been a disaster; everyone snapping at each other, no one taking the wish list seriously and then Carrie's shock exit. Sarah wouldn't be surprised if she never saw Jo again.

She stepped blindly over the pile of trainers in the hall and pushed past the washing basket.

She stopped in front of the hall mirror. An angry pulse pounded at her right temple. She looked grumpy. She felt grumpy. The problem was that wherever she was, she felt like a failure: she wasn't the fabulous mother she thought she'd be and she wasn't the competent professional she wanted to be either. Jo didn't understand what it was like to juggle a home, a career, a baby. She'd even admitted when they first met that she was a workaholic. What the flippin' heck did she know about it?

'I'm doing nothing wrong,' she whispered to her reflection. 'I'm a mother and a woman who cares about her career. I'm doing my best. So there.' She poked her tongue out at her reflection and went in search of the comfort of her family.

In the kitchen, Zac was banging on his high chair with a spoon and Dave was making aeroplane noises.

She placed a hand on Dave's shoulders and kissed the top of Zac's head.

'Hello, beautiful boy.' His fine baby hair tickled her nose.

She peered into Zac's bowl. 'That's very . . . orange.'

Zac's face was smeared with his dinner, as was the high chair and his bib. Dave had some in his hair and the red quarry floor tiles hadn't escaped either. Or the kitchen wall.

She kissed her husband lightly on the lips. 'Hello, beautiful man.'

'It's butternut squash and parsnip. I made a huge batch and froze it today. High in vitamin A and calcium, you know,' said Dave, trying to negotiate a clear path with the spoon to his son's mouth.

She didn't know. A wave of self-doubt washed over her. She was missing out. On cooking Zac's food, on seeing his first attempt at crawling, on check-ups with the health visitor . . . Her son was growing up without her. The thought struck her as viciously as if someone had hit her in the stomach with an iron bar. She turned away quickly to the sink so Dave didn't see her stricken face and rinsed a flannel under the hot tap. The clean water splashed on to their dirty breakfast and lunch dishes; porridge and beans on toast by the look of it.

'Let Mummy wipe your mouth.' Sarah forced a smile at Zac, who whipped his head from side to side to avoid the flannel. 'It's very chunky,' she said, peering into the bowl.

'It's fine. He can do big lumps now.'

'Can he?' She swallowed a massive lump in her own throat. 'That's good.'

'Can you light the fire, babe? I haven't had a chance.'

'Or I could finish feeding Zac?' she suggested hopefully.

'We're nearly done,' said Dave. 'Just put a match to the kindling and leave the door open for a bit.'

'OK,' she replied, stifling a sigh.

She opened the living-room door and almost gagged. What a stench. Urgh, she was going to be sick. And the mess! What had he been doing all day? Toys all over the place, changing mat on the sofa and a full stinking nappy sack lying on the floor. Dave hadn't got the first idea about hygiene. She shouldn't have to come home to this.

She kicked some toys towards the toy box angrily. If she was at home all day with the baby, it would be a different story; the house would be spotless. A little voice in her head that sounded uncannily like Jo's reminded her that it was her choice not to be at home all day.

'Oh, sod off,' she muttered.

This was not how it was meant to be.

As she opened her mouth to yell at Dave, he appeared in the doorway with Zac, both happily ignorant that they were still smeared in food. Her spirits plummeted. What was the point? It would only start a row.

'You do the fire.' Sarah handed the nappy sack to Dave and reached out for Zac. 'I'll do bath.'

Two hours later over dinner, Sarah had just started to relax; the house was halfway to being tidy again, Zac was asleep and Dave had poured her a glass of wine. Just as she took a long sip he dropped his bombshell.

'Guess what!' His eyes flicked to hers briefly. 'I'm working tomorrow. An old contact has called in a favour. Cash job so I couldn't say no.'

'Tomorrow?' Sarah lowered her glass. 'Dave? What about Zac?'

He helped himself to more broccoli.

'I managed to get him in to nursery for the morning.

The job is only a small room, so I'll be finished by lunch-time.'

'Dave! We said we didn't want our child brought up by strangers. The horror stories you read in the papers . . . No! How could you?'

Her cheeks flamed with indignation. So Rebecca had been right about Zac going to nursery. Nice of Dave to discuss it with *her*, before his own wife. Decisions about her son were being made without her and she hated it. She didn't feel like a mother at all. She felt like . . . she felt like . . . a father.

'No, we said we didn't want him going to nursery full time until he's one.' Dave laid his fork down on the edge of his plate and looked directly at her.

'I said I didn't want him to go to nursery full stop,' she retorted.

'We liked the nursery,' said Dave calmly. 'We liked the atmosphere and the staff. It was clean, the kids were happy and it's only for half a day.'

'But if I'd known you were going to paint some stupid room tomorrow, I'd have taken a day off and spent some quality time with my own baby. Now it's too short notice.'

Dave reached across the table for Sarah's hand.

'Don't get upset,' he said quietly, bringing her fingers to his lips. 'I need this. I need to work. I try my best to be a house husband but,' he gave her a lopsided smile, 'I'm crap at it.'

A vision of the living room earlier flashed into her mind and she managed a feeble laugh despite her frustration. She sat back in her chair, dinner abandoned, and blotted the tears from her face with kitchen paper.

She would never be able to concentrate at work tomorrow, worrying about whether Zac was being looked after properly.

'What are we going to do?' she said in a small voice.

Dave got up from the table and pulled her into his arms. She felt her body sag in defeat.

'Our best, babe,' he said. 'That's all we can do.'

The next morning Sarah scurried along the corridor towards Eleanor's office and prayed her boss was in a good mood.

She was so pleased with herself that she could scarcely keep the grin off her face. The solution to her domestic problems had come to her in the middle of the night. It was so obvious; she could kick herself for not thinking of it before. To give credit where it was due, it was Rebecca who had given her the idea from something she said in the park a few weeks ago: *Oh, I think we all have a choice*, she'd said snootily. And actually, she was right, Sarah did have a choice, and today she was going to make it.

She would simply ask to work from home. Dave could get his business back up and running again and work, say, four or five days a week, she would set up her laptop on the kitchen table and only go into the office whenever she had a meeting.

It was the best thing to do, she was sure of it. Poor Dave; the expression on his face last night when he'd admitted he hated staying at home had broken her heart. Secretly, she was pleased that he wasn't perfect at being a house husband; it wasn't exactly normal, was it? Her father would have been appalled. Not that that mattered for one instant. She felt a flush to her cheeks and took a deep breath.

Focus, don't think about him.

She forced herself to get her thoughts back on track . . . And with more money coming in they'd soon be able to afford that extension. It would all be perfect, absolutely perfect.

She was about to knock on the door but paused, doubting herself for a moment. But she flicked the fear away. Eleanor would understand. She was a mother; she'd be fine about it. She knocked and Eleanor called her in.

'Have you got a second?'

Eleanor's eyes flicked to her watch and she nodded, Sarah closed the door and took a seat opposite her.

At the moment, Eleanor was the only female partner out of five. She had a rapier-sharp brain for figures, nerves of steel when it came to negotiations and seemed to slice through her workload like a blade through butter. The downside of working for a superhero was that Eleanor had blazed such a trail for females at Finch and Partners that it was a bit daunting for mere mortals like Sarah to keep up.

Eleanor was waiting.

Sarah smoothed her skirt down with clammy hands. She had had her little speech all figured out, but now she was here, in front of the boss, her reasoning seemed flawed and she doubted her own ability to put a strong case forward.

'Is this about the bakery accounts?' asked Eleanor. 'I hope they're nearly ready?'

Sarah crossed her fingers under the desk. 'Ninety-nine per cent there. Just one final check through and . . .'

Her voice faded as she caught sight of what Eleanor referred to as her wall of fame; a series of framed photographs cataloguing her finest moments: Eleanor drinking champagne with the board on becoming a partner, Eleanor shaking hands with the Prince of Wales when he thanked her for services to charity, Eleanor at the launch party for her own accountancy textbook, Eleanor holding her newborn granddaughter after her daughter-in-law went into labour and she had had to deliver the baby with instructions over the telephone from the emergency services.

She was probably wearing a red and blue spandex corset under that suit.

Eleanor cleared her throat pointedly.

Oh God. Sarah's stomach churned. Whatever had possessed her to think this was a good idea? Oh well, she was here now. She took another deep breath.

'I was wondering if you would – if the board would – consider letting me work from home two days.' She caught sight of Eleanor's nostrils flaring. 'I mean *one* day a week. Just for a few months. Until Zac is a bit older.'

Bad move. She just about resisted biting her lip; that would really show weakness.

Eleanor stared at her, a look of confusion etched across her smooth brow. Sarah hated it when people stayed silent; it was rarely a good sign. She toyed with the idea of telling the truth.

Help. I need your help. I'm totally failing at life, spreading myself too thin. I shouldn't have come back to work so soon and definitely not full time. I'm a rubbish accountant and I'm a crap mum too.

Her heart lurched with longing. One day a week she would love to sit down to breakfast with Dave and Zac, together, as a family, instead of dashing out of the house with a cereal bar in her bag, leaving them both still in their pyjamas. For once she would like not to have to sit for an hour in a queue of cars all nosing their way slowly along the commuter treadmill towards the city.

Her gaze fell on the plaque Eleanor used as a paperweight. It was engraved with the inscription '1992 Nottinghamshire Business Woman of the Year'. Eleanor's own children would have been small then, how had she managed to stay at the top of her game?

Sarah's stomach fluttered with nerves. She glanced at the door, wishing she had never started this.

Please say something, Eleanor.

'I'd miss the camaraderie, of course,' she said, to fill the silence.

'Of course.' Eleanor inclined her head slightly but didn't break eye contact and didn't smile.

Sarah's mouth had gone dry now. She licked her lips and racked her brains for something positive to say.

'I think it would help me to raise my productivity. I

could motor through tax returns without the constant interruption of the telephone ringing. It would be a godsend at peak times, when we're sorting out all our last-minute clients. I'd be on top of my monthly reports and it would help me to be more efficient on the days I am in the office.'

Eleanor appeared to be listening, which she took to be a good sign.

'It's the future,' said Sarah, getting into her stride. 'Lots of companies are seeing the benefits of home-based workers. Reduced absenteeism, improved staff morale. Fewer lost hours due to bad weather and traffic jams. Saving on fossil fuels . . .' She closed her mouth, sensing that she had started to veer into weird territory.

Eleanor leaned her elbows on the desk, linked her fingers and circled her thumbs.

'I do understand how you feel. I remember those days myself when the children were small and I can see you've given it a lot of thought.' She lowered her voice and leaned forward. 'The problem is, Sarah, that the rest of the board are men. They'll see this request as a sign of weakness. That you aren't partner material after all.'

Sarah looked at her boss in alarm. 'I think I've proved that I am, and I cut my maternity leave short to come back when you needed me, and—'

Eleanor held up a hand to stop her.

'The way they'll see it is like this: once we let one woman do it, the floodgates will open. You'll be setting a precedent. Word will get out that this company is a soft touch and all the female staff of child-bearing age will want to work part time – I mean work from home.' Eleanor gave her a knowing smile. 'And there'll be no one in the office to answer calls and take client meetings.'

A soft touch? Hardly. Her mouth had gone dry with nerves; this hadn't gone to plan at all.

Eleanor picked up her fountain pen and pulled a stack of papers towards her.

'I'm sorry. It's a no, Sarah, and I'll do you a favour and pretend we didn't have this conversation.'

Sarah held Eleanor's gaze for a long moment. She was being dismissed. She needed to say something quickly to redeem herself. If she lost her chance to become partner, she couldn't bear it. She had worked so hard to come this far.

'Eleanor,' she inched forward on her chair, 'can I just reiterate that I'm one hundred per cent—'

There was a knock at the door. Ben walked straight in without waiting for an answer. Eleanor beamed at him.

'Ah, Ben, take a seat.'

There was only one visitor's chair. That was her cue to leave. Sarah walked out, digging her nails into her palms and suspecting she may have just shot herself firmly in the foot.

Chapter 13

Jo had been cooped up in her office for hours and for the last thirty minutes she had been staring at the wages spreadsheet. She rubbed her eyes and sighed. Every employee was listed, along with their salary and number of weekly hours. If there was a way of cutting the costs without making redundancies, she was damned if she could spot it.

The two biggest earners were herself and Patrick. She could hardly make herself redundant and the thought of Gold's without Patrick was too awful to bear. Besides, since his divorce, Patrick needed his salary more than ever. He was renting a tiny terraced house for himself and Holly at the moment, and although he hadn't complained, she knew he was struggling to get back on the property ladder. She had even overheard him laughing with Len, saying that he hoped Holly didn't want to go to university because he couldn't afford it, and she suspected he was only half-joking. She owed it to him and Holly to safeguard his job for as long as possible.

Next month, she would forfeit her own salary. It was a drop in the ocean, but at least she would feel like she was doing something. She saved the changes to the document and sighed; she could do with asking Sarah's help about cost-saving, if they were still on speaking terms, that was. Jo's know-it-all comments on childcare last time they met had been harsh, even by her own standards.

'Knock, knock.' Bob Gold stuck his head around her office door, looking relaxed in his blazer and jeans.

'Dad!' Jo closed the top of her laptop and jumped up to greet him. 'This is a nice surprise.'

He kissed her cheek and tucked an arm around her. 'I was in the area . . .'

'Yeah, right.' She laughed at the feeble excuse; Gold's was on the edge of town in an industrial estate and on the road to nowhere.

He grinned sheepishly. 'Your mother was threatening me with the ironing pile and I had a sudden urge to see these fancy new shoes I've been hearing about!'

Jo had only told him the bare minimum about the Josephine Gold collection, preferring to wait until they had got the final order through from Shaw's. She was under no illusion: this wasn't a social call; Dad was checking up on her. Her stomach lurched in panic. She hugged him back and wondered if information was being leaked to him from anyone else on her team.

Liz arrived with a tray of coffee, the best cups and a plate of biscuits.

'Teresa says you're supposed to be cutting down,' she said with a conspiratorial wink at her old boss, 'but I'm sure one won't hurt.'

Bingo. There was her answer. That was the problem with having a secretary who used to work for your father and was still good friends with your mother. Jo bit her tongue and left them to chat while she collected the mood boards and samples from Cesca's office.

She found her father sitting in her chair when she got back and her laptop was open again. This had been his old office, it probably felt natural to him to sit behind the desk, but Jo found it oddly disconcerting to be sitting in the visitor's chair.

She took a sip of her coffee and jiggled her foot under the table. So far, her dad hadn't given much away as she took him through the new collection. She tried to read his various expressions as he studied the boards and took every single sample out of its box.

'Very brave,' said Bob, turning a mink suede ankle boot round in his tanned hand.

Jo considered his remark carefully.

'Brave as in innovative or brave as in barmy?' she asked finally.

'There are too many copycat brands out there,' he said. 'Developing a sub-brand might give Gold's a point of difference.'

Might.

'Thanks, Dad, that's exactly what I am hoping to do.' She leaned across the desk and pressed her cheek against his. The wages spreadsheet was open on her laptop; she wondered if he'd been snooping. She sat back down and bit her lip.

'You don't think we're completely mad to try and manufacture them in our factory then?'

'I would be happier if the collection was half the size, Jo. It's a big risk. The question is,' his eyes scanned hers, 'can you afford to?'

Jo felt her face flush and hoped he wouldn't notice. 'Shaw's needs a big range to fill the shelves. It does push up the price, but it would be fantastic to keep them British-made, wouldn't it?'

'The wages bill has been creeping up, I notice,' he said, nodding at the laptop.

'You're not spying on me, are you?' she said, keeping her voice neutral.

He ignored her and pulled the laptop closer. 'Who's on the list for the chop then, if things get worse?'

'It's all under control, Dad, trust me.'

He didn't trust her, though. Would he have been here poking around if Jo had been his son? Somehow she doubted it. Perhaps it was her fault for not standing up to him. She felt her hackles rise.

Right on cue, Patrick knocked on the glass panel in the door and held up a hand in salute to Bob.

Hallelujah! She could have hugged him. She almost ran to the office door to usher him in.

'Dad just popped in to see the new samples.'

Bob shook Patrick's hand and slapped him on the back. Patrick winked at her over Bob's shoulder and she rolled her eyes. It was no secret that Bob thought the world of him.

'Teresa says to tell you to call in with Holly sometime and that if you're ever in need of a babysitter . . .'

Jo couldn't look Patrick in the eye; her mother was so transparent. This wasn't her first attempt to throw her and Patrick together now that Melissa was off the scene.

'That's very kind of her.' Patrick rubbed a hand through his hair until it stood up in peaks. He looked as uncomfortable as Jo felt. He cleared his throat and nodded towards the new collection.

'Len's making some more samples for Shaw's in the workroom, if you'd like to come and see, Bob?'

'Sure, lead the way, son.' Bob put his hand back on Patrick's shoulder and followed him out of Jo's office.

Jo let out a long breath that she hadn't even realized she'd been holding.

Five minutes later they were back, Bob's face red and set firm in contrast to Patrick's pale expression.

'A word,' he said, closing the door and shutting Patrick out. He shrugged an apology through the glass panel.

'What's wrong?' said Jo, trying to keep her voice light.

'Shaw's haven't placed an order and yet you're making all these one-off shoes for them?' He glared at her, hands on hips.

'True, but Ed has given me a verbal agreement.'

Bob gave a patronizing laugh. 'Which means nothing.'

Jo's jaw was rigid and her heart was pounding but she wasn't going to be bullied over this. 'We're going out for dinner next week to celebrate. The deal is as good as done. They just need some shoes for their photo shoot.'

'The number of materials in some of those styles is crazy; the manufacturing costs will be astronomical. Have you done your cash flow?'

'Of course,' she retorted, hurt that he displayed such little faith in her.

Bob was already round her side of the desk again, trying to take control of her laptop and nudging her out of her chair. 'Let's have a look.'

'No, Dad!' She sprang out of her seat, scooped up the computer and shut it into a desk drawer.

This was her collection, her new venture, and she felt both inordinately proud and protective over it. A small part of her wondered if Bob's reaction was fuelled by envy because he had never done anything quite so dynamic when he had been in charge.

'You're not the boss any more,' she said calmly, backing away. 'I'm trading my way through the downturn like you said. The Josephine Gold collection is the start of a new era for the firm. The Shaw's opportunity could be exactly what we need to set us on an even footing.'

Bob leaned forward, scowling, his fingertips splayed on the desk, taking his weight.

'It could also ruin us. You're forgetting something; I'm still the major shareholder,' he said, raising his voice. 'This is a time to be conservative. Not throw caution to the wind.'

Jo's stomach flipped; the partition walls in this place were only thin, the entire company would be able to hear his outburst.

'I'm going to do this, Dad,' she said defiantly, narrowing

her eyes. 'And when I make a success of it, you're going to apologize.'

Bob shook his head, strode to the door and pointed a finger at her. 'You've got until September to show me some profit.' He put his hand on the door handle and pulled it open.

'And if I don't?'

'Then you're out.' He turned his steely eyes to her. 'This will be my office again.'

He couldn't do that to her, could he?

She felt the blood drain from her head and sank down in her seat; she already knew the answer to that one.

Chapter 14

Carrie sat down at the desk in the little bedroom and turned on the computer. She covered her face with her hands while she waited for it to come to life. Since the whole Jordan Lamb fiasco, she had been on edge, miserable, full of anger and ready to lash out at someone. Her behaviour at the Pear Tree was a prime example. She had had the perfect chance to tell Jo and Sarah the truth, but instead she had flounced out like a sulky child. They would probably never want to see her again.

She tapped in her password and contemplated sending them both an apology. Maybe later. Today she was on a mission and she didn't want to get distracted. She had stuck to her diet rigidly, but it was such hard going and she was convinced there must be a way she could speed it up. She took a sip of water and typed 'easy ways to lose weight' into the Google search bar.

Using the internet hadn't been half as difficult as she'd imagined. It was a real eye-opener too. She would definitely be doing her clothes shopping online from now on; it was the perfect way to shop. She had suffered years of humiliation at the hands of thin changing-room attendants. All pretending they didn't know she was still in there as they whisked the curtain back to reveal her partially clad body and then yelling, 'Have we got this in a size twenty for this woman?' and have the rest of the queue straining their necks to see which cubicle the fatty was in.

She was getting used to email as well. She realized she might have been a bit hasty choosing the user name 'Carriebikinibod' but she didn't know how to change it. Besides, it had seemed like such a bold gesture at the time and she still got a laugh out of it every time she clicked on her inbox.

It was amazing how many emails she received, particularly rude ones from strangers. She deleted most of them, but she couldn't resist keeping one from a man called Pedro. He was currently a resident of a correctional facility in Ohio, and had asked her to be his pen pal. He seemed very friendly. She was thinking about it.

Her Google search for weight loss had given her one hundred and fifty-five million results in a fraction of a second. She scrolled through the first couple of pages of websites, but it was a small advertisement on the third page that caught her eye.

Discover the secret of successful, effortless weight loss. We use hypnosis to help you understand your over-eating and change those eating patterns for ever. Free yourself from the tyranny of food and take control of your life!

Call Michelle Terry today to take the first step towards a slimmer, happier you.

Carrie frowned. What was there to understand? She did like her food, that was true enough, who didn't? The way this Michelle Terry was talking it was as if over-eating came from something deep within. Which was ridiculous. She simply had a slow metabolism. And big bones, like Sarah said. Trying to blame something or someone else for the size of her appetite was a concept Carrie had never considered.

On the other hand, if this hypnotherapist could guarantee

effortless success, maybe it was worth a shot? She clicked on to the website, read every testimonial and sent her a message . . .

A week later Carrie lay back in the hypnotherapist's chair and closed her eyes as instructed. She was beginning to regret being quite so impulsive. The upstairs room in the modern family home was dimly lit and warmed by a two-bar electric heater in the corner. Plinky-plonky oriental music filled the silence. She had been expecting a clinical room with white walls and a long couch.

'Counting down now from ten to one,' said Michelle Terry in her gentle, mesmerizing voice. 'With each number you will feel more and more relaxed and by the time I reach one, your subconscious mind will be totally open to my suggestions, which will help you in your quest for a slimmer, healthier body.'

Carrie wouldn't feel less relaxed if she was being dangled over the edge of a lion enclosure on a frayed piece of string. She tried to resist opening her eyes for a peek. So far she'd endured the weigh-in and the tape-measure torture, when Michelle had invaded her personal space in order to reach around Carrie's middle.

'Oh, the classic apple shape,' the consultant had pronounced brightly.

A very red apple. She felt a brief pang of sadness for the apple. How unfair to be all fresh and perky, only to be compared to fifty per cent of the obese population of Britain. She didn't feel sorry for pears and their unhappy association with big bottoms. Pears were unpredictable; either chin-dribblingly over-ripe or hard and grainy. Unless they were poached in red wine and served with a blob of clotted cream. Yum.

'Focus on your body now, become aware of your breathing and with every breath sink deeper into the chair. Notice how your muscles are relaxing.'

Carrie had an itch on her cheek. Keeping her eyes closed, she rolled her head to one side and tried to scratch it discreetly against her shoulder. It didn't work. Her muscles were more tense than ever and all she could think about was her itchy face. She raised her hand and rubbed her face violently. Now her skin really stung. She began to feel hot and wondered if she dared look at her watch.

'That's good,' said Michelle, in her soft, melodic tones, apparently without irony. 'Just relax.'

Carrie wasn't even sure why she had come. It wasn't as if there was some huge dark secret in her past that would make everything clear as soon as she confronted it. She was just a greedy pig. But she was here now in a leather chair, with her legs on a footstool. It was quite comfy. Carrie tuned back in to what Michelle was saying.

'Notice your arms, notice that one arm may feel heavier than the other . . .'

Imagine if one was actually heavier than the other. Imagine if she lost loads of weight off one arm and the other one stayed fat, with a solo bingo wing and one dimply elbow. When she walked, her fat arm would swing faster than the other. It would throw her off course, until eventually she would fall into the road and get crushed under a lorry. On the other hand, if she could only have one thin arm, she would like it to be her left one; she hadn't been able to get her engagement ring off for years.

'Well done, Carrie, you're now completely relaxed . . .'

She hoped not. What if her bowels completely relaxed? She couldn't face another yoga incident. Jo still blew raspberries every time she bent down.

'From now on, you will only eat when you're hungry and STOP WHEN YOU'RE FULL!'

Carrie flinched at Michelle's raised voice and her hand flew to her heart. Well, that wasn't very relaxing. She opened one eye. Michelle gave her an encouraging smile.

'I want you to travel back in time. Keep going back and

back until you come to the first time you can remember over-eating. Keep thinking.'

Carrie suppressed a sigh. This wasn't achieving anything. It was impossible to remember when she had first started comfort eating. *Comfort eating?* Was that what she was doing? Her heart thumped as the realization hit her and then her subconscious took over and started divebombing her with memories, moving further and further back in time.

Tarte Tatin eaten secretly in the kitchen at one of her dinner parties because she felt too embarrassed to rejoin the party. Worried her guests would look at her eating dessert and judge her.

Further back to the early years of her marriage, buying a box of doughnuts every day after she gave up her job at the florist, because she missed being busy and feeling valued, and didn't know who she was any more.

Before she met Alex, treating herself to a family-sized bar of chocolate to cheer herself up because she was living on her own in a poky flat and had forgotten how to make friends. Eating and eating and not noticing how sick it made her feel.

Further back still, waiting until her housemates had gone off to uni, then sneaking down and taking a box of cereal back to bed with her. Waiting to feel better. Waiting for the pains in her stomach and the hollow in her heart to disappear. Until sleep overtook the nausea and desolation and self-disgust.

And later, lying in the semi-darkness, eating crisps until they returned, their noisy laughter filling the house with the hubris of student wisdom.

They knew nothing about the real world, Carrie had thought harshly.

Food gave her a focus, an excuse for the new curves, the rounded belly. Her friends had stopped asking what was wrong, or when she was coming back to lectures or what was causing the tears that continued long into the night.

Nothing mattered any more. Ryan Cunningham hadn't wanted to know her after their one-night stand. She had been so flattered when Ryan, a third-year student, had joined their group, buying her drinks, making her friends laugh and singling her out as the chosen one.

Losing your virginity was supposed to be special, wasn't it?

The next morning, she'd woken up in a strange bed with the hangover from hell and a boy who couldn't even remember her name. He had thrown some coins in her direction, pointed out the way to the bus stop and sent her packing. That was the last time he had spoken to her. He ignored her at university and when she sent him a text informing him she was expecting his baby and asking him to come to the clinic with her, he didn't even respond.

From somewhere outside of her head, she heard a soft voice talking to her.

'Good, Carrie, let it go, let the tears come, there's nothing to fear. Your eating was the way your subconscious coped with whatever happened. And this behaviour helped you. But now you are ready to make changes to your life.'

Michelle's voice continued softly and gradually faded away.

She had only been nineteen. Without the maturity to cope with aborting the baby, she had floundered. Too shy to talk to her friends and too ashamed to approach her parents, Carrie retreated into a world of solitude and food.

At the end of term, she swapped a cosmopolitan student life and a planned teaching career for a studio flat and the minimum wage at a florist. Meeting Alex a year later provided her with a new start but the damage had been done.

'You are walking in a park, Carrie. There's a man ahead of you selling helium balloons. I want you to imagine that you buy three balloons from him. Notice the colour of them, which ones will you choose?'

Red, thought Carrie, definitely red, bright and bold.

'There's a bench along the path in front of you. Now, sit down and think of three reasons, perhaps three excuses you give yourself, for eating too much.'

This was getting tricky; food was her friend, it made her forget, it made her feel better. Carrie thought hard. And finally, finally, she gave herself over to Michelle. The noise of the traffic outside faded, the sensation of her own body reclining in the chair disappeared, she floated away until the only Carrie was the one in her head holding three beautiful, red balloons.

Carrie sat on the park bench and pondered.

There was a huge oak tree ahead of her, so big that a young mother and her daughter were playing hide and seek around its trunk. The mother was laughing and changed direction to trick the little girl. But even though she ran all the way round the tree, she didn't catch up with her daughter. The smile slipped from the mother's face and she frowned, putting up a hand to her forehead to shade her eyes. She called her daughter's name over and over again, fear creeping into her voice, louder and louder. But the child was gone. The mother sank to her knees and cried as if she knew the child would never come back.

It was June.

If Carrie hadn't aborted her baby, it would have been born in June.

Guilt. Sadness. Emptiness.

'Reach into your pocket, Carrie. Take out a marker pen and write each of your reasons on a balloon.'

Carrie checked her pockets. Remarkably, she found a black marker pen and wrote on the balloons.

Guilt. Sadness. Emptiness.

'It's time to let these reasons go, Carrie. They have served a purpose. But you don't need them any more. Because you don't need to eat when these feelings come over you.'

Carrie held on to the balloons, the strings wrapped

tightly round her fingers and her heart bled for the life she had chosen to end. *I'll never forget you, but please forgive me, because I need to forgive myself.*

One by one, she released the balloons and watched them float higher and higher on the breeze until finally they were nothing but tiny specks in the distance. Oddly she felt as light as a balloon herself.

Let it go, Carrie, let it go.

Chapter 15

Jo pulled up outside Patrick's house and tooted the horn. She took a deep breath and forced herself to relax. No chance. Her blood pressure had been hovering somewhere near 'explode' since her darling father had publicly humiliated her last week.

Tonight's plan was that she was driving them into Nottingham for dinner with Ed Shaw and his wife, and Patrick was driving them home. It had been his idea, saying that that way she could have a couple of glasses of wine. Under the circumstances, she wasn't sure whether Patrick encouraging her to drink alcohol was entirely the right strategy. Then again, the way she felt right now, she wasn't going to argue.

There was no sign of Patrick so she reached into her clutch bag and reapplied her lipstick in the visor mirror. She tweaked a few strands of hair into place; she'd opted for a messy look tonight, tousled and sexy, smoky eyes and nude lips. She was quite pleased with the result; it made a change from the swept-back look with bright red lips she normally went for.

She snapped the visor back up and tutted. Not that anyone would appreciate her efforts. Patrick treated her like a mate and Ed obviously wasn't interested. Anyway, her mission to get to know Ed up close and personal had been aborted indefinitely.

Tonight had one purpose and one purpose only. The

order from Shaw's needed to be big. Huge, in fact. Shaw's would have to back the Josephine Gold collection with everything they'd got. Dad had thrown down the gauntlet and she was going to take great pleasure in proving him wrong. There was no way she was going to allow him to take over at Gold's again. She had worked too hard, sacrificed too much, to let that happen.

The worst of it was that her team had overheard the whole debacle and her father had planted a seed of doubt in everyone's mind. That initial bubble of hope that the new collection had created was now in danger of bursting and people were tiptoeing round her looking worried.

Her pulse was racing again. For God's sake, where was Patrick?

Just as her palm hovered over the car horn for a second time, the front door flew open and Holly ran out, arms flailing and dark wavy hair flying behind her. Patrick was close behind her. A woman in jeans and a T-shirt stood in the doorway, arms folded. Jo was intrigued; she hadn't seen her before. Was this who the new smart Patrick was trying to impress? She squinted to get a better look, but the woman stepped back into the shadows.

Jo opened her car window and laughed as Holly wrapped her arms round her neck and pressed a cheek against Jo's.

'It's my birthday soon,' said Holly, moving back and failing to pull off an innocent look.

'I know.' Jo grinned. That was the great thing about kids. No qualms about getting straight to the point. She should maybe spend more time with Holly; she might get some tips on where she was going wrong. 'What do you want this year?'

Holly glanced over her shoulder at Patrick who was nearly at the car.

'I've put a wish list on Insta,' she hissed, adding in a louder voice, 'Do you think Dad looks sexy for your date, Auntie Jo?'

'Er, yes,' said Jo vaguely, wondering at what point children had begun using Instagram to send out their birthday lists.

'Told you.' Holly folded her arms and grinned at Patrick mischievously.

Jo looked at Patrick properly. He seemed to be hiding his face in Holly's hair as he kissed her goodnight. Bloody hell! He actually looked really smart. He smelt good too.

'Don't use that word,' he said, nudging his daughter playfully back towards the house.

'Which one – date?' Holly called cheekily over her shoulder, waving goodbye to Jo.

'Sorry about Holly,' said Patrick, climbing into the car.

'Don't apologize, you do look good. New suit?'

Patrick concentrated on doing up his seat belt and wouldn't meet her eye. 'Holly thinks it's time I move on – up my game, as she calls it – and get back out there, wherever "there" is.'

Jo started up the engine and grinned, she couldn't take her eyes off him. That woman had to be something to do with it; he must be making an effort for her. She wasn't sure how she felt about that; she must admit, the two of them had been getting on better than ever since he split with his wife. Jo would miss that closeness if he started going out with someone new. *But he deserves to be happy*, she thought with a pang.

They both waved at Holly as they drove off; she was sticking both thumbs in the air and bouncing on the spot.

'So who's the lady friend?'

'Oh, babysitter.' He lifted one shoulder casually, but he couldn't hide the flush to his face. 'Just one of the mums from school. Holly thinks she's old enough to be left at home by herself. I do not.'

Jo kept her mouth shut, the poor man was uncomfortable enough and if there was something going on between him and the babysitter, it was none of her business.

Patrick tugged on his collar. 'Should I have worn a tie? I was going to but Holly said I should loosen up a bit.'

Jo glanced at his navy suit and matching navy shirt.

'Holly was right. You look pretty cool, McGregor. I feel underdressed.' She paused, waiting for Patrick to compliment her on her cream minidress, but he was still fussing with the buttons on his jacket.

'Do you like my shoes?' She lifted a foot up and the car lurched to one side. Patrick grabbed the steering wheel and she batted him away.

He looked down. 'Very nice, Paul Smith?'

She grinned. 'Spot on. Expensive, but I really want to make a professional impression tonight.'

'Right, in that case, you might want to, um . . .' He inclined his head towards Jo's lap, eyes averted.

Jo glanced down to see that her dress had ridden up, revealing a triangle of lacy knickers. Blood rushed to the tips of her ears. Very professional.

The restaurant was in the middle of a noisy, brightly lit multi-media complex. As they arrived, a group of teenagers was running up and down the escalators throwing popcorn at each other.

'I feel *over*-dressed now!' muttered Jo as Patrick steered her to the lift. She hated lifts. She felt her stomach lurch as she glanced at the buttons; how high up were they going exactly?

'I Googled it,' said Patrick. 'It looks a nice place inside.'

She sneaked a look at his profile. He poked his tongue out while he decided which level to go for. She smiled, thinking how like Holly he looked when he did that. His wavy sandy hair was flecked with grey at the temples. That was new, but it suited him. And the sticky-up tuft at the back had been tamed for the night. He really had made an effort.

The restaurant had a nice vibe, unobtrusive music, darting waiters and an eclectic interior. Jo scanned the place for the Shaws. She was used to being single, confident at walking into places alone, but for once it was nice to have Patrick's solid presence at her side. And a lift home. The first drink couldn't come soon enough.

'Over there.' He pointed to where Ed was standing at the bar with his wife sipping champagne.

'Holy cow,' Jo muttered softly.

Patrick sniggered. Lisa Shaw was waving at them as if they were long-lost relatives appearing at airport arrivals.

Ed was, as usual, the picture of nonchalance in tan-coloured jeans, a checked shirt and a lazy smile. Lisa grabbed the bottle and sloshed some champagne into two clean glasses. She had a curvaceous figure, red hair pinned up into a bun and wore a low-cut pink dress.

'Oh, don't you two make a gorgeous couple; I'm so excited to meet you!' she said in a broad Lancashire accent. 'Ed has told me so much about you both. Haven't you, love?'

Jo brushed cheeks with Ed in a self-conscious greeting and smothered a giggle as Lisa yanked Patrick towards her and kissed him like an old friend.

Introductions complete, Ed proposed a toast to the success of the new Gold/Shaw collaboration and the four of them settled into a blend of industry chatter and common-ground conversation.

'This is *so* nice,' said Lisa, grabbing Jo's arm and giving it a squeeze. 'We should double date again!'

'It is nice,' said Jo tactfully. 'But it's not a date.'

'We're not a couple,' Patrick added.

'Aww,' said Lisa, nudging Ed and looking at them like they were a pair of newly-weds. 'Are you staying in a hotel in town, making a night of it?'

'No,' said Jo tightly. 'Because we are just colleagues.'

No wonder Ed had resisted Jo's charms if this was the sort of woman he went for. Jo and Lisa couldn't be more different if they tried.

Patrick smiled at Lisa politely. 'And I've got to get back for the babysitter. I have a daughter.'

'Oh! What's her name?' asked Lisa undeterred.

'Holly.'

'Holly! That's lovely! Was she born at Christmas?'

'No.'

Lisa screeched with laughter. 'Did you hear that, Ed?' she nudged her husband several times in the ribs. 'I said, "Holly? Was she born at Christmas?" and Patrick said "No"!'

Ed smiled affectionately at her. 'I heard.'

'I'll get the next round,' said Jo, swapping places with Ed to get closer to the bar. Sod her resolution to only have a couple of drinks; she was going to need more booze to get through this evening. Thank God for Patrick and his good manners.

'Have you got children?' he asked Lisa.

'Two. A boy and a girl.' Lisa bent down to her handbag, exposing her considerable cleavage, and took out a small photograph album.

Patrick's face was a picture; Jo turned away to catch the barmaid's attention and hide her smile.

'This is Tiffany,' she said, holding up the pictures to Patrick. 'Ah, babe, do you remember? That was where we—'

Ed intervened swiftly. 'Lisa, I don't think we need to go into that.'

Jo ordered more champagne. The barmaid tore the foil off the cap and removed the cork with a muted pop.

Lisa, however, was not easily silenced. 'We called her Tiffany because that was where Ed proposed.' She squeezed her husband's arm, treating them all to a flash of her diamond ring as she did so.

Jo froze. Ed had proposed to his wife in Tiffany's? A shiver ran down her spine. That was her secret fantasy: to be proposed to in Tiffany's. Or even just with a ring from Tiffany. He would drop down on one knee, everyone would stare, indulgent smiles on their happy faces . . .

'Anything else?' The barmaid tweaked the fifty-pound note from between Jo's fingers.

'No, no, thanks,' she stuttered.

She swivelled from the bar, blinked furiously and held out the bottle.

'Top up, anyone?'

'I'm driving, remember?' Patrick raised an eyebrow. 'Have a large one for me.'

She bit back a giggle, handed him a glass of water and they shared a look of solidarity.

'So, Tiffany?' Jo turned to Lisa. 'On Fifth Avenue?' It was like picking a scab; painful but she couldn't help herself.

'Well, no,' said Lisa, sucking her cheeks in. 'Heathrow airport, we were on our way to Glasgow.'

A bubble of laughter threatened to escape and Jo held her glass up to her mouth to hide her smile.

'Still Tiffany, though,' argued Ed, putting an arm round his wife's waist and pulling her in for a kiss. He winked at Patrick.

'Ah, my little Eddy-bear,' cooed Lisa, snuggling up to him.

Jo stared at them. Thank God she hadn't already eaten; she was in danger of being sick soon.

Patrick cleared his throat. 'And what about your son? What was he named after?' he asked, catching Jo's eye.

'His name's Brad,' said Lisa proudly. 'After one of Ed's idols.' She jerked her head towards her husband. 'Ed bumped into him in the Gents at the motorway services at Watford Gap when I was pregnant.'

Jo's eyes widened.

'You met Brad Pitt in the toilets at Watford Gap?'

Ed spluttered and choked on his champagne and Lisa collapsed with hoots of laughter.

'Not Brad Pitt!' she cried. 'It was Brad What's-his-name, the rugby player. Tell her, Ed!'

'Brad Barkley. I was at the urinal and this big fella appeared next to me and started to pee. I couldn't believe it, I'm a massive rugby fan. We exchanged a few words, but I couldn't even shake his hand or get his autograph.'

Patrick grinned and shook his head in sympathy.

'Why not?' asked Jo, bewildered by the whole, Tiffany-slash-Brad-Pitt let-down.

'We both had our hands full, didn't we?' said Ed with a shrug. 'Some of us more full than others.'

Jo was speechless and didn't even want to think too deeply about that last comment. Patrick breathed a sigh of relief as the waitress approached them.

'Your table on the terrace is ready for you,' she announced.

Jo's stomach flipped over at least twice. The terrace? But they were at least four floors up.

'Ooh, fantastic,' said Lisa, patting her stomach. 'I could eat a cow on a crust.'

The waitress smiled politely. 'Follow me, please. It's a mild evening and the heaters are on, so you should be nice and cosy with fabulous views across the city.'

Lisa grabbed hold of Ed's hand and whispered something in his ear. They both laughed as they walked away. The waitress held open the door and the Shaws stepped out on to the terrace.

Jo followed behind with Patrick, fighting the urge to grip his arm. She watched as Lisa Shaw placed both her hands on the glass balustrade and leaned over towards the city streets below. Then Lisa lifted one foot off the ground and pretended to throw herself over.

I can't do it. The blood drained from Jo's head and her vision went blurry. Beads of sweat popped out on her forehead and her hands turned clammy. Patrick stepped on to the terrace and turned to smile at her. His face dropped and he lunged towards her, grabbing her round the waist.

'Jo? Are you OK?'

'I can't . . . I can't,' she gasped.

She felt her knees tremble and she braced herself against his chest.

'Patrick, there's something I need to tell you.'

Ed turned back and caught her eye.

'Don't mind us!' he shouted, and gave them both a lusty wink.

Jo groaned. Tonight was getting better and better.

Chapter 16

From: Carriebikinibod@gmail.com

Dear Jo and Sarah,

I am mortified at my behaviour at the pub. I don't know what came over me and I can't apologize enough. I've been so miserable since then that I can't eat (so it's not all bad!). If you both want to abandon the wish list, then I understand. But I hope you don't! To make it up to you, please come round for dinner next week and I promise not to bite your heads off again.

Carrie xx

From: Jo Gold (work)
CC: SarahDaveZac

Dear Carriebikinibod,

No apology needed. I'm not proud of that night either. I upset both of you and I'm sorry. Also I had a massive panic attack whilst on the fourth floor of a very public place, so I'm still in. To help you even further with your diet, why don't you both come to Northampton instead and I'll feed you (I hesitate to use the term cook). One taste of my food is usually enough for anyone!

Jo x

PS might end up being a takeaway

From: SarahDaveZac

Me too. I think I might have been a bit bossy, sorry about that. I've made a total hash of my wish and it would be good to get it off my chest. And if I'm honest I'd love to have a snoop round your flat, Jo! Carrie – I'll pick you up if you like.
   Sarah x
   PS Jo – don't forget I'm a veggie

From: Jo Gold (work)

Vegetarian?? Definitely a takeaway then!

Jo was quite fond of her flat. It wasn't as homely as Carrie's place or as cute and quirky as Sarah's but it was compact, easy to keep tidy, and was only on the first floor, so as long as she didn't hang out of the windows she could just about cope with the heights thing.

She cast an eye over the living room, propped two takeaway menus up in the kitchen and checked that there was plenty of wine in the fridge. Preparations complete, she even had time for a run. It was late May and although there had been some rain that morning the streets had dried up in the early-evening sun. Perfect conditions for running.

Stripping off to her underwear, she pulled a pair of trainers from her shoe cupboard and took her running gear out of the drawer. She was about to slip into her T-shirt when there was a knock at the door. They were early; she smiled to herself, the run would have to wait. *So much for security,* she thought idly, someone must have let them in through the main entrance.

'Coming, ladies,' she called, jogging down the hallway. She squinted through the spyhole to check she wasn't opening the door to a random salesman. A pair of dark eyes was focused on her door.

'Bloody hell, Patrick! What are you doing here?' she

called through the door, automatically wrapping her arms round herself. 'Hold on, I'm not dressed!' She ran back to her bedroom, threw on her dressing gown and dashed back to let him in.

'Bad time?' he asked, his eyes flicking past her to the bedroom door.

'I was just going running, if you must know.' She stood aside to let him in. 'What's up?'

He had been here before, to drop her off or pick her up, but never unexpectedly.

'I've got some bad news.'

She studied his face and her heart skipped a beat; his usual good-natured smile was missing and he looked really uncomfortable.

'Patrick, what's wrong? Is it my dad, has something happened?'

He shook his head. 'Can we talk?'

'Sure.'

She tried not to panic and walked into the kitchen, gesturing for him to follow. Out of habit she put the kettle on, but Patrick declined the offer of a drink. She leaned back on the kitchen cupboards and tightened the belt of her dressing gown.

'Spit it out, McGregor, the suspense is killing me,' she said with a shaky laugh.

Patrick raked a hand through his hair and unfolded a piece of paper from the inside pocket of his jacket.

'We've had an email from Ed Shaw about the contract for the Josephine Gold collection.'

Jo let out a harsh breath and relaxed her shoulders. 'Oh! You had me so worried, I thought—'

He shoved it towards her. 'Read it.'

She held his stare as she took the sheet of paper from him. He was acting very strangely. Her eyes went straight to the bottom of the page where the order value was highlighted in bold. She whistled. That was a big number.

Shaw's had done them proud, ordering more pairs than she'd dared hope for.

'And?' She looked at Patrick and frowned. 'This is good, isn't it?'

He folded his arms.

'Paragraph three,' he said quietly. 'Exclusivity to Shaw's. Did you agree to this?'

'You're kidding?' Jo scanned the relevant paragraph, shaking her head in confusion, her pulse racing. 'Of course not. The bastard!'

According to this email, Shaw's was prepared to stock the collection in all its stores, feature it in radio and print commercials and run a special staff incentive scheme. Which was all fantastic except that in exchange they were demanding three months' exclusivity on the collection. If Jo agreed to this, Gold's wouldn't be allowed to sell the range to any other high-street retailer until December.

The blood drained from Jo's face. 'Can he do this?'

Patrick shrugged. 'He can ask for anything he likes. But we don't have to agree to his terms.'

She felt sick; there was no way she would be going for a run now.

'I need to sit down.' She brushed past him and dropped on to the sofa in the living room.

Patrick joined her, perching on the other end, his arms resting on his knees.

Her father would have a field day with this; making a profit on the new collection was always going to be tight, but at least they had assumed that some of their other customers would take the range too, to bump up the numbers. Making the shoes exclusively for Ed's stores would be financial suicide.

She groaned and turned to Patrick.

'We could refuse to abide by these terms, tell him to get stuffed.'

Patrick rubbed his face, his complexion was grey and he

looked as devastated as she felt, which was some small con-solation. 'We could, but he has us over a barrel and he knows it. We've invested so heavily in the collection; we'd be idiots to risk losing the contract altogether.'

'Oh, I don't know.' She attempted a smile and punched his arm. 'Who needs Shaw's anyway, eh, McGregor? Let's tell him to bugger off. Look on the bright side; at least we won't have to have dinner with them again.'

'Jo.' His voice was serious and it worried her. 'By Septem-ber the company won't be able to trade profitably. The cash flow is stretched as it is and so far autumn orders are OK but not as good as I'd like.'

And she would be vacating her office to make way for Bob Gold's return. She nodded, the miserable reality sink-ing in. She dropped her head into her hands.

'Promise me you won't breathe a word of this to Liz — it'll get straight back to my dad and I need to get my head around it first before he comes barging in.'

'Promise.'

She looked at him and they shared a rueful smile.

'I know you don't want to hear this but . . .' He let out a long breath and held her gaze for what felt like an eternity. 'Well, redundancies are now the only option.'

'Shit. I know you're right but . . . it stinks.'

Jo felt her throat constrict. How was she going to break it to her staff? They would hate her. She was a total failure. Three years at the helm and all she had succeeded in doing was lose money. So much for her fresh new direction, the sub-brand that was going to herald a new future for the firm. She clasped her hands round her knees and willed herself to stay strong in front of Patrick, blinking hard to ward off any tears.

Maybe it was time to wind up Gold's and strike out on her own. Maybe she could start a new venture. Perhaps Pat-rick might even consider joining her; after all, they made a good team.

Patrick cleared his throat and looked down at the floor.

'There's something else.' He puffed out his cheeks and turned to face her. 'Ed Shaw has offered me a job as his General Manager. I think it's best, under the circumstances, if I accept.'

Time seemed to slow down, the air in the room grew heavy and Patrick's face drifted in and out of focus. Jo shook her head to clear her vision. Did she just hear that right?

'You're not serious. I thought you hated him?' she said, her voice barely more than a whisper. She stood up from the sofa, holding the edges of her dressing gown together, and willed him to say it was a joke.

'He's a good businessman. Shaw's is a sound company.'

'Yeah, look what he's done to us!' She threw her hands up in the air.

'Be honest, Jo.' He got to his feet and took a step towards her. She backed away. 'We both know my job will be on the line if sales continue to fall. I have myself to think of, and Holly.'

She was too het up to think about his financial security just now. First her dad, then Ed Shaw and now Patrick . . . Did none of the men in her life have any faith in her?

She refused to meet his eye and picked at a loose thread on her sleeve. 'Do the words rats and sinking ship mean anything to you?'

'Don't say that.' Patrick inched closer to her and gently placed his hands on her arms.

Jo held her breath. In all the years she had known him, he had never really touched her. She wasn't sure whether to collapse on his chest and hope he'd give her a hug or kick him in the balls.

'I'm on three months' notice,' he said, looking into her eyes. To be fair, he looked as dreadful as she felt. 'I'll do whatever I can in that time to try and turn the business round.'

Except retract his resignation presumably. Jo shrugged

off his hands. She felt exhausted, drained and incredibly, inexplicably sad. 'Just go away, Patrick.'

He hesitated for a few seconds and then walked to the living-room door.

'I do think it's the right decision.'

'For you maybe,' she muttered, turning her back to him and looking out of the window.

She heard him walk to the front door and open it. Then there was a yelp and the sound of women laughing. Bloody marvellous; Carrie and Sarah had arrived.

She could hear them giggling in the hallway – Patrick must have let them in.

'Look at me! I've even got it on my feet. I'll make the floor sticky!'

'Take your shoes off then. Hurry up, Sarah. I want to find out who that man was. Jo?' Carrie called. 'The door was open, can we come in?'

Jo squeezed her eyes shut and took a deep breath.

'Yes, sure. I'm in here,' she called in a wobbly voice.

Sarah poked her head into the living room, closely followed by Carrie, hidden behind a huge bunch of flowers.

Sarah was holding a dripping plastic carton.

'I've made fruit salad. For dessert.' She appeared to be wearing it too; her floral tea dress had a wet stain all down the front. 'Except I've had an accident.' She bit her lip. 'Sorry. That man came out of your flat and made us jump. The lid must have been loose.'

Carrie nudged past Sarah and laid the flowers on the coffee table. She bent and pressed a kiss to Jo's cheek.

'Thanks,' mumbled Jo.

'He had ever such a sexy voice,' said Carrie, taking her cardigan off and fanning her face. Then she noticed Jo's stricken expression and her face fell. 'Oh, love.'

'He only said one word.' Sarah was still hovering, looking for somewhere to dump her fruit salad. 'But, yeah, I admit,

181

even that was sexy. Who is this sound and vision of gorgeousness, Jo?'

Carrie stared at Sarah, who was in turn staring at Jo, with a mischievous grin on her face.

'Aye, aye? Have we just interrupted something?' said Sarah, pointing at Jo's dressing gown.

Jo's shoulders sagged. 'Yeah. The worst day of my entire life.'

Carrie took one look at Jo's pale face on the verge of tears and dropped on to the cream leather sofa to give her a hug. Sarah reached for her voluminous handbag. She rummaged through it, muttering that she was sure she had some tissues somewhere. She produced a battered packet of Kleenex and handed one to Jo.

'This is the beginning of the end,' Jo said between sniffs, 'for me and for Gold's, and it's all my fault. Dad was right all along.'

Carrie's heart went out to Jo; she'd never seen her look so vulnerable.

Sarah squeezed herself on to the sofa on the other side of Jo and took hold of her hand. 'Come on, it can't be that bad. Want to talk about it?'

Jo swiped at her face angrily with the tissue, as if cross with her own weakness. 'Where do I start?' she mumbled glumly.

'I'll make us some tea,' said Carrie, 'and find a vase for these.'

She bustled off to the kitchen, cross with herself for reverting to type: as soon as things got tough, Carrie Radley headed for the kitchen.

Jo would probably have asked for a glass of wine, given the choice, but what she really needed was a cup of reviving tea. It felt a bit odd being in someone else's kitchen, but if Jo could rummage through *her* cupboards, Carrie could do the same. Besides, Sarah was probably much better at wheedling out the problem than she would be.

The kitchen was all black and white and glossy. White cupboards beneath an unbroken run of black granite counter tops and a black-and-white tiled floor. There were no wall cupboards and aside from the built-in hob and oven, no obvious appliances either. She located the kettle without problem. White canisters labelled tea and coffee sat on the worktop next to two takeaway menus. That would be dinner, then; she wondered whether Chinese or Indian food had the fewer calories.

She opened a cupboard looking for mugs. With the exception of six tins of soup, it was bare. Further investigation led her to a cupboard containing crockery and glassware. A meagre pile of plates was outnumbered considerably by an impressive collection of glasses for every possible alcoholic drink. Carrie bit back a smile; Jo might not be a cook but she was definitely a party girl. She couldn't help but contrast it to her own fragrant kitchen stuffed with herbs, spices and every possible baking ingredient you could ever need. She selected the largest glass in lieu of a vase and arranged the flowers.

In the fridge, which was cunningly disguised as another cupboard, she found milk along with six Granny Smith apples and a mini Stilton cheese still in its Christmas packaging. Carrie couldn't resist checking the freezer when she eventually found it. Just as she thought: empty except for a bottle of vodka, some ice cubes and a gel-filled eye mask.

By the time she returned to the living room with the tea, Jo was a little bit livelier. Carrie put mugs down on the coffee table. The room was minimalist to say the least. Just a sofa, TV and coffee table. But oddly, three cardboard boxes sat in the corner.

'Is everyone having fun?' Jo asked with a wry smile. She let out a heartfelt sigh and picked up her tea.

Carrie settled herself back down and peered at her two friends over the rim of her mug as a warm rush of affection for them washed over her. Something had clearly upset Jo, and that was terrible, obviously. But at least they were all together and on speaking terms. The last time they'd met at the pub had been awful and Carrie had been really worried that she might never see them again.

'OK, Miss Gold. We want details. Like who was the mystery man we almost met?' Sarah demanded.

'He's Patrick McGregor, my right-hand man, without whom I don't know how the hell I'm going to manage. He came to deliver some bad news.'

'Are you and he . . . ?' Sarah raised her eyebrows.

'No,' said Jo emphatically. 'Although he has just broken my heart.'

Carrie sent a confused look to Sarah, who responded with an equally confused shrug.

'The footwear business is really tough at the moment and I thought we were going to have to lay off some of our staff. Then at the eleventh hour, Shaw's – you know – the shoe retailer, came up with a suggestion that I thought would potentially protect our jobs.'

Jo briefly explained about Shaw's new image, and the new Josephine Gold collection.

'That all sounds great so far,' said Sarah encouragingly.

Jo heaved a big sigh. 'It was all going so well,' she agreed. 'Until about half an hour ago when Patrick came round to deliver the killer blow. Well, double blow, in fact.'

Jo set down her mug and smoothed out the crumpled email. 'We went out to dinner to celebrate our partnership the other day—'

'Was that when you had your public panic attack?' asked Carrie.

'Exactly, more on that later,' said Jo. 'But after letting us celebrate, Ed Shaw sent through the contract and he has demanded exclusivity.'

She dropped her head into her hands. Carrie was confused; that all sounded very positive.

'Exclusivity is a good thing, surely?' she asked naively.

'It is for the bloody retailer!' retorted Jo. 'But Shaw's has only got seven branches. We can't produce an exclusive range of shoes for just seven shops. If we can't sell them elsewhere as well, we can't afford to make them at all. We might as well just set fire to a pile of cash!'

'What's your break-even point?' asked Sarah, frowning.

Jo puffed her cheeks out. 'It's about . . . we'll need to sell . . . they cost . . .' She flapped her hand as if she was defeated by the effort. 'I can't remember now. That's Patrick's department.' Her eyes filled with tears. 'Or was.'

Carrie was filled with admiration and sorrow for the usually intrepid Jo. Most of what she was talking about, quite frankly, went over her head and she was at a loss to know what to say to make matters better. She put an arm round her shoulders.

'Have you had to make Patrick redundant?' she asked, tutting with sympathy. 'No wonder he looked so upset when he left.'

'No!' Jo cried. 'That's just it. He's leaving me – I mean us. He's resigned and to make matters infinitely worse, he's going to work for Ed Shaw.' She shook her head slowly. 'That man has got me over a barrel. And to think that only a week ago, Ed Shaw having me over a barrel would have been quite appealing.'

Her lips twitched into a smile and Carrie and Sarah exchanged relieved looks.

'Anyway, enough about my woes,' Jo said firmly. 'I suppose I'd better feed you.'

'Unless you'd rather we left you alone?' said Sarah.

'No.' Jo reached a hand out to them both. 'Stay, please. I want you to.'

An hour later, they were tucking into an Indian takeaway, which Jo had insisted on paying for. Carrie was balancing her plate on her knees and felt very on edge. Her fingertips were already stained bright orange; goodness knows what would happen to the cream sofa and cream carpet if she dropped so much as a morsel. They always ate in the dining room at home.

Alex grew up without home-cooked meals and always cherished the fact that they ate together at the table every night. Jo didn't even own a table, so that was that.

As Carrie gamely nibbled on her plain chicken tikka, which was far spicier than she would have liked but seemed to be the healthiest option, she remembered that they were supposed to be checking up on each other's wish list progress.

'How is your plan to get promoted going, Sarah?' she asked, watching them both tuck into a plate of poppadoms and pickles and bowls of creamy korma – chicken for Jo and vegetable for Sarah.

'Absolute disaster on that front.' Sarah heaped some lime pickle on to the edge of her poppadom and crunched into it. 'Wow.' She dabbed her nose with her napkin, her eyes watering. 'That one packs a punch! You won't believe this, but I actually asked to reduce my hours in the office.'

She explained that Dave had started taking on some work, which meant putting Zac into nursery against her wishes and that asking her boss if she could work from home had not been well received.

'There's one bright spot, though: Zac absolutely loves nursery and he was so shattered when he came home that he slept through for ten hours straight.'

'Wow,' said Jo, chinking her wine glass against Sarah's water. 'I bet you and Dave didn't know what to do with yourselves.'

'We did actually,' said Sarah, going pink. 'Has everyone finished? Who'd like fruit salad?'

Jo laughed and clinked her glass against Sarah's.

'So tell us about this celebration dinner with Shaw's,' said Carrie, watching a still blushing Sarah serve the fruit salad.

'Oh,' groaned Jo. 'The restaurant was practically in the clouds and of course our table *had* to be outside on a glass-fronted balcony.'

'Ah,' said Sarah, handing Jo a bowl and a spoon. 'I think I know the one. I take it you didn't feel comfortable, then?'

'I thought I was going to faint and ended up in Patrick's arms, telling him all about my fear of heights. I felt such an idiot!' Jo shuddered.

'It's the best thing to do, though,' said Carrie, accepting some fruit salad from Sarah and refusing the offer of cream. 'The book I read says you should enlist the help of friends.'

'Patrick's not a friend,' muttered Jo. 'Although he was good. He ran after the Shaws and pretended that he suffered with really bad hay fever and asked if we could sit inside. He then proceeded to sniff and sneeze.' She began to chuckle. 'It was quite funny, actually, I mean, hayfever, four floors up! I think Lisa Shaw thought he was mad.'

'What a gentleman.' Sarah smirked.

'He must really care about you to act like that,' agreed Carrie. 'I mean, he must have looked a bit pathetic, not wanting to sit outside.'

'A gentleman?' stuttered Jo. 'Care about me? He's just resigned, remember!' She shook her head sadly. 'I thought he would always be part of my life, I mean, of Gold's.'

'Maybe resigning is his way of showing he cares too. Think about it. Not having to pay his salary is bound to have an impact on the profit margin. And as you said yourself, if you don't make a profit, you have to plan for redundancies. Perhaps Patrick wanted to help?'

Jo sighed and pushed her bowl on to the table.

'But without Patrick, I—' She clamped her mouth shut before opening it again in a yawn.

'We should go,' said Carrie, collecting the empty bowls. 'You're tired.'

'Me too,' said Sarah, beginning to yawn herself. 'But

listen, Jo. If I can help, let me know, even if you just want to talk through your options.'

Jo showed them to the door and kissed them both goodnight. 'Thanks for tonight. I'm not much of a one for girlie bonding and I'm a rubbish hostess, but I'm so glad you came over.'

Carrie was glad too. She didn't feel like she had helped much but at least she had been there for her friend.

As she and Sarah set off along the corridor towards the stairs, a thought struck her and she turned back. 'Jo, why is all your stuff still in boxes?'

Jo shrugged. 'I've just never got round to unpacking. Homemaking's not my thing, I guess.'

She smiled and Carrie detected a touch of wistfulness in her eyes, which made her wonder whether her bachelor-girl lifestyle was, in fact, all part of an elaborate defence mechanism.

Chapter 17

Sarah had had misgivings about attending the networking lunch with Eleanor. Partly because she had so much to do at the office and partly because she was going with Eleanor. The stern dressing-down she was receiving from her boss in the car on the way wasn't helping matters.

'Your vintage look is all well and good for weekends, but not the office,' said Eleanor, giving Sarah's outfit the sort of scrutiny she hadn't had since leaving school. 'And those clumpy lace-ups are really more building site than boardroom.'

Sarah took exception to the comment about her Doc Martens. Every other woman at Finch's was virtually crippled by five o'clock, stumping round in ridiculous heels. She, on the other hand, was walking on cushioned air.

They stopped at a red light. Eleanor quickly whipped out a lipstick and reapplied it without even needing a mirror.

'You might want to rethink your image.'

That was plain rude. Sarah shot her a sideways glance.

'I thought my image was rather distinctive.' Besides, who wanted to blend in and look like another corporate sheep?

'We like to present a professional front at Finch and Part-ners. Not that you aren't professional,' Eleanor was at pains to add.

Well, that was something at least. Perhaps this was Eleanor's way of grooming her for promotion. In which case perhaps she ought to sit up and listen.

'But sometimes your choice of clothing singles you out.'

'And that's bad?' Sarah frowned.

'Correct.'

Eleanor accelerated away from the traffic lights and Sarah was forced back against her seat. She stole a glance at the speedometer. Fifty in a forty zone. Naughty. Eleanor did everything fast: work, speak, drive and cut her staff down to size.

'I've finished the tax investigation for Bertie's,' said Sarah in an attempt to show herself in a better light for once.

'Good.' Eleanor nodded. She even nodded fast. 'How many hours?'

'Um, off the top of my head . . . Can't remember. Quite a few, though. But I had to be thorough.' Sarah tried a conspiratorial laugh. 'You can't rush HMRC.'

'Rubbish,' scoffed Eleanor. 'Anyway, I happen to know you logged forty hours. Will you invoice the client forty times your hourly rate?'

'Oh gosh no! That's far too much . . .' Her voice faded away and she could feel her face getting hot. Point taken. Eleanor's lips were tightly puckered. Sarah pressed her cheek against the cool glass and prayed they were nearly there.

'In future, I'll try to do a thorough job without being quite so . . . thorough,' she said.

Eleanor did her are-you-taking-this-seriously face and put her foot down on the pedal again.

Things improved considerably over lunch. Sarah's marketing skills were on fire; she handed out all her business cards, though unfortunately she seemed to have only brought four with her, and made appointments for a tattoo artist and a cupcake maker to come into the office to talk to her. The best bit was that both of them had approached her to compliment her on her dress. Sarah only wished Eleanor had been within earshot at the time.

The session ended with a round of applause for the motivational speaker, who had urged all the women to 'be who they want to be'. Sarah clapped loudly. It was as if the speaker were talking directly to her. That was exactly what she was trying to do.

She beamed at Eleanor and excused herself to go to the ladies.

She shut herself into a cubicle and tried to remember all the skills listed on that job advertisement she had found months ago.

Apart from the unfortunate 'working from home' conversation that she now regretted bitterly, Sarah thought she had a good chance of making partner when Mr Buxton retired. She had marketing skills and people skills and, as even Eleanor had to admit, she was professional.

Making a profit was still a bit of an issue. But she could work on that. And she did have business acumen. She'd proved that the other week by pointing out to Jo that maybe by handing in his resignation, Patrick was helping her out. The loss of his salary, being one of the largest at Gold's, was bound to improve the profit margin. Patrick might be falling on his sword to save the company.

Jo still didn't seem very happy about losing Patrick, but sometimes people were too close to their own problems to see the obvious solution.

Sarah flushed the loo and unlocked the door. She washed her hands, dried them and out of habit, applied a squirt of antibacterial gel. She glanced up at the mirror and her reflection took her by surprise. For the first time in months, she looked like her old self: confident, smiling and not tired. Even her curls were behaving themselves for once.

I'm back, Sarah Hudson is back in business.

A wave of happiness washed over her. She looked around for someone to share it with and grinned inanely at the next person who walked in.

Life was beginning to feel normal again, it was a new normal, but whatever, it was welcome and long overdue.

She went back into the meeting room and located Eleanor at the networking table, pilfering marketing literature from two other accountancy firms.

'Research,' hissed Eleanor, secreting all the rivals' brochures in her briefcase and replacing it with Finch and Partners' material.

'Well done today.' She looked at Sarah with genuine praise in her eyes. 'I'm impressed.'

'Thanks for inviting me, Eleanor.' Sarah smiled calmly. Inside she was air-punching and hi-fiving herself. 'I've really enjoyed it. And I picked up some new business leads.'

Eleanor linked an arm through Sarah's, drew her away from the scene of her crime and checked her watch.

'Look, it's after three. By the time we get back to the office it'll be four o'clock. I think we both deserve an early finish, don't you?'

'That's very generous of you,' replied Sarah carefully, not wanting to fall into any traps.

'I'm sure there'll be plenty of emails and so on you can be getting on with at home.'

'Absolutely,' Sarah replied graciously, thinking that she was more likely to catch up on playing peekaboo with Zac.

'And you'll be all right getting the bus from here, won't you?'

'Of course.' She supressed a sigh. At this rate she'd barely be home any earlier than normal. Never mind. It was the thought that counted.

It was Zac's teatime when Sarah finally let herself into the house ninety minutes later. Dave had the radio on in the kitchen.

'Surprise! I'm home early, well, earlier!'

She dropped her bag and jacket in the hall and frowned as she caught snatches of the latest news report coming from the radio in the kitchen. *Two elderly pensioners have suffered a vicious attack* ... Sarah burst into the room and switched it off.

'How long has he been listening to that?' She glared at Dave and dropped a kiss on to Zac's sticky cheek, checking his face for emotional damage.

Dave stared at her, a mixture of fear and confusion on his face. 'What?'

The feeding spoon in his hand hovered in the air a fraction too long. Zac seized his opportunity and flicked it from his father's grasp, covering them both in cheesy pasta.

'Oh, hell.' Dave set down the bowl, stood and reached for the cloth. Sarah spied it first and picked it up between two fingers. It was grey, smelly and dripping with brown liquid.

'Yuck.' She wrinkled her nose and threw it straight in the bin. 'Did you know that a dishcloth is one of the most germ-ridden things inside the home?'

'You may have mentioned it before,' he said flatly as she passed him a new cloth from the bumper pack under the kitchen sink.

She picked up the surface cleaner and started spraying around the kitchen sink. It bothered her that it claimed to only kill 99.9 per cent of all known germs. That meant that the other 0.1 per cent were free to multiply by the millions in their house and live the life of Riley. And what about the *unknown* germs, parading round, scot-free like invisible escaped convicts smearing themselves all over Zac's vulnerable little face?

She could feel herself starting to panic and forced herself to take deep breaths. Zac was singing and waving his arms. He was healthy and smiling and absolutely fine.

'Why did you turn the radio off?' Dave looked warily at

her. He was dressed in his football kit and had cheese sauce running down his shin. Sarah's hand twitched around the spray gun and she fought the urge to spritz his leg. She held herself back; he already looked annoyed.

'He's too young to hear the news, it'll traumatize him. The reporter was talking about violent crime.'

'Sarah, he's eleven months old—'

'Exactly, I don't want Zac worried about the world he's growing up in.'

'All he's bothered about right now is finishing his dinner.'

Dave shook his head, switched the radio back on and sat down opposite Zac.

'I am a man, you know, I have needs,' he said, frowning up at her.

'Dave!' She jerked her head towards Zac.

He rolled his eyes. 'I mean, I can't listen to Peppa Pig all day.'

'Whoops, sorry,' she giggled. 'But we parents have to make sacrifices, I'm afraid.'

'Oh yeah? Haven't noticed you making many,' he muttered under his breath.

Her chest tightened with frustration. 'I'm working hard so you can swan around all day at home, actually.'

She could kick herself; that wasn't fair. Dave's face told her that she had gone too far. If she could have taken the words back she would. Where were her excellent people skills now? Dave curled his lip and stared at her so hard that the hairs on the back of her neck stood up. He shoved his chair back and handed her Zac's bowl.

'Well, now you're home, you can swan around while I'm at football.'

'I'm sorry, I didn't mean it.' She sprang up, stood on her tiptoes and threw her arms round his neck. The baby food tipped out of the bowl on to the floor and Zac shrieked and pointed. 'I'm a neurotic, OCD control freak and I don't know why you put up with me.'

Dave tugged distractedly at his left eyebrow. Sarah recognized the signs. He always pulled his eyebrow hairs out when he was agitated. A couple of years ago, he removed an entire eyebrow when Nottingham Forest lost 5–1 to Burnley. It didn't start growing back until they'd had a 2–0 win against Middlesbrough three weeks later. What was she doing to her lovely man?

'Dave?'

He stared at her for a long moment and her heart nearly thumped its way out of her chest. She reached up and kissed his lips, brushing her fingers through the short soft hair at the nape of his neck.

'I'm sorry too,' he said, returning her kiss.

'Thank you,' she murmured. 'You get ready for football and I'll clear up.'

'Thanks. Paul will be picking me up in five minutes.'

It was only five-a-side, but at least he got some exercise and some male company for a couple of hours. Bless him, he deserved it.

He took the milk out of the fridge, poured himself a glass and placed the empty carton by the back door for recycling.

'Oh no,' she groaned.

Dave sighed and checked his watch. 'Now what?'

'You've finished the milk!'

He looked at her incredulously. 'I always have milk before football.'

He opened the fridge again. There was no new carton. 'It was just milk.'

'It wasn't *just milk*,' said Sarah. They had only made up a moment ago, she didn't want another row, especially in front of Zac, but she was so mad with him. Why didn't he notice anything?

Dave's eyes scanned hers as if looking for the answer to a trick question. He held his arms out. 'I give up. What was it then?'

'It was organic milk and it was the milk for my morning cup of tea, the milk for my cereal, and now it's gone.'

It was only a small thing. But sometimes, it was the small things that really mattered. Especially after a day of being made to feel as though she was permanently in the wrong: wrong clothes, wrong work ethic, wrong parenting values . . . A wave of frustration welled up inside her.

'Come here.' Dave put his arms around her and she leaned against him wearily.

'And because we live in this stupid village, miles from civilization, we can't pop to the shop and buy any more.'

Dave lifted her chin so he could see into her eyes. 'Is that how you feel about living here?'

'Yes,' she said in a small voice. 'No. I don't know.'

Her shoulders drooped. Everything was so confusing. She didn't know who she was half the time, let alone what she wanted.

'I'll get some on the way back from football,' he promised.

'Organic?'

'I'll try.'

'Because there was an advert on TV that said if you only switch to one organic thing it should be milk.'

A beat passed between them before he spoke.

'I won't come home until I have found organic milk, OK? And Sarah?'

She smiled at him, much calmer now the milk crisis was averted.

'I can't put up with you like this for much longer.'

'What's that supposed to mean?' Her stomach plummeted. 'Dave?'

A car horn sounded outside. Dave slipped on his hoodie, his eyes not meeting hers. And then he was gone. Five minutes later Sarah realized she was shaking. She forced herself to smile as she freed Zac from his high chair and let him play on the floor in the spilled food, for once not worrying about the mess or the germs.

This time she might have pushed her mild-mannered husband too far.

Chapter 18

House check complete, Jo stepped from the cool of Abi's hall to the warmth of the pavement. Abi seemed to have fallen on her feet with her Monday to Friday tenant. A businessman, apparently, who disappeared somewhere up the motorway at weekends. Shame. She would have quite liked to have met him; he'd left Abi's house and garden looking immaculate so was house-trained and obviously not averse to a bit of gardening either. Probably married. She locked the front door, inhaled the lavender scent from two terracotta pots flanking the step and pulled her sunglasses back down over her eyes.

She turned to face her car and pressed a hand to her shoulder. The early June sun was already turning her pale skin pink. She was urgently in need of a bit of colour. It would have to be a spray tan, though; there was no chance of a holiday at the moment. She was working longer hours than ever and getting more desperate for a solution to the company's cash flow problem.

Keys in hand, she contemplated her next move. It was too nice to go to the gym, she couldn't bear the thought of spending another Saturday in the office and her parents' house was a no-go zone since her dad's visit to Gold's. She wasn't going there until he apologized. Her poor mum was at her wits' end with the two of them.

Maybe Sarah would be at home? She shoved the keys

back in her bag and headed towards Rose Cottage in search of a cold drink and a chat.

She lifted her hand to knock on Sarah's door but a voice halted her.

'No one in.'

Jo looked into the next-door neighbour's garden. An ancient mongrel, with more bald patches than fur, sat panting on the path. Jo raised her eyebrows and the dog cocked its head to one side.

'You've just missed 'em, duck.'

An old man stood in the open doorway of the cottage next door. His brown cardigan with leather buttons reminded her of one her granddad used to wear. It also made her feel distinctly underdressed in her T-shirt and denim shorts.

Jo walked back to her car, wishing it had converted into a convertible in her absence. Today was a day for whizzing along country lanes, wind in your hair, feel-good music blaring out and drinking Pimm's in the garden of a quaint little pub. She felt restless and in need of company.

She would try Carrie's house next and maybe even meet that mysterious husband. Jo jumped in the car and set off for Fern House, keeping her fingers crossed that the Radleys were both in.

A couple of minutes later, she waited in the shade in front of Carrie's house. The sudden change of temperature brought her out in goosebumps and she rubbed the top of her arms. The scuff of footsteps approaching across the tiled floor sounded male. Good; it must be Alex.

From the little things Carrie had said about him, Jo imagined a surly, pompous old fart who liked his woman to be in an apron at all times. She was quite looking forward to locking horns with a man like that. As the heavy oak door opened she glanced down at her chest. Oh great; her nipples were sticking out like a pair of coat pegs under her lacy bra. If he was as stuffy as Carrie made out that wouldn't go down well. She stuck her hands on her hips and decided to style it out.

A totally gorgeous man appeared at the door and Jo stared in surprise, trying not to let her jaw drop open.

This was Alex Radley?

The man had a look of amusement on his handsome face. His full lips twisted upwards in a lopsided smile, his black eyebrows raised in question. Even his deep brown eyes were full of humour.

Jo swallowed and glanced at the engraved slate sign by the doorbell. This was definitely the right house. Thank goodness her sunglasses were shielding her eyes.

'Sorry to turn up unannounced.' Her voice cracked. God, he was very attractive; she had lost the power of speech. 'Is Carrie in?'

'She is, who shall I say . . . ? Ah.' Realization dawned on his face. 'You must be,' he paused, looked her up and down and smiled, 'Jo?'

'Correct.' She smiled back, dying to ask what Carrie had said about her. *Get a grip, this is Carrie's husband. Don't even think about flirting.*

'Alex,' he said, extending a hand. 'Pleased to meet you. Come on in. Carrie's in the garden.'

Jo couldn't take her eyes off him as she followed him through to the kitchen. The soles of her Converse squeaked across the tiles and she tried to tiptoe. Alex was well-built and broad-shouldered, his thick hair was showing signs of going grey but it suited him. Jo approved.

'Can I get you a drink?' He stopped in front of the fridge and opened it.

'Thanks. Water please.'

The kitchen door was open and Jo looked out into the garden for any sign of Carrie.

'I'm so glad to have met you,' Alex said. 'I've heard a lot about you and Sarah. Carrie talks about nothing else. She certainly has come out of her shell a bit these last few months. And this diet business . . . She's obsessed.'

Jo scrutinized his face. She had imagined Carrie's husband to be domineering and stand-offish. But the eyes that smiled back at her crinkled at the corners. She was perplexed; he seemed nice. In fact, he was absolutely charming.

'She looks amazing, doesn't she?' Jo probed, accepting the glass of iced water gratefully.

He nodded and smiled proudly. 'Beautiful.'

'Is she out this way?' She gestured towards the door with her head.

'Of course. Sorry.' Alex made it to the door in three strides. 'Carrie?' he boomed. 'Someone to see you, petal.'

Petal? Sweet. Jo grinned as he graced her with another of his devastating smiles.

'She's up at the top. We're on a bit of a slope, as you can see.' He pointed to the far end of the garden. 'Among her precious roses. Her other passion. I come a miserable third these days. Can you take this glass for her?'

Jo was aware of Alex's eyes on her back as she made her way up the garden with the two drinks. Carrie stood up, pushed a huge floppy sunhat out of her eyes and looked down towards her. Her face lit up.

'Oh my God!' Jo murmured as she handed her a glass and kissed her cheek. 'Your husband is gorgeous.'

She held her friend at arm's length, noticing how Carrie squirmed at the mention of him.

'I know,' she said with a sigh. 'I know.'

Jo looped her arm through Carrie's and they walked to a white wrought-iron table and matching chairs in a sunny area of the garden surrounded by a flower bed full of big floppy pink blooms. Jo angled her chair towards the sun and fanned her face with both hands. 'He is hot! You dark horse,' she continued. 'Here was me thinking you were married to a monster and it turns out you've bagged yourself your own George bloody Clooney.'

Carrie picked up her glass and grinned. 'What's he doing married to a moose, you mean?'

'Oh shut up,' Jo scoffed. She slipped her feet out of her shoes and wriggled her toes in the cool grass.

'Bliss. Firstly, your husband clearly adores you. You should have seen him in there, all gooey over you. Secondly, forget moose, you're positively gazelle-like these days!'

'Pff.'

Jo studied Carrie's eyes under that big hat. She was still sure she was hiding something. What was it? Surely her husband wasn't violent towards her? Jo flicked her eyes over Carrie's body – what she could see of it; she was wearing one of her shapeless baggy dresses.

'Carrie . . . ?' she began tentatively.

As if sensing the conversation was about to turn personal, Carrie jumped in quickly. 'So to what do I owe the pleasure?'

Jo paused, recognizing Carrie's pleading expression as a bid to change the subject.

'I promised Abi that I'd check up on the house for her every now and then. The last thing she needs is to come back from Australia to a wreck.'

Carrie nodded, looking more relaxed now the conversation had turned away from her marriage. 'It's a lovely house.'

'Then I was at a loose end so I thought I'd call in here and we could sunbathe topless in your garden and ogle your husband.' Jo grinned as Carrie spluttered on a mouthful of water. 'Joke.'

'I've never sunbathed topless,' said Carrie nervously, glancing back towards the house.

'You should try it, it's very liberating.' Jo laughed. 'Actually, I wanted to talk to you about Sarah. I had a text from her saying that she had had a row with Dave and she thought he was fed up with her.'

'Oh.' Carrie winced. 'That's not good. Do you think it's true? I mean, she can be a bit dramatic.'

'Don't know.' Jo shrugged and grinned wickedly. 'Perhaps he wants his balls back.'

Carrie bit back a smile. 'I shouldn't laugh, but for such a tiny person, she is very bossy.'

Jo tilted her face up to the sun and closed her eyes. 'Perhaps he's not getting enough?'

'Jo!'

'I'm just saying, you know, she's working, she's tired . . .'

'Knowing Sarah, I'm sure she has a schedule for sex in her notebook.'

'Or a signed contract!' They both laughed.

Jo opened her eyes and leaned forward. 'I wonder how long it takes your lady garden to get better, you know, after giving birth.'

Carrie shuddered.

'You are a prude!' Jo snorted.

'It's not that, I . . .' Carrie paused and brushed a strand of hair from her face and tucked it behind her ear. 'It takes months to get over the trauma. I should imagine,' she added.

Exactly. What did either of them know about it? Jo took a deep breath of fresh air and exhaled, and lazily took in her surroundings.

The garden was charming; it was quite big and terraced to make the most of the slope. Next to the house was a yellow flagstone patio, with a wooden, ivy-covered pergola. A central path cut through an immaculate lawn. But the most prominent feature was the mass of flowers. With the exception of the roses and possibly a few others, Jo couldn't begin to name them. But it seemed that blooms of every shape, size and colour had a place in Carrie's garden. The effect was magical.

'Your garden is amazing,' she said. 'It's like being at the Chelsea Flower Show here. I didn't know you were a gardener?'

Carrie's face glowed with pride. 'I'm not really. I'm just addicted to flowers and this is my favourite time of year when nearly all of them are out.'

Jo grinned. Carrie looked so happy and at home. Now she thought about it, Carrie nearly always presented her and Sarah with flowers. Jo had assumed they were shop bought. But obviously not. She stood up and pulled Carrie to her feet.

'Come on.' She slipped her sunglasses back on. 'Educate me.'

Ten minutes later, they were back in the kitchen, Jo's arms full of flowers and her head buzzing with Latin plant names. She passed them gently to Carrie, who filled the sink and rested the stems in water.

'Next lesson,' said Carrie, fishing a large glass vase out from a cupboard. 'Flower arranging. Don't groan! And while I'm doing that you can tell me about your fear of heights therapy.'

Carrie had eventually admitted to Jo and Sarah about her sessions with the hypnotherapist. Jo had been so impressed with Carrie's success that she had contacted Michelle Terry and had begun hypnotherapy herself.

Privately, though, she didn't think it was working for her. When the therapist was supposedly 'talking to her sub-conscious', as she put it, Jo found she was drifting off and thinking about something entirely different. Men usually, or shoes. Or in the case of Patrick, both. She was still no closer to working out what she was going to do without him. It was catch-22 : she couldn't manage without him and she couldn't afford to pay him more to persuade him to stay either.

'Fill this with water and you can do your own arrange-ment,' said Carrie, handing her the vase.

'I'd rather just watch you,' Jo grumbled.

She turned the tap on too forcefully and cold water spurted out, bouncing off the sink and soaking them both.

They squealed; Jo's face and arms were wet but the front of Carrie's dress was soaked.

Jo rubbed herself down with a towel and laughed at Carrie, who held her arms out to let the water drip on to the floor.

'You'll have to take it off!' She laughed, throwing her the towel.

Carrie looked horrified.

'Off, off, off,' chanted Jo, tugging at the hem of Carrie's dress.

Carrie turned to the wall and peeled off her wet clothes, preserving her modesty with a tiny kitchen towel.

'Bloody hell!' said Jo, unable to drag her eyes off Carrie in just her underwear.

'What?' Carrie mumbled, her face ablaze. 'Haven't you seen a fat girl without any clothes on before?'

'You silly moo!' Jo shook her head. 'How much weight have you lost, exactly?'

Carrie gripped on to the towel and lifted one shoulder. 'About two stone.'

'That's amazing! So why dress in sacks all the time?'

Ignoring the question, Carrie darted out to the utility room and came back wearing another similarly unflattering dress.

'I mean it, Carrie. You look fantastic. I'm so proud of you.'

Carrie's eyes shone as Jo pulled her into a hug.

'Right. Come on, then. Let me show you how to arrange these flowers.'

Jo fell silent, watching as Carrie selected stem after stem, slotting them into the vase, standing back to assess, adding another and so on. Somehow, without Carrie even appearing to think about it, she created a work of art. The contrast between the large flowers and the tiny ones, the balance of the petals and the foliage, seemed completely natural to her.

'All I normally do is hack a bit off the stems and plonk them in water,' Jo said admiringly.

Carrie grinned. 'So I can arrange flowers. Big deal. You run a company, for heaven's sake.'

Jo groaned. 'That's debatable. Where did you learn to do all this?'

Carrie pushed a strand of hair off her face. 'I used to be a florist. Unplanned career move. But when I dropped out of uni, it was the only job I could get. As it turned out, I loved it.'

Jo was struck by the depth of sadness in those deep brown eyes.

'You said you'd had a dead-end job. But that wasn't true, was it? Why on earth did you give it up?'

Carrie was doing her best to feign indifference but Jo could sense she was holding back on her.

'Oh you know,' she said vaguely. 'I had to work one Mother's Day. You can imagine how busy it was, that and Valentine's Day are the two maddest days of the year. But it was our first wedding anniversary too, unfortunately, and Alex tried to insist that I took the day off and I wouldn't. He'd booked a restaurant for lunch or something. We had a terrible row and it upset me so much that I gave up work shortly after that. It just wasn't worth it.'

Jo bristled with anger on Carrie's behalf. So that was the problem; Alex was a bully behind that charming exterior.

'It was wrong of him to make you give up a job you loved,' she urged. 'You're entitled to a life too.'

Carrie pressed her lips together and said nothing.

'You've got passion, talent—'

'It's not like that.' Carrie smiled sadly. 'It sounds so black and white when you say it but . . .'

The phone in the hall rang and Carrie, with a look of relief, raced to answer it.

'Hello, Vicar?'

Jo followed her out to the hall. 'Give him my number!' she mouthed, tapping Carrie's arm.

'Shush!' Carrie giggled and turned her back on Jo.

'Oh no, the poor thing! Oh goodness. Hold on a moment.'

Carrie's eyes were wide as she looked at Jo.

'He's got a bride with him,' she hissed, covering up the mouthpiece with one hand. 'She's getting married next week and her florist has let her down. He wants to know if I can decorate the church. What shall I say?'

Jo's heart squeezed for Carrie; this was just the sort of confidence boost she needed.

'Yes! Bloody hell, Carrie, say yes!' She jumped up and down on the spot, tempted to rip the phone out of Carrie's hand and answer for her.

Alex appeared in a doorway, his eyebrows raised in question. 'What's going on?'

'Carrie's got a job,' said Jo triumphantly.

'Hello again,' Carrie took a deep breath and with a trembling voice replied, 'I will.'

Chapter 19

Carrie looked round the elegant city-centre bistro and tingled with anticipation. She could get used to this. Walls lined with old black-and-white photos of films stars, eclectic mirrors, marble-tiled floors and a pianist playing Sinatra songs; she never normally went anywhere without Alex. It was about time she did more of this.

The waitress showed Carrie to a corner table and she settled in a chair with her back to the wall to watch for the others. The waitress came back almost immediately with a jug of water and the bread basket. She waved the bread away firmly. She was early and had already had texts from both of them to warn her they were running late; the last thing she needed was to fill up on stodge while she was waiting.

Carrie studied the other diners, trying to guess their relationship to each other and their reasons for lunch. Business meetings were easy to spot with their phones and tablets cluttering up the table. A group of girls were giggling and gossiping over a bottle of Prosecco. Two lovers were leaning so close together that they were nose to nose. Judging by the number of times the woman checked furtively over her shoulder, it was possibly a clandestine lunch date.

For once Carrie didn't feel uncomfortable sitting on her own people-watching and the thought made her proud. Meeting Sarah and Jo had been the best thing that had happened to her in years. They had made her see how much she was missing out on, that her cushioned, reclusive life was really no life at all. That she was capable of making some real, positive changes. This was only the beginning, she decided. She smiled up at the waitress and accepted a menu.

She smoothed her slate-grey cotton dress over her stomach. It was a new online purchase. She hadn't summoned up the courage to go shopping in real clothes shops yet. She wondered whether Sarah and Jo would approve of her new outfit. Probably not; it was still fairly shapeless. Carrie could feel the rolls of flesh underneath the fabric. She knew she was still overweight, but the uncomfortable folds of her belly had gone and her boobs were now two cup sizes smaller.

She was still one of the plumpest in the restaurant. But not actually the biggest, she noticed with a shiver of satisfaction. Not any more. She ran a hand over her new shiny bobbed hair. Gone was the straggly pony tail, instead there were short layers at the nape of her neck, long wisps at the front. She had only had it cut that morning and every time she caught sight of her reflection a whole new Carrie smiled back.

Still no sign of Jo and Sarah.

She took her phone out of her bag and slipped a pair of headphones into her ears. A couple of minutes listening to her hypnotherapy track now might help her resist making any bad choices over lunch. She'd never done it in a public place before, but no one would know. She wouldn't even close her eyes, that way as soon as she saw the other two, she could turn it off and they would be none the wiser. Carrie pressed play and the chatter and clatter of the restaurant disappeared, replaced by the gentle voice of the therapist. 'From now on, you will be satisfied with smaller amounts of food . . .'

Jo bumped into Sarah at the door of the restaurant and nearly gasped at the sight of her. Gone were the kooky clothes, wild hair and cute shoes. Instead, Sarah's hair was pulled up into a tight knot, she wore a classic grey suit with a slinky cream camisole and grey stilettos. If that wasn't enough to shock her, Sarah also had deep blue smudges under her eyes and her skin was so pale that her freckles stood out like a dot-to-dot picture.

'New directive from above,' Sarah said, reaching up to kiss Jo's cheek. 'I'm supposed to look corporate, whatever that means. Still,' she plastered on a smile and hefted a huge patchwork bag on to her shoulder, 'if that's what it takes to get promotion, then that's what I'll do.'

But at what price? Jo had never seen Sarah look so miserable, although she had to stifle a smile at the sight of her ridiculous hippy handbag. Not totally conformist, then.

A waiter directed them to where Carrie was fast asleep in the corner, head tilted back, earphones in and a silly grin on her face.

Sarah giggled and was about to wake her, when Carrie suddenly yelled 'Yes!', slapped the table and opened her eyes with a jolt. She blinked at them both, turned a vivid shade of red and clapped her hands over her face.

'Oh, heck. Did I say that out loud?' She pulled the headphones out of her ears roughly, fumbled to turn off her phone and shoved the lot in her handbag.

'Yes,' said Jo with a laugh as she and Sarah sat down.

She leaned across and kissed Carrie's cheek.

'Looks like we interrupted a *When Harry Met Sally* moment. Or should I say when Sally sat on her own enjoying herself?' she said, taking a napkin from the table and laying it over her lap.

Sarah gave Carrie a hug. 'Your hair is lovely; you look loads younger.'

Carrie took her hands away from her flaming cheeks and gave her head a self-conscious shake. 'Thanks. I've kept it long for years to hide my face, but the time has come for a new image.'

'Suits you,' said Sarah with a tired smile, tugging at her grey skirt. 'Unlike my new image.'

Jo handed the menus round and Sarah scanned it quickly.

'I've only got fifty minutes. I've got tons to get through this afternoon,' she said with a sigh. 'I wonder if they'll do me a sandwich.' She looked round to attract the attention of a member of staff.

Jo frowned and caught Carrie's eye, wondering if she had noticed how distracted and uptight Sarah seemed. Carrie raised her eyebrows slightly in response.

'So what's new with you, Sarah?' enquired Jo, determined to get to the bottom of her friend's mood.

'Nothing.' Sarah shrugged and deflected the question. 'Nice dress, Carrie!'

The waitress interrupted them at that moment to take their food order. Jo eyed Carrie's dress dubiously. She begged to differ; it looked like a nun's habit. As soon as the waitress swanned off, unimpressed with their request for three house salads, as quickly as possible, Jo tried again.

'So. Busy at work, Sarah?'

Sarah looked at her with such a pained expression that for a moment Jo thought she was about to cry.

'Busy at work and really, really worried at home.'

Sarah's shoulders sagged and she lowered her head. Jo immediately flagged down another waitress and added a bottle of Pinot Grigio to their order.

'Nothing's going right. My perfect boss criticizes everything I do, or say, or wear.'

'She sounds awful, not perfect,' said Carrie.

'And I'm permanently tired. It's nearly Zac's first birthday and I haven't even organized a party for him. There just isn't enough of me to go round.' Her voice cracked and Carrie put an arm round her and stroked her hair.

'Also,' Sarah looked at them both and bit her lip, 'Dave thinks I'm neurotic. He even admitted it. I think he's had enough of me.'

Jo tried and failed to find some suitably appeasing words.

In her experience, it didn't take much for married men to stray. And if Dave was truly fed up with his home life, who knew?

The waitress set a bottle of wine on the table and Jo poured them each a glass, while Carrie murmured soothing words to Sarah. There was no point her trying to offer advice, Jo mused. Her love life was as disastrous as her new footwear collection. Her stomach turned over queasily and she took a gulp of her wine.

Sarah shook her head. 'We never get a chance to talk.'

'What about organizing a babysitter and having a night out?' suggested Carrie. 'I'll come over if you can't find anyone else.'

Sarah smiled sadly and she squeezed Carrie's hand. 'I think that's exactly what we need. It's ages since we've been out on a date. A night of romance.'

'Three house salads.' The waitress handed them their plates. 'Dressing on the side for you, madam.'

'Thank you,' said Carrie, going pink.

A night of romance.

Jo racked her brains to think of the last time romance had appeared on her agenda and drew a blank. A night of any description, with any man? The only recent event that sprang to mind was the night that she and Patrick had spent poring over the accounts recently, working out how long they would be able to pay the staff before the firm's cash flow caved in under pressure.

A wave of panic washed over her. *Patrick*.

She couldn't afford to think about him now, or she'd be as depressed as Sarah. A whole month had gone by since his announcement and the idea of losing him still filled her with horror. She was angry with Ed Shaw for poaching her director, angry with Patrick for deserting her and angry with herself for letting it bother her so much. She wished she could offer him a better deal than Shaw's but it was out of the question. She wished . . .

Jo thought back to the ridiculous wish she had made in Sarah's cottage in February. Standing on the observation deck of the Empire State Building was as far from reality as being swept off her feet by the man of her dreams. Not. Going. To. Happen.

She was thirty-four. Not quite ready for comfy shoes and cardigans, but getting there. She knew there was still plenty of time left to meet someone, but her single-girl lifestyle had completely lost its appeal; she wanted to meet someone now.

She caught sight of her reflection in the mirror behind Carrie. Was it time to soften her image? The tough and sexy persona she had affected for work, after her father retired, was intended to send out a 'don't mess with me' signal. Perhaps that was the problem? She glanced at the other two. Sarah had cheered up a bit and was telling Carrie a story about Zac emptying all the books out of the bookcase. They were both giggling. Jo felt a pang of jealousy. For all their husbands' faults, at least Sarah had Dave and Carrie had Alex.

A couple on the other side of the restaurant, who had been glued to each other's faces ever since she had arrived, stood and wandered to the door. Oblivious to those around them, they kissed goodbye, a long, lingering embrace, before moving in opposite directions, their fingers touching until the last possible second.

She turned back to the mirror and was shocked by her own melancholic expression. Jo Gold, spinster of the parish. She sighed dramatically. Quite simply, Jo had had enough of being alone. Lonely. *Toute seule*. She wanted to be loved. Embarrassingly, her eyes pricked with tears. She blinked them back, shocked. Jo didn't cry. Ever.

Carrie and Sarah stopped chattering and stared.

'Everything all right with your salads?' asked the waitress in a tone that implied that she didn't care either way, but felt obliged to ask.

'Jo?' Sarah shuffled her chair nearer and placed a hand on her arm.

The waitress harrumphed and walked away.

Jo swallowed. It was June; she had known these two for five months. They were friends but had they really opened up to each other? Jo certainly hadn't been completely honest and she had doubts about Carrie and Sarah too.

'I've got a confession.' She took a deep breath. 'About the wish list. I told you a white lie about my wish.'

She studied their faces, twisting her napkin into a rope and winding it through her fingers.

'You mean you aren't scared of heights?' asked Carrie, a frown of confusion creasing her forehead.

'No, no,' said Jo swiftly, not wanting Carrie to think that she had wasted her time researching coping strategies and dragging her up the stairs in car parks. 'I am. I'm petrified. That's not it.'

Sarah did her usual scrabbling around in her handbag and took out the dreaded notebook and pen. 'You don't want to climb the Empire State Building?'

'No, I do. But . . .' Jo sighed, frustrated by her inability to find the right words. She rested her elbows on the table and buried her face in her hands. She thought for a moment and lifted her head. 'OK, here's the thing.'

Sarah sat with her pen poised, ready to make notes.

'Put that notebook away, this is for your ears only.'

Sarah lowered her pen and took a big gulp of her wine.

Jo placed her hands on the table.

'OK,' she said calmly, 'confession time. My name is Jo Gold and I'm a hopeless romantic.' She risked a quick look at their faces. As predicted, they looked stunned. 'And what I really wish for is my very own *Sleepless in Seattle* moment. There, I've admitted it. And now you probably think I'm an idiot.'

'We do not,' Carrie retorted.

'Carry on,' said Sarah. She topped up their glasses, checked the time and gave a little gasp.

Jo paused to take a drink.

'I always assumed I'd meet someone special when I was older,' she began. 'A man who would sweep me off my feet. The whole happy-ever-after that little girls dream of. I've watched *Sleepless in Seattle* a million times and you know that bit at the top of the Empire State Building where their eyes meet? Well, that's what I want.' She looked up. 'Pathetic, isn't it?'

'No!' Sarah shook her head.

'It's totally adorable,' said Carrie.

'But taking over my dad's business three years ago has taken over *me*, over my whole life. He drummed into me pretty much since puberty that I needed to keep a clear head to run a business. Attachments of the alpha-male kind were strictly off limits. Since I turned thirty, I can probably count my romantic encounters on one hand. I mean, I've had—'

She looked at their sympathetic faces and stopped short of saying the word 'affairs'. In the past, she had let the men carry all the guilt for cheating on their wives. Now she had seen Sarah's anguish, she felt ashamed. No more attached men. Ever.

'Well, I've had some action, obviously. I've not been entirely celibate.'

Carrie and Sarah both smiled.

Jo ploughed on, desperate to get the whole thing off her chest. 'But I want to fall in love. I want to share my life with someone. And now I've started to think that it's never going to happen.'

'Why didn't you stand up to your dad?' asked Sarah, spearing a fork into her salad. 'Sounds like a bully to me.'

'Not a bully,' said Carrie swiftly. 'I'm sure he thought he had your best interests at heart.'

Jo looked at the two of them and wondered how they'd each have responded to Bob Gold's sermons. Sarah would

215

probably have ignored him and Carrie in all likelihood wouldn't have wanted to take the business on at all.

'You're right, Sarah. I should have stood up to him. Long before now. I guess a part of me just thought he was right.'

Carrie looked subdued and Jo managed a smile.

'Before you ask,' she reassured her, 'the trip to New York is still on; I've got to go for work anyway. We can go shopping, sightseeing, a bit more shopping . . .'

'But no skyscrapers?' asked Sarah.

'I don't want you two to miss out,' said Jo carefully. 'I bet the views across the city are amazing. But even if I could handle the height, I don't think I could cope with the anti-climax. No offence, but in my imagination I'm there with some delicious hunk, not my two mates.'

'Hey,' said Sarah brightly, 'you might have met a hunk by then.'

Jo shook her head sadly. 'I'm the career woman. Spiky, sharp and sarcastic. Hardly every man's dream, am I?'

'Er, hello?' Sarah pointed at the mirror, forcing Jo to examine her reflection again. 'Stunning, ballsy, wicked sense of humour and legs to die for. What's not to like? Or love, in fact?'

Jo picked at her thumbnail without looking up. 'You don't think I'm too intimidating?'

'You do ooze sex appeal,' said Carrie diplomatically. 'And you do scare our vicar. But the right man wouldn't be intimidated.'

'I'll cross the Vicar of Woodby off the list then, shall I?' Jo smiled, feeling faintly cheered by the compliments. 'So who's next? Anybody got anything they'd like to share, anyone else not quite truthful with their wish?'

Sarah buried her head back in her salad bowl and began to plough her way through iceberg lettuce and Carrie shook her head.

'Oh,' said Carrie, changing the subject, 'the flowers for that wedding went really well, Jo.'

Jo noticed the spark in Carrie's eyes. This could be just the push she needed to get back to work. 'Sarah, you should see Carrie's garden, it's amazing. Did you know she used to be a fl—'

'Knickers!' Sarah jumped up from the table, knocking over her empty wine glass. 'Look at the time! I'm so sorry, but I'm going to have to rush off. Can I settle up with you next time?'

'Of course! You go,' said Carrie.

She leaned over to kiss them hurriedly, grabbed her bag and tottered off on her heels, overturning a stool on her way out.

'Book that babysitter!' Jo shouted to Sarah's back. Sarah raised a hand in response and disappeared out into the sunshine.

Chapter 20

That evening Jo sat next to Patrick in his office. A white-board completely dominated one wall. It was blank except for the words JOSEPHINE GOLD COLLECTION in its centre and circled with marker pen. The two of them stared up at the board in silence, waiting for inspiration to strike. It was after six o'clock and most of the staff at Gold's had gone home. Jo had nothing better to do and no one to do it with so she didn't mind working late. She wasn't so sure about Patrick. He had been drumming the marker pen against his thigh for a full five minutes. If he didn't stop soon, she was going to shove it up his nose.

Patrick sighed and stopped tapping. 'It's not too late to pull out.'

Jo risked a quick glimpse at him and held her breath. Was he thinking of retracting his resignation? This was the conversation she had been hoping for. She shifted in her seat and waited for him to continue.

At first her reaction to him handing in his notice had been blurred by her fury over the exclusivity demands from Shaw's. After that, she was a bit cool towards him, but he had demonstrated that he was every bit as committed to saving Gold's as she was and she hadn't been able to stay cross with him for long. At the end of the day, who knows, she might have had no choice other than to make him redundant in September. Far better this way, with him making the decision to leave.

For the past few weeks, it had been business as usual and other than discussing her annual trip to New York and whether he would still be with Gold's by then or not, they had hardly mentioned his departure. But inside she was counting down the weeks with dread, unable to contemplate running the company and standing up to her father without his confident handle on all the figures.

'I mean, Shaw's wouldn't be happy, but it isn't too late, is it?' he repeated, turning to look at her.

Jo swallowed, mentally crossing her fingers. 'What are you thinking?'

He leaned forward, fixing his grey eyes on hers. 'There's nothing to stop us withdrawing the Josephine Gold collection entirely. We simply tell Ed that financially it doesn't stack up.'

Jo's heart sank. She pretended to herself she'd known all along that was what he was referring to. A ball of thwarted hope gathered at her feet and she kicked it into touch. Of course he wasn't going to stay. She half wished she could bugger off and leave Gold's too.

Liz stuck her head round the door. She rested her shopping bag on the floor while she pulled her cardigan over her neat blouse and skirt. 'I'm off now. I've switched the phone to night service; you can pick up any calls from Patrick's phone. Don't stay too late.'

'OK, Mum,' Jo and Patrick said in unison.

Liz tutted at them as if they were recalcitrant teenagers and pulled the door to as she left.

'Oh, it definitely doesn't stack up,' said Jo.

She took Patrick's marker pen from him and walked around the desk to the whiteboard. She drew an arrow from the centre and wrote HIGH STREET, underlined it and added 'Shaw's' underneath. She folded her arms and turned back to Patrick.

'Ninety per cent of our customers are high street stores. The Shaw's contract stipulates we can't sell to any of them.

Even if we sold the Josephine Gold collection to the other ten per cent who *aren't* on the high street, it still wouldn't be enough to make production viable.'

Patrick was staring at her. She wondered if he could read her mind, could see that the fight had gone out of her. She was usually such a ball of energy, enthusiastic to the last. *Come on, Jo*, she urged herself, *don't give up*.

'The Shaw's order is big,' she continued. 'It's the biggest on our books. The idea of canning the collection is killing me, and not only that,' she gave him a twinkly smile, 'I really want to prove my dad wrong. Help me out here, McGregor, I need one of your brilliant ideas.'

'Hmm.' Patrick rocked his chair back on to two legs and flattened the tip of his nose with his forefinger. She could almost hear the cogs whirring in his head. 'There has to be a way to get round this exclusivity clause. Something we haven't thought of yet.'

'Well, that was worth waiting for,' she said with a smirk and turned back to the board.

She drew another arrow and wrote 'materials', under-lined it twice and then scribbled a list of the new fabrics, leathers, suedes and embellishments needed for the Josephine Gold collection.

'That is a long expensive list.' She frowned. 'I'm guessing you've got to place orders for all these new fabrics and leathers in a couple of weeks?'

Patrick nodded. He pushed his chair back, walked around the desk and took the pen from Jo's hand. On the opposite side of the board to her lists he added NON-HIGH STREET.

'That's what we've got to concentrate on. We need orders from somewhere not on the high street.'

Jo perched herself on the desk and managed a weak smile. 'Notonthehighstreet.com?'

'Exactly,' said Patrick. 'Websites, mail order—'

'Patrick,' Jo interrupted wearily, 'I don't mean to sound

negative, all ideas welcome, obviously. But most footwear websites are spin-offs from retail stores that *are* on the high street.'

'Calm down, Gold!' He grinned. 'Exports then? We recruit agents in key territories and expand the business across Europe, maybe even further with the right team.'

Jo cocked an unconvinced eyebrow at him. 'In two weeks? We can do all that and it's a good idea, but have we got time?'

Patrick sat beside her on the desk.

'Jo, leaving the new collection to one side for a moment, the main range has done pretty well. Most of our customers want to bring in the autumn/winter styles early because the summer has been so wet. It's only July and orders are up on this time last year.'

So there was a glimmer of hope. Thank God. She pushed herself up, walked to the fridge in the corner of his office and helped herself to a bottle of water. She held one up for Patrick and he nodded.

'And can we supply them early? Will the stock be here in time?' she asked, glancing up at his wall planner and handing him his water. The wall planner was decorated with coloured stickers in some unintelligible code understood only by Patrick, denoting when container-loads of footwear would be arriving from India and China. Her heart twisted and she wondered who'd take the time to do such meticulous planning when he'd gone.

Patrick pulled a face and took a long drink from the bottle. 'I think so. And that will ease cash flow no end. By September, we'll have shipped out all the autumn shoes and we'll be starting on winter boots.'

'And you'll be gone,' said Jo simply. She stared at him. Why was it that although she was usually so forthright in her opinions, she couldn't just speak her mind?

Don't go.

She felt like crying. God, she was turning into an emotional wreck. Out of the blue, she felt an ache of loneliness

221

so strong it was almost physical. She couldn't do this on her own. Month after month, crisis after crisis. The constant battle to retain staff, pay suppliers, chase customers for payment. She was ready to call it a day.

Jo walked back to her chair to avert her eyes from Patrick's gaze. She rubbed her face; her eyes felt tired and gritty. She couldn't speak; even if the lump in her throat would allow it, her pride wouldn't.

The silence lengthened and grew heavier until Patrick cracked.

'That's months away yet,' he said.

She gave him a wry smile. They both knew that wasn't true.

'Right now what we need is a new chain of stores opening up on out-of-town retail parks. Ergo . . .' He paused and grinned. Jo narrowed her eyes irritably, she hated it when he used corporate jargon. 'Ergo,' he repeated with relish, 'not breaking the exclusivity clause.'

Now he was just being silly. She folded her arms and crossed her legs, revealing a flash of ankle under her black linen trousers. Patrick stared at her ankle chain, a present from Carrie. Sarah had one too; it had a fairy charm on it to remind them of the wish list. She pressed her lips together trying not to smile; a fairy was probably the last thing he'd be expecting to see her wear. What she wouldn't give for a bit of fairy dust now to make everything right.

The phone rang loudly, making them both jump. Patrick looked at Jo in surprise.

'A cold-caller probably,' said Jo. 'Ignore it.'

Patrick held up his crossed fingers. 'Or it could be Kate Middleton looking for a pair of shoes.' He stabbed the hands-free button so that Jo could hear the call too.

'Gold's Footwear; can I help you?' He grinned as Jo rolled her eyes.

'Patrick? Ian Hamilton. Long time no speak, mate!' A raucous Essex accent boomed across the office.

222

'Ian! Er, great to hear from you. I'm just—'

'Still poncing round in women's shoes then, eh?' Ian laughed. Jo raised her eyebrows at Patrick who looked a little pink.

'Thought I'd find you at work, you sad bastard!' Ian obviously found this hilarious and much guffawing followed.

'Actually, Ian, I am quite busy, so could I—' Patrick tried valiantly to take control of the conversation, but Ian wasn't listening.

'Heard on the grapevine about you and your missis. Shame, that. Still got the hots for—?'

Patrick started coughing violently and grabbed the phone as Ian got to the interesting bit. Jo listened as he eventually managed to convey to his friend that he was in a meeting with his boss, yes the female one, and could he call him back after work.

'Jo, he says it's a business call after all,' said Patrick, placing a hand over the mouthpiece. He looked faintly uncomfortable. 'I'll put it back on speakerphone. He wants to know if we manufacture in Britain.'

There was a sparkle in his eyes that filled her with warmth and sent a tingle all the way down her spine.

Her eyes widened. 'Sure.'

Patrick introduced Ian Hamilton as an old friend from university who was now the finance director for Global Duty Free, the largest retailer within the UK's airports, with branches in all the major terminals from Belfast to Bristol and most importantly, Heathrow and Gatwick.

'We had nearly seventy million people through the door at Heathrow last year, mate, all with dosh jingling in their pockets. The retail operation is massive and we're developing it all the time,' Ian explained.

'And duty free is not high street,' Patrick said slowly, staring directly into Jo's eyes.

Jo's stomach fizzed with interest.

'Er, no, because it's *duty free*, Patrick,' Ian enunciated

slowly, as if he was talking to a child. 'We're launching a major "Best of British" campaign in the autumn. Honestly, mate, you wouldn't believe the uplift in sales of British stuff at the moment. Stick a London bus on a tea towel and it sells itself.'

He paused and Jo heard his chair creak.

'So how can we help?' Jo asked.

'Footwear is one of our sticking points. We don't do much at the moment. It tends to be travel-related: flip-flops and flight slippers. We want a proper women's footwear range; stylish and high quality. Price doesn't matter too much, but it's got to be made in Britain. Can you do that and are you interested?'

Jo's heart started to beat so loudly she wouldn't have been surprised if Ian could hear it down the other end of the phone.

'Absolutely!' she said, trying to keep the squeak out of her voice. 'We've been making shoes in Northamptonshire for thirty years. It's what sets Gold's apart.'

Patrick frowned. 'But aren't you the finance director, Ian? Surely it's not your decision?'

'Yeah, that's right, it's not up to me. You've got to go through the whole sales presentation thing with the buying team. There'll be other companies invited too. But I asked if I could put you on the pitch list.' Ian hesitated. 'Interested?'

Jo and Patrick exchanged excited smiles.

'Definitely,' Patrick stuttered. 'In fact we've got a new label, Josephine Gold, which would be perfect for airport shopping.'

'Good stuff,' said Ian. 'Short notice, though. The presentation is in three days' time.'

'No problem,' said Jo, sticking her thumbs up at Patrick. 'We'll be there. Thanks so much, Ian. I really appreciate this.'

Ian talked for another couple of minutes, giving them details about the rest of the board and arrangements for the presentation, and then Patrick ended the call.

'Oh my God,' he murmured.

They fell silent, staring at each other, the atmosphere between them crackling with electricity.

'Did that just really happen?' Jo said, excitement bubbling up inside her. And to think that only a few minutes ago she'd been ready to give up.

He grinned and nodded. 'Surreal, but yes.'

She jumped up, grabbed hold of his shirt and plonked a smacker of a kiss on his cheek. He stared at her.

'Sorry,' she said, feeling quite giddy. 'I don't know what came over me. I can't believe it; it's like a dream come true.'

He touched his fingertips to his face. 'It is,' he said gruffly.

'Just think,' she said with a sigh, 'if we're successful, the Josephine Gold collection will be on view to . . . Tell me the number again?'

Patrick checked his hastily scribbled notes. 'More than two hundred million passengers a year.'

'This changes everything.' She jumped up, went back to the whiteboard and started a new column for *Duty Free*. 'We can make the packaging a bit more obviously British, see if we can negotiate a better price on materials if we order larger quantities, perhaps think about adding another colourway to the Carnaby collection . . .'

Patrick laughed. 'Let's concentrate on winning the order first, shall we?'

Jo dashed to the shoe rack and scooped up an armful of samples. She was so excited she could burst.

'Look at these shoes. They're fantastic. High quality, stylish, made in Britain . . . They'll win the order for us,' she said, laughing breathlessly. 'It's our time, Patrick, we deserve this.'

'I agree.' He nodded.

She scanned his face, trying to read his expression; there was a softness to his eyes instead of his usual mickey-taking sarcasm.

A strange sensation crept up the back of her neck as if

someone was blowing on it. She shivered. All of a sudden she needed to get out of the office. She rolled her shoulders back to release the stress and without stopping to question herself, said, 'I want to celebrate; sit outside a pub in the fresh air, with a nice glass of wine. Fancy joining me?'

The look of panic on Patrick's face appalled her. She'd obviously crossed a line. She would have taken her words back in a heartbeat if she could.

'I can't,' he stammered. 'I've got to pick Holly up from Girl Guides later.'

'Of course,' said Jo hurriedly, feeling her ears grow hot. 'Stupid idea. Probably too wet outside anyway.'

She busied herself with the whiteboard, drawing a star around 'Duty Free'. Her heart was dancing a tango in her chest. *Get a grip, Jo!* It had only been an invitation for a drink, not a marriage proposal. This was Patrick she was talking about, they were mates. Before his divorce, she'd been out with him and Melissa regularly. She was his daughter's godmother, for heaven's sake.

But for some reason it felt different tonight.

Patrick thrust his hands in his pockets and jingled the coins.

'Unless I could try and get someone else to pick her up . . . Oh.' His voice tailed off as he looked at his watch and winced. 'Actually, I've left it a bit late to organize now.'

'Let's forget it.' She gave him a brief smile then picked up her things, said goodnight and walked away, heart thundering at her ribs. She paused briefly at the door, just long enough to hear him swear sharply under his breath.

Chapter 21

Sarah stood at the end of the busy bar waiting for Dave to be served. She smiled happily to herself. This was such a good idea of Carrie's to get a babysitter and go out. OK, it was only dinner at the Pear Tree pub in the village, but even so. This could be the start of a whole new era of socializing, romantic nights out and a chance to be a couple again. *Heaven.* She hadn't wanted to confess to Jo or Carrie, but she and Dave hadn't been out on a date since Zac was born. But now they had found the marvellous Rosie: eighteen, nursery nurse extraordinaire and completely gaga over Zac.

There was a couple nearby, a man and woman in their fifties, sitting side by side, gazing in to the bottom of their glasses wordlessly. She and Dave would never be like that. They had fun together, had loads to talk about and still fancied the pants off each other – well, she fancied *his* pants, she couldn't speak for Dave. He could well be eyeing up someone else's pants, for all she knew.

Of course he wasn't. She took a deep breath and forced herself to calm down. Her hand snuck into her bag and pulled out her phone. No messages from Rosie. *Phew.*

She had resisted Dave's attempts to organize a night out before now. What with the strict bedtime routine, money being tight, her not wanting to be tired in the morning and – she might as well admit it – not trusting anyone else to look after Zac.

But now she had.

'They've only got Pinot Grigio,' called Dave, from further along the bar. 'That OK?'

'Perfect,' she called back. 'Large, please.'

Her heart fluttered at the sight of her man in amongst the crowd at the bar. They'd both made an effort with their appearance tonight and Dave was even wearing proper shoes instead of trainers. She'd thought for a moment earlier they might not be able to come; Zac had had a slight temperature at five o'clock and had been a bit grizzly, but after a dose of medicine and a biscuit he soon rallied. Rosie and Zac had been having a lovely time playing in the bath when she and Dave left them earlier. Sarah wished she had done this months ago; a few relaxing hours together was exactly what they needed.

As she tugged on a strand of hair and wrapped it round her little finger, an awful thought struck her. The staircase in Rose Cottage was very steep. What if Rosie slipped carrying Zac downstairs and they were lying there unconscious in a heap right now? She slipped a hand into her handbag and pulled out her phone again; still no messages. But what if that was actually a *bad* sign?

Should she tell Dave, get him to nip home and check? Sarah caught sight of her frowning face reflected in the mirror behind the optics and froze.

And that, Sarah Hudson, is why Dave gets so annoyed.

She was winding herself up over nothing again. Zac would be asleep by now and Rosie would be watching TV and sending messages to her friends. Everything would be fine. And if there was an emergency, they could be home in five minutes.

Dave handed a ten-pound note to the barman and held out her wine to her.

'The table will be ready in five minutes.'

She wiped her palms on her skirt before taking the glass. Why was she so nervous? All she had to do was be herself (minus the OCD tendencies, preferably), stop thinking about Zac and concentrate on her husband.

'Thanks.' She couldn't think of a single thing to say and gulped at her drink.

'You look beautiful tonight, easily the best-looking girl in here,' murmured Dave close to her ear.

'Oh Dave, thank you!' She reached up and kissed his cheek and her heart flipped as she inhaled his familiar scent. 'You're not so bad yourself.'

They smiled shyly at each other. Sarah was still walking on eggshells a bit since the stupid row about organic milk, but both of them had apologized and had been making an effort with one another recently.

'New parents?' asked the barman, presenting Dave with a perfect pint of Guinness.

Sarah nodded, wondering how he knew.

'We look that knackered, do we?' asked Dave, slurping the head off his pint.

The barman grinned. 'You're both doing that rocking thing. As if you're still holding a baby. I recognize the signs. Me and my girlfriend used to do it all the time.'

'It's true, Dave, we are!' Sarah laughed. 'We're not used to going out without him.'

'But that was before we found a babysitter,' Dave added. He leaned closer to Sarah and whispered in her ear. 'Now we're here, I sort of miss the little man.'

'Oh, me too!' she groaned. 'Do you think we should ring home . . . ?'

They looked at each other nervously until Dave shook his head.

'He'll be fine. Cheers!' He clinked his glass against hers.

'Cheers,' she replied, thinking how lucky she was.

Dave was a wonderful dad, and though she hated to admit it, he was a much better parent than she was. Her eyes burned suddenly. Her emotions were running so high; it felt as if they were just underneath her skin, as if they might escape at any moment. Tears or laughter; it could go either way. She took a deep breath. The Guinness had left a creamy moustache on his upper lip. She brushed it away with a finger and kissed him softly on the lips.

'You're right, he'll be fine,' she said. 'Weird, isn't it? Twenty minutes ago, I couldn't wait to get out of the house. Now I miss him.'

'You must be used to leaving him,' said Dave, just like that, as if it wasn't the most hurtful thing he could have said if he tried.

Sarah stared at him, her heart hammering against her ribs. 'I'm still his mum. I miss him all the time. You've no idea how much I hate waving goodbye to him in the mornings.'

Dave put an arm around her shoulders, pulling her close. 'Course you miss him. I didn't mean it like that.'

Sarah took a deep breath. She'd been longing to have Dave to herself for the night, to have proper adult conversation and prove to him that she wasn't a neurotic headcase. Five minutes in and she was already ruining it. It was like being on an awkward first date. If this *had* been their first date, she thought gloomily, there probably wouldn't have been a second.

A waitress appeared holding menus. Sarah looked at her and plastered on a smile.

'Your table is ready if you'd like to come through to the restaurant.'

Sarah and Dave managed to keep the conversation flowing over dinner. She told him about Carrie's amazing diet, Jo's eleventh-hour rescue opportunity from the airport company for her new shoes and details of the trip to New York the three women had planned for September, and he filled her in on a couple of painting jobs he had picked up, a funny story about Zac losing his socks and some morsels of village gossip. They oohed and ahhed over the menu, she chose mushroom risotto and he had a steak and they shared a warm chocolate fondant.

Somewhere into their second bottle of wine she finally relaxed. The other people in the restaurant faded out of view and she gazed at her husband's familiar handsome face. Impulsively, she pulled him towards her by his shirt and kissed him full on the lips. Dave responded, as she hoped he would, not caring that anyone could see them. For the first time in months, she felt sexy again and it felt fantastic. They came up for air and grinned at each other.

It was time to share the news she'd been keeping to herself all evening.

'Guess what?' said Sarah, leaning closer and squeezing his hand.

'What?'

'I'm going to wake up extra early in the morning. I've got a really lucky feeling about tomorrow.'

'Oh yeah?' Dave gave her a cheeky grin and slid his free hand under the table to her leg.

'Not that sort of lucky.' She laughed nervously. 'Eleanor has asked me to come into the office early. There's been something in the air all week. I think it's an announcement about the partnership. I'm sure they are going to offer it to me. Imagine!' She stared at him, expecting him to be happy for her.

'Yeah, imagine.' Dave removed his hand from her leg. 'You're already knackered when you come home, a partnership will put more strain on you. On us.'

He picked up his glass and took a long drink.

'I thought you'd be pleased,' she said, her heart beginning to race.

'Correct me if I'm wrong but you have to buy a partnership, don't you?'

'Oops! We're out of wine, shall we order another bottle?' she said innocently.

Dave looked at her, his jaw set.

'Have you thought about where the money will come from for you to buy your share?'

'Well,' she swallowed, 'I'll earn my way in partly, you know by taking a cut in salary, and er, take out a loan for the rest.'

'Oh my God, Sarah!' Dave placed his glass down on the table and rubbed his hand roughly over his cropped hair.

She could hear her pulse whooshing in her ears and wished she'd kept her mouth shut.

'What?' she said shakily.

'You wanted to move to the country, so we did,' he said in a dangerously low voice. 'You wanted to go back to work early, so you did. Last week you were talking about wanting an extension on the house and now you're planning on borrowing money to pay for your partnership. You won't let me go back to work full time and you already work long enough hours. What about Zac, what about me – *your family*?'

'OK, OK, calm down,' she said, smiling at him to ease the tension.

Dave glared stony-faced and then looked away with a tiny shake of his head.

Sarah's heart sank. This was supposed to be a romantic date. Time together as a couple, as Carrie had suggested, not a night out with Mr Stroppy. It was on the tip of her tongue to back down, tell him to forget she had ever spoken, but then she remembered her wish.

'Come on, Davey, you knew I was ambitious when you married me. Surely you wouldn't want me to be a boring, stay-at-home drudge . . .' Her words faded away at the sight of Dave's thunderous expression.

Any romantic spark that may have keen rekindled had been well and truly extinguished. All that remained was a damp patch of regret. Her and her big mouth; she could have killed herself.

He stared at her for what felt like hours. 'Thanks.'

Her insides trembled and she had an awful feeling she

might be sick. She thought of a few things to say, but rejected them all. She waited for him to speak, her heart in her mouth.

Dave scratched at his stubble; looking totally fed up.

'Sometimes,' he said gruffly, 'I look at Zac and the love I feel for him is so immense it's almost painful. And caring for him should be enough. But when you leave the house in the morning, I'm jealous of your freedom.'

'Freedom?' she exclaimed quietly. She felt anything but free. 'Trapped' would be a better word.

'I'm not going to say *emasculated*,' he continued. 'That's one of those poncy words they use in women's mags. "My husband feels emasculated by my success." Isolated maybe. Embarrassed definitely. And I did it for you, because I know your work is important to you, far more so than mine is to me.'

She attempted to disagree, but he held up a hand.

'But to hear you describe my role in this marriage as boring drudgery . . .' He shook his head and finished in a hoarse whisper. 'It hurts.'

They sat in silence, staring into their glasses while the waitress collected their plates. Only an hour ago she'd thought that she and Dave would never run out of things to say; now look at them.

She scooted her chair around the table next to his and snuggled up to his rather unyielding shoulder.

'Saying exactly the wrong thing is a skill that I think I've nearly perfected now. Wouldn't you agree?' She nudged him. Dave didn't reply so she tried again. 'I just want to be somebody. And it might sound snobby but status is important to me.'

Dave stared into her eyes.

'So Zac and I aren't important.'

'Of course you are; that's not what I meant. It's just I've got a lot to prove, you know, to my dad. I told him before he died that I was going to get to the top of my game and I have to do that. I cannot fail to do that.' Her chest felt tight with emotion and she forced herself to breathe deeply.

Surely he could understand? He knew how she felt about her dad. After a moment, Dave wrapped his arm around her and kissed her temple. The relief escaped out of her in a long breath.

'When I asked your dad's permission to marry you, he made me promise something too. That I'd always do the right thing by you. So I'm saying no.'

'What?' Her jaw dropped and her head whirled with the enormity of his words.

'No. I don't want you to take the partnership if they offer it to you.'

They glared at each other. That wasn't fair. He couldn't ask her to give up her dream. She had made a wish, signed a contract. It was what she had given up so much for.

'I mean it.' He unwound his arm from her waist and drained the last bit of his wine. 'I'm putting my foot down.'

Had she suddenly been plucked from the twenty-first century and inserted into a Charles Dickens novel? She stood up too quickly and grabbed the edge of the table as the room began to spin. No way. He could put his foot where he liked, but this wasn't his decision to take.

'Can I get you anything else?' trilled the waitress.

'The bill please,' muttered Sarah.

'A brandy,' said Dave blackly, at the same time.

The waitress looked from one to the other, pencil poised and then retreated.

'I'm not saying no for ever,' he added, reaching out a hand to her arm. 'I know you're determined and I admire that in you. But now is not the right time for us. And some-times . . .' He paused and seemed to search for the right words. 'Sometimes, I don't think your job even makes you happy.'

Well, he had that wrong for a start, she thought, conveni-ently forgetting how she'd mentally described herself as trapped only a few minutes ago. Most of the time, her job gave her immense satisfaction. Unless she had a run-in with HMRC, or she got in a mess with her timesheets, or she got told off for wearing the wrong clothes. But by and large ... Anyway, work wasn't supposed to be fun.

Sarah clenched her jaw, determined not to cry at the injustice of it all. Their date had been a disaster. The sooner she could get home and get tonight over with, the better.

She picked up her handbag. 'I'm heading off home. It's late.'

'It's ten o'clock,' said Dave sarcastically. 'Even Cinderella stays up later than that.'

The date had gone on long enough as far as she was concerned.

'It's the babysitter's first time,' she said, not meeting his eye. 'I don't want to leave her for too long. Have you got some cash on you?'

Sarah flinched as Dave shot her a filthy look. 'I'm not so strapped that I need hand-outs from my wife, I'll pay the bill myself.'

'That wasn't what I meant,' she retorted.

Dave gave a mirthless half-laugh. 'Right.'

The waitress approached with the bill and a brandy. Dave pushed his chair back roughly, took both from her and strode off into the bar.

Sarah stared after him, her heart heavy with sorrow. How had they come to this? He had been to the cashpoint to get the money for the babysitter; now she'd have to pay Rosie by cheque. *That* was all she had meant.

'Did you enjoy your meal?' asked the waitress nervously.

'Not really,' she said, swallowing hard.

Chapter 22

Sarah was up at six the next morning. She hadn't had a wink of sleep and had tried in vain to block out the noise of the dawn chorus when it started up two hours ago. Zac had woken up screaming with a temperature at one point and she had almost been glad of the company. Now her head was thumping and there were lumps of sleep in her eyes the size of Rice Krispies. *Still, looking on the bright side*, she thought, as she snuck out of their bedroom, leaving Dave to sleep off his hangover, at least she was up early for Eleanor's meeting.

Dave, her Lord and Master, withholder of independence and mover of goalposts, had stumbled in at midnight, waking her up. He mumbled something about a job he had picked up from the pub, before collapsing starfish-style on to the bed and conking out.

Sarah had had to give the babysitter a cheque seeing as he had had the money to pay her in his pocket. Rosie had stared at the rectangle of paper and asked if Sarah did PayPal.

She looked in on Zac before she left. He was in a deep sleep with one arm outstretched and the other clasped around his toy giraffe, the blankets tucked around his tummy. Damp tendrils of fine hair stuck to his hot forehead. She peeled back the blankets, stroked his face with her fingertips and bent right into his cot and kissed him goodbye.

She contemplated leaving a note for Dave, telling him about Zac's temperature, but last night's argument was still raw and she couldn't even bear to write to him, let alone speak. Besides which, he was perfectly capable of looking after their son without her interference.

Sarah left the house, got in her car and drove away as quietly as possible.

Her heart twisted with guilt about her plan to defy Dave's wishes as she drove off through Woodby and into Nottingham. Mr Buxton was retiring in two months' time and it made sense that succession planning needed to be firmed up pretty soon. If Eleanor offered her the chance to take up a partnership today, she wouldn't turn it down. She just couldn't.

Dave was right; she would have to buy her way in to the partnership. But borrowing the money would be a cinch, he was worrying about nothing. And she would be earning more as a partner; she would soon pay it back. Zac was nearly one, he could go into nursery every day then and Dave could get his painting and decorating business back up and running. Sorted. There was absolutely nothing to stress over.

Anyway, who did he think he was telling her she wasn't allowed to take promotion? Hadn't he heard of smashing the glass ceiling? She turned on the radio and put her foot on the accelerator to get herself in a rousing mood but a massive tractor pulled out in front of her at that moment and she was forced to slow right down.

'Farm vehicles shouldn't be allowed on the road when normal people are trying to get to work,' she muttered crossly under her breath as she ran down the deserted corridor and skidded to a halt outside Eleanor's office. She was late, hot, out of breath and her hair was probably all over the place. She took a second to smooth down her curls then lifted her hand to knock, but the door swung open. The office was empty.

Dammit. Now what?

She swung round and looked down the corridor and couldn't resist a smile as the skirt of her new dress swirled round her legs. She loved this dress; it was pale blue and printed with little white birds. Her outfit wasn't one hundred per cent business-like, as she'd been advised to aim for, but it made her feel confident and after last night's argy-bargy with Dave, she needed all the bravado she could get.

Her breathless panting was so loud that she nearly missed the faint noise from the far end of the corridor. Voices, chattering and laughing coming from the boardroom. It sounded like the whole firm was in there. Except her. They must be waiting for her.

Oh Lordy.

A fluttering sensation started in her stomach and made its way up to her throat. Major promotions were always celebrated in the boardroom. A bubble of excitement threatened to burst free and she pressed her fingers to her lips to keep the squeaks in. Eleanor must have organized a surprise.

Slowly, using the precious few seconds to get her breathing to revert to normal, Sarah made her way to the boardroom. She pushed her shoulders back, lifted her head up, and with a huge beaming smile, she stood in the doorway and waited for the applause.

A champagne cork popped. People whooped and clapped and Sarah stared in dismay. Blood rushed to her head and all she could hear was the whooshing sound of her wish to become partner disappearing. Seconds seemed to lengthen as the occasion sank in, the facts took hold and her career plan fell apart. It was like watching a silent movie; Ben, centre stage, was being handed a glass by Mr Buxton, slapped on the back by one of the other partners and kissed by Eleanor.

The Golden Boy had taken her crown.

She knew with certainty that her chance of making

partner at Finch's was almost nothing now; this would have been the perfect time, but she had been overlooked.

Game over.

Eleanor spotted her first; her eyes flicked to the wall clock and she beckoned her over. Sarah dragged herself across the thick carpet feeling suddenly childish in her summer dress amidst the sharply creased suits, the ties and the high heels.

Someone handed her a glass of champagne. She took a desperate swig and lifted it in congratulations to Ben. She attempted a smile too, but her cheeks had got that post-dentist numbness and refused to lift. He grinned back, a smarmy grin that made Sarah want to slap him. She turned back to her carrot-dangling boss and thought that she had never despised anyone quite so much in her life.

'He's young,' said Eleanor, unable to drag her eyes away from the chosen one, 'but he's got everything. Charisma, drive, dedication . . .'

Everything except family commitments, Sarah thought bitterly.

'Absolutely,' she said, a fixed smile threatening to lock her jaw. 'Please excuse me, I've got an awful headache.'

She smiled apologetically at Eleanor, set down her glass and fled back to her office.

By the time her new business appointment called to say she was running late at lunchtime, Sarah had re-categorized her thumping head as a migraine of crippling proportions.

She swallowed some paracetamol and vowed to dispatch the cupcake maker she had met at the networking meeting as soon as possible and go home to sleep it off.

'I'm so sorry I'm late,' said Heather McCloud when she eventually arrived. She dropped into the chair opposite Sarah with a sigh. She had dark wavy hair and plump rosy cheeks. 'I forgot how long it takes to drive into the city centre.'

Sarah smiled despite her headache; even if she hadn't

known Heather ran a catering business, she could have guessed: she had flour in her hair, and lumps of coloured icing stuck to her cardigan. Sarah poured her a cup of coffee and nudged the sugar bowl towards her.

Heather shook her head and took a noisy sip of her coffee.

'And I've been up since five, preparing for this afternoon. I'm doing gluten-free today and I've been experimenting with different types of flour. I've brought you some cake to try.'

Her new potential client opened a large cake tin and offered Sarah a muffin.

Sarah's mouth watered at the aroma of fresh baking. She accepted a small one and set it to one side for later.

'Shouldn't really,' she said, patting her stomach. 'I'm still trying to lose the baby weight.'

'Well done you!' said Heather.

'Not really, I'm still flabby under these clothes.'

'No,' she laughed, 'I meant coming back to work with a young baby. That must be tough?'

Sarah felt her cheeks redden. 'We're coping.'

At least she assumed Dave was coping; they hadn't been in touch with each other today. She was dreading their next conversation, if she was honest.

'Best thing I ever did was to set up my own business,' said Heather through a mouthful of cake. 'No easy ride, mind you. But at least it gave me a bit of flexibility when I needed it. Like when my three all went down with chicken pox.' She shuddered. 'I still can't stand the smell of calamine lotion.'

Flexibility: music to Sarah's ears.

'Tell me about your business, Heather.'

'I run baking parties, for kids' birthdays mainly. It has really taken off,' said Heather, sounding amazed at her own success. 'I'm planning on building a franchise network over the next five years. If it all goes well, "Kids in the Kitchen" could go national.'

Sarah smiled; Heather's enthusiasm was infectious. Perhaps that was the answer? Be her own boss, choose her hours and find a better way to juggle her career with motherhood. Anything had to be better than feeling like such a loser as she did now. But she had zero business experience and seemed to have an aversion to making a profit. She sighed inwardly and scanned her notes.

'And you're looking for a new accountant?'

Heather nodded, opened the tin and took out another muffin.

'We live in a little village. My accountant used to pop round to collect my books and drop them back off when he had finished. But he's retired now and I can't find anyone else locally who will offer the same service. So – no offence – but I'm forced to come into town to find a new accountant. It's such a waste of time when I've got today's party at four.'

'Why did he come to you? That's quite unusual, even in a small village, I would have thought.' Sarah frowned.

'He worked from home. I think he liked to get out and about, see how firms were run, you know. He was quite hands-on, lots of practical ideas on saving money. And he always managed to turn up when I'd just baked. Used to joke that he had more of a nose for pie than profit!'

Sarah could never work from home; Rose Cottage barely had enough room for her to open her laptop, let alone open a business. Still, it was nice to dream.

'I'm not the only one who misses him,' Heather continued, retrieving crumbs from her cleavage. 'There are loads of small businesses that used him. And people used to go to him with personal tax problems too.' She sighed. 'He really got involved with the community.'

'Sounds like a lovely little business,' said Sarah, nodding fervently. That was something she wanted to do, get more involved in village life.

'Anyway, I got in touch with WiRE and they suggested I

should try networking to find a new accountant. And I spotted you in that lovely dress and I knew straight away that you were the one for me.'

'Wire?'

'Women in Rural Enterprise. It's a business support group. I couldn't have set up without their help. I was in purchasing before, didn't know the first thing about working for myself.'

Sarah pressed a hand to her temple. Her head was getting worse; there was a distinct possibility that she might even be sick. She jotted down a few notes, took the necessary details from Heather and ushered her out of the building as quickly as she could.

On her way back to her office, she heard Ben bragging on the phone to someone: 'Youngest partner in the history of the firm, would you believe . . . ?'

Sarah quickly shut her office door to drown out the sound of his voice. Bad move. Even the noise of the door made her head pound. Ben would be impossible to work with now. Or work for. *Oh God.*

She dived into her handbag for some different painkillers and found her mobile phone. It was beeping with alerts; the battery was nearly flat and there was a missed call from Carrie. Ringing her back would have to wait; Sarah wasn't sure either she or her phone had enough energy right now. But still no word from Dave. So she guessed they were officially not speaking. She tossed two ibuprofen into her mouth and swallowed them with a gulp of water.

Two huge files had appeared on her desk, topped with a note from Eleanor marked 'urgent'. Sarah pushed them to one side; anything from her boss was always urgent. She sank down into her chair and forced herself to focus. The dream to become a partner at Finch's was over.

Time for Plan B.

Sarah pulled her notebook towards her, wrote 'Options', underlined it twice, sighed and tapped her pen on her cheek. Stay or leave the firm. That was it really. And if she went, then what? Her eyes strayed to the framed photograph of her mum and dad on the corner of her desk. Her mum had always been so proud of her achievements. Sarah would give anything to have her back, one hug, one soothing word. She blinked back tears and picked up the other photograph frame. It was one of her, Zac and Dave taken at Christmas, just before she had come back to work. It had been such a happy family time. Her chest heaved; she should phone Dave, let him know the news that she hadn't made partner, although she had a sneaking suspicion that he wouldn't be too bothered, given the argument they'd had last night.

Everything was going wrong and she couldn't for the life of her figure out what she had done to deserve it. She squeezed her eyes shut and when she opened them the four walls of her office seemed to be closing in on her. They were trapping her, hemming her in . . .

Air, she needed air. It was just her headache playing tricks on her.

Plan B would have to wait. Today wasn't the day for making life-changing decisions, her head hurt too much, for starters. She set the frame down and scooped up her bag. The only thing she was going to study this afternoon was the inside of her eyelids.

Perhaps it was the sheer relief at being away from Finch and Partners, or maybe it was the sugar rush from Heather McCloud's raspberry and white chocolate muffin – either way, Sarah didn't care – but on the drive back to Woodby her headache started to lift and as it did so, her mind drifted back to the wish list.

The thing she would most regret not doing.

Whichever angle Sarah came at it from, the answer was the same; being successful in her career was key to her happiness. She loved being a mum, she loved Dave and she loved their little family. But she wanted a career too. Did that make her a bad person? She didn't think so.

But it did mean that she needed Dave to be on her side.

She drummed her fingers on the steering wheel impatiently. The sooner she could get home and sort out this silly argument the better. The day might have gone disastrously so far, but she wasn't going to write it off just yet. They both might have strong personalities apart, but they were even stronger together. In the grand scheme of things, that was all that mattered.

By the time she passed the sign for Woodby she felt a bit of a fraud; her headache had gone and she was humming along to the radio.

As she drove past the old post office she saw a man erecting a sign and slowed down to see what it said. The post office had been shut since they moved into Woodby and for goodness knows how long before that. The sign was wobbling about a bit as the man hammered it into position, but Sarah could still read it: *To let – shop with flat above.* Her spirits lifted; how fabulous it would be to have a shop in the village. No more three-mile dash for a carton of milk.

As she indicated to turn left into her lane, a pushchair on the pavement ahead caught her eye. It looked exactly like Zac's and it was outside Rebecca's house. She stared at it; it was Zac's and he was in it. In the split second before she made the turn, she saw her husband standing under the porch with Rebecca pressed tightly up against him. They were kissing.

Dave was kissing Rebecca.

Sarah couldn't breathe; a tight band formed around her chest and she gulped at the air. For the second time that day, time seemed to slow right down as she took in the scene in front of her and she lost concentration. The car swerved, mounted the curb, narrowly missed a lamp-post and dropped back on to the road. She yelled out loud, jerked the steering wheel and turned the corner. Thirty seconds later, heart pounding, she found herself outside Rose Cottage.

With trembling hands she let herself in through the front door and charged upstairs. She couldn't stay. She couldn't face him. Not today. She was in no fit state to deal with this on top of the humiliation over Ben's promotion. Tears cascaded down her face as she grabbed her overnight bag from the top of the wardrobe and began stuffing it with clothes. She could barely see straight, let alone think straight.

She felt sick as she slipped her toiletries in the side pocket. This had been her hospital bag. The last time she had used it, she and Dave had packed it together, marvelling over the tiny vests and nappies and laughing about Sarah's OCD typed birth plan. She closed her mind to the memories and wiped her eyes.

He could be back at any moment. She had to leave before then, because there was no way she'd be able to resist confronting him. And then he would admit that he was having an affair and it would all be over. Her marriage would be over. After all, it wasn't as if he hadn't warned her.

'I can't put up with you like this for much longer,' he had said.

Get back in the car. Drive. Give yourself space.

Sarah threw her bag in the boot and set off for Northampton, deliberately driving the long way out of the village to avoid Rebecca's house. A night in Jo's no-nonsense, clutter-free and more importantly *man-free* flat was exactly what she needed.

Chapter 23

Jo slid the portfolio case out of the back seat and locked her car. She glanced round the nondescript industrial estate and at the faceless single-storey building that apparently housed the headquarters of Global Duty Free.

'Are you positive this is it?' she asked Patrick.

They had worked their backsides off for three days to prepare for the presentation of their lives, she had dashed out and bought a new confidence-enhancing outfit and the satnav had brought them to an unlikely location on the outskirts of Liverpool. She wasn't altogether sure that it wasn't a huge wind-up.

'All buying decisions are made here, apparently,' said Patrick, wheeling a huge sample bag specially designed for shoes towards an inauspicious pair of aluminium doors. 'Have you got the USB stick?'

'Yes, in my handbag.' She frowned, still unconvinced. 'I thought we'd be in some glitzy boardroom in an airport, not in an ugly warehouse in the middle of nowhere.'

He chuckled. 'Sorry to disappoint you, Miss Gold.'

She stuck her tongue out and hoisted her bag over her shoulder.

'They keep it unnamed for security purposes. This place is stuffed with luxury goods. There'd be a major risk of theft if there was a sign above the door.' He rang a discreet doorbell and the door buzzed open. He bowed deeply. 'After you, ma'am.'

Jo reported in to the receptionist and took a seat next to Patrick in the waiting area. A group of Japanese businessmen made a vignette of grey suits as they lined up to have their picture taken in front of a gigantic chrome Global Duty Free logo mounted on the wall behind them. An older man with glasses, grey hair and a round face looked over at her and barked something in a staccato voice at one of the younger men in the group.

Jo raised her eyebrows at Patrick in mock alarm. 'Do you think we nicked their seats? Because I'm not moving.'

Patrick shot her a look. 'Behave. Please.'

'*Moi?*' she said innocently. The young Japanese man approached them and she lowered her voice to a whisper. 'Ooh, hello.'

'I am sorry to disturb you,' he said in an American accent, 'but Mr Yamamoto would like to know what you have in the case.'

Jo pointed to the case and looked over to the senior man. 'In here? Shoes.' She pointed to her own feet for added clarity. She bowed as an afterthought and heard Patrick stifle a snort of laughter.

'Ah, shoes!' repeated the Japanese party, accompanied by a round of nodding at each other.

There was another machine-gun round of speech from the older man.

The young man cleared his throat and, looking uncomfortable, said, 'Mr Yamamoto thought that might be so and would like to see them.'

Jo looked at Patrick, shrugged and began to unzip the case. 'They're in order,' he whispered, looking anxious. 'Don't mix them up.'

'Relax,' she said with a grin. 'What can go wrong?'

Ten minutes later, the receptionist ushered them into a

large boardroom. There were shelves along two walls, lined with tempting displays of luxury duty-free products, including all Jo's favourite perfume and cosmetics brands.

'Holly would be in heaven,' Patrick hissed, nodding to a giant box of Swiss chocolates.

'Ditto,' Jo muttered back.

A group of people in cool designer brands were standing around the refreshment table at the far end of the room. Not a stiletto or a pinstripe between them. Jo pulled at her tight shift dress, feeling quite starchy by comparison. Even Patrick looked more the part than her in his linen trousers and open-necked shirt. He was a picture of calm: relaxed and confident, his boyish smile never far from his lips. She, on the other hand, was a bag of nerves.

His old student buddy, Ian Hamilton, sauntered over to say hello. His Superdry T-shirt and vintage jeans didn't quite work with the rest of him. He had a little round tummy, plump cheeks, gold-rimmed glasses and scarcely any hair. Jo glanced at Patrick's mop of thick fair hair; he had definitely aged better.

Patrick introduced Jo to Ian who in turn introduced them to the rest of the group and led them to the front of the room where the IT equipment was set up for their presentation.

'Good of you to come at such short notice,' he said, thumping Patrick's back. 'Our American colleagues are only here for one more day and they've insisted on seeing all the brands for the British campaign. Jo, can I get you a drink?'

She accepted a glass of water gratefully and Ian left them to get set up.

Patrick winked at her and began to arrange the Josephine Gold collection on the allocated shelving unit at the front of the room. Jo inspected the laptop which had been set up for their use, inserted the USB stick and waited for the presentation she'd spent hours preparing to load. A flash flood of panic swept through her body as the contents of

248

the USB stick appeared on the screen: *Staff headshots © First Shot Photographic Studio.*

Oh hell. Her stomach flipped. She'd picked up the wrong USB stick.

This one had arrived yesterday from the photographer. Patrick had suggested they had some new headshots taken for a press release about the Josephine Gold collection. She frantically tipped up her laptop case with shaking hands, but even as she did so she knew she wouldn't find the other USB stick. She remembered picking this one up off the desk earlier this morning. The correct one must still be lying there.

Now what. *Think, Jo, think.*

Her head swirled with all sorts of thoughts, none of them useful.

She cleared her throat and Patrick caught her eye. In under a second he was at her side.

'Problem?' he muttered. Global's management team had now taken their seats and were waiting silently.

Jo quickly flashed a nonchalant smile around the room. 'Bear with!' she trilled. 'Just sorting out the technology.'

'I've brought the wrong USB stick,' she hissed through gritted teeth. 'Look.'

'Bugger,' said Patrick unhelpfully.

'What are we going to do?' squeaked Jo. 'There's no time to ask Liz to email the presentation, we'll miss our slot.'

This was unbelievable. She was always prepared, unflappable and totally cool under pressure. Today was different. Today felt like it was her last chance to save Gold's. It was thanks to Patrick that they had got this opportunity; it was up to her to make sure the contract landed in their laps.

'Forget the presentation.' Patrick touched her arm gently, his cheeky grin replaced with fierce determination. 'Remember what you said before? About the shoes winning the order for us? We're going to let the shoes do the talking. Speak from the heart, Jo. From the heart.' His eyes bored into hers and she gazed back, absorbing some of his calm. 'You can do it.'

'Thank you,' she murmured, as her own heart performed somersaults.

He was right. Of course she could do it. Jo pulled herself up to her full height and took a deep breath. Besides which, she really had no choice, she thought, reaching for the first of her mood boards.

Fifteen minutes later, Jo was on a high. The pitch had gone really well and she was ready to wrap up her speech.

'We believe that what we have created in Josephine Gold is a high-end, luxury British brand that captures the zeitgeist in terms of fashion for the confident woman. Thank you.' She finished and smiled at everyone in the room.

And breathe.

All of the samples were being passed around under the scrutiny of the panel. If she had to guess, she would say they were happy. Not exactly whooping and hollering, but some raised eyebrows, minuscule nods and lots of note-taking. She and Patrick had done well, despite her earlier mammoth hiccup. She exhaled and smiled at Patrick, who winked back.

Hopefully no one could see that her whole body was trembling. Now they just had to answer any questions that the panel might have.

A woman with a light tan and sparkling white teeth raised her hand.

Jo beamed at her. 'Yes?'

'I'm Tori, buying director from the States.'

Director? She looked barely old enough to be out of school.

'We're looking for new brands that really represent the

Best of British for our campaign. Why should we choose Josephine Gold?'

Because if you don't, there probably won't even be a Gold's shoe business in twelve months.

She shuddered. That was unthinkable. All her father's hard work, years of building up the Gold's brand, up in smoke. All because she had made a complete mess of it. She stared at the panel, aware that this was the clincher, her last chance to make an impression. She needed this more than she had needed anything in her life.

'Thank you for your question, Tori. Well, I guess what makes our brand special is . . . um . . .'

She opened her mouth again but nothing came out. Heat rose to her face and she had a sudden image of herself collapsing in floods of tears in front of this cool young American. Only a few seconds ticked by, but it felt like an eternity to Jo. Tori shifted in her seat.

Say something, for God's sake!

A tapping noise made her spin round. Patrick was doing something on the laptop. His warm, friendly smile as his eyes met hers told her to relax, that he had it covered. He gestured for her to step to one side and she jumped out of the way gratefully.

'To answer that question,' said Patrick smoothly, 'I'd like to introduce you to the Gold's family.'

Her family? Jo threw him a puzzled frown. He grinned back. She had no choice but to let him run with it, but if he revealed embarrassing details about her and her parents, she would quite possibly shrivel up and die.

Patrick picked up the remote control to operate the projector screen, opened the company's headshots folder on the USB stick and set it to slide show.

'This is Len,' he said, 'the workroom manager.'

Jo's heart squeezed at the sight of one of Gold's oldest and most loyal employees. Immediately she saw what

251

Patrick was about to do: he was selling the team behind the Gold's brand. She sneaked a sideways glance at him. *Patrick, you're a genius.*

'Len has worked with leather since he was sixteen,' Patrick explained. 'He crafted the samples you see here today by hand. Some of them have thirty individual pieces of leather. There is nothing you can teach this man about craftsmanship.'

There was an impressed whistle from Ian.

'Here's Francesca,' he said as the slide show continued, 'our very own in-house British designer. She has a love of fashion that borders on the obsessive and an instinctive talent for designing beautiful, commercial shoes.'

Patrick clicked again.

'The team in the workroom,' he said. 'Men and women whose attention to detail, fine stitching and time-honoured skills help to create a level of quality that imported footwear can never hope to compete with.'

Jo gradually released the breath she had been holding. Patrick's pitch was perfect. She could kiss him. The panel was loving it and asked him to go back so they could see images of the factory and warehouse again.

'This is the admin team,' said Patrick. 'These ladies would be your day-to-day contacts. They are so efficient that they scare me to death.' He grinned and was rewarded with a round of laughter.

'The staff are so dedicated to Gold's that they recently offered to work for nothing if they had to.'

Jo glanced at him; she didn't know that. Her throat was aching with emotion. Sometimes she felt like the only one who could solve the company's problems, but Patrick was right: they were a family and she was humbled that they would come up with such a generous solution.

'And finally our Managing Director.'

Jo noticed a row of tiny beads of sweat on his forehead and felt slightly better about her own nerves. He paused the slide show as her own picture filled the screen, surrounded by Josephine Gold shoeboxes. The photographer had captured a moment of proud happiness on her face.

'We set out as a team to breathe new life into the Gold's brand and create footwear that women will covet. The Josephine Gold collection embodies that goal. I truly believe that there is no one in this industry more passionate about footwear, about her staff and her company, than Jo Gold herself.'

He sounded pretty passionate himself. Jo wanted to look at him but didn't dare; her own eyes were doing battle with some very persistent tear ducts. She looked at the audience instead: Tori looked impressed and the others were pulling positive faces without giving too much away.

'Quite simply, everything that's right about British fashion right now,' he prodded the table in front of him for emphasis, 'you'll find at Gold's.'

He made eye contact with everyone before delivering his parting shot. 'Gold's *is* the Best of British. Thank you.'

Ian led the group in a round of applause and within ten minutes was showing them back out into reception.

'Thanks, mate,' he said to Patrick, shaking his hand and simultaneously slapping him on the back. 'You didn't let me down. And you've done yourself proud there.'

'We really appreciate you putting us forward for this,' said Jo.

'No worries,' Ian said airily, pumping her hand up and down between his pudgy ones. He flared his eyes at Patrick with a grin. 'It was good to meet you finally; Patrick has mentioned you a few times.'

'Really? All good, I hope?' said Jo, amused to see Patrick squirming.

'So. When will we know if we've been successful?' said Patrick, punching Ian on the arm and changing the subject swiftly.

'It'll be a quick decision.' Ian rubbed his arm. 'Today, probably, before the Yanks go back. I'll call you on your mobile as soon as I hear, OK?'

Outside in the car park, Patrick adopted a cocky swagger as they headed back to the car.

'It's in the bag, I'd say.' He loaded their cases back in the boot and grinned.

'No thanks to me,' Jo replied flatly.

'You were great and the Americans lapped up all that British stuff. I'll drive,' he said, swiping the Lexus keys out of her hand.

She shook her head and sighed. Buoyed by his own performance, he was going to be impossibly smug for the rest of the journey.

The two of them climbed into the car and Patrick tapped instructions into the satnav to direct them back to the office and then turned the radio on.

'"Born in the USA",' he said with a broad grin as the Bruce Springsteen track came on. 'It's a sign.'

Jo couldn't help but smile; his happiness was contagious. The presentation had gone extremely well in the end. There was no doubt about it; they did make a good team.

But that was going to come to an end soon.

Her good mood faded. She couldn't imagine what it would be like not to have him to talk to, not to have someone around whom she trusted so implicitly. Whatever crisis she found herself in, Patrick always seemed to have exactly the right words to talk her down from her panic. The thought of not seeing him every day sitting in his office, ready with a joke and a smile, filled her with dread. He was almost as much a part of Gold's as she was.

'Hey, have some faith!' said Patrick, misreading her glum face. 'They loved us.'

'Oh, McGregor.' Jo spontaneously threw her arms

around his neck and pulled him towards her, planting a huge smacking kiss on his cheek.

'Wow.' He put a hand to his face.

'Are you blushing?' she teased. 'Thanks for today. I fell apart and you were amazing. If we do get this contract, it will be down to you and you alone. I cocked it up well and truly.'

Patrick stared at her so intensely that her heart began to thump.

'You,' he said, reaching for her hand and bringing it to his lips, 'are much more impressive than you think.'

Jo's breath caught in her throat, confused at the effect Patrick's touch was having on her insides.

'Anyway.' He released her hand and started the ignition. 'I meant what I said in there. You deserve this.'

He steered the car out of the car park and they left the industrial estate behind.

For the next thirty miles, Patrick's line of conversation was variations on a theme of how convinced he was that Gold's would win the contract, repeating 'it's a done deal', 'it's a no brainer' and back to 'it's in the bag', until Jo wished he had a mute button like the car radio. She was glad he felt this way, but she couldn't quite share his confidence; there was too much riding on this and she didn't want to tempt fate.

'Chewing gum?' She pulled a packet out of her bag and offered him a piece, as much to shut him up as anything else.

'Yes please.'

He opened his mouth and she popped it in, her finger-tips brushing against his lip. From nowhere a tingling sensation rippled through her body. *Wow.* She swallowed, totally thrown for a second.

'I wish I hadn't worn this stupid dress, it's too tight and businessy,' she said, in a bid to change the subject and hide her blushing face. 'Everyone else looked really trendy. Even you.'

She smoothed down the skirt, already grinning, expecting a smart retort.

'You look lovely,' Patrick murmured gruffly. 'Always.'

There was something in his tone that made her glance at him. Their eyes met, just fleetingly, but the look that he gave her made her stomach quiver. She looked away and pressed a cool hand to her face, aware that her pulse had speeded up. What was going on between them today? They kept having these little electrically charged moments. Her heart was thumping against her ribs. It was too weird. This couldn't be happening. Not with Patrick. He was almost family. Father of her god-daughter.

'How's Holly?' she managed to stammer.

Patrick exhaled. *He felt it too*, thought Jo, trying to focus on his words. But did that make it worse or better?

'Holly's good, thanks.' Patrick nodded vigorously. 'Yes. Very good. She often asks after you.'

'Really?'

'Oh yeah, there's some serious hero-worship going on there.'

'I hope you set her straight!'

'For her homework last month, she had to write about a woman who inspired her. She chose you.' Patrick flicked a glance at her.

Jo was flattered into silence.

'We'll have to make sure we keep in touch, you know, when you leave Gold's,' she said finally. 'Do you think she'd like to go shopping with me one day?'

Patrick chuckled. 'Er, eleven-year-old girl, shopping, do you need to ask?'

'I'd like that.' Jo settled back in her seat, relieved that they had navigated their way past the tricky moment they had just shared.

'She's lucky to have you in her life,' said Patrick, with a smile that threatened to bring her blushes back. 'I'm happy about that too.'

What did that mean? Happy that Holly had Jo in her life or happy that *he* had Jo in *his* life? It was all so confusing. She wanted to ask but just at that moment her mobile rang, and besides, she wasn't sure she was brave enough to hear the answer.

'Carrie? Slow down, I can't understand you.'

Chapter 24

It was all right for skinny people. Shopping for clothes might be fun if you had a body like Sarah or Jo.

Carrie emerged from the lift into Nottingham's Victoria shopping centre and stared at all the thin people striding along purposefully. She dithered in the corridor, getting in people's way, and toyed with the idea of getting back in the lift, driving home and buying something online.

Come on, Carrie, it's just one thing.

She took a deep breath and began to walk.

The hypnotherapist, Michelle Terry, had given Carrie some rules and made her promise to honour them. Going shopping for one item was one of the rules. She still hadn't admitted to Michelle that her ultimate goal was to wear a bikini in public this summer. Michelle had a habit of asking Carrie to picture her 'new slim self'. The last thing Carrie wanted to do was to imagine herself dressed only in a bikini. She might have managed to lose over two stone in the last six months, but she was still a long way from being the type of woman to strip off to a few flimsy triangles of fabric.

Carrie's stomach lurched. Who was she kidding? She would never be that sort of woman. No matter how thin she was, she would always be clothed in a blanket of self-doubt. Perhaps she should imagine Jo on a beach in a skimpy bikini instead. She would be entirely comfortable with her own body, prowling along the shoreline, scouting for gorgeous men to impress. Jo would lower her sunglasses a fraction, purr 'hello' seductively and have all the lifeguards eating out of her hands in seconds.

Carrie stopped in front of a shop window and focused on her reflection. She had chosen her outfit with comfort in mind: three-quarter-length black leggings and a long white T-shirt. Easy to whip on and off in the changing rooms, but not very flattering. Jo would tut with exasperation if she was here and Sarah would try to get her to wear something more colourful. Her eyes travelled upwards and once again she was struck by how lovely her hair looked with its new swingy bob.

She turned her head from side to side, letting her hair flick across her face. She moved closer to the glass.

'Hello,' she mouthed in what she hoped was a good imitation of Jo's seductive drawl.

More eyebrow, she decided. She said it again, trying to arch her brow, but she couldn't isolate just one and both of them arched at the same time making her look curious rather than sexy. She tried it once more, this time lowering her chin and pursing her lips. 'He-llooo.'

'Are you all right?' A sales assistant popped her head out of the shop. 'The door is over here, if you wanted to come in.' Her smile was polite but there was a tremble in her voice as if she was on the verge of giggling.

Carrie gasped. 'I'm fine, thanks,' she managed in a high-pitched voice. 'Just looking at the . . . er . . . dresses.'

There was a collective snigger from two other members of staff standing behind the sales assistant. Carrie stepped back from the window and noticed the display properly: impossibly thin mannequins wearing wisps of Lycra masquerading as clothing. She was nearly twenty years too late and at least four dress sizes too large for this shop. She hurried away, desperate to hide her burning face, and caught a pitying comment of 'Ah bless,' and a few more giggles coming from inside.

Focus on the rules, she told herself, as she hurried past the shops for stick insects. That was why she was here. She imagined Michelle beside her, reminding her just how well she was doing.

Rule number one, the most important rule, was to eat only when hungry and stop when full. That was going very well. Carrie had been amazed to find how much she had been eating without even noticing. The secret, she had found, was to keep her hands busy. She had downloaded some games on to her new smartphone; that was helping. Shamefully, she seemed to have swapped one addiction for another. Alex had got so fed up with it he had banned her from bringing her phone to the dinner table. He wanted to talk to her at mealtimes, he said, not listen to her phone beeping away.

The second rule was to drink two litres of water every day. Not so easy, actually. It meant she was running backwards and forwards to the loo constantly. Carrie sat down on a bench and took her water bottle out of her bag automatically, holding it to her still-warm cheeks before taking a small sip. If she was going to be trying on clothes, she didn't want to fill her stomach up too much. The flatter the better.

It was the third rule that Carrie had so far rebelled against: buy yourself something to wear in a smaller size. Jo and Sarah had both said that she would feel better for treating herself to some new clothes. But to buy a size too small, in the hope that she would slim into it, seemed crazy to Carrie.

In front of her was a shoe shop. Now, that was an idea. Shoes would be easier to buy. She didn't mind shopping for shoes. That was hardly embarrassing at all. Except for buying boots. She shuddered, remembering all the times when she'd struggled to do up the zip, and the occasion when it had taken two members of staff in Clarks to help yank off a boot that she had managed to pull on but couldn't get back off.

Michelle had not stipulated specifics, but Carrie was pretty sure shoes that were too small were not what she had in mind.

She sighed and stood up. It would have to be something to wear, but not too expensive. That way if she didn't manage to lose any more weight, it wouldn't be a waste. Just a summery top, something a bit brighter than she normally wore. Still baggy, though; even if she did go down one more dress size she would still be big.

Blending in with the lunchtime crowds, Carrie left the shopping centre behind and headed for Clumber Street. It had been so long since she had wandered through the city centre that she could hardly remember where all the nice shops were. She stopped outside the first clothes store and peered in, careful not to pull any strange faces this time.

'We sell size four!' a sign in the window proclaimed.

That couldn't be healthy, surely? Carrie eyed up a skirt on display that would barely stretch around one of her thighs. It looked like one of those sports supports you put on for a dodgy knee. She shook her head and moved on. It was the same story at the next shop: tiny clothes for pre-pubescent girls. Where were the shops for real women with hips and boobs? Or perhaps the small ones *were* the real women and it was Carrie who was the imposter?

The grey clouds opened and it started to drizzle. She dashed into a pretty little shopping arcade for shelter. There were fewer people here, which she preferred, but the shops were smarter and the browsing public slightly more up-market too, which made her feel a bit self-conscious. She paused outside an art gallery to wipe the rain off her face. The painting in the window was priced at over two thousand pounds and depicted a plump woman sitting on a man's knee in a pub.

Hurrah for big girls, she thought, feeling cheered. Of course she was a real woman. And real women came in all shapes and sizes. Not everyone liked skinny girls. Alex certainly didn't seem to mind her size. Mind you, Alex had stopped noticing her years ago. He rarely mentioned her weight loss unless she asked him a direct question.

In the early years of their marriage, they had only had eyes for each other. She had been well-padded even then but Alex had appreciated her curves and revelled in her sweet nature, loving the fact that she was a 'home bird' who was content to set him at the centre of her world.

How boring that made her sound, she thought as she walked through the arcade, heading vaguely towards the department store, where the clothes and the changing rooms were bound to be large enough for her. And how much more she wanted for herself now. Alex was still the most important person in her world, but over the last few months since meeting Jo and Sarah, she'd realized how insular she'd become and how dependent on Alex too. Her world had opened up and she liked what she saw, and maybe, just maybe, the time might be coming for her to venture out wider.

Just then Carrie passed a little boutique and something in the window caught her eye.

'Oh, my word!'

She stopped in her tracks and stared. Carrie was rarely affected by fashion but the dress on the mannequin was possibly the most beautiful thing she had ever seen. It was a coral-pink silk shift dress with a butterfly print on the front, cap sleeves and tiny tucks around a scoop neck.

If only she was braver, that would be her dream dress. The low neckline would elongate her own neck and the tucks would help the fabric to skim over her stomach. Her pulse quickened with longing. Clothes had been a necessary evil for so long. This was the first time in years Carrie wanted something so badly she would starve herself if necessary to fit into it.

She'd never shop in a place like this: a posh boutique where staff hung round you trying to be helpful. And coral pink? That wasn't a Carrie colour; she was more monochrome – black, grey and beige at a push. Besides, she was meant to be buying something too small. How could she get away with trying on a smaller size? She could try one on in her own size and then just buy a smaller one. Though what if the assistant noticed and pointed it out? That would be so mortifying.

But she couldn't drag her eyes away.

Maybe if there were no other customers, she would go in and have a look around.

Carrie moved closer to the glass and shielded her eyes with her hands to look past her own reflection and into the store.

It didn't look too busy: a couple browsing a rail of clothes at one side and one member of staff sitting at the till. Carrie could just sidle in, pick up the lovely coral dress in two sizes and dash off to the changing rooms at the back before the shop assistant had a chance to challenge her.

The couple moved towards the doorway. The woman was older than Carrie, slender and elegant with a waterfall of caramel-blonde hair. She looked graceful and supremely confident in her linen trousers and belted cardigan. Carrie felt frumpy and ridiculous in her Lycra.

The woman pulled a jacket off the rail and held it up for inspection. The man, who had his back to Carrie, laughed. It was a deep, throaty and horribly familiar sound. One that Carrie would recognize anywhere. She stared at the man in confusion.

Alex?

An urgent pulse started beating in her right temple:

thump, thump, thump. Her vision went fuzzy at the edges, the inside of the shop twisted out of focus until all she could see was the woman placing her hand on Alex's arm and leading him across the sales floor.

Her husband was shopping with another woman.

Carrie stumbled, gasping for air, sideways to the far edge of the shop window out of sight. All thoughts of the coral dress evaporated like a dream. She clung to the window frame for support.

Alex was having an affair.

Why else would he be laughing and joking with this picture of loveliness in a ladies' clothes shop?

Carrie tried to breathe in and a great heaving sob escaped. She clapped her hand over her mouth to hold in the ugly noise. For ten years she had been married to this man. She couldn't remember the exact words of their marriage vows but she was almost certain that fingering flimsy fabrics with another woman wasn't included. Forsaking all others was definitely in there somewhere, and so was being faithful as long as they both shall live.

Despite how much it hurt, Carrie stole another look inside the shop. Alex and his lady friend were looking into each other's eyes, standing far too close for Carrie's comfort. Alex took out his phone and tapped away, grinning at the woman shyly like a schoolboy.

Carrie had never looked at another man like that since her wedding day.

She tried to recall the last time Alex had taken her shopping, other than to a garden centre or a supermarket.

She stood, jaw tight with the effort of not crying, and stared. The two of them were at the cash desk now. Carrie lifted a hand to her face just in case Alex spotted her, not that he would. *I am invisible to him*, she thought again. He was still laughing. He was never that animated with her. Not any more.

She began to walk away, feeling light-headed. She left the arcade and went out into the damp muggy air, no longer caring about the rain. She walked as far as the nearest bench and sat down on the wet wooden slats.

She dialled Sarah's number but it went straight to voice-mail, so she tried Jo.

Jo answered instantly.

'Jo? Oh, thank goodness! I've just seen Alex; I don't know what to do. Do I go in, do I walk away? Nothing like this has ever happened to me before—'

'Carrie? Slow down, I can't understand you.'

'I'm in town,' cried Carrie. 'And—'

'Good. Are you going shopping? Have you bought clothes? Do not, under any circumstances, buy anything that makes you look like a Greek widow.'

'I saw a dress I liked in a window and—'

'Right. Listen to me, Carrie, I want you to go in and—'

'I can't.'

'You *can*! Anyway, why are you whispering? Are you crying?'

'I can't go in the shop because Alex is in there. With a woman. Jo, he's having an affair!'

'Oh shit. Are you sure?'

'Of course I'm sure. He's in there mooning all over her. He never takes me shopping. I've lost all this weight and he chooses now to be unfaithful. Or perhaps . . . perhaps this has been going on behind my back for years?'

A sudden wave of nausea hit her and she let out a moan. A smartly dressed woman looked over at her with concern. Carrie turned her face away.

'What are you going to do? Don't do anything silly.'

'I'm going to buy myself the biggest bag of crisps and a giant bar of chocolate and I'm going to stuff my face. And then . . . I don't know what I'm going to do then!' Carrie groaned. 'Nothing will ever be the same, ever again.'

'Oh love,' soothed Jo. 'Try not to panic. Go home and ring me when you get there, OK?'

'Home,' said Carrie with a sob in her voice. 'Oh God.'

She ended the call to Jo abruptly and ran faster than she'd run for years back to the car park, vaguely grateful that her comfy clothes had finally come in useful. If Alex left her she would no longer have a home; she owned nothing, earned nothing, deserved nothing.

What a stupid, stupid woman.

Chapter 25

A buzzing noise in Carrie's head forced her to lift her cheek off the kitchen table. After a few seconds it stopped. *Thank goodness*. She'd been crying for so long that she'd given herself a headache. She probably looked awful; her eyes would be swollen and bloodshot and she felt sick too. In front of her was an empty wrapper from a giant bar of chocolate. A rising tide of nausea surged from her stomach up to her throat. She couldn't have eaten the whole thing, could she?

The noise started again, rattling insistently at her brain. She pressed her hand to her temple but the sound wasn't coming from inside her head after all. There was movement in front of her; an empty, family-sized bag of Maltesers danced its way across the table. Please say she hadn't eaten them as well? She stared at the bag for a moment before she spotted her mobile vibrating beneath it.

Willing her hand to cooperate, she reached for the phone but changed her mind at the last second. She wasn't convinced she could hang on to her stomach contents *and* talk so she let it ring. It would be Jo checking up on her. Or Sarah returning her call. Thank God she had friends to turn to at a time like this.

She belched, loud and gassy. How ladylike, she thought, grimacing. She cast her eye over the table. An empty bottle of full-fat Coke. No glass. Fantastic – bingeing and swigging. Disgusting. She knew without even reading the packaging that she had managed to put away over two thousand calories in one sitting. And after all her hard work over the past months. No wonder she felt sick.

She heaved herself up from the table and poured a glass of water from the tap. Her poor stomach was threatening to rebel at any moment and she clutched it, shuddering as the cold water trickled down her throat and into her belly.

A cold shower. That's what she needed. She would take her water and a bowl in case she was sick, go upstairs and let the jets of icy water shake her from this nausea while she rehearsed what she was going to say to Alex. She was definitely going to confront him about his lunchtime tête-à-tête. No more Mrs Nice Guy, it was time to take a stand.

Carrie got as far as the doorway before remembering the missed call. She picked up her phone and listened to the message. It wasn't from the girls, it was from Alex.

'I'm coming home early tonight; I've got something to tell you.'

Carrie threw up all over the floor, completely missing the bowl.

Ten minutes later, she was on her third bucket of detergent and still finding splashes of vomit in hard-to-reach places. She would never, ever eat chocolate again as long as she lived. She doubted she would ever be able to stand the smell of cola again either.

If only Sarah would miraculously knock on her door armed with some antibacterial wipes and a pair of rubber gloves. She could do with a friend at this precise moment; she felt completely out of her depth. The thought of Alex coming home and confessing his affair was enough to make her feel sick again. Carrie needed help; she didn't know what to do or say at all.

Sarah would know what to do. She sat down at the table and called Sarah's mobile. She would be at work, but Carrie was sure she wouldn't mind the call, not for an emergency like the end of her marriage. A sob caught in her throat as Sarah's phone switched to voicemail. She hung up without leaving a message.

She stowed the mop and bucket back in the utility room and checked the kitchen clock. Alex had said he'd be home early. How early was early? It was four o'clock already. He could be home any minute.

She wandered out into the hall, feeling weak and hollow, and stopped in front of her favourite pink roses in the vase in the hallway. She pulled a few dead petals away and re-arranged the stems. She buried her nose in the blooms, inhaling their scent. Pink symbolized gracefulness. She lifted her head and caught sight of her reflection in the mir-ror behind the vase. If she hadn't felt so awful, she might have laughed. Her face was pink, but she looked anything but graceful. Also, the long front pieces of her hair had gone crisp. Gross. She shuddered, realizing what was stuck in her not-so-shiny bob.

And you wonder why your husband is being unfaithful?

The slam of a car door on the drive almost made her heart explode in panic.

Alex was home.

Carrie gave a yelp. She wasn't ready to face him; she was speckled with vomit and hadn't worked out what she was going to say yet. All clarity of thought vanished as she darted into the living room, then back out, then into the kitchen. With seconds to spare she ran along the hall bent double in case he could somehow see her through the two-foot-thick brick walls, scrambled up the stairs and dived into bed, squealing with inexplicable fear as Alex's key turned in the lock.

'It's me,' he called.

Carrie held her breath as she heard her husband drop his keys on the hall table.

'Are you home, petal?' he called.

Petal? How dare he call her that? Carrie threw back the

269

covers and jumped out of bed indignantly. The bedframe squeaked, revealing her location. *Damn.*

'You're up there, are you? I'll come up.'

Carrie's heart was pounding in her ears. How could he sound so normal? So cheerful?

She grabbed a hairbrush, desperately trying to sort out her hair in the remaining ten seconds before Alex appeared at the bedroom door. But the bristles got tangled in her matted locks and she threw it down in frustration.

'Hello, been having a little nap, darling?' Alex chuckled, taking in the messed-up bed.

Her mouth opened and closed silently as she took in his easy smile, heart-stopping gorgeous dark eyes and unruffled appearance. This was awful. A part of her had always known this would happen – that he would leave her – but this was so much worse than she could ever have imagined.

A shadow of concern crossed his face. 'You're not ill, are you?'

'No,' she said with difficulty; her mouth felt like sandpaper. 'Not ill.'

I love you. Give me another chance.

She swallowed down her thoughts and took a deep breath. He might have caught her on the hop, but she had to remain dignified. She wanted to look back at the day they split up and know that she had behaved admirably. He'd hate it if she caused a scene.

'Glad to hear it. Oh,' he produced a bunch of sweet peas from behind his back, the ends wrapped in silver foil, 'I brought you these. Didn't buy them, obviously, I passed Mr Ogden in the village and—'

A surge of anger spilled out of her before she could stop it.

'*Sweet peas?* How could you?!'

She leapt at him, knocked the flowers out of his hands and beat his chest with her fists.

'What's wrong with them?' Alex's jaw dropped and he staggered backwards.

'Thank you and goodbye!' cried Carrie. She pushed past him into the en-suite bathroom and locked the door.

'What are you talking about, petal?' came a bewildered voice through the bathroom door.

'That's what sweet peas mean,' sobbed Carrie. 'And don't call me petal.'

'You're not making sense.'

'It's subliminal. That is what you wanted to tell me, isn't it? Thanks for the good times but now it's over?'

Carrie could hear some scrabbling coming from the other side of the door. Dammit, these doors were so easy to force open. She sat on the loo, grabbed some paper and dabbed at her face as Alex forced the bathroom lock open with a coin.

She looked up at his concerned face and her shoulders slumped. *Oh, what the hell.* What was the point of trying to hang on to him? He deserved someone beautiful, like that elegant creature in the shop. Carrie could never hope to compete with her, no matter how much weight she lost. She sighed, her breath coming out in shuddery bursts, and resigned herself to letting go of her husband, the only man she had ever truly loved.

'Darling?' said Alex softly, kneeling in front of her and taking her soft hands in his. 'What's the problem? One minute you're in bed and the next you're attacking me with a perfectly innocent bunch of Mr Ogden's flowers.'

'The problem is, I already know,' Carrie sniffed. 'I already know why you're home early.'

She lifted her head to meet his eyes and then looked down at her lap again. There were two wet patches on the knees of her leggings from where she'd been kneeling on the kitchen floor. No wonder Alex had looked elsewhere. Frankly, he was a saint to have hung around this long.

His lips twitched. 'I don't think you do . . .'

Carrie glared at him and shifted uncomfortably on the lid of the toilet. Her marriage was going down the pan and Alex found it funny?

'I saw you today,' she blurted out in a wobbly voice.

'What?' His eyes widened. 'Where?'

'In town.'

'Oh.' Alex tutted. Carrie watched as his face changed from confusion to disappointment. A wave of sadness washed over her. Had he so desperately wanted to break the news to her himself? Was he cross that she had spoilt his big announcement?

She could just see him, with an earnest expression, explaining how he hadn't meant to hurt her, how this new love was too powerful to ignore and even though it caused him pain to do so, he needed to be with his flaxen-haired filly. Carrie was livid. Alex was a big . . . self-centred . . . *pig*.

Without a second thought, she leaned forward and shoved Alex backwards. He yelped in pain as he toppled awkwardly into the shower cubicle. Then she dashed from the bathroom and ran down the stairs.

Forgetting her earlier promise to forgo chocolate for ever more, Carrie dragged a chair over to the tallest kitchen cupboard and raided the top shelf for her emergency, unopened box of after-dinner mints. She ran a fingernail along the cellophane and, still standing on the chair, grabbed a handful of individually wrapped chocolate squares and slipped one in her mouth.

What did it matter if she was fat? What did it even matter if she made herself sick? When Alex left, there would be no one here to criticize her, there would be no need to please anyone else. She was going to be living on her own after today and she could do as she damn well liked, starting right now.

'Jesus Christ!' Alex recoiled at the smell, his eyes taking in the chocolate wrappers on the table. 'What's been going on, Carrie?'

'I've been sick. That's what, Alex.' Carrie wiped a trail of sticky mint fondant from her chin and dropped the box on to the worktop. 'Sick at the sight of you and your . . . your . . . I bet you thought you were safe, didn't you?' She pelted him with a handful of chocolates and he retreated to the doorway nervously.

'That you wouldn't be spotted. Well, ha! I did see you and you have broken my heart.'

She stopped, out of ammunition and out of breath. What was she doing? She had vowed not to make a scene, to behave in a self-respecting manner, gracious even in the face of her husband's betrayal. Instead, she was standing on a chair, with snot and tears running down her face, hair crusted with vomit, pelting him with After Eight mints.

Her head started to spin and she lurched forward. Alex immediately rushed over and tried to help her down.

'Get off me!' she hissed. He would put his back out. Another amusing anecdote to tell the new mistress.

Carrie couldn't stay here. She was a laughing stock. An embarrassment. She pushed past him, picked up her handbag from the hall and fled to her car.

'Do not follow me,' she yelled. 'I mean it, Alex. Stay away from me.'

As she started the car and began to reverse off the drive, she caught a glimpse of Alex in her rear-view mirror, hands on hips and shaking his head.

Jo's flat. That's where she would go. She might even get drunk and stay the night.

Chapter 26

Despite the heavy Friday afternoon traffic, Jo and Patrick made it back to Gold's before five o'clock. Patrick steered Jo's car into her personal parking space and handed her the keys.

There had been no word from Global Duty Free. But on the plus side, Patrick had calmed down and had stopped asking her to check his phone for messages. Carrie hadn't rung again either. Jo was worried about her and furious with Alex. Carrie had really begun to build her confidence over these last few months; whatever Alex was up to, this was bound to knock her progress. She had always suspected there was something going on there. Jo made a mental note to call Carrie as soon as she could. But right now, she needed to focus all her attention on securing the Global Duty Free order.

'We must play it cool when we go in,' said Jo, as they were lifting the bags out of the boot. 'The staff are counting on this deal, I don't want to raise their hopes only to dash them again.'

Patrick nodded. 'Agreed. Although I do think it's in the—'

'If you say "it's in the bag" again, McGregor, I shan't be responsible for my actions.'

Patrick mimed zipping his lips and the two of them crossed the car park giggling.

Liz was waiting for them in reception. She darted forward and took one of Jo's bags.

'You two look happy. It went well then, I take it?'

'Really well,' said Jo, instantly breaking her own rule. 'Patrick was brilliant. He saved the day.'

'Your hero, eh?' Liz winked and gave her a nudge.

'Um,' Jo stammered, feeling her ears turn red. Patrick forged on ahead up the corridor.

'Say no more,' said Liz, beaming. 'I've saved you some sandwiches in case you haven't eaten.'

'Thanks, you're a star.' Jo rested a hand on the older woman's arm. 'And Liz, I'd rather my father heard company news from me in future.'

'Oh, of course,' said Liz innocently as two pink spots appeared on her cheeks.

Over a pot of coffee and a plate of sandwiches, Patrick helped Jo carefully unpack all the samples. The shoeboxes were still only at mock-up stage and didn't stand up to too much handling. As they stacked them on Jo's purpose-built shoe racks, she couldn't help fantasizing that soon these boxes would be on display in airports all over the country.

It was the end of a long week and in theory, time to go home, but by unspoken agreement, neither of them was going to stray far from Patrick's mobile phone until Ian Hamilton rang.

'Knock, knock!'

Cesca stood in the open doorway. Since being given the title of Designer, she had fully embraced her creative role; she was dressed from head to toe in black and her brown eyes sparkled beneath a long shocking-pink fringe.

'Liz said it went really well?'

Jo and Patrick exchanged looks.

'We're optimistic,' said Patrick, holding up his crossed fingers.

'They made all the right noises, Cesca,' said Jo with a

smile. 'But whatever happens, you are a very talented designer. Remember that.'

'Text me as soon as you know,' said Cesca and waved them goodnight.

Len was next to pay them a visit. 'Spill the beans, then!'

'No news yet, Len,' said Patrick. 'But the signs were good and I think you've even got your own fan club up there.'

'Well done, lad,' said Len, pumping Patrick's hand and slapping his shoulder.

He turned to Jo and gave her a big smile. 'You've done your dad proud, young lady.'

'Thanks, Len.' Jo stepped forward, assuming he was going to shake her hand too, but he gave her a self-conscious hug instead.

Her heart bounced with emotion. Len knew better than anyone how hard she worked to please her father – he was a pretty tough nut to crack himself. Jo could have had no finer compliment.

She showed Len to the door and closed it behind him.

'So now we wait,' she said, looking at Patrick.

He stood against the wall, arms folded, rocking backwards and forwards on the balls of his feet. His linen trousers were a bit crumpled now, his face bore a shadow of stubble. He was a good-looking man, she thought with a jolt. It had been a long day, but he looked so alive, so energised by events.

She pulled out a chair from the meeting table, sat down and studied her nails.

'Patrick, how do you feel about going to work for Ed Shaw?'

He sucked in a long breath and dropped heavily into the chair opposite. She waited so long for him to reply that she thought perhaps he wasn't going to. Maybe the pause said it all. She mentally crossed her fingers. Looking up, she met his earnest gaze and unexpectedly felt her throat thicken.

'It's a great opportunity,' he began quietly. 'I've only

worked for one company since I left university and I guess I've realized that I'll never get any further here.'

Their eyes met. There was a tone to his voice that she couldn't quite interpret: regret, sadness . . . ?

'And financially, it stacks up for me,' he finished.

So that was that; his mind was made up.

'Then I'm pleased for you,' she said stoically. 'I never thought of you as ambitious, but you are, aren't you?'

He shrugged and grinned at her, but there was something behind his eyes that she couldn't quite read.

'Time to stop worrying about what I can't have and concentrate on securing a future for Holly and me.'

So he wanted her job; to be Managing Director. Oh, the irony. Jo would give it up in a heartbeat. To be free of the responsibility of Gold's – not to have her father breathing down her neck with his ultimatums and lack of confidence in her. Perhaps she should be the one to go? She could take the Josephine Gold collection and strike out on her own, let Patrick take over. Her dad might actually prefer that, she thought bitterly. He'd referred to Patrick more than once as the son he'd never had.

'Just bear in mind that this deal would give us a reprieve,' she said, 'the chance to sort out the cash flow. No redundancies. No one would have to leave. Not even you. *Especially* not you.'

Patrick stretched a hand across the table that divided them. Jo held her breath. For a second, she thought he was about to take her hand. And for that heart-stopping second, she wished he would. She blinked and wetted her lips with the tip of her tongue. Her heart dipped with disappointment; he pressed a finger to his phone and checked the screen for messages.

'I'm very grateful to you, to Gold's: taking me on after university, training me up in the business. But lately . . .' His voice died away and he raked roughly through his hair, leaving it standing in little peaks.

'There's stuff I've never told you ... About me and Melissa.'

Jo couldn't drag her eyes from him. This was the first time he'd opened up about his divorce. 'Go on.'

Patrick's mobile started to ring loudly. They both jumped and she let out a breath she hadn't realized she was holding.

'It's Ian,' said Patrick with a gulp.

He snatched up the phone, stood up and pressed it to his ear. Jo leapt round to his side of the meeting table and leaned as close to him as she dared. Her heart was thumping and despite being desperate to eavesdrop on their conversation, she couldn't help noticing how divine he smelled; woody and fresh. She closed her eyes and concentrated on Ian's voice.

It was bad news.

After only five seconds, Jo edged away, her heart plummeting, along with her hopes for saving the business. Ten seconds after that, Patrick ended the call.

The dream was over; Global Duty Free had turned the Josephine Gold collection down.

'Shit.' Patrick dropped the phone on to the table. He covered his face with his hands, rubbing fiercely at his eyes.

'We lost,' whispered Jo.

'I'm so sorry.' He groaned and turned to face her. 'It was between us and a new brand, Hooray Henry. Ian said it was close but they went with them because they've got a celebrity designer.'

'I've never heard of them.' Jo racked her brains but the events of the last few minutes had made her mind go fuzzy and she couldn't think straight.

'It has been set up by a rich girl from one of those reality TV shows.'

Jo felt a wave of fury at the injustice of it all. 'And Global chose them over us? So much for integrity and British craftsmanship.'

Patrick nodded. 'Ian was gutted. He said it was the Americans who voted against Gold's. You know how impressed they are with the whole celebrity culture thing.'

'Well, that's that, then.' She swallowed hard. 'The last chance saloon has closed its doors.'

The energy seemed to drain from her body and her shoulders sank.

Patrick stepped closer and placed his hands on the tops of her arms.

'Don't say that,' he murmured.

She rested her head against his broad shoulder, relishing the feel of his solid presence, the soft fabric of his shirt against her cheek. She squeezed her eyes shut and contemplated Gold's' next move.

Perhaps this was a sign. Maybe she should start something new. Call time on her father's business and start from scratch.

She locked eyes with Patrick. He looked so apologetic, it broke her heart.

'It's not your fault,' she said quietly.

'Even so, I'm still sorry.' He hung his head. 'I was so bloody cocksure of myself. I was convinced we'd win.'

They sprang apart at the sound of the door opening.

'Oops, excuse me!' Liz beamed at them from the doorway.

Jo groaned. No doubt this would be all over the company by Monday morning.

'I'll leave you to it, but just wanted to say I'm off now. See you Monday.' Liz winked, performed an excited little shimmy and closed the door behind her.

Jo rubbed her face, 'I'm not sure I can do this anymore.' *Especially not without you*, she added to herself. 'And I'll have to tell Dad.'

'Not yet. Don't give up yet,' Patrick urged. 'We've still got options.'

She rolled her eyes impatiently. 'We're running out of time. The cash flow has trickled to nothing.'

'I'll go to the bank. Talk to them about an overdraft, show them the projections.'

She sighed. 'Patrick . . . What's the point?'

He reached across and squeezed her arm. 'Please, Jo. Let me try.'

'OK. Whatever,' she said wearily, too tired to argue. She collected her things, managed a small smile and headed for the door.

She unlocked the car and slung her bag on the passenger seat. Thank goodness the drive from Gold's to home was short. She planned to have a quiet night in; she'd watch a romcom and drown her sorrows with a bottle of wine. But as she pulled into the car park outside her flat, she had a feeling that her evening would be anything other than quiet.

There, sitting on the pavement outside the communal entrance, were Carrie and Sarah, looking as miserable as she felt.

Chapter 27

'This is a lovely surprise,' said Jo tentatively, registering the smudged mascara hiding Sarah's freckles, and Carrie's pale face and matted hair. There was also a distinct whiff of vomit coming from somewhere.

'Our husbands are having affairs,' Sarah said with a sniff.

'So we wondered if we could move in with you,' added Carrie.

Today just keeps on giving. Jo's heart squeezed for them. She jerked her head at the entrance door. 'You'd better come up.'

Ten minutes later, Jo had made everyone tea, listened to their woes and shared her own. She carried a tray into the living room and set it down on the coffee table.

'So, in summary,' she said, squeezing between the pair of them, 'you two have lost your husbands, Sarah's lost her chance at becoming a partner and I have as good as lost the business. An outsider could be forgiven for thinking that our wish list hasn't exactly been a resounding success.'

From their positions, huddled either end of her sofa, neither Sarah nor Carrie smiled. Jo felt a rush of warmth towards her two friends. In spite of the fact that their presence had successfully put the kibosh on her own plans for self-indulgent misery, she was secretly flattered that they had both fled to her in their time of need. She would feed them, make up the spare bed, listen to all their problems . . .

and generally keep herself so occupied that she wouldn't have time to think about Patrick, or shoes, or her father until tomorrow. Now she thought about it, having their company felt a whole lot better than an evening on her own.

'You're right,' said Carrie glumly. 'I've lost weight but at what cost?'

Sarah took a mug and spooned two spoons of sugar into it.

'In the space of one day,' she said, stirring her tea in slow motion, 'I've lost everything: my career dream, my marriage, maybe even my home.'

'You've still got Zac, you won't lose him,' said Jo helpfully.

'Won't I? Oh God!' Sarah gasped and dropped the teaspoon on the coffee table, creating a small puddle of tea on its surface. 'Do you think Dave will want custody? He will. And he'll probably get it. I mean, Dave has been Zac's main carer since Christmas.'

Carrie wiped the spilt tea up with a clean tissue.

'Before you get too carried away,' she said calmly, 'there could be an innocent explanation for kissing Rebecca, like . . .' She glanced at Jo to back her up. Jo shrugged; in her book there was no such thing as innocent kissing. 'Like perhaps he wasn't even kissing her, it just looked like it,' Carrie suggested.

Jo nodded. 'Yeah. Perhaps he had something in his eye and she was getting it out?'

'With her tongue?' Sarah eyed them cynically.

Carrie chewed her lip. 'Don't you think if he had something to hide, he wouldn't be doing it in a public place?'

'Like a shop?' said Jo, raising her eyebrows pointedly at Carrie.

'That's different,' Carrie replied. 'Dave was virtually on his own doorstep; Alex would never expect to see me in a shop.'

Tears trickled down Sarah's face and Carrie's face crumpled.

'Sorry, Sarah,' Carrie murmured.

Jo felt a lump the size of a conker in her throat too.

'I've been a terrible wife and mother,' continued Sarah. 'If it wasn't for the fact that he'd chosen Rebecca to do it with, I wouldn't even blame him.'

'Rubbish,' Jo retorted.

'I think we're going to need more tissues, Jo,' said Carrie in a wobbly voice.

Jo jumped up and fetched them all a loo roll each. Not very classy, but it did the job. No one spoke for a few seconds while they all had a mop-up. Jo felt at a loss to help her friends, especially as her own heart was breaking after the Global Duty Free disappointment, but she felt as if they were both giving in a bit too easily. Weren't their marriages worth fighting for? A little voice in her head reminded her that she hadn't exactly been fighting to keep Patrick at Gold's. She shook the thought away. *Men.* As soon as you start realizing just how nice it is to have them around, they're off . . .

'Did you confront your husbands?' she asked.

Sarah shook her head. 'No. I packed a bag and drove straight here; he doesn't even know where I am.'

'And I did the same,' added Carrie. 'Although I sent Alex a text to let him know where I was going.'

'Which reminds me,' Sarah rifled through her handbag and pulled out her mobile, 'do you have a charger I could borrow? My phone's dead.'

Jo retrieved her charger from the kitchen and Sarah found a socket and plugged her phone straight in.

'Alex's mistress is gorgeous, with lovely silky hair.' Carrie sighed and raked a hand through her own hair, wrinkling her nose when she reached the crusty ends at the front. 'I should probably have a shower.'

'Of course,' Jo said with relief, she'd been wondering how to put it politely.

Suddenly Sarah's phone came back to life; it beeped and flashed in her hand.

'I've got loads of missed calls. The office, home, Dave's mobile . . .' Her face paled. 'I can't talk to him yet. If he rings, you won't make me talk to him, will you?'

Carrie reached for her own phone. 'You're lucky,' she said flatly. 'Alex hasn't bothered to text me back. He's probably moving Goldilocks into my house as we speak.'

Right on cue, Sarah's phone rang. She threw it up in the air like a hot potato and yelped. 'It's Dave.'

'I think you should talk to him,' said Jo. 'He doesn't know that you know about Rebecca and he'll be worried that you didn't come home.'

Carrie nodded in agreement as Sarah pressed herself back into the sofa cushions and bit her lip.

'Will one of you answer it?' she asked.

Jo crossed the floor to the phone.

'Sarah's phone? Jo Gold speaking.'

Dave's voice was so full of panic that Jo could hardly make out what he was saying. All the same, a prickle of fear spread its way from Jo's knees to her scalp and her heart began to pound. She looked across at Sarah who'd gone pale.

'Hold on, Dave,' Jo said after a few seconds. 'I'll put her on.'

She held out the phone with a shaky hand. 'Sorry, Sarah. Dave's at the hospital with Zac.'

'Oh my God.' Sarah grabbed it off her. 'Dave? What's wrong?'

Zac had suspected meningitis.

Dave had taken him to the doctor, concerned about his high temperature and a rash on his stomach. The GP had taken one look at the baby boy and phoned ahead to let the hospital know Dave was on his way. Now they were in the children's accident and emergency unit and Dave had been frantic with worry about Sarah's whereabouts.

After that phone call everything seemed to speed up. Sarah went a bit hysterical, gulping at the air and declaring herself to be the worst human being ever. Jo and Carrie had calmly gathered her things, dried her face and forced her to breathe deeply. As soon as they could, they all ran outside to the car park and Sarah threw her bag on to the passenger seat.

'Let me drive you,' Jo begged, unconvinced that Sarah was in any fit state, but she shook her head desperately.

'I want to be on my own. I've let my little boy down,' she whispered.

Her face was so pale her skin was almost transparent and her eyes had taken on a haunted look. 'If I had been there for him, this might never have happened. If . . . if . . . I'll never forgive myself.'

Jo kissed her cheek.

'Children get ill,' she said, putting on a brave voice, despite feeling sick with worry for the little family. 'Don't blame yourself, and stay safe on the journey to the hospital.'

'And phone us as soon as you know anything,' Carrie insisted, pulling her in for a hug.

Jo linked her arm through Carrie's and after waving Sarah off, they made their way back inside.

'Poor Sarah.' Jo sighed. 'Motherhood seems to be fraught with dangers and problems.'

'It is,' said Carrie darkly.

Jo looked at her sharply and opened her mouth to question her further but Carrie interrupted her.

'Can I have that shower now, do you think?'

'Sure.'

Carrie threw her arms round Jo's neck. 'Thanks for making me feel so welcome.'

This flat used to be an oasis of tranquillity, Jo mused with a warm glow as Carrie disappeared into the bathroom. But tranquillity, she decided, was so overrated.

Chapter 28

Carrie's head was aching with the tumultuous events of the afternoon. This was all so different from her normal gentle routine of an hour spent in the garden amongst her flowers before turning her attentions to dinner. Her heart ached too: for Sarah and her poorly little son, and for Alex.

Stay away from me, she had yelled at him before driving off. And he'd done exactly that, she thought ruefully. She stripped off and caught sight of herself in Jo's bathroom mirror. Gone were the rolls of fat that had so sickened her back in January after Fréd's funeral. She was curvaceous, probably always would be, but she couldn't help feeling a flicker of pride at what she'd achieved.

If only Alex had felt the same.

Tears began to prick at her eyes and she cast her glance away from her reflection and turned the shower on full blast. She stepped into the cubicle, whacked the heat up as high as she could bear and tilted her face up to the shower head. As a distraction, it worked. For five minutes she was in too much discomfort to think about anything other than dodging the needle-like water jets. She lathered her hair with Jo's *Blondes Have More Fun* shampoo, hoping the sentiment would rub off and emerged squeaky clean and an awful lot more fragrant.

Jo certainly knew how to pamper herself, she thought, smoothing a generous dollop of coconut body butter on her legs.

Feeling almost human again, Carrie wrapped a voluminous fluffy towel around her body, made a turban for her head with a smaller one and stared at the pile of her clothes on the bathroom floor. Jo wouldn't thank her for putting those back on; perhaps she could borrow something.

She opened the door to call for Jo and nearly had a heart attack. Two faces were looming right outside the bathroom.

'Oh my Lord,' she squealed.

Jo, hands clasped together, was looking worried, and next to her, looking even more worried, was Alex.

Carrie panicked and slammed the door, gasping for air. She gripped her towel round her and sat down with a thump on the loo. What was he doing here? She wasn't ready to face him yet.

'Sorry, Carrie, but he was very persuasive,' Jo called through the door.

'Darling, I was worried about you,' Alex was saying. 'Just driving off like that, especially when you've never driven on a motorway before.'

'What? Is that true?' Jo sounded amazed.

It was true. Carrie had never been brave enough to use a motorway. Alex always drove if they went somewhere together and over the years it had become more and more of an issue until today when she'd decided that she couldn't rely on Alex any more. For anything.

'We need to talk, don't you think?' said her philandering husband.

'Are you all right, Carrie?' Jo again.

Her insides fluttered; she was going to have to face him sometime and at least Jo was here to fight her corner if she needed her to. She slowly opened the door, wishing she was wearing something other than a towel.

'Yes, I'm fine.'

Alex's face sagged with relief. 'Thank you.'

'I've made up the spare room for you, Carrie, and left

some clean clothes on the bed,' murmured Jo, giving her a hug. 'I'll be in the living room if you want me.'

'Wait there, Alex,' said Carrie, pushing past him without meeting his eye. 'Don't move.'

He threw his hands in the air and sighed as she shut herself into Jo's spare bedroom and pulled on a pair of jogging bottoms and a T-shirt.

Two minutes later she opened the door and took a deep breath.

'OK, you can come in,' said Carrie. 'Let's talk.'

She tentatively raised a hand to her head; she had taken off the towel-turban but hadn't been able to find a comb. Her hair was sticking up in damp straggly clumps and she attempted to push it back off her face and tried not to think of that woman's waterfall of shimmering hair.

Alex entered the room and shut the door behind him. Her body was trembling and a pulse beat insistently in her ears and she was unsure of the protocol all of a sudden. They had been together for eleven years, married for ten, but now the atmosphere between them felt strange and different and charged with so many feelings that she didn't know how to *be* around him any more.

And judging by the way he simply stood there, gazing at her, a frown on his face, he was having the same problem too.

Jo's spare room was large enough for a double bed and a single wardrobe but there was very little floor space, most of which was being taken up by Alex. Carrie pressed herself up against the wardrobe, folded her arms and fought the urge to flee.

'I have examined your extreme outburst at home from every possible angle,' said Alex. He sank down on to the bed and rested his elbows on his knees. 'But I haven't got a clue what's got into you.'

Carrie gawped at him. 'I catch you with another woman in that shop and I'm supposed to accept the end of our marriage without making a scene?'

Alex blinked at her for a long moment and then his eyes lit up with understanding. He jumped up off the bed and pulled her gently towards him.

'Oh, Carrie,' he murmured, planting a soft kiss on her forehead, 'I was on my own in town today.'

The feel of his hands on her body was such an utter relief that she had to stop herself from stepping into his embrace. She inhaled the scent of him, so familiar and so intoxicating that it was almost too much to bear; cinnamon and citrus and warm man.

'No, you weren't,' she said, heady with confusion. Had that only been today? It felt like ages ago. And her brain might have gone a bit hazy but he was definitely with someone. 'I . . . I . . .'

'I went shopping alone, I promise. It must have been the shop assistant you saw me with.'

'Oh Lord.' She pressed a hand to her forehead. 'I need to sit down.'

He guided her to the bed and sat down so close to her that she could feel the tiny hairs on his arms. Her chest was pounding and she concentrated on getting her breathing under control while she processed his words.

If he had been on his own – and it hadn't looked like that to her – but if he had, then why? Why wander round a boutique? An awful thought struck her: perhaps he was having a mid-life crisis and turning into one of those cross-dressers? For all she knew, he could be parading round in her underwear every time she left the house. She shot him a sideways glance. She couldn't see it somehow; he wasn't that type.

Alex cleared his throat.

'Were you . . . ? When you saw me . . . ?' He shifted awkwardly and rubbed at an invisible mark on his trouser leg. 'What I mean to say is, were you jealous?'

Carrie stared at him incredulously until huge tears filled her eyes and she couldn't see his features any longer.

'Of course I was jealous,' she said huskily. 'I was devastated, but not surprised. I mean, who could blame you? You could have your pick of women.'

Alex shook his head sadly.

'Carrie, for the last couple of years, you've kept pushing me away. Whenever I compliment you or tell you I love you, you brush me off. And the last few months have been even worse. I thought . . .' He paused and she couldn't be sure but there might have been a tremble in his voice. 'I thought you were fed up of me. I thought I was too old and boring for you.'

Carrie gave a sharp, incredulous laugh and swiped away at her tears.

'I was ashamed of my size and worried about embarrassing you. Everyone thinks it. You can see it on their faces. "What is he doing with *her*?" people think. Meeting Jo and Sarah has made me realize that I've wasted years of my life. I've just eaten my way through the days getting fatter and fatter and more and more miserable and . . .' She met Alex's gaze and left the tears to roll down her cheeks. 'I'm sorry. I didn't mean to push you away. I love you so much. I lost this weight mainly for myself, to be more healthy and confident, but also for you. I wanted to make you proud.'

Alex cupped Carrie's face with his hands and kissed her mouth. She felt her entire body light up as if he had flicked a switch and her heart swelled with desire and love for this man.

'I love you exactly the way you are, darling, I always have. You are the kindest, most loving person I know. I don't think you realize how beautiful you are. Your gentle smile, your sparkling eyes, I could look at you all day. It used to make me cross when you put yourself down all the time.'

Carrie blushed, recognizing the self-defence mode she had adopted for the last ten years: to joke about her size before someone else did.

'I don't care what you weigh,' he murmured, kissing her again. 'You are still the same wonderful person I fell in love with when you were twenty-one.'

Carrie managed a watery smile.

'So why were you in that shop?' she asked quietly.

'I wanted to buy something for you.' He laughed, wiping tears from her cheeks. 'Seeing as you never let me come shopping with you.'

'That's not true.' Carrie huffed indignantly.

Alex raised an eyebrow and she flushed. Maybe he did have a valid point. Unpleasant recollections wafted through her mind of Saturday afternoons in changing rooms trying on too-tight clothes, refusing to come out and show Alex who was loitering patiently outside with the other husbands.

'Any good?' he'd ask benignly. 'No,' she'd mutter as she rammed hangers full of clothes on to the reject rail and made a hasty exit. Eventually she'd banned him from accompanying her in her humiliating attempt at shopping for big girls' clothes. So, yes, it was true.

'Oh.' She looked back at Alex, feeling like a fool. 'That was such a lovely thought. But how did you know what size I am? I'm not even sure myself any more. You know how much I hate shopping.'

'Aha,' said Alex, grinning with such pride she thought he might burst. He took his wallet from his back pocket and removed a small card. 'I thought as much, so I Googled "personal shoppers" and I found that boutique in town. I've made you an appointment. I hope that's OK?' He peered at her, running a hand through his thick hair.

'It's a lovely idea. I've been such an idiot,' said Carrie, mortified.

All the poor man had tried to do was arrange a surprise, and in return she'd accused him of having an affair, pelted him with chocolates and forced him to drive across three counties to retrieve his runaway wife.

Shyly, she slid her arms around his neck. Alex responded by turning his body towards her and taking her face in his hands. She closed her eyes, lifted her lips to his and—

A sharp knock at the door had a rather crowbar-like effect on the pair of them.

'You all right in there?' yelled Jo.

Carrie leapt up and opened the door.

'We're absolutely fine,' she said, unable to keep the smile off her face.

'Good. I'll tick you off the to-do list, then,' smirked Jo, flicking her eye over Alex, who'd turned a delicate shade of pink.

Jo shut the door and Carrie grinned at Alex. 'Now where were we?'

Chapter 29

By the time Sarah had reached the motorway, her wish list had changed beyond recognition and she spent the next forty-five minutes sending prayers to anyone she could think of from God to the tooth fairy: *Please let my baby boy be OK.*

It was seven in the evening by the time she reached the hospital campus and the car park was barely half-full. She abandoned the car and fumbled with the keys as she tried to lock the door. Her palms were clammy, there was a trickle of sweat running down her spine and she had almost no recollection of her journey.

She ran across the hospital grounds. Her brain was travelling faster than her feet, churning out accusations and apologies, regrets and recriminations, and she felt almost delirious with fear. How could she have disappeared off to Jo's without sparing a thought for Zac? He had been under the weather during the night, warm when she'd left him this morning – all the signs were there, for goodness' sake! She had to be the most selfish, self-absorbed, self-indulgent person on the planet. If he got through this – *He will get through this* – she would never leave his side again.

She aimed for the main entrance, scanning all the signs for the children's A and E department, the sound of Dave's voice whispering 'meningitis' like a witch's curse over and over in her head until the guilt threatened to undo her completely.

Her face burning with anxiety and shame, she gave her details to the receptionist and asked where she could find the rest of her family. She followed the woman's directions down the corridor to a bay, screened from the others by a long brown curtain. Her legs were shaking and her stomach was clenched so tight that she could hardly breathe. She tweaked the curtain back and nearly collapsed at the sight; her baby lay still and lifeless in a cot. Dave was slumped in a chair, leaning over it.

He lifted his head as Sarah entered the cubicle and a look of relief passed over his exhausted features.

In a fraction of a second, he was out of his seat. He scooped her up into his arms and squeezed her until she thought her ribs would crack. A shuddering sob vibrated through her.

'Sarah, thank God. Where have you been?'

Her chest felt tight; she couldn't answer that now. None of that mattered. Instead, she eased herself out of his arms and bent over her son, covering his face with fairy-light kisses, so as not to wake him. Her heart clattered with fear and she gripped the sides of the cot.

'How is he? Is he going to be all right?'

Let me swap places with him. I'll do it in a heartbeat. Just let him be OK.

'I'm waiting for news.' Dave put an arm round her shoulders.

Zac's breathing was rapid, but he was asleep. Even wearing only a nappy, he looked hot; his hair plastered with perspiration and one arm thrown up above his head. Apart from the small plaster on his arm, he looked exactly like he had that morning when she'd left home early, full of hope that today would be the day she got her partnership. She squeezed her eyes shut; all that seemed so trivial, so pointless now . . .

She reached out and stroked his arm; it was clammy to the touch and there was a swathe of tiny purple spots across his stomach. Zac made little sucking noises in his sleep, he looked so peaceful that it was almost unimaginable that such a nasty virus could be rampaging through his blood-stream at this very moment.

'What happened?' Her mouth was so dry she could barely speak. She turned to look at Dave properly. His skin was grey, his lips were colourless and he seemed to have aged in just a few hours. He looked awful. And alone.

He sank down into a chair and rubbed his face. 'He's been on Calpol all day to get his temperature down. He was warm even when he woke up this morning.'

She nodded, but didn't speak as a shudder of guilt rippled through her. She'd known that but instead of doing anything about it, she'd simply left the house.

'He seemed a bit better this afternoon,' Dave murmured, 'but after we came back from the park, it was way up high again. Then I noticed that rash on his tummy so I took him straight to the doctor's. The GP did the tumbler test against the spots and said he didn't like the look of it.'

Sarah felt her eyes burn with tears. After *we* came back from the park?

Focus, Sarah, none of that matters. Only Zac.

She was dying to pick her baby up, but she didn't dare, as if by not being here when she was needed, she had some-how forfeited the right to be his mummy.

Dave must have read her mind. 'The doctor said to leave him to sleep.'

'You said *suspected* meningitis, when will we know? What are they doing for him?'

'They've done tests; I don't know how long the results will take.'

There was a sudden scraping noise as the curtain swished back on its rail and a girl in a white coat appeared, scrib-bling notes on a clipboard. Dave jumped up and put his arm around Sarah's waist. She pressed against him grate-fully and held her breath.

'Right. Hi, Mr and Mrs Hudson? Zac is a poorly little chap, but the good news is it's only a virus and he'll be fine in a few days.'

Sarah clutched at Dave with relief. 'It's not meningitis?'

The doctor gave them a brief weary smile and leaned into the cot, shaking her head. 'It's a bacterial virus from the same family, but nothing like as serious.' She took Zac's temperature and made a note of the reading.

'Thank God.' Sarah turned her face into Dave's shirt and let the tears come. Dave's shoulders were shaking too.

'Your GP did the right thing,' said the doctor briskly. 'It's not always easy to isolate the symptoms on babies. Take him home; give him plenty of fluids, Calpol, the usual. He might not have much appetite and he'll be fractious for a few days. But he should be OK soon.'

Another smile, a nod to sign off and she was gone.

Sarah and Dave looked at each other. Her heart was still thundering and her legs felt like they could collapse any second. *Zac was going to be OK.* She wrapped her arms round Dave's waist, grateful for his solid body against hers, not caring for the moment about Rebecca. Whatever happened next, they were Zac's parents, they loved him and he needed them.

For a full minute they stood tight within each other's arms, just breathing, lost in their own private thoughts and gradually Sarah's fear began to subside. Zac stirred and started to whimper.

'He's waking up.' Sarah darted to the cot and lowered her voice to a whisper. 'Hello, little boy.'

Zac was still dozy with sleep and she lifted him up ten-derly, holding him close and breathing in his baby smell.

'Mummy loves you,' she murmured. 'Shall we go home?'

'Let's all go in the van,' said Dave. 'We can leave your car in the car park and collect it in the morning.'

Twenty minutes later, Sarah climbed into Dave's van with a very drowsy Zac in his car seat between them. The evening sky was tinged with bands of red and orange and from the top floor of the car park, Nottingham's landscape shimmered in the fading light. It was a beautiful end to an otherwise ugly day.

Sarah took one of Zac's hands and stroked his warm skin, soothing him back to sleep. She chewed the skin around her thumbnail and peered at Dave, watching as he drove the van out of the hospital campus. The events of the last twenty-four hours were so far from the norm that in her emotional state, she wasn't sure what was real and what wasn't. Had she really seen him kissing Rebecca?

'So where were you?' he asked. 'I was getting a bit desperate not being able to reach you.'

The words leapt out at her in the silence, making her jump.

'At Jo's,' she stuttered. 'My battery died on my phone. I'm sorry about that, Dave. I really am, I'll never forgive myself for not being there.'

She should ring them; Jo and Carrie would both be worried about Zac. And her.

He frowned at her. 'Did I know you were going there? Because if you told me, I completely forgot.'

She stared at him, her stomach twitching with nerves.

Part of her wanted to get everything off her chest, the other part wanted to crawl into bed and erase the day from her memory banks permanently. She shuddered; no matter what happened next with her and Dave, the image of Zac in that hospital ward would stay with her for ever. Maybe now wasn't the time.

But it was a bit like a scab: once the urge to pick it had occurred to her, she couldn't leave it alone.

She took a deep breath.

'It was a spur-of-the-moment thing. I had a bad day at work, left early with a migraine . . . and got back to Woodby to see you kissing Rebecca.' She paused. 'I couldn't face confronting you about it so I ran away instead.'

Dave made a choking noise. 'Bloody hell, Sarah. If I wasn't so knackered, I'd laugh.'

She glared at him. She could think of many words to describe this situation. None of them was funny.

'I've pushed you away, I realize that. But I'm so sad that you've cheated on me. I know Rebecca's a much better mother than me.' Sarah stared down at her lap, determined not to let any more tears fall. 'She'd probably be a much better wife too.'

'I haven't cheated on you.' He gazed at her, bemused. 'And none of the rest is true either. She's gay, for a start.'

Sarah blinked rapidly. 'Oh. She doesn't look gay.'

Dave raised an eyebrow.

'You don't deny kissing her, then?' said Sarah, feeling like the list of her own mistakes was getting longer and longer by the minute.

'I found a little teddy bear in the park with "Ava" written on its T-shirt so I dropped it in on the way past. Rebecca was really grateful; it was Ava's favourite and she'd turned her house upside down looking for it, apparently.' Sarah could feel his eyes boring into hers. 'So she kissed me. Simple as that.'

Sarah turned her face to the car window and pressed her hot cheek against the glass. What an idiot. She couldn't have got today more wrong if she'd tried.

'How do you know? About her, I mean?'

Dave shrugged and kept his eyes focused on his driving. 'We both feel like misfits in the village sometimes. She's a gay single mum. I'm a house husband. There aren't many of us around; in fact, it's a club of two.'

She reached across and squeezed Dave's hand.

'I'm sorry I doubted you,' she said quietly.

Dave brought the van to a halt as they approached red lights. He lifted her hand to his lips.

'After the way I behaved last night?' He shook his head. 'It's me who should be apologizing. I should never have told you to turn down the promotion. I ruined our first date in ages, then to compound it, I got drunk and came home late and missed saying sorry to you this morning. I've felt bad about it all day, but I was too ashamed to call you. I thought I'd make it up to you tonight but then all this happened with Zac.'

They looked at each other and her heart swelled with love for him. 'We haven't really talked properly in ages, have we?'

He groaned suddenly. 'God, I'm sorry, I haven't even asked. Did you get the partnership?'

'No. But do you know what, I'm glad.' She laughed at his shocked expression. They were fine; everything was going to be OK. 'You were right; the job is making me miserable.'

She glanced down at Zac as he snuffled in his sleep and felt an enormous weight lift from her chest.

'I've had my priorities wrong ever since I went back to work. But that's all going to change. I don't know how yet, but from now on I'm going to get the balance right.'

Dave wove his fingers through her hair, pulled her in close and brushed his lips softly against hers.

'I love you,' she whispered.

The lights turned to green and a car tooted behind them.

'Hold that thought,' said Dave with a grin. 'We'll be home in ten minutes.'

Chapter 30

Carrie and Alex both kissed Jo goodbye at the door of her flat.

'You are both welcome to stay in my spare room, you know?' said Jo, keeping hold of Carrie's hand. She looked genuinely disappointed to see them go.

The thought of the making-up she was planning to do later brought colour to Carrie's cheeks.

'Thank you, but now we know that Zac is going to be OK, we'll get back to Woodby. I want to call round early tomorrow to check up on Sarah and Dave, see if they need anything.'

Her eyes flicked to Alex; she hadn't filled him in on Rebecca's situation yet, sensing that one alleged affair was enough for one day.

Carrie followed Alex's car carefully back up the motorway to Nottingham. Motorway driving was another of the many things she had shied away from in adulthood. It was late now and the road was empty; so much less frenetic than her journey down this afternoon. It had been a bit hair-raising at times, but she couldn't help being proud of herself for giving it a go. The summer sky was still light, the last of the sun's setting rays tingeing it with a warm glow and matching her mood perfectly. The radio was tuned into the love songs show and she sighed happily as a Michael Bublé number filled the car with 'Crazy Love'.

Back at Fern House, Carrie put away her car keys and her handbag, topped up the water in the vase of roses in the hall and tried to ignore the wild horses that appeared to be charging through her body. Today marked a turning point in their relationship. She and Alex had let themselves drift further and further apart and she was determined to put that right tonight. She was a different person now to the troubled twenty-one-year-old he'd fallen in love with. Then, she'd desperately needed someone to rely on. But now she was a grown woman who craved independence. But that didn't mean she loved Alex any less; all they needed was to look at their marriage with fresh eyes and she felt sure that they would have a happy future together.

Alex poured them both a drink and smiled at her from the dining-room doorway.

'Gin and tonic?'

She took the glass from him gratefully and knocked it back in two large gulps and before she had time to change her mind, then she nodded her head vaguely in the direction of upstairs and said, 'Shall we, um . . . ?'

Her cheeks were flaming; it was the first time she had ever initiated anything in the bedroom. But she was determined to change, to show Alex exactly how much she loved him. As he came forward to kiss her, she caught a glimpse of her reflection in the hall mirror and gave a yelp.

She had never got round to combing her wet hair. Now she looked like a complete mess.

'Actually, can you just give me a minute?' she said and dashed up the stairs to do battle with her hair straighteners and a black mascara wand, with the sound of Alex's deep throaty laugh ringing joyfully in her ears.

An hour later in bed, Carrie lay with her head on Alex's chest, blissfully relaxed. Her fingers twirled his chest hair, which she noticed with a rush of love, had started to show threads of silver. She was floating on air, she thought, smiling to herself; every nerve was tingling and her whole body was fizzing with happiness. She lifted her head and looked at her husband. His eyes were closed but there was a contented smile on his face.

'Was that OK?' she murmured.

He squeezed her tight and she snuggled in closer. 'You were amazing.'

Carrie sighed. 'That's what they all say. Ouch!' She giggled as Alex pinched her arm playfully. 'Seriously, though, I'm getting my confidence back, you know, since losing weight.'

'That's great, Carrie, really,' said Alex, pulling her towards him for another kiss.

She propped herself up on her elbow before he got carried away.

'I've been thinking about getting a job. Now, I know you didn't like it when I worked before,' she said hurriedly, 'but—'

He rolled over to face her, frowning. 'I never minded you working.'

'Alex! You did!' said Carrie in disbelief. 'That's why I gave up.'

He stared, mouth open. 'I don't believe this.'

'You were so cross about me not taking time off on our first wedding anniversary, when you'd booked us lunch somewhere,' she countered. 'But it was Mother's Day and—'

She caught sight of the frustration etched on Alex's face. She was in danger of ruining the mood again. She should have kept her mouth shut.

'It wasn't just lunch,' he said after a moment's silence. 'I'd booked flights and lunch in Paris. As a surprise. *After*,' he stressed, 'checking with your boss first. But you refused, said you couldn't leave her to do all the Mother's Day bouquets on her own.'

'No wonder you were angry,' she said in a small voice.

'I was a bit cheesed off,' admitted Alex.

Understatement of the decade, thought Carrie. He hadn't spoken to her for two days.

'But it just confirms what I said earlier,' he said with a smile. 'You are totally selfless. Most people would have jumped at the chance of a day off on a busy weekend.'

'Paris,' breathed Carrie dreamily. 'How romantic. It was a lovely thought. I'm sorry I spoilt your surprise, like I did today too.'

Alex regarded her face earnestly and shook his head sadly. 'I'm sorry that we got our wires crossed over it. I would never have made you give up your job at the florist's; I could see how much it meant to you.'

Carrie nodded wistfully, remembering how she had revelled in combining different flowers for her customers according to the message they wished to send; thanks, friendship, love, passion, and there was even an art in striking the right note for sorrow. Doing the wedding flowers for that couple a few weeks ago had brought it all back. Seeing the bride gasp in wonder had filled Carrie's heart with joy.

'Don't worry,' soothed Alex, assuming she was lamenting the lost weekend in Paris. 'We can go this year. I could book some flights. August, perhaps? What do you think?' His eyes shone and he stroked her cheek with his thumb.

Carrie laughed and kissed him, thinking how like an excited little boy he looked. She suddenly remembered the wish she had made to wear a bikini this summer. She had never had the confidence to wear one on their honeymoon, but maybe this year would be different.

'How about somewhere warmer instead? How about Marbella? In September?' she said, thinking that she would still like to lose a few more pounds. Maybe it could be a second honeymoon.

Maybe – the idea tugged at her heart – they could talk

about starting a family? She wouldn't mention it tonight, not when their relationship was still so fragile. That conversation had kept for ten years, a few more weeks wouldn't hurt.

'Your wish is my command.' Alex grinned wolfishly. He tugged at the thin sheet that was protecting Carrie's modesty and she resisted the urge to dive back underneath it. 'Now, before I have my wicked way with you again . . . Is there anything else you need to get off your chest?'

Carrie hesitated, only for a micro-second and shook her head. But it was long enough for Alex to notice.

'Come on, Carrie, after what you've accused me of already today, you can't shock me. Spit it out.'

'Well,' she said awkwardly, unable to meet his eyes. 'You criticize my cooking. Sorry, but it's true.'

Alex looked thoughtful for a few moments and Carrie held her breath, wondering if she had gone too far. He started to nod slowly.

'I can see why you might think that,' he conceded.

'Alex, anyone would think that,' said Carrie with a tut.

'In my defence,' he gave her a guilty smile, 'you asked for feedback on your cooking.'

'Once,' she corrected. 'Before we were married. You were much more knowledgeable than me at the time and I wanted to learn.'

He winced. 'I've become a food snob, haven't I?'

She bit her lip and nodded. 'A bit.'

'Sorry. No excuse, I know, but the standards at Cavendish Hall are so high. I guess I've been bringing my work home too often.'

Carrie snorted with laughter. 'I was a terrible cook when you met me, wasn't I?'

'Remember that recipe book you used to have?' he laughed softly.

'*One Hundred Ways with Mince*? How could I forget?' Carrie cringed. 'I think I tried ninety-nine of them out on you.'

'I came round to your flat once and found you in floods of tears under a mountain of split cabbage leaves. The place stank to high heaven.' He chuckled at the memory.

'Oh yes,' she giggled, 'every time I tried to roll the leaves up, they tore and the mince fell out. The book went in the bin that night, I seem to remember. We had Chinese take-away instead.'

'Well, that's in the past and I will never be rude about your food again. Promise. Anyway, you're a fantastic cook.' Alex leaned forward to kiss her but Carrie wriggled free.

'Even my pastry?' She raised an eyebrow pointedly, thinking back to the funeral. 'You said it was heavy.'

'I take it all back. Your pastry is soft and buttery.' He lifted a strand of her hair and kissed her neck. 'And delicious.' He continued a line of kisses down towards her collarbone. Carrie shivered in delight. 'And melts in the mouth.' He looked up at her, his eyes dark with desire. 'Just like you.'

Carrie squirmed with pleasure at the sensations he was awakening in her body. 'I love you, Alex.'

'Oh yeah?' he said, laying her back against the pillows. 'Show me.'

And with a new twinkle of confidence in her eyes, Carrie pulled her husband towards her and did just that.

Chapter 31

Sarah hurried along Main Street armed with a tape measure, notepad and camera and came to a halt outside the post office in Woodby. Her stomach performed an impressive tumble routine – nosedive, backflip and forward roll – as she checked her watch for the fifth time since leaving Rose Cottage.

She was a few minutes early. Good. Just time to catch her breath and go over her questions.

Eleanor – in a rare show of empathy – had approved Sarah's last-minute request for annual leave and she had spent a few delicious days at home enjoying being part of a family. Zac had made a full recovery in time for his birthday today and, with his mummy and daddy's encouragement, had taken his first steps. Sarah was chilled out for the first time in months and it felt wonderful. The time off had given her a chance to consider her future career plans. And her future, she had concluded, was not at Finch and Partners.

Instead, a new idea had begun to whirr away and the two things – or rather one thing and one person – which she hadn't been able to shake from her mind were the old post office in the village, which was available to rent, and Heather McCloud with her successful catering business.

It was probably not the best time to be viewing business premises, she mused, when guests were arriving for Zac's birthday party in just over two hours. But this had been the earliest available appointment with the estate agent and she was so fired up about the possibility of a new venture that she simply couldn't wait.

Speaking with her accountant's hat on, if she were to set up her own business, as Heather had done so amazingly, the sensible thing to do would be to start off from home to keep the overheads down. But Rose Cottage was just too small and so the post office was the next best thing.

She pushed against the heavy metal door handle, expecting it to be locked. To her surprise, the door, creaky with disuse, swung open and an old-fashioned bell tinkled to sound her arrival. The interior was dark and cool and the air smelt damp and musty. It was not especially inviting, but it was nothing that Dave with his decorating skills couldn't fix.

The shop was narrow, with two small windows flanking the glass front door, but it extended back a long way. The shabby fixtures and fittings revealed that the post office had once sold everything from cigarettes to fireworks.

Sarah followed the well-worn groove in the old red quarry tiles towards the back of the shop.

'First-class stamp, madam?' boomed a jocular voice from nowhere.

'Jesus!' Sarah clutched at her chest and her tape measure, camera and notebook clattered to the floor.

A middle-aged man with dark slicked-back hair and a navy suit sprang up from behind the post office counter, clearly delighted with his little joke.

'Made you jump, did I? Sorry.' The man flipped up the hatch in the counter and strode forward to greet her.

Sarah shook his hand and wondered how to wipe the clamminess off without being too obvious.

'Colin Hanley, estate agent. And you must be . . .' He rifled through his papers until he found a yellow sticky note.

'Sarah Hudson,' she supplied.

He beamed at her. 'Miss, Mrs or a politically correct Ms?'

Several responses to that hovered at the tip of her tongue, not all of them polite.

'Mrs,' she said, wondering what her marital status had to do with anything.

'Good, good.' He looked up from his clipboard and over her shoulder. 'And will your husband be joining us today?'

She blinked at him. Good grief, what year did he think they were in, 1973?

'No. He's at home looking after the baby.'

'Righto.' Colin's face dropped. He'd clearly already written her off as a time-waster.

'Would the owners mind if I took out the old post office counter?' Sarah asked.

The building itself had lots of lovely old features, but the interior was very 1970s and not at all appealing.

'I'll check,' mumbled Colin reluctantly.

She crossed to the shop window, measured the area just in front of it and noted it down.

'And this greeting cards fixture would have to go. In fact, we'd probably want to strip everything out and replaster. Would that be a problem? And has the property got any heating?'

At that moment, Rebecca stopped outside the window with Ava in her pushchair and posted a letter through the original Royal Mail postbox fitted into the door. There was a dull thud as it landed. Sarah waved to attract her attention. Rebecca's mouth formed an intrigued 'ooh' shape, she crossed her fingers and held them up to the glass.

Sarah smiled and waved back. Rebecca was really nice when you got to know her. A bit prickly about her choice to be a single mum, but Sarah understood what it was like to make difficult decisions as a parent. She and Ava had been round for coffee and Sarah felt at long last like they might actually be making friends.

'And there's still a mail collection from here,' noted Sarah. 'Could that be moved?'

'I'll check everything.' The estate agent scribbled some notes on his clipboard. He coughed importantly to herald the start of his sales patter. 'The building dates back to the early nineteenth century and has got many original features.'

It was nice, but all a bit gloomy; in her heart of hearts, Sarah simply couldn't see herself working here. Although she was surrounded by windows, bushy trees on the opposite side of the road cast heavy shade over the little shop.

An old couple in matching beige overcoats, despite the July heat, halted outside and pressed their faces to the glass, their hands around their eyes as if holding binoculars.

Not very private either.

'So, what were you thinking of, love? A café? That's what people want, a cup of tea and a sticky bun with a slice of village life thrown in. Ha! You could call it that. "A slice of village life".' He swept his arm out and gazed into the distance, as if visualizing the sign above the shop door. Then he pointed at her notepad. 'Get that down. You can have that one on me.'

'Actually, I'm an accountant.'

'Oh, right.' He looked doubtfully round the shop. 'Well, I'm sure good accountants are always in demand. We all hate the tax man, don't we?'

'Almost as much as we hate estate agents,' she muttered through gritted teeth.

The shop wasn't right for her. It was no good pretending. It was too . . . . shoppy. Disappointment trickled through her as she felt her pipe dream evaporate.

Her sketchy plan had been to run her accountancy practice from downstairs and find a tenant to rent the little flat above to help cover the costs. She could have walked to work, nipped home for lunch and been back at Rose Cottage by five past five each evening. It all seemed perfect on paper.

'Do you still want to see the flat?' asked Colin in a lack-lustre voice.

His lack of enthusiasm was catching but she nodded anyway; she was here now, she might as well.

As soon as she got to the top of the stairs her spirits soared.

'This is lovely!' she exclaimed.

In contrast to downstairs, the flat was bright and airy. A big window in the open-plan living area let in loads of light and the view across the road skimmed the treetops to the meadow beyond where two handsome horses grazed.

'The kitchen,' said Colin superfluously, indicating the tiny area in the corner, separated from the rest of the room by a breakfast bar. 'Bedroom and bathroom through here.'

Sarah poked her head into the other rooms.

'Shower room,' she corrected him. 'No bath.'

'Ah yes.' Colin nodded gravely. 'That's what modern tenants want these days. Commuters, and whatnot. Just wash and go, eh?'

She nodded vaguely, adrenalin coursing through her. It *was* living accommodation, which was all wrong, but somehow Sarah knew it was exactly what she wanted.

She could already see the layout as an open-plan office: meeting table in front of the window to make the most of the view, filing cabinets in the corner – she would even buy one of those trendy coffee machines to put in the kitchen area. The bedroom could be her own private office, just change the door for one with a glass panel, and the shower room . . . Well, a quick scrub and it would be fine – shell pink, but fine. She might just get rid of the 'his and hers' toothbrush holders . . .

'Only one bedroom, but that makes it more attractive, I think. Very common now, living on your own.' Colin was still wittering on.

'Could you operate a business from up here?' Sarah demanded.

310

'I'd have to check.' Colin sighed as if he had better things to do with his time, but dutifully made a note.

'Will the owners split the lease, do you think?' She crossed her fingers behind her back and held her breath. The lease was for the shop *and* flat. She only needed the flat.

Colin Hanley sucked in his breath sharply. 'Unlikely; there's another interested party who would take the lot. That proposal *is* for a café. They've got a meeting with the planners next week. They've asked me not to tell the owners yet, until they know the result of that meeting.'

'Oh.' Her heart sank a little as she followed him back downstairs. 'It would make a lovely café.'

'Yes. Prime retail space, this,' he said, slapping his hand on the underside of the staircase, sending a cloud of loose plaster dust into his hair.

'So I see,' said Sarah, coughing. 'But in any case, I'll give you my card.'

She rummaged round in her handbag for a business card but could only find one of Zac's baby flashcards with a dog on it. She really must get round to sorting this bag out. 'Never mind. If I put together a proposal for your clients, would you be so kind as to forward it to them?'

The estate agent gave her a smile that couldn't have been more patronizing if he'd patted her on the head. 'Of course. But don't get your hopes up.'

'Fine,' Sarah lied. Her hopes were well and truly up and ready to fly . . .

Chapter 32

Two hours later the sun was still shining and Sarah and Dave were nearly ready for Zac's party.

Thank goodness it's a nice day, thought Sarah, frantically flicking a tea towel over plastic garden chairs; trying to shoehorn everyone inside Rose Cottage would have been a nightmare if it had rained.

Dave emerged from the kitchen wearing an apron over his shorts and T-shirt and carrying a tray of large utensils.

'Is it time to get this on, do you think?' She lifted the lid on the new stainless-steel barbecue and peered at the charcoal that Dave had already piled up.

'Step aside,' he said, puffing his chest out. 'This is man's work.'

She laughed. 'I'll leave you to it. Oh, by the way, Jo's coming and she's bringing a man.'

'Phew, says I, on behalf of the men of Woodby.' He grinned at her and added some chunks of firelighter to the charcoal.

Sarah went into the kitchen, smiling as she heard Dave singing 'Maneater' loudly to himself. Things had been so much better between them since Zac's hospital scare. The air had been well and truly cleared and she felt like they were both on the same team again. They had agreed that Dave would start rebuilding his decorating business, starting with a big contract for some show homes that he had picked up in the pub last week. And when she returned to work on Monday, she would be handing in her notice at Finch and Partners to focus on her new business idea.

Her own accountancy practice; the very thought sent shivers down her spine. She knew exactly how she wanted to run it: every client would be made to feel special, no matter how small; she would give each job as much time as it needed (profit notwithstanding – Jo had taught her that); and most importantly, the family would come first. Flexibility, as Heather had said, was the key.

All she had to do was keep her fingers crossed that the other party interested in the post office changed their minds and took their café plans elsewhere, and that she could convince the owners of the post office to split the lease.

She paused from chopping cucumber into toddler-sized sticks and strained her ears. Zac had woken up from his nap and was shouting for her. She dried her hands and went to fetch him. He had been in nursery that morning while both she and Dave were busy and Sarah had to admit, he did enjoy it. Rosie, his favourite nursery nurse, said he especially loved 'messy play', which basically entailed being stripped off to his nappy and smearing himself in jelly or shaving foam. At least he could indulge his creative flair outside of the cottage, Sarah thought, running a damp cloth along the stairs banister on her way up.

'Bababa,' said Zac, as Sarah carried him downstairs in his clean birthday-party outfit.

'Yes, we're going to blow up some balloons.' She dropped a kiss on his fluffy head. 'And Auntie Carrie's bringing you a cake. Any minute, hopefully.'

There was a knock at the door and Sarah opened it to see Carrie looking radiant in a coral-pink silk dress with a butterfly on it and holding her trademark bunch of flowers. Alex stood behind her beaming proudly, weighed down with bags and a Peppa Pig birthday cake.

'Look at you!' Sarah gasped, taking in Carrie's beaming smile. 'One gorgeous lady!'

Carrie blushed. 'This old thing. Happy birthday, Zac. Let's have a birthday cuddle.' She swapped the flowers for Zac and kissed his cheek.

'Come in, come in,' cried Sarah, ushering them into the hallway which had been de-cluttered for the occasion.

Alex went into the garden to help Dave, and Carrie and Sarah stared at them for a few moments through the kitchen window.

'We are so lucky, aren't we?' sighed Sarah, looping her arm through Carrie's.

Carrie nodded. 'If only Jo could meet someone.'

'Ooh, I forgot to tell you,' said Sarah with a twinkle in her eye. 'I've had a text. She's bringing Patrick to the party!'

'Do you think she's a bit in love with him?' said Carrie slyly.

Sarah lifted a shoulder. 'Not sure, and I don't think even she can answer that one.'

Sarah and Dave had only invited about twenty adults plus children, but the garden was full to bursting with bodies. Their first party and it was going really well; Sarah grabbed three glasses of Prosecco and headed for Jo and Carrie.

'Cheers!' She chinked her glass against theirs. They had commandeered a section of the garden wall to perch on and Sarah sank down for a rest gratefully.

'This has worked out splendidly for me in the end.' Jo smiled wickedly. 'I wouldn't have been able to drink if I hadn't got Patrick as a chauffeur.' She sighed and took a long sip. 'You don't mind him tagging along, do you?'

'We're delighted you've brought a plus one.' Sarah swapped a gleeful glance with Carrie. 'Does this mean . . . ?'

'No it does not,' said Jo tartly. 'We've come from a meeting together, that's all. Probably too little too late, but Patrick has taken it upon himself to launch a one-man rescue plan for Gold's. He set up an appointment with some dusty old government department about exports. And that is all there is to it.'

She sniffed, signalling the end of the matter.

The little garden was a suntrap and the women fell into a contented silence as they basked in the heat. Dave was a little bit red-faced but still expertly churning out burgers, ribs and sausages for the children. He even had a veggie selection for Sarah and Rebecca. She had a lot more in common with Rebecca than she could have imagined, she mused, watching as Rebecca wiped Ava's hands with a wet-wipe. Alex, the self-appointed barman, had become a hit with the older children by mixing non-alcoholic cocktails and decorating beakers with fruit, parasols and straws.

Patrick had manfully blown up the paddling pool that Jo had bought Zac for his birthday and was entertaining the little ones by bouncing them in turn down the slide and into the water.

Jo was observing Patrick playing with the children with a look of pure happiness across her face. Sarah nudged Carrie and they exchanged conspiratorial looks. Jo turned back to them to speak and narrowed her eyes.

'Oh, seriously,' she huffed. 'Don't even go there.'

Carrie and Sarah held up their hands in mock surrender. 'Whatever!' said Sarah.

Jo could protest all she liked, but there was definitely something in the air.

'So tell me about this personal shopper, then?' said Jo, refusing to be drawn.

They listened as Carrie regaled them with the whole litany of misunderstandings between her and Alex, which seemingly had started as soon as they'd met, and how she had spent a whole day with a personal shopper who had educated her on shopping for her body shape and totally revamped her wardrobe. Carrie was so bubbly and happy; it was a pleasure to watch. Especially as her eyes kept darting over to Alex with unconcealed adoration.

'Well, you look amazing,' said Jo, raising her glass again.

Carrie tugged at her dress self-consciously. 'I do feel

better about myself. And my marriage. And you know what, I've realized something about my wish. I don't need to lose weight to wear a bikini, I'm never going to be a stick insect like you – no offence, Jo.'

'Obviously.' Jo smirked.

'I should simply be myself and be happy in my own skin.' She paused and pulled a face. 'Well, that's what I keep telling myself, anyway.'

'That's the best news I've heard for weeks.' Sarah hugged her and thought how fortunate she was to have such a lovely friend living so close by.

'Talking of news,' Carrie continued, 'I'm thinking about going back to floristry properly.'

'She's fantastic with flowers,' confirmed Jo with a nod. 'You should see her garden.'

'I've had more requests to do flowers for events. So I'm going to ease myself back into it gently.' Carrie looked down at her knees shyly.

'Good for you,' smiled Sarah. 'I could do with your green fingers in this little patch; the flowers have just been growing wild this year.'

'Gladly,' said Carrie. 'Although I think you might have a little helper already. Look.'

The other two turned to follow her gaze; Zac was on his knees pulling the heads off all the marigolds in the border.

They laughed and Sarah began to top up their glasses when there was a loud splash followed by some loud bawling. Ava had fallen face first into the paddling pool and given herself a shock.

'No harm done, my little mermaid,' laughed Rebecca as she fished her out.

Sarah jumped up to fetch a towel and topped Rebecca's glass up too. She returned to her spot a few minutes later.

'I have news too,' she said, fizzing with excitement. 'I'm leaving Finch and Partners; I'm going to set up my own accountancy practice.'

'That's fab,' said Jo, 'and I'm sure your dad would have been even more proud of you for striking out on your own than if you'd been promoted at Finch and Partners.'

Sarah's stomach did a little flip. There was an image of her dad's angry face seared into her memory banks and it had just as powerful an impact on her now as it had when she was eighteen.

'You're wasting your time,' he'd said harshly, dropping her off at the coach station for her first term at university. 'And you're a fool to turn down that apprenticeship at the hairdresser's I got for you.'

She'd tried telling him that she could scarcely tame her own curls and that surely her straight As in every mathematics exam she'd ever taken told a different story? But he wouldn't listen. He'd managed all right without a fancy degree, he'd said, and she'd be married with kids before long anyway so what was the point?

She'd spent every day of her life since proving him wrong.

'Me and my dad . . .' She swallowed, trying to find the right words. 'Let's just say he wasn't exactly a feminist. When Dad was made redundant from the local pit along with the other miners, Mum got a job for a few hours a day in the corner shop to help make ends meet. When he found out, he came in and dragged her out by her hair, accusing her of showing him up in public. Everyone would think he couldn't support his own family.' She popped an olive into her mouth and looked away, her stomach trembling at the memory of her mum's silent tears.

'God, Sarah, I had no idea,' said Carrie, rubbing her arm.

'Sounds like a right charmer.' Jo frowned. 'Did your mum leave him?'

Sarah shook her head. 'Amazingly, no, she adored him. When he died of a stroke, she passed away six months later of a broken heart.'

'So when you said you wanted to be a partner, was that to spite your dad or did you mean it?' Carrie asked.

'You've hit the nail on the head,' Sarah replied with a rueful smile.

She looked across the garden to see Patrick holding Zac's hands and supporting him while he tiptoed over the grass and her heart twisted. Her dad had been the motivation behind many of her actions. She had even cut her maternity leave short knowing that he would have expected her to give up work completely once Zac came along.

'Jo, I owe you an apology. When you admitted that you'd told a white lie about your wish, you asked whether anyone else had not been quite truthful with their wish. You were right. Even back then I was having my doubts that striving to be a partner was the right thing for us as a family, but sticking a metaphorical two fingers up at Dad had been my driving force for so long that it clouded my judgement. But really that job was squeezing the joy from me.'

It sounded ridiculous when she said it out loud. At least now she'd recognized it for what it was: a meaningless goal that had caused more harm than good.

'So I hope nobody minds,' she said with a surge of pride, 'but I'm changing my wish, I'm no longer going to let my dad rule my life.'

Jo lifted her glass. 'Bloody hell. I'm with you on that. Cheers!'

'So my next move is to find premises.'

She told them about wanting to move into the flat above the old post office and turn it into an office, if only the other party didn't get in there first.

'They won't get planning permission for a café,' said Carrie, reaching for the crudités to nibble on.

Sarah frowned. 'What makes you so sure?'

'The owners tried that themselves a couple of years ago.' She crunched on a carrot stick. 'Got turned down. Planners said there wasn't enough parking and it would result in congestion or something like that.'

Sarah stared at her open-mouthed. This was brilliant news, particularly as something Carrie had said sparked an even more amazing idea. The sensible thing to do would be to mull it over and consider this brainwave from every angle. But knickers to that.

Sarah's face broke into a broad smile. 'Carrie, are you free next Friday?'

Carrie nodded, intrigued.

'Good. There's something I'd like to show you,' Sarah said mysteriously. 'But now it's time for birthday cake.'

Chapter 33

From: SarahDaveZac
To: Jo Gold (work)
CC: Carriebikinibod@gmail.com

Guess what?? Carrie and I have got a surprise for you!
Can you meet us on Friday night in Woodby at the old
post office?

From: Jo Gold (work)

Will there be wine? If so, yes.

From: Carriebikinibod@gmail.com
To: Jo Gold (work)

There'll be champagne. You OK, Jo?

From: Jo Gold (work)
To: Carriebikinibod@gmail.com; SarahDaveZac

Absolutely marvellous. Not. Time is running out for
Gold's and I'm running out of ideas.

Jo came back from a quick lunch break to find Ed Shaw
waiting in her office.

'Hello?' She summoned up a polite smile.

'Surprise!' he said with a boyish grin.

On balance, she decided, after an awkward air kiss, it was not a nice surprise. Three weeks had gone by since the meeting with the Department of Trade and Industry on the day of Zac's party, and as much as she recognized that government departments had to be thorough, unless they hurried up, she was going to run out of time for the export of Gold's Footwear to have any impact on her September deadline. And seeing Ed's perky smile was like rubbing salt into a particularly nasty wound.

'No Patrick today?' said Ed, ignoring the chair that Jo pointed him to.

Jo shook her head. 'He's at a meeting.'

With the bank. Trying to negotiate a bigger overdraft – thanks to Shaw's.

'All set for the big launch, then?' He rubbed his hands together gleefully.

She gave him a tight smile. She couldn't for the life of her see why she had been so enamoured with him when they'd first met. He was aiming for the casual, nonchalant look, but in truth he was simply scruffy. Designer brands maybe but still scruffy. A crumpled Ralph Lauren polo shirt hung loosely over a pair of marked Armani jeans. Even his Paul Smith brogues needed a polish.

'The three-month exclusivity period plus the impending departure of our operations director has hit us where it hurts, Ed,' she said, forcing herself to keep her voice calm.

He irritated her with his lazy smile and the way he was wandering around her office picking up her things, studying them and putting them back down in the wrong place.

'I don't know what your father would have thought of the way you're doing business,' she said, folding her arms, 'but I know mine won't be impressed.'

Ed laughed. 'Don't tell me you still go running to Daddy with your problems?'

She bit back a retort and clenched her fists. She was so close to telling him where to stick his order.

'You'll have to make do with just the shoes for September; the boots will follow in October. And our credit terms are strictly twenty-eight days. Any later and Shaw's forfeits the exclusivity.'

Ed's eyes widened and he sucked his breath in sharply. 'Twenty-eight days is a bit steep. We might not have sold many shoes by then.'

'Maybe not,' said Jo, tilting up her chin, 'but we will have bought the materials and manufactured the shoes, packaged them and delivered them to you. Besides, you promised Patrick a glitzy advertising campaign; don't you have faith in your ability to turn that into sales?'

Ed set down the paperweight that he had been throwing carelessly from one hand to the other and dropped down into the chair opposite Jo.

'Thing is, Jo,' he said silkily, 'with all this new shop fit expenditure, our cash flow is taking a real bashing.'

'*Your* cash flow?' retorted Jo. 'Look at this!' She pulled a folder towards her and flicked through the pages. Showing a customer her financial statements was unorthodox, but she couldn't see another way of getting through his thick skull.

'These are our set-up costs to produce the Josephine Gold collection.' She jabbed the paper with a manicured finger and flicked on to the next page.

'This is the price of the logo and packaging design.' She turned the page once more.

'And these are the unit costs to make each shoe, which due to the very small numbers, are exceptionally high.'

She snapped the folder shut, making him jump. 'So don't you tell me about cash flow. I'm sorry, Ed, you've done a great job with Shaw's but restricting sales of our new collection to your stores this autumn is crippling us.'

Ed sat back in his chair and rubbed his nose. 'I can see

your dilemma. Actually, I wanted to talk to you . . . Um, any chance of a coffee?'

Liz was in with a tray of coffee and biscuits before Jo could say 'caffeine fix'. She set it on the desk and gave Jo an encouraging wink.

Jo sipped her coffee and watched as Ed swirled a biscuit around in his mug, lifting it out at the last second before it disintegrated. He shoved it in his mouth whole and gave her a cheeky grin.

All right, maybe he was attractive. But he was still married and after seeing the damage that even *thinking* their husbands had been unfaithful had done to Carrie and Sarah, Jo had turned over a new leaf in that regard. No more married men. Ever.

In fact, from now on, she'd only date men who'd give her all their attention; she wasn't interested in sharing. She wanted someone to love and who'd love her in return. God, she was beginning to sound like Carrie . . .

'Jo? Hello?' Ed waved a hand in front of her face and laughed. 'I said, I might have been overzealous with the exclusivity demands.'

He reached for another biscuit and glanced at Jo sheepishly.

'You think?' she said, giving him a loaded stare.

'Look. This is my first proper season of buying shoes. It has been quite good fun, placing orders,' he admitted. 'I thought insisting that we were the only ones allowed to sell your new stuff made good business sense. But you're right. Dad wouldn't be impressed with me making these sorts of demands. I mean, what difference does it make to Shaw's if your range is available in London or Bristol? We haven't even got branches there.'

Jo felt her mouth go dry. She liked the way this conversation was going and hardly dared speak in case she ruined it.

'So . . .' Ed spread his hands out on the desk in a gesture of peace. 'I know it's probably too late to be of any use, but I retract the exclusivity requirement.'

'Thanks,' said Jo shakily, letting out a breath. 'You're right, it might be too late, but I really appreciate it. It just might make the difference we need.'

He shrugged and his humble moment was over. 'To be honest, in the cities where we operate, our stores are so much better than the competition that frankly there *is* no competition, some of them are so out-dated that—'

'Well, thank you again,' Jo interrupted. She needed to get rid of him straight away. There was no time to lose; they would get everyone on the phones, even the workroom. Cesca could design an eye-catching mail-out and they'd email it to all the independents today . . .

'Am I forgiven now?' He smirked at her. 'I'm surprised my coffee hasn't frozen over with the icy looks you've been giving me.'

Her lips started to twitch. He was such a charmer. But no, he wasn't forgiven. There was something else he had done, something that had hurt even more than the exclusivity demands . . .

'Not quite.' She gave him a steely glare. 'Why poach my staff?'

Ed looked shifty. He exhaled at length, ran his fingers through his unruly brown hair and then folded his arms, mirroring Jo's defensive posture.

'He's the best in the business, but then you already know that,' he said simply. 'I'll see myself out.'

Jo showed Ed to her office door, his words running over and over in her mind on a loop. They shook hands. Ed reached the end of the corridor and pushed open the door to the reception area. He looked back at her and lifted a hand.

'And I thought I was doing you both a favour,' he said with a grin.

She gasped with frustration. 'Favour. Are you kidding me?'

'You know what they say.' He tipped her a tiny wink. 'Absence makes the heart grow fonder.'

She watched him cross the car park, wondering what the

hell he was talking about. Whatever, she didn't have time to dwell on Ed Shaw's games. She charged down the corridor to Liz's office.

'Can you get everyone together, please?' she said to her startled secretary. 'Staff meeting. Five minutes! Oh, and check how long Patrick is going to be. Thanks,' she finished with a grin.

Jo dashed back to her own desk and pulled the phone towards her. August might be a bit late in the day to sell in the autumn range, but if she were to stand a chance of showing her father a profit by September, she owed it to the whole team to try.

Later that evening, Jo called goodbye to Abi, closed the door to her friend's cottage and set off along Main Street to the old post office, armed with a bottle of Prosecco.

Abi and Tom had just arrived back from Australia and looked sunkissed and happy, or at least Tom did. Underneath Abi's tan Jo detected deep-rooted grief suggesting that she was far from over losing Fréd. Unsurprising really; Fréd had been there all Abi's adult life. Coming back to the home they'd built together had hit her hard. All Jo could do was be there; to listen, to lend a shoulder to cry on, but that didn't feel like much and seeing her friend so sad had taken the edge off her own good mood after the most positive day she'd had at work for weeks.

Still, she had no doubt that Sarah and Carrie would cheer her up; Sarah had sounded so excited on the phone earlier. She stopped outside the post office and smiled. It didn't take a genius to work out what the news was and Jo felt inordinately proud of her.

She peered through the windows expecting to see Sarah hopping around like a woodland sprite, but the place was oddly deserted. She pushed the door open and a bell tinkled above her head, but there was still no one in sight.

'Hello?' Her heels echoed on the tiled floor as she stepped into the shop.

Upstairs a cork popped and two familiar voices shouted, 'Surprise!'

Two sets of rapid footsteps then charged down the stairs. Carrie appeared first, her face wreathed in smiles. Jo couldn't help but smile back; Carrie was so different these days to the awkward mouse she'd met in January. Sarah was right behind her.

'Welcome to the new commercial hub of Woodby,' Sarah cried, pouring them each a glass of champagne. 'You're our first visitor.'

'Thank you,' said Jo with a laugh, raising her glass. 'Congratulations!'

'This is going to be my very own florist's,' said Carrie, waving an arm around the space.

Jo's jaw dropped. 'Wow, really?'

'And I'm converting the flat upstairs into an accountancy practice,' added Sarah, doing a little shimmy.

Jo laughed. They were already halfway to becoming a double act. 'Congratulations to both of you. I'm seriously impressed.' She clinked her glass to theirs. 'Come on, then, tell me more.'

The evening sun cast a golden glow through the shop's windows. Jo leaned on the old post office counter and Sarah wiped the dust from the low windowsill and perched on it as Carrie darted here and there, demonstrating what she was going to do with the place.

'I'm going to leave the counter where it is, but take out the glass panels,' she explained. 'I can keep the cash register there and do the arrangements and stuff along this area. The shop is quite shady so the flowers can go in buckets in the windows. Over here, I thought I might sell a few greetings cards, you know, to go with the flowers.' She waved her arm towards one wall and then stood back with her hands on her hips, looking totally exhilarated. 'And I'm going to do online orders too.'

Jo sipped her champagne. Carrie was so excited and she

was delighted for them both. Absolutely. She was. But their success served to highlight her own lack of progress.

Everything seemed to be going to plan for Carrie and Sarah. Their wishes might have altered over the last few months, but they had both managed to change their lives for the better. She, however, was still in the same place as she had been when they met: a workaholic, with a non-existent love life and an annoying fear of heights. She had given up smoking, she supposed, but to be honest, she hadn't been a heavy smoker anyway. Although she could do with one now.

Sarah linked her arm through Carrie's. 'What do you think?'

Jo raised her nearly-empty glass.

'I think it's bloody amazing!' She grinned, bemused. 'When did this all happen? Five minutes ago Carrie was going to start up slowly and this place was on its way to becoming a café.'

'Carrie was right,' said Sarah happily. 'As soon as the owners knew that the potential tenants wanted to apply for planning for a café, they rejected their offer. I couldn't afford to rent the whole place, just for my accountancy business—'

'So she asked me to go halves,' Carrie finished off.

Sarah giggled. 'Anyone would think I'd asked her to jump off a cliff naked. It took Dave, me *and* Alex to persuade her, over dinner, to give it a go. The lease is initially for twelve months. If it doesn't work out, we don't renew it.' She shrugged casually.

A pang of jealousy prodded at Jo's heart. *Over dinner.* She tried to tell herself it didn't matter. She realized it was childish, but she felt left out. *Would they have invited me if I was one half of a couple?* she wondered.

'Good for you, Carrie.' She plastered on a smile. 'Show me upstairs, then.'

After a tour of the delights of the shell-pink bathroom and small bedroom, they settled into three deckchairs, on loan from Carrie's garden.

Carrie ripped the foil off a second bottle, giggling nervously in case the cork made a bid for the ceiling. Jo noted her long eyelashes, radiant smile and high cheekbones. She had always thought Carrie was a natural beauty, but being in such a happy place had highlighted her good looks even more.

Sarah had come clean about her hidden motivation to be so ambitious, Jo had admitted her penchant for happy-ever-afters, and yet she couldn't ignore the feeling that Carrie was still hiding something. Why had she taken so long to do something with her life?

She accepted a refill from Carrie and took a fortifying gulp.

'It's great to see you so positive about life, Carrie, but what I don't understand,' she said gently, 'is what led you to be unhappy in the first place? You had a lovely husband, beautiful house and yet . . .'

'Yeah,' Sarah added, frowning with curiosity. 'You were practically a hermit when we met.'

Carrie shrank back immediately and Jo's heart sank, worried that they had probed too much, but to her surprise, after a moment's hesitation, she spoke up.

'My unhappiness started at university, when I met a boy called Ryan Cunningham.'

With the help of the rest of the champagne and an entire packet of tissues, Carrie filled them in on the regretful night out at university that had defined the next thirteen years of her life. The one-night stand that had resulted in an unwanted pregnancy, an abortion she bitterly regretted and the unborn baby she had grieved for ever since.

'I had no one to turn to.' Carrie sniffed, twisting a tissue round in her hands. 'My friends were all still partying and having fun and I felt detached from everyone, even from myself. I dropped out of uni to try to shake the depression, to force myself to start afresh. And it worked, sort of. But until I started hypnotherapy, I'd never forgiven myself.'

'But what about when you got married,' Sarah asked softly, reaching for Carrie's hand. 'Didn't Alex help?'

She nodded. 'He loved me and that made me feel better about myself to begin with, but then I saw a way to cut myself off from real life by retreating to being a homemaker. His own mum worked hard but was never very homely. So I cooked, I looked after him and I made our house a home – and Alex loved that. But along the way I lost my purpose, my identity. She'd have been twelve now. A girl on the cusp of becoming a woman, friends of her own. A life of her own.'

The sun had sunk from the sky and Jo sat in the shadows, united with Sarah in their sadness at Carrie's story.

'Why didn't you tell us?' asked Jo quietly.

Carrie shrugged nervously. 'You two are such strong independent women. When we met and decided to start a wish list, I saw an opportunity to start living my life to the full again. But I thought if I told you the truth, you wouldn't want to know me. Especially you, Sarah, being a mum. So I guess we all told a bit of a white lie.'

Jo and Carrie smiled at each other.

'You daft thing! Of course I would have wanted to know you.' Sarah leapt up and threw her arms around Carrie's neck. 'Anyway, can you remember how desperate I was to meet people back then? I would have made friends with an axe murderer given half a chance.'

Jo snorted into her champagne.

Sarah clapped a hand over her mouth. 'Not that you— I didn't mean it like that, Carrie. That came out all wrong.'

Carrie burst out laughing. 'Remind me about your impeccable people skills again?'

Suddenly all three of them were laughing hysterically and Jo could have kissed them both for lifting her out of her bad mood. They were possibly the most unlikely friends, but, she realized, she loved them and was truly overjoyed to see them doing so well.

'But . . .' Sarah began and then bit her lip. 'Forget it.'

'Go on,' said Carrie. 'Ask me anything, I quite literally have no more secrets.'

Sarah looked dubious. 'OK. Well, I was going to say that you're still young enough to have children if you wanted to.'

Carrie went pink and nodded. 'I told Alex about the abortion when we met and said that I didn't want to go through anything like that again, that I couldn't see myself as a mother and he said that that was fine by him. We both admitted recently that in fact that's not true and we would like to give it a go. But even if we do, Sarah, I still want to be a florist, so don't worry.'

Sarah held her hands up. 'Not worried. I'd be thrilled for you both.'

Jo's heart twisted with happiness for her, even if there was a little twinge of jealousy mixed in there too.

'If it's not too un-PC,' she said, reaching for the Prosecco she'd brought with her, 'I think that deserves another toast. Oh, also, I just remembered . . .'

She delved into her handbag and tossed a small package wrapped in tissue paper and tied with ribbon into Carrie's lap. 'Catch!'

Carrie tore into the parcel to reveal a black and silver bikini. Jo had chosen something both elegant and flattering for the fuller figure. She held her breath, hoping Carrie approved.

'Do you like it?' she asked. 'Alex helped with the size.'

Carrie gasped. 'It's beautiful. But I don't think . . . I mean, I was a bit hasty.' Her cheeks had turned a delightful shade of rose pink and she wafted her face with her hands.

'A trip abroad in September, Alex tells me?' said Jo firmly. 'I'm really proud of you, Carrie. You're so close to making your wish come true.'

Carrie swallowed and nodded reluctantly.

'Thank you. I love it,' she said, giving Jo a hug.

'Next up. The village show,' announced Sarah. 'I thought I should enter something, as a way of introducing my new business to the village. Any ideas?'

'Yes, jam!' said Jo. 'Believe it or not, I've got some tips. I was in the pub the other night with an old friend from school and I overheard . . . What?'

Sarah and Carrie looked at each other and laughed.

'I do go to pubs without you two, you know,' Jo said, pretending to be offended.

'It's not that.' Sarah grinned.

'We just never expected to hear jam-making tips from Jo Gold,' said Carrie.

'I've surprised myself, to be honest,' Jo said wryly. 'Anyway, I overheard a group of women talking about some competition or other and one of them said that to win over the judges, you should put alcohol in your jam.'

'Ooh, now you're talking,' said Sarah, draining her glass. 'Champagne and strawberry jam maybe?'

'Or whisky and raspberries?' suggested Carrie.

Sarah thought about it for a moment. 'It would be nice to use some local produce. Did the woman in the pub say what she was making?'

Jo frowned. 'Yes! It was damson gin jam. That's quite hard to say after three glasses of champagne!'

'Damson gin jam,' the other two repeated with a giggle.

'Hey, it could become my sales gimmick,' said Sarah. She rifled through her handbag, extracted a notebook and jotted something down. 'You know: if you're ever in a financial jam, come and see Sarah Hudson. I could put a proper logo on the jar.'

'Perfect, so damson gin jam it is,' said Carrie, clapping her hands. 'Who's got damsons we can pick?'

'There's probably a tree in Abi's orchard. I'll ask her when I get back.' Jo looked at her watch. She ought to get back to Abi's; it felt rude to be staying over at her friend's house and not spend the evening with her.

'Gosh, how is Abi? I feel awful for not asking earlier,' said Carrie, frowning.

'OK, all things considered,' said Jo with a sigh. 'Very tanned. A bit anxious, though. Tom starts school next month and I don't think she knows what she'll do with herself then.'

'She can join our gang,' said Carrie merrily. 'We'll have her making ridiculous wishes before she knows it. Mention it to her.'

That was a lovely thought. Jo's heart tweaked at Carrie's kind gesture.

'She must come out with us next time, if she feels up to it,' Sarah added. 'Send her my love. I did call round this afternoon, but there was no one home.'

'I will.' Jo stood up and gave them both a kiss. 'I'd better go. Abi's cooking me dinner.'

'Are you growing your hair?' asked Sarah, studying her closely.

'No . . . Well, yes, a bit.' Jo's hands fluttered self-consciously up to her fringe and pulling it across her forehead.

'Very girlie,' said Sarah.

Carrie nodded. 'Much softer; it suits you.'

'It's part of my new persona,' Jo said flatly. 'Seeing as the old one wasn't working.'

'Oh, I don't know.' Sarah looked slyly at Carrie. 'Patrick seems very smitten.'

'Whoa.' Jo held her hands up. 'He's a colleague. At most a friend. That's as far as it goes.'

Carrie smiled at her. 'Well, I think he's lovely.'

'No, I mean it,' Jo warned, aware that her heart had just speeded up. 'I don't want to talk about Patrick. He leaves next month and I don't think I can bear it.'

She felt her throat tighten and made a show of checking her mobile phone, pretending not to notice as Carrie and Sarah exchanged the most unsubtle nods and winks.

'Have you tried telling him how you feel?' asked Carrie.

Jo chewed her lip and shook her head. Admit her feelings to Patrick McGregor? She wasn't sure she was ready to admit those to herself yet.

Chapter 34

It was bank holiday Monday in August, and the English weather had lived up to its reputation with the utmost accuracy. The pavement was shiny with recent rain and a vindictive wind was blowing the first autumn leaves up and down in relentless spirals. But that hadn't deterred the people of Woodby and thereabouts from turning out for the annual event of the year. The village hall car park was overflowing and the roads either side were lined with cars as far as the eye could see. Sarah clutched Dave's arm as he wove the pushchair through the parked cars.

'I look ridiculous in this flowery dress and my face looks like rice pudding,' Sarah pouted. 'My hair is so frizzy that it actually looks like it has been in a fire and it's *cold*. It's still August, why is it so cold?'

'It's not that cold. Your body is in shock, that's all.'

She glanced up at his handsome face and the smile he gave her plucked at her heart.

'Oh, Dave. I do love you,' she said, squeezing his arm tightly. 'Thank you for coming to my rescue.'

'I love helping out a damson in distress.'

'Funny.' She managed a smile. 'If my head wasn't banging quite so hard, I'd laugh.'

Zac spotted a dog on the other side of the road and started to shriek. Sarah clutched her head in pain. She was sure the entire cast of *Riverdance* were in there having a dance-off.

Images of her drunken self head-banging to heavy metal round the kitchen last night kept creeping up on her. She remembered straining off some of the gin, dancing round the bubbling vat of jam, pretending to be a witch and taking quite a few sips of the damson-infused liquor. After that it was all a bit fuzzy. She shuddered. She would never drink gin again. Or eat damsons. Jam was possibly a no-go zone too.

At nine thirty this morning, the time that entries had to be delivered, she had still been sleeping off her hangover. If it hadn't been for Dave who ran down to the village hall and entered on her behalf, she would have missed the deadline altogether.

She had woken up at ten, with jam on her face, in her hair, and even on the bedroom floor. The kitchen had come off worse: every surface was sticky, the unwashed jam pan lay abandoned in the sink and a row of rejected unlabelled jars filled to various levels had glued themselves to the table.

'Looks like the whole village is out in force,' said Dave. 'It'll be a good opportunity to speak to people about your new business.'

Sarah grunted. 'Can't speak at all at the moment.'

The sky was as grey as her mood. She was so cross with herself. Dave was right: this should have been her big moment. In her mind's eye she had seen herself skipping gaily through the hall with a wicker basket on her arm, buying cakes and plants and exchanging friendly gossip with her neighbours, along the lines of, 'Yes, I'll be opening my new accountancy business in September.' Or, 'Of course I'd be happy to help you with your tax return, pop in any time.' And then, of course, 'First prize for my jam? Me? I don't know what to say!'

In reality, she could barely stop shaking, she didn't have the energy to walk around the stalls and the only words on her lips were: 'Pass me a bucket.'

Dave deposited her at a table with a cup of tea and a scone and tactfully whisked Zac off to the face-painting stall where Abi was turning a little girl into Batman. Tom was already sporting a black-and-white Dalmatian face. Sarah caught her eye and waved. She'd go over later and have a chat with Abi. Just as soon as she felt a bit more human.

'Hi, Sarah, guess what?' Carrie dropped into the chair next to her, elegant and tanned in a cream shift dress and matching cardigan. 'Oh heavens! What happened to you?' She recoiled in horror at the sight of Sarah's face. 'You look green!'

'That lethal damson gin jam happened, that's what!' Sarah groaned.

Carrie bit her lip apologetically. 'So sorry I couldn't help you, we only got back from holiday yesterday and I've been up to my eyes in the floral displays for the show.'

'S'all right,' sighed Sarah. She slurped her tea as a thought occurred to her. 'Did you wear your bikini?'

Carrie wriggled uncomfortably in her seat. 'Only in our room.' She leaned forward and whispered, 'I felt a bit, you know, overexposed.'

'Pictures?' asked Sarah. 'Because if there's no evidence . . .'

Carrie twisted her wedding ring round. 'I'll have to check with Alex,' she mumbled.

'You are such a poor liar!' Sarah rolled her eyes, feeling slightly better. 'I have such an awful hangover,' she confided. 'Promise me you'll never let me touch gin ever again?'

'OK, promise. Now come and have a look at the prizes!'

Sarah's resistance was no match for Carrie's exuberance and they were soon wandering amongst the locally grown produce, giggling at the size of Mr Ogden's marrow and marvelling at the handmade corn dollies.

'You're the two girls taking on the old post office, then?' asked a whiskery elderly man. His unlit pipe bobbed between his lips as he spoke. 'Good to see the place opening up again. Well done.' He lifted his pipe in a salute and nodded.

Sarah raised her eyebrows in surprise at Carrie.

'Nothing stays secret in this village for long,' Carrie laughed. 'Which reminds me, Rebecca wants to talk to you about going self-employed and what to do about tax and stuff. I said you'd go and find her later.'

'OK, thanks. My first customer!' This was going far better than she expected. The people in the village were lovely. Such community spirit! The veil of cloud began to lift from Sarah's head and she squeezed Carrie's arm tightly. 'I'm so glad we did this wish list. It has really made me realize what is important to me. Well, eventually, anyway.'

'Our two businesswomen!' exclaimed the lady running the secondhand book stall. 'Congratulations, both of you! Good luck.'

Another woman pricked up her ears and waved at them. 'Ah now,' she cried.

Sarah shot Carrie a quizzical look.

'Marjorie from the Women's Institute,' hissed Carrie. 'Be very afraid and don't agree to anything.'

'Ladies!' Marjorie beamed at them. 'I hear that we have two entrepreneurs in our midst. Can I put you down to come and talk at our October meeting?'

'I'm not sure I'd be any good at public speaking,' stammered Carrie.

'Absolutely!' said Sarah, ignoring Carrie's frantic gurning. 'We would love to.'

Carrie laughed nervously as the woman recorded their contact details on her clipboard.

'Don't worry,' Sarah whispered, 'I've had loads of practice at that sort of thing. I'll do the talking and you can do a flower-arranging demonstration or something. At this rate, we won't need to do any advertising!' She sighed happily and linked her arm through her friend's as they walked away, suddenly aware that her nausea had vanished.

'Here's my advertising,' said Carrie proudly. 'What do you think?'

They had reached the floral displays. There were six different categories arranged along one long trestle table.

'You are so talented.' Sarah gasped as she moved along the table, reading the placings, which were written on cardboard stars. Carrie's entries had come first in five of the categories and second in the sixth.

'Second place, Carrie?' she said with a tut. 'What happened there?'

Carrie nudged her playfully. 'I've already had a request to do the flowers for a ball in October,' she said happily, her cheeks calming down to a more pleasing pink. 'I'm so excited.'

'Well done you,' said Sarah. 'Oh! Does this mean the prizes have been announced for the jam too? Come on!'

She dragged Carrie over to the preserves table as fast as she could without wishing to appear too eager. She spotted her own nearly black jar of jam from a distance.

'It's half empty!' she squeaked, squeezing Carrie's arm. 'That's got to be a good sign.'

'I've come second,' said Abi, squeezing between them. She looped her blonde hair behind her ears and smiled wistfully. 'It was Fréd's recipe for raspberry conserve; he'd have been really proud.'

'Congratulations,' said Carrie, plonking a kiss on her cheek.

Sarah beamed at her. 'And I bet you didn't trash your entire kitchen making it, did you?'

'Thanks,' said Abi. 'So how did you do?'

Sarah pulled a face and picked up the card next to her jar of jam.

'You've got to be kidding,' she gasped, reading the judges' comments.

'Third!' cried Carrie, looking over her shoulder. 'Oh, well done.'

'No, that's not what I mean, look! It's not my jam, apparently!' Sarah jabbed her finger at the name on the card: Dave Hudson.

Abi bit her lip and looked at Carrie. 'Whoops.'

After all that effort, pricking three million damsons with a cocktail stick, soaking them in gin for a week and boiling them up into a gloopy mess, not to mention the crippling headache she had incurred as a result of rigorous tasting, her husband had muscled in at the last moment and stolen her glory.

'He entered the jam as his own. The cheeky . . . Oh, speak of the devil.' Sarah folded her arms and gave her husband a pointed look as he arrived carrying a mini Spider-Man.

'I hope that face paint is all right?' said Abi nervously. 'I haven't done anyone that small before.'

'It's fab.' Sarah chuckled despite herself. Zac had a red and black spider's web on his forehead and cheeks, white eyes and a little black spider on his nose.

'Mama!' yelled Zac, wriggling in his father's arms.

'Aw, cute,' said Carrie anxiously.

Sarah took Zac from Dave and stared at him.

'What?' asked Dave innocently, trying not to drop Zac.

'Thanks a bundle,' she harrumphed. 'You know how hard I've worked to make that . . . ffffflippin' jam!' She wouldn't swear in front of Zac, he was starting to repeat words. Only yesterday, she had heard him say something that sounded distinctly like 'bugger'. She had been mortified.

'Sarah, I haven't got the faintest idea what you're talking about.'

'*Your* name. *My* jam.' She waved the third-prize certificate under his nose.

'What? Not on purpose, the lady must have got the wrong end of the stick when I delivered it. She was very scary and I got a bit flustered.' He paled suddenly. 'Oh Christ, it's her.'

An officious-looking woman with steely grey hair propelled herself towards them at speed. She was wearing reading glasses that dangled from a string and bounced dangerously on her vast bosom.

'Sarah Hudson? Our new professional accountant?' the woman barked at her.

Sarah beamed, flattered to be recognized. 'Yes. And this is Carrie Radley, the professional florist.'

Carrie smiled shyly.

'I wonder if I could impose upon you to present our prizes in the children's category?'

'Me?' Sarah gasped. 'Why? I mean, I'd be happy to help, but why me?'

'It's the vicar's job usually,' explained the woman, 'but he's had to rush off for emergency dental treatment after breaking his tooth.'

'Oh, that's terrible,' said Carrie. 'How did he do that?'

The woman gave Dave a stern look. 'Mr Hudson failed to mention that he had left the damson stones in his jam.'

For one tiny fragment of a second, Sarah considered owning up to the jam's real provenance. But presenting awards, on the stage . . . being introduced as a professional . . . well, she felt like a local celebrity. It was probably best if she didn't make a fuss about the jam. After all, what was done was done.

'I'd be delighted.'

Carrie gave her the thumbs-up and smiled.

Sarah grinned. They were going into this new venture together; they should share this moment in the spotlight too. 'As long as Carrie can help,' she added.

The woman nodded, hooked her glasses on to the end of her nose and consulted her clipboard. 'Four awards, you can do two each.'

'But I do feel so sorry for the vicar. Dave!' Sarah shook her head at her husband, tongue wedged firmly in her cheek. 'What an oversight. How could you?'

'Please send my apologies to the vicar,' he said, feigning sincerity. 'It was my first batch; I'll know for next time.'

'Yes, well.' The woman hitched up her bosom and sniffed. 'This way please, Mrs Hudson, Mrs Radley, we must get a move on.' And she ushered them towards the stage.

'Apart from the damson stones,' asked Sarah, hurrying behind her, 'did the jam taste all right?'

The woman flicked her eyes at Dave and huffed. 'If it hadn't nearly broken the vicar's jaw, it would have been the star of the show!'

Sarah turned back to Dave, Carrie and Abi and punched the air.

'The Lord works in mysterious ways,' she whispered innocently.

Chapter 35

Jo waved a last goodbye to her father as he pulled out of the drop-off zone and made her way through the glass departures doors at Heathrow airport. *And breathe.* A ninety-minute car journey with Dad had done nothing for her stress levels.

Jo's mum had offered to drive her to the airport, and Jo had been looking forward to nothing more taxing than her mum's unsubtle reminders about body clocks and the usual newly single and totally adorable man she had found at the golf club. But at the last minute her mum said she felt unwell and had persuaded her husband to go in her place, thus forcing Jo and her dad to sort out their differences as they sped down the M1. Full of concern, Jo had called her mum who had apparently made a miraculous recovery and was busy shopping. The words 'stitched up' and 'kipper' came to mind.

Instead of gentle gossip, Jo had been subjected to a painful interrogation about the state of the company's cash flow and whether or not Jo could pull Gold's out of the red and into the black.

It had started off well: her dad had grunted with reluctant approval at the appointment of additional sales agents and the development of the new website. But Bob Gold wanted to see profit, which so far had remained elusive. Progress on that score seemed to be one step forward and two steps back. A major retail website had agreed to stock the Josephine Gold collection, but only if Gold's handled the shipping to consumers. They had been forced to turn the order down or the sales office would have spent half of their day parcelling up shoes. Then they had received a big order from Germany, only to find out that the cost of delivery wiped out virtually all their profit. It was maddening; Jo was trying so hard to lift the company out of the red and getting nowhere.

She cast her eye over the departures board, sought out the check-in desks for her British Airways flight to New York and marched off to join the queue.

Were her efforts enough to keep her father off her back?

Oh no. Not Bob Gold. He could have done better. *Obviously.*

Jo massaged her jaw; she must stop grinding her teeth. At her last visit to the dentist, he had threatened her with wearing a gum shield at night if she continued to gnash her teeth. That would be a passion killer if ever she had heard one. She could see it now:

'Goodnight, Jo, my little love muffin.'

'Ugg ugg slurp.'

No thanks.

Suitcase dealt with, boarding pass in hand, Jo sidestepped the holidaying family groups and headed for passport control. She switched her mobile phone to mute, slipped off her shoes and placed her watch and jacket in a plastic tray on the conveyor belt.

Looking on the bright side, i.e. charcoal grey as opposed to black, Dad had reduced his threat of returning to work from full time to one day a week. That was as close to an apology as she was ever going to get. Jo had remained tight-lipped when he delivered the news. Even coming in one day a week was effectively a vote of no confidence in his daughter.

'Cheer up, love,' said the security guard, beckoning her to come forward.

'What for?' she muttered crossly. She was thirty-four, more single than a Trappist monk and her own father was about to demote her. What, precisely, had she got to be cheerful about?

She tensed automatically as she walked through the X-ray machine. *Imagine if the machine could detect emotions: lonely, scared of heights, wants a baby . . .*

Jo inhaled sharply. It wouldn't do to start wallowing immediately before a lengthy flight; she wasn't an easy flier at the best of times. She collected her tray of belongings, turned her phone back on and perked up as two devastatingly handsome pilots crossed the concourse towards her.

Her mobile phone rattled in the tray. She tutted, glanced at the screen briefly and rejected the call. *Not now, Patrick, I'm busy*, she thought, turning her attention back to the uniformed pair.

'Ooh sorry!' she exclaimed, tripping over a pile of bags. She bumped into an old lady and dropped her passport. 'I wasn't watching where I was going.'

One of the pilots stopped in his tracks and picked up her passport. A whole scenario instantly flashed through Jo's mind in which the pilot, who of course would be the captain of her flight to JFK, upgraded her to Business Class, plied her with champagne and invited her to keep him company in the cockpit.

'Thanks, that's mine,' said Jo, catching his eye. She felt better already.

'Hello, er . . .' He flicked open her passport. Dammit, he was looking at her picture. Jo tried hard to maintain her smile even though her photograph bore more than a passing resemblance to Coco the Clown.

'Josephine.' He grinned and handed back the passport, reading her boarding card as he did so. 'Off to New York?'

She nodded and held his gaze as long as she could manage. 'You?'

He shrugged. 'Edinburgh.'

Bang goes that fantasy.

A tannoy announcement in the distance distracted her momentarily: 'Would passenger . . .'

The name sounded vaguely like hers but she dismissed it: she was travelling alone, hadn't lost anything and was locked in eye contact with a very attractive man. It was simply too good a moment to interrupt.

She gave him what she hoped was an enigmatic smile, affected her best slinky walk and set off in the direction of the bookshop.

I am such a flirt. She sighed under her breath, remembering too late that she was supposed to have turned over a new leaf where men were concerned, and went in search of the self-help book for acrophobia that Carrie had told her about.

Nine hours later Jo had safely landed in New York. She aimed a kick at her suitcase, moving it along to keep up with the immigration queue. Juggling her paperwork and passport in one hand, she stooped to retrieve a cardigan from her suitcase to stop herself from shivering. The sun might be shining over JFK airport but in this windowless room, the air conditioning must have been turned up to maximum.

The flight had been non-eventful; she had read and slept through much of it. She yawned and rotated her stiff shoulders. Now she was fidgety and anxious to get to her hotel for a shower. She wanted to call the office too before everyone left for the day, although that was looking increasingly unlikely. It would already be nearly seven in the evening in Northampton.

It was Patrick's last week already. When she'd left Gold's early this morning, he had been clearing his desk, cramming ten years' worth of diaries, mugs, broken pens and old catalogues into black bin bags. God knows what he was going to do with it all. He didn't usually suffer from the

Monday morning blues, but she had never seen him in such a bleak mood. The next time she saw him, it would be Friday – his final day with the company.

A thought hit her, set her imagination into overdrive and her stomach on to full spin: she hadn't returned his call from hours ago and there *was* that tannoy message . . . What if it *had* been for her? What if something was wrong? What if . . . he had changed his mind about leaving?

She peered along the queue and fought the urge to stamp her foot. How long did it take to let a few tourists into this country, for God's sake?

Checking over her shoulder, she slid a hand into her handbag surreptitiously and turned on her phone, then instantly regretted it. *Shit.* The obligatory text messages informing her she was now abroad kept on coming, reverberating around the busy, but eerily quiet, hall. She barely had the chance to register a string of missed calls from Patrick when she felt a meaty hand on her arm and jumped guiltily.

'Ma'am?' A burly customs officer released her and pointed to the huge sign forbidding the use of mobile phones.

'Oops. Sorry.' Jo squirmed. The people either side of her in the queue, in the absence of anything else to do, decided to stare at her vacantly.

What the hell was taking so long in this line? Jo folded her arms and tapped her foot against her suitcase until the man in front of her whirled round and glared at her for fidgeting.

'Come on, come on,' she chanted under her breath, suddenly desperate to speak to Patrick. 'I've got to get out of here.'

Thankfully there was no queue for taxis outside arrivals and Jo jumped straight into a yellow cab.

'DoubleTree Hotel in Times Square please,' she called to the driver, sinking gratefully into the back seat.

Right. *PatrickPatrickPatrick*. Her fingers fumbled with her phone and she shook it impatiently as she waited for her roaming service to connect. Her heart was beating wildly. Please God, let nothing have happened to her dad on the drive back up the motorway. Or a fire? Perhaps Gold's had burned to the ground and there were casualties and . . .

No sooner had the AT&T symbol appeared in the corner of her screen than the phone rang, making her jump. She practically stabbed the green button in her haste to answer the call.

'Patrick?'

'Jesus, Jo! That was quick. You frightened me to death. Are you OK? How was the flight?'

She let out a breath of relief. He sounded smiley. There was nothing wrong. She slumped back against the leather seat, cross with herself for overreacting. But pleased at the same time. Whatever Patrick wanted, she was sure from his greeting that there was no life-or-death situation lurking across the pond.

'Fine. I'm in a taxi on my way to the hotel.'

'I've been trying to get hold of you for hours; didn't you get my call or hear the tannoy at the airport?'

'Yes, no, sorry.' She was so glad he wasn't here to see her pink ears.

'Never mind. I've got something exciting to tell you.'

Jo stared out of the window, only vaguely registering the traffic on the Long Island Expressway. He had decided not to leave Gold's? She bit her lip, heart pounding, not daring to speak in case she jinxed his next words.

'Remember Mr Yamamoto?'

'Who?' Jo was thrown momentarily. What was he talking about?

'The Japanese businessman we met at Global?'

'Oh, yeah, yeah, I remember.' Jo frowned and rubbed her gritty eyes. Fresh off a long flight and the most pressing thing Patrick had to tell her was . . .

'Did you also know he's head of a chain of fifty shoe shops in Japan? That's five zero shops.'

This conversation was getting surreal. Shoe shops in Japan? Jo's travel-weary body began to tingle; she could tell from his voice that he was doing his James Bond face, all raised eyebrows and wonky smile.

She laughed softly. 'No, I didn't know that. What else don't I know?'

There was a pause down the line.

'There's a lot you don't know, Gold.'

She smiled a bittersweet smile; she was going to miss their banter.

'But let's stick with the Japanese for now,' he continued. 'When we met Mr Yamamoto and his team, they were in the UK sourcing luxury brands for their stores. Some government body had organized the trip for them. Which was lucky for us.'

'Was it?' asked Jo tentatively, crossing her fingers.

'Oh yes, because according to the translator, who we also met that day, Josephine Gold is the perfect archetypal British footwear brand.'

'Well, I'd have to agree!' cried Jo, drumming her feet excitedly in the back of the cab. The driver eyed her nervously in his rear-view mirror.

'Patrick, you're loving this, aren't you?' She laughed down the phone. 'Are you walking round the office doing your swagger?'

There was a slight pause down the line and she heard the squeak of his leather office chair.

'Er, no, I'm sitting down.'

'Yeah, now you are.'

'This could be even bigger than the Global contract, Jo. Do you realize that?'

The taxi joined a seething mass of cars all competing for which of them could edge closest to the car in front without actually hitting it. Ahead, Jo could see the Queensboro

Bridge spanning the East River like a huge metal spine. The turquoise cloudless sky, the iconic Manhattan skyline and the glittering river . . . no matter how often she visited New York, the magic was still there. Carrie and Sarah were going to love it.

Around them drivers were honking their horns and she could barely hear Patrick. Her taxi driver wound his window down and started to yell indiscriminately at the cars in front.

'. . . meeting on Wednesday . . . want to get deal signed . . . only opportunity before flying . . .'

Jo pressed a hand over her free ear and strained to listen. What was he saying?

'Close your window, please!' she shouted at the driver.

'Jo, can you hear me?'

His voice was breaking up. A ball of frustration began to build in the pit of her stomach. *Hell, this is important.* Her heart was thumping and she was an inch away from completely losing it.

'Patrick, are you still there?'

Mercifully, the taxi pulled on to the bridge and the traffic started moving again.

'So, Wednesday?' Patrick repeated clearly. 'Shall I agree to the meeting?'

'We can't! I'll still be in New York,' she shouted. This was a nightmare.

'I know,' explained Patrick patiently. 'The Japanese are in America too. They're in Atlanta at the moment. They'll be arriving in New York tomorrow and want to meet up.'

The cars were quieter now they were on the bridge, thank goodness; she had barely been able to hear herself think.

The impact of Patrick's news began to sink in. In the back of her mind, she had always considered the possibility of exporting to Japan. They were barmy about British brands, apparently. But she simply didn't have the resources to investigate any further. Mr Yamamoto could be the answer to their prayers.

'Jesus Christ, Patrick, this is amazing. Josephine Gold in Japan! Imagine,' laughed Jo incredulously. 'Have you booked your flight?'

'Me?'

'Of course! You don't leave the company until Friday, you know.'

'Jo, you know I'd do anything you ask,' said Patrick quietly.

Then don't leave.

She took a deep breath. 'Get yourself on a flight, McGregor. I can't do this without you.'

More to the point, she admitted, she didn't want to do it without him. 'I need you, anyway,' she added brightly.

'I'm flattered,' said Patrick gruffly. 'And I'd love to be involved.'

'Yeah, I need you to bring all the samples out with you,' she teased.

'Oh. Right.'

Oh bless, he sounded all deflated. 'Patrick?'

'Yes?'

'Thanks for this and thanks for trying so hard to get hold of me and . . . just thanks. But now get off the line. I'll call Liz and get her to organize you a flight. Carrie and Sarah are coming tomorrow; we'll book you on the same flight. Now go and pack!'

It was too busy and noisy at the airport for Carrie; she felt a bit intimidated by the crowds. She had never left the UK without Alex and she was used to him organizing all their travel arrangements. And Sarah was so excited that she was no help at all.

'Look at this!' Sarah chirped, pointing to her groin. She hopped from one foot to the other, making her curls bounce.

Carrie eyed her with amusement. She had been bursting

with energy ever since they had checked in. She was exhausted just watching.

'My teensy weensy, tiny little bag,' Sarah continued merrily, now swinging her body from side to side, smacking Carrie with the bag in question.

'Come on,' laughed Carrie, dragging her friend towards the coffee shop.

'You've no idea how liberating this is,' Sarah said with a blissful smile. 'Just my passport, ticket and purse. No toys, drinks, nappies, spare vests and . . .'

'Wipes?' Carrie finished for her.

'Oh gosh,' Sarah gasped. 'I need hand-sanitizer for the loos on the plane.' She shrugged herself out of Carrie's grasp. 'Just popping to Boots, meet you back here.' She darted off with a wave.

'I'll go to the bookshop then,' said Carrie to no one.

Back at the coffee shop thirty minutes later, Carrie emptied the contents of her carrier bag on to the table to show Sarah.

'Richard Branson's biography, two books on the language of flowers and one about marketing for dummies,' she said, pleased with her haul.

Life had never been so exciting and she was intent on making the most of her first transatlantic flight.

'Wow.' Sarah raised her eyebrows over the top of her latte glass. 'That's quite a lot of reading for one flight.'

Carrie laughed, realizing it made her look pretty antisocial. 'I promise I won't ignore you. I've never flown long haul before. We can chat away, maybe watch a movie . . .'

'Here's my in-flight entertainment.' Sarah grinned. 'Tadah!' She waved a small Boots bag in front of Carrie. 'Eye mask, ear plugs, herbal sleeping tablets, caffeine tablets. Oh, and of course, hand gel. So don't worry, I won't be interrupting your reading!'

'Won't those pills cancel each other out?'

Sarah shook her head. 'Sleep on the plane, then wide awake when we get there. I am not going to miss a single moment of this trip.' She sighed dreamily. 'Two days, two nights and no responsibility.'

A familiar face caught Carrie's eye as an attractive man with fair hair approached them carrying a tray. She nudged Sarah and lowered her voice. 'Look who's here!'

'Hello, ladies.' Patrick smiled. 'Jo said I might bump into you.'

It was one o'clock in the afternoon when Carrie, Sarah and Patrick caught their first sight of Manhattan as their shared taxi retraced Jo's route of only twenty-four hours ago.

'It's exactly as I imagined it,' breathed Carrie, her nose pressed up against the window.

'I'm so excited!' Sarah squealed. 'It's gorgeous. Are you excited, Patrick?'

He nodded modestly and then scrabbled to reach inside his pocket as his phone began to ring.

'It's Jo,' he said, answering the call and leaning as far away from Sarah as he could. Carrie and Sarah openly stared and leaned closer.

'We're in a cab,' said Patrick. He laughed. 'All three of us. What? OK.'

He held out the phone and pressed a key. 'You're on loudspeaker, Jo.'

'HI, JO!' yelled Sarah.

'Wow, someone's excited!' Jo's laugh echoed around the cab. 'OK, here's the plan . . .'

Carrie readied herself for instructions.

'Go to the hotel first and check in. Patrick, you put your stuff in my room.'

'Whoo-hoo, it's your lucky day, Patrick,' Sarah cackled, slapping his thigh.

Carrie pressed her lips together, watching as Patrick squirmed in his seat and turned a cute shade of pink. Why

351

hadn't Jo seen it? He was mad about her, it was so obvious. And they made such a lovely couple.

'Control yourself, Sarah.' Jo tutted. 'There wasn't another vacant room, so Patrick can have mine and I'll share with you two, the rooms are massive anyway.'

'Ah,' said Sarah. 'He looks really disappointed.'

Jo went quiet. Patrick looked about ready to expire with embarrassment.

Carrie rolled her eyes. 'I apologize on Sarah's behalf,' she said. 'She's been popping caffeine pills like Smarties since we landed, I don't think she'll sleep at all this side of the Atlantic.'

Jo laughed down the phone.

'You've probably heard from Patrick that we've got a meeting to go to tomorrow, so as it's such a lovely day, we could . . . Oh God, I can't believe I'm even suggesting this . . . We could do the Empire State Building?'

Carrie's heart fluttered. The Empire State Building was the highlight of her trip. She thought she would have at least another day to work herself up to it. 'You're going to do it then, Jo?'

'Er, well, I'll meet you there. I'm about to go into a meeting with a footwear design studio on West Thirty-fifth, so I can walk to Fifth Avenue from here. We can have some food first, if you like?'

'What about Patrick?' asked Sarah, turning to look at him.

'You're welcome to join us?' offered Jo.

Carrie and Sarah nodded at him.

'Thanks but no. You girls enjoy yourselves. Holly has given me a shopping list; I'm off to Fifth Avenue to find Abercrombie and Fitch.'

Chapter 36

Jo had booked them a table at the Heartland Brewery. It was in a prime window position, with a view straight on to Fifth Avenue. Perfect for a spot of people watching, although Sarah and Carrie had had so much to tell her about their day so far, that she had barely glanced out.

'I'm so full,' groaned Jo. 'I'm not used to eating lunch. Not super-sized portions like that, anyway.'

She tugged at the waistband of her flared skirt.

What she needed now was a lie-down. After all the excitement of Patrick's call about Mr Yamamoto, the brilliant meeting she had had this morning with a design studio and then the girls arriving, it was all starting to catch up with her.

'You should have had the salad,' Carrie said primly, dabbing her mouth with her napkin. 'Have I got spinach between my teeth?' She flashed them a quick look at her pearly whites and tucked her hair behind her ear.

Sarah shook her head. 'You're fine. I'm stuffed too. The ravioli was to die for but I'm not sure I can move.'

'There's no rush,' said Jo, flicking an eye over her mobile-phone screen. No calls. Not that she was expecting any; it was late evening back in the UK, the office would be closed.

'Aww, hasn't he phoned?' Sarah teased.

'Who?' Jo knew full well who she meant; both she and

Carrie had brought Patrick into the conversation at every conceivable juncture for the last hour. The poor guy; she bet they'd grilled him to death with questions at the airport this morning and in the taxi into Manhattan.

'The gorgeous Patrick I've-got-the-hots-for-Jo McGregor, obviously,' said Sarah, who with her hair tied up in a polka-dot scarf, Capri pants and fitted blouse looked like an extra from *Grease*. She pushed her chair back until it was balanced on two legs and grinned cheekily.

Jo rolled her eyes.

'I think I preferred you when you were miserable,' she said, only half-joking. She picked up her water glass and took a sip.

'He's flexing his credit card; he'll be too busy to call,' said Carrie. 'Sarah and I were asking the concierge for directions to Fifth Avenue and he joined us to do the same. We walked up together and he disappeared in the direction of Tiffany and Trump Tower.'

Jo spluttered and sprayed water on the remains of her lunch. 'Tiffany? He's going shopping for Holly in Tiffany?'

'No,' said Sarah, sticking her hand up to attract a waitress, 'that's just his landmark to aim for; he's looking for Abercrombie and Fitch, opposite.'

'My god-daughter has got him well trained.' Jo smiled at the thought of Holly giving Patrick strict instructions on where to go.

But Tiffany. Jo's insides turned to marshmallow at the very sound of the word. The story of Ed Shaw proposing to his wife in the Heathrow branch of Tiffany popped into her head. What a let-down. Fifth Avenue on the other hand . . .

Jo inhaled so much for a big sigh that her shoulders lifted a full six inches. She let the breath out and sank back into a slump. Carrie and Sarah exchanged curious glances and she felt her ears heat up.

Surely Tiffany in New York had to be the most romantic

place on the planet to get engaged? Unless, of course, you counted . . .

'Perhaps we should give the Empire State Building a miss?' she blurted out, wriggling in her seat. 'It won't be good for our digestion. All those stairs.'

'Nice try.' Carrie gave her a stern look. 'But it's only an elevator ride all the way.'

'And the Heartland Brewery is actually *underneath* the Empire State Building, so technically, we're already here,' added Sarah.

Jo's stomach flipped. This was going to be harder to get out of than she thought.

Sarah reached for her hand. 'Won't you feel proud if your wish comes true? You can do it, I know you can. My wish has worked out perfectly,' she paused and pulled a face, 'once I'd realized what it was I really wanted. And look at Carrie! She's a different woman; she's confident, gorgeous and a budding entrepreneur. You've supported us both all the way, Jo. Now we want to help your wish come true.'

'Sarah's right.' Carrie adjusted the straps of her dress. 'My life has improved beyond my wildest dreams. And we're all here for each other.'

Jo shrugged. 'There's no point. You know I only told you half the story about wanting to reach the top of the Empire State Building. Being up there on my own – well, it would feel like a failure to me.'

The last eight months had confirmed what she had already known: she was a businesswoman first and foremost. Her personal life definitely took a back seat. And she didn't mean normal-car back seat. More like stretch-limo back seat.

Sarah and Carrie stared back at her with solemn, disappointed faces.

'We won't go if you don't come,' said Carrie in a small wheedling voice.

'Is that the bikini top I bought you?' said Jo, changing the subject. She leaned forward and pulled at Carrie's straps.

Carrie's face turned scarlet. 'Shush! Yes, I didn't have a halter-neck bra to go under this dress.'

'So. What are you ladies doing next?' The waitress beamed at them as she stooped to collect their plates.

'Empire State Building,' said Carrie, before Jo had the chance to argue.

'Oh, good choice! It's nearly three o'clock, you've picked a quiet time, so it shouldn't be too crowded.'

'Yes, I know, I researched it. Right, let's go.' Carrie dropped her share of the bill on the table and stood up. 'Come on.' She flapped her hands at them. 'Up, up!'

Jo felt like an escorted prisoner, clamped between the other two as they emerged on to Fifth Avenue. All she needed was a set of handcuffs to complete the look.

'Entrance between Thirty-third and Thirty-fourth Street,' Carrie read aloud from the guidebook, marching along as if her life depended on it.

'Miracle on Thirty-fourth Street, more like, if I make it up there,' muttered Jo, pressing a hand to her trembling stomach.

'There are two observation decks,' said Carrie. 'The eighty-sixth floor has an indoor viewing area as well as the outdoor bit. And the one hundred and second floor is indoors only.'

'Wow!' Sarah shielded her eyes against the sun with her hand and looked up. 'It's massive.'

Jo tipped her head back and followed the line of the building upwards, past row after row of windows. Carrie and Sarah gripped on to her as she stumbled, her legs weak with terror.

'I feel dizzy. I can't do it!' She gulped at the air. 'It's too high. It must be halfway to the moon.'

'Nearly a quarter of a mile, apparently,' said Carrie unhelpfully, referring back to the guidebook.

Sarah prodded Carrie in the ribs. 'You're not helping.'

'Jesus,' said Jo, through gritted teeth.

'Are you going to be sick?' asked Sarah, fumbling in her tiny bag. 'I think I've got some Rescue Remedy.'

Jo shook her head and headed for the wall of the building to catch her breath. 'And there are revolving doors. I hate revolving doors.'

'Jo.' Carrie gazed into her eyes pleadingly. 'I know it's an irrational fear and you can't help it. But I really, really want to go up there. I've been looking forward to it for months. Please. For me.'

'I might fall off,' Jo replied in a small voice. Her hands had gone clammy already and they weren't even through the doors yet.

'Impossible. There is a huge spiky fence all round the observation deck. There aren't even any benches you could stand on and then fall off,' Carrie explained patiently.

'People might push me near the edge,' Jo mumbled.

'You are a brave, confident woman. You can do it,' Sarah said, gripping her arm.

'Can't.'

'Oh, I give up.' Carrie folded her arms. 'You're a cowardly selfish woman and you're ruining my day.'

'Carrie!' gasped Sarah, who had a handful of tissues and a nappy sack at the ready. 'I do think you could be a bit more sympathetic.'

Bollocks. She was going to have to do it. Jo made a vow never to make a wish in public again. Neither of them got it. It wasn't about the bloody tower.

Jo took in Carrie's pouting face and held up her hands.

'All right,' she snapped. 'I'm coming. But only as far as the first deck on the eighty-sixth floor. And I'm not going outside.'

'Yes!' Carrie beamed. 'My reverse psychology worked.'

For a moment, Jo thought her crab cakes were on their way back up as she processed 'only' in the same sentence

357

as 'eighty-sixth floor'. She narrowed her eyes at her friend. She wasn't sure she liked the new assertive Carrie any more.

'Good. Let's do it,' said Sarah, smiling nervously at them both.

Jo felt a prickle of sweat at the back of her neck as the lift reached the eighty-sixth floor. She gripped harder on to both Carrie's and Sarah's hands as her stomach swooped and dived. The lift doors drew back. Carrie disappeared straight outside and she allowed Sarah to lead her gently out into the window-lined indoor gallery.

Keep your eyes down and forget where you are.

Her heart was pounding as she smiled at Sarah. 'Go on, you go outside, I'll be fine. I'll just sit on this seat and close my eyes.'

'If you're sure,' said Sarah, patting her hand. 'I'll try to keep it brief, although I've got a feeling Carrie might be difficult to chivvy along today.'

Jo checked her watch again. Thirty minutes they had been out there. How long did it take to look out over four sides of one bloody tower?

The other people in the elevator that brought them up had all left ages ago. Probably to go up to the very top. At least Sarah had popped back once to check she was OK. But no sign of Carrie. She was behaving very oddly, all jittery and snappy. Jo wished they would both hurry up. It was so embarrassing waiting on her own. It looked like she'd been stood up.

Like Meg Ryan in *Sleepless in Seattle*. Oh, the irony.

In fact, the best five minutes she'd had so far was when a tall blond Danish guy started chatting to her. But then even he left her for the allure of the outside observation deck. It wouldn't be so bad if she had got the guts to actually look out through the glass. But every time she lifted her head from the information panel in front of her, adrenalin crashed like waves through her body.

A beautiful Asian girl smiled at her and held out a camera questioningly, pointing at herself and her boyfriend. Jo smoothed down her skirt, pleased to be asked, and obliged. That was the fourth time she had been handed a camera. Her new demure look was definitely making her more approachable. Usually other women glanced at her cleavage and dragged their men away.

The Empire State Building was impressive, no doubt about it, especially the art deco lobby. They had all taken photos of the gold mural. That had been her favourite part. But that had been ages ago; now she was fed up.

With this indoor gallery and with her own company.

The niggling thought that she had let herself down wouldn't go away. Sarah could confidently tick her wish off the list. So could Carrie. Not that they'd seen actual evidence that she'd bared her bikini-clad body in public, but the rest – weight loss, confidence, a new business . . . There was no denying Carrie's success.

Technically, her own wish had come true. She was near enough at the top. But lurking about on her own, desperately trying to ignore the fact that she was here? Well, it didn't feel like success.

Jo braced herself and forced her eyes to focus on the nearest window. Through the glass, Jo watched parents hold their kids up to get a better view, groups of friends laughing as they shared the huge fixed telescopes and lovers posing for photographs. She felt nauseous just watching them.

Bugger it. She was so jealous.

Jo stood up and huffed and puffed crossly. What was actually stopping her from going outside? It was plainly safe; otherwise none of those people out there would look so happy.

Maybe she could just stand a bit closer to the door?

She shuffled her way to the exit, keeping her focus on the man in the burgundy uniform outside the door and not the view beyond. Carrie and Sarah were still nowhere to be seen.

The liveried security man beamed at her and held the door open.

'Welcome to the top of the world, ma'am!'

Jo smiled stiffly and clung to the open doorway.

'I wasn't . . . I mean, I can't . . . I'm scared of heights,' she managed to squeeze out with a wavering voice.

'Well, you just stand by me and get the measure of the place first,' suggested the man, tipping her an encouraging wink.

Jo nodded. Sliding one foot in front of the other, she took her place next to him and pressed her back against the glass. She had made it. She was outside. A warm breeze ruffled her hair and she could feel the sun on her face. She stared down at the floor. She had never been so terrified in her life. Her breathing was ragged and her chest was heaving with the effort of controlling her panicky lungs. The oxygen must be thin up here.

Breathe in, breathe out.

Jo remembered snatches of the self-help book she'd read on the plane. Apparently she should try to rate her fear on a scale of one to ten.

Right now, her fear level was ten out of ten at least.

The security man's presence was quite comforting, she thought, peeking at his burgundy blazer and cap. He smiled back at her and she took the bold decision to re-categorize her fear. *Nine out of ten.* She wondered if she could ask to hold his hand. Probably not a good idea. He seemed friendly enough, but she doubted that hand-holding was part of his duties.

'You can't come this far and not enjoy the view, can you? I mean,' he said, chuckling softly, 'you'd regret it for the rest of your life!'

Jo nodded and focused on her breathing. In and out. Repeat until calm. *Eight out of ten.*

The thing you would most regret.

He was right, dammit.

'I'm tired, Mommy.' A little boy plopped himself down near Jo's feet and her heart pinged. Oh good grief, he had scruffy dark brown hair and was the spitting image of Jonah in *Sleepless in Seattle.*

'OK, honey,' called a plump woman, who had a tiny baby strapped to her front in a papoose. 'I'm right here.'

'Why are you standing back there?'

Jo glanced down to find a pair of solemn brown eyes staring up at her.

'If you step up closer to the edge,' continued the little boy, clearly not interested in the answer to his own question, 'you can see the Statue of Liberty.'

'Really?' She raised an eyebrow. Her breathing was almost normal now. *Seven out of ten.*

'It's the Roman goddess of liberty,' he recited. 'A memorial to our independence. We just did it in school,' he added as an aside. 'See it?'

'Yes, I can see.' Jo flicked her eyes quickly out to the right over the river and back to meet his challenging stare.

'No, you can't.' The little boy rolled his eyes at her as if he'd just caught her out lying about washing behind her ears.

She laughed at his cheekiness. The fear factor had slipped a notch. She was now down to six. Six, if she was honest with herself, was naff all. She must have been at around nine out of ten that time she realized she'd switched USB sticks at Global and she'd survived that ordeal, hadn't she?

Her stretch of the observation deck was pretty empty, just herself, the boy and the boy's mother, who was scanning the horizon through the viewfinder of the telescope. Carrie and Sarah must be round the opposite side somewhere. She wished they could see her now; they'd be so proud. Jo took a shaky step towards the edge. The wind had picked up a bit; she shivered and pulled her cardigan tight.

'Way to go, ma'am,' said the security guard, nodding encouragingly at her.

'Closer. You need to go right to the edge,' the little boy urged her.

'OK, OK,' snapped Jo.

She lurched in one fast movement towards the metal fence and clutched on to it. Her heart was hammering so hard in her chest that she had to look down to check it wasn't actually visible through the fabric of her T-shirt.

Deep breaths, deep breaths. She inhaled and exhaled until her grip on the fence lessened. She'd done it. She, Jo Gold, had made it to the top of the Empire State Building. By herself. OK, with a small amount of input from a bossy child and a security guard. She laughed out loud with pride. All she had to do now was open her eyes.

'Jo!'

She released one hand from the fence and whirled round to come face to face with Patrick. He was grinning at her, red-faced and a bit sweaty and weighed down with shopping bags.

'Patrick!' she gasped, realizing that she was completely overjoyed to see him.

'Urgh,' muttered the little boy. He turned away and folded his arms.

'I've just seen Carrie and Sarah round the other side. They said you were indoors. Aren't you terrified of heights?'

Jo cast her eye through the fence, feigning nonchalance. 'I was.' A rogue wave of dizziness caused her to sway precariously. 'Still am.'

'Whoa!' Patrick dropped his bags and caught hold of her waist. 'I've got you.'

'Thank you,' she whispered. Her heart was doing that hammering thing again, but this time it had nothing to do with the fact that she was nearly a quarter of a mile above New York.

'What would you do without me, Gold?' he quipped, grinning at her.

This was her cue to tease him, say something like how she could manage perfectly well without him, thank you very much. But her mouth was dry, her head was spinning and her legs felt leaden.

He was looking at her very strangely, with a sincerity that made her cheeks flush. He had lovely eyes, she thought. Why hadn't she noticed that before? Sort of smoky and intense.

Patrick still had his hands round her waist. Her hands were braced against his chest. It should have been awkward but it wasn't. It was reassuring. It felt right. She took a deep breath and blew out sharply. *Stay brave, Jo*, she told herself, although inexplicably, her fear had crept back up to seven out of ten and adrenalin was doing a Zumba class through her veins.

'I had to come and find you,' he said.

He was still smiling but his voice was trembling. Unfit, obviously.

'Did you?' Various worrying scenarios raced through Jo's mind. She forced herself to calm down; he was smiling. It couldn't be bad news. Which meant by a process of elimination that it must be good news. Relax. *Six out of ten.*

She was glad she had flat shoes on. In heels, she was nearly the same height as Patrick. It was quite nice looking up at him for a change. She felt uncharacteristically girlie.

Patrick's grin grew wider. 'Global Duty Free have cancelled their order with Hooray Henry. Ian phoned me while I was in . . . while I was shopping.'

'Oh my God!' She swallowed and nodded for him to continue.

'The so-called celebrity designer has checked into rehab for drug abuse. Global can't risk having anything to do with them if there's even a whiff of scandal. So . . .' He paused for dramatic effect, his lovely eyes shining with excitement. 'The Josephine Gold collection is going to be stocked for the Best of British campaign! They've placed the order already.'

Patrick increased the pressure on her waist with his hands. The unbelievable announcement he had just made, along with the delicious sensations produced by his touch, were almost too much for her brain to deal with and her pulse had slipped into overdrive.

'We're back in business,' marvelled Jo, her voice all husky with emotion. 'Oh my GOD, PATRICK!'

No way could her dad justify a return to work now. The two of them grinned wildly at each other.

'Are you gonna kiss her?' a little voice piped up. Patrick looked down at the small boy and back to Jo with a bemused expression.

Well, are you?

Jo blushed at her inner thoughts. Where had that come from? Did she mean it? She must be getting carried away. This was her ultimate romantic fantasy, her magical moment. The top of the Empire State Building, a cloudless sky, panoramic view of Manhattan, and in the arms of . . . Patrick.

'Sorry about him.' Jo's eyes flicked briefly to the Jonah lookalike, who drummed his fingers on one knee impatiently and stared back at them. 'He's very nosy.'

'Jo, I need to tell you something,' stammered Patrick, still staring at the boy.

'Let's go, honey.' The mother held out her hand, the boy climbed to his feet and they began to walk away.

'Kiss her!' said the child, over his shoulder.

Suddenly she was struck by a realization so strong that it simply took her breath away: there was nowhere else in the world she would rather be than here, in Patrick's arms. It didn't matter how high up she was, or how scared, or how difficult the situation was; as long as Patrick was by her side, she would be OK. Goosebumps sent a shiver down her spine and her heart fluttered as she gazed up at the face she knew so well. This man had been her confidant, her friend and her supporter.

But he was so much more than that.

And on Friday she was letting him walk out of her life.

What an idiot she had been! Why had she only just worked it out? Maybe if she had been more honest with him, told him how devastated she had been when he resigned, she might have changed his mind. Maybe it wasn't too late.

'Jo?'

His dark eyes were searching hers. And in a moment of absolute clarity, Jo knew that he wanted her as much as she wanted him. The strength of his feelings was unmistakable. The girls had been right: he did have feelings for her. Her body started to tremble.

'You heard the boy,' she murmured.

Patrick loosened his grip on her waist and slowly cupped her face in his hands. Her skin tingled at his touch. She closed her eyes and felt her body melt into his as their lips met for the first time. As if following some inaudible instruction, they took a tiny step towards each other until their bodies were completely entwined. Jo slid her hands round his neck and wove her fingers through his hair, savouring their closeness, not wanting this precious moment to end.

'Whoo-hoo!'

A round of applause eventually broke into Jo's consciousness and she reluctantly pulled herself away from Patrick's kiss. He let go of her face and took her hands in his.

'Yes, ma'am!' The security man smiled at her and gave her the thumbs-up.

Her previously empty section of the deck was now heaving with a group of shivering twenty-something girls, who judging by their skimpy bumblebee outfits, were part of a hen party and they were all swarming round the pair of them.

'Wow,' she whispered shakily, vaguely aware that her ears were burning. 'We just kissed.'

'Jo, I . . .' There was a look of confusion on his face. Jo held her breath.

Please don't say that was a mistake.

It might have come out of the blue, but that had been the most perfect kiss of her life. She wanted nothing more than to grab him and do it all over again. She would be devastated if he didn't feel the same way.

Patrick rummaged around in the shopping bags at his feet and produced a small turquoise box.

'Tiffany!' squealed one of the bumblebees.

'Aww!' shrieked a girl whose sash declared her the queen bee. 'Oh my God! He's gonna propose!'

The other girls began to jiggle and clutch each other, their antennae getting all tangled in the fray.

Jo swallowed nervously. She was gripped by panic as one fear was replaced by another. This was going too far the other way. He wouldn't, would he? *Please don't ruin it*, she muttered inwardly. It was only a kiss. One kiss. Ten minutes ago she hadn't even realized she was in love with him.

In love with him? Bloody hell, this was moving fast. But she was. Definitely. She loved him so much that she almost couldn't contain herself.

'I had planned on giving you this at my leaving party on Friday.' He held out the box in front of her. 'That way if you turned me down, I could have disappeared into the sunset to lick my wounds in private. But up here, just you and me . . .' he grinned, jerking his head at their audience ' . . . and the rest of the hive, it seems like the right moment to tell you how I feel—'

'Please . . .' Jo interrupted, her heart pounding in her chest. Being proposed to, up here, well, it was a dream come true, but . . . what the hell was she going to say?

Patrick snapped open the box and her heart swooped with relief.

'It's beautiful!' she breathed, looking at the delicate heart pendant on an elegant silver chain.

'It ain't a ring!' yelled the queen bee in dismay. The message was quickly relayed around the group and thankfully they buzzed off, leaving Jo and Patrick in relative peace.

'No. It ain't a ring.' Patrick grinned at her. He slipped the necklace out of the box and fastened it round her neck. Jo could feel his hands trembling.

This was the moment. This was her chance. She could be the person she wanted to be; she didn't have to always be the hard-headed businesswoman. She remembered what he had said to her in that presentation at Global a few weeks ago: *Speak from the heart, Jo. From the heart.*

'Don't leave!' she blurted out.

Patrick relaxed his shoulders and rewarded her with a euphoric smile. And, if she wasn't very much mistaken, his eyes looked a little bit misty.

The silly sod.

He gave the tiniest nod. 'You have my heart now, Josephine Gold. I won't leave you.'

'You are so cheesy, McGregor,' she said, laughing.

He pulled her towards him and kissed her again.

For ages.

She leaned up against him as they looked out to the southern tip of Manhattan. Her fear of heights had almost evaporated. Perhaps it had something to do with trust, or maybe she had finally let go of the reason for her fear? Or perhaps the joy she was experiencing at sharing this moment with Patrick was so huge that she didn't have room for any more emotions. A thought struck her suddenly.

367

'It was a bit of a fluke that you found me here, wasn't it?'

He shook his head. 'Not really, Carrie told me she wanted to be here at around now. She'd researched the quietest time, apparently.'

The security man's two-way radio crackled into life.

'Go ahead,' he shouted, holding it to his ear. 'A streaker? Location? OK. On my way.'

Jo caught hold of the security man's burgundy sleeve as he prepared to dash off. 'What is it?'

'No need to be alarmed, ma'am,' said the security guard, patting her hand as he removed it from his arm. 'Some joker has started to strip on the west side. Assistance required.' He gave her his best action-hero smile and darted off, elbowing his way through the crowds. Within seconds he had disappeared out of sight. Jo and Patrick stared at each other in disbelief.

'Come on,' Patrick said, laughing as he scooped up his bags and caught her hand in his. 'This we have got to see.'

A crowd had gathered on the west side of the observation deck, around the central telescope. There was clapping and cheering and people were holding their cameras, phones and camcorders high up above the sea of heads.

Jo and Patrick arrived just as a familiar Marks & Spencer's halter-neck dress billowed up into the air and got caught on a metal spike of the safety fence.

'Bloody hell!' Jo froze, her jaw somewhere near her knees, and pointed ahead. 'That's Carrie's dress.'

And straddled rather precariously astride a coin-operated telescope was Carrie, arms akimbo, wearing nothing but a teeny-weeny bikini and a radiant smile. Sarah was gazing up at her in awe and hanging on to her thighs for safety.

'My bikini body!' Carrie yelled triumphantly. 'It may not be perfect, but it's all real! Take a look, people. For one day only.'

'What's your name, honey?' cried a tall man, busily snapping away with his camera. 'And where are you from?'

'Carrie Radley.' She beamed, waving at the flurry of camcorders that were pointing in her direction. 'I'm a florist. Visit Carrie's Blooms in Woodby for the most beautiful flowers in England!'

The crowd cheered even louder. Someone tossed a bunch of sunflowers into the air and Carrie caught them.

'Sunflowers,' she cried, blowing the onlookers a kiss. 'The boldest, brightest flowers of all!'

Jo clapped a hand over her mouth as Carrie waved the bouquet in the air.

Some people called out her name to get a better picture. Taller members of the crowd jumped up to try to reach the dress. There was an almighty tearing sound as the fabric tore down the middle, leaving a tiny scrap of fabric on the jagged tip of the fence.

Two uniformed men pushed their way to the centre of the action. Carrie dived neatly into the arms of one of them like a crowd-surfer, whilst Jo's friendly security guard removed his jacket and slipped it round her scantily clad body.

Sarah sprang into action, whipped open her bag and began distributing a pile of newly printed business cards to the audience.

'Please tag us on Facebook,' she yelled, above the clamour of the crowds and the continuing flash of cameras, 'Carrie Radley and Sarah Hudson, as in the river. As in that river down there!'

'Jesus,' Patrick murmured. 'What the hell is going on?'

Jo was laughing so hard that tears were trickling down her face; Patrick looked totally bewildered. 'She's making her wish come true,' she said, wiping her eyes. 'We all made a wish months ago. Hers was to wear a bikini in public. I had no idea she was planning this, though.'

'What was yours?' Patrick asked, raising a quizzical eyebrow.

Her heart was leaping around like a demented frog. *Careful, Jo*, she told herself. She could not mess with this gorgeous man's head. He wasn't a married man after an illicit squeeze, she couldn't love him and leave him and forget it never happened. She was Holly's godmother, for heaven's sake. She took a deep breath. If she kissed him now, she would have to do that big scary commitment thing. But that wouldn't be so bad, would it?

'Come on, Gold,' he laughed.

She pretended to huff. 'You just missed it. But I *suppose* I could do it again.'

With a backdrop of New York skyscrapers set against a perfect cerulean September sky, Jo wrapped her arms around Patrick's neck and kissed him long and hard.

'What a coincidence,' he murmured, gazing into her eyes. 'I've been wishing for the same thing for years.'

'Really?'

He nodded. 'Even Melissa knew how I felt about you. She was brilliant about it really and knew I'd never be unfaithful to her, so she set me free.'

Jo nodded thoughtfully. That would explain why Melissa had been frosty towards her in the last year of their marriage. 'But you were still prepared to leave Gold's?'

'I told you a bit of a white lie there.' He gave her a bashful smile. 'It was Ed's idea. He guessed straight away that I had the hots for you and told me to man up and come clean. He also suggested that you'd appreciate me more if I left the company.'

'But you're not, are you?' she asked nervously, tightening her grip round his neck as she pulled him in for another kiss.

'Urgh. Please.' The little boy was back.

Jo leaned away from him reluctantly, her heart bursting with the rush of love she felt for this man. She and Patrick looked at each other and laughed. The mother smiled an apology. Behind them stood Sarah and Carrie, fizzing with excitement, hands clasped to their hearts like emotional aunties at a wedding, albeit oddly dressed and, in Carrie's case, flanked by security guards.

A mobile phone began to ring. Everyone, from the onlookers, to security, even to Jonah's mother, started patting down pockets and fumbling through handbags.

'Mum!' said Jo breathlessly, answering her phone after a frantic search. 'Is everything OK? You'll never guess where I am: the top of the Empire State Building!'

'Yes, we're fine and well done, darling, and you're all right? Not tempted to throw yourself off?'

Jo looked at Patrick, her eyes shining with love. 'No, not at all and guess what else? I've met someone in New York!'

'Oh finally, that's marvellous, darling! I'd better get knitting. Tick tock!'

'Knitting? Mum!' She looked at Patrick and shook her head in despair.

'For baby's layette.'

Jo smiled. 'I think people go to John Lewis these days.' Why was she even having this conversation?

'Anyway, can you put him on, please?'

Yeah right, so her mum could quiz her new fella about his prospects, previous relationships and emotional baggage? Not likely.

'Now why would I do that?'

'Because Holly wants to ask his permission to go on a school trip.'

'What! You knew who it was?'

'Darling, the only person who didn't know was you. Until now, apparently.'

Out of the corner of Jo's eye she saw Patrick grinning sheepishly, Sarah still mooning at her all dewy-eyed and Carrie having a heated conversation with two security men about being unable to get dressed due to her clothes being in tatters, hanging from barbed wire and suspended over Manhattan.

They all knew.

Which in some ways was oddly disconcerting and in others, weirdly comforting.

'Even Dad?'

'Your father's delighted.'

'I wouldn't go that far.' Dad's voice boomed in the background.

'Chop, chop!' said her mother. 'It's already past Holly's bedtime.'

Jo handed over the phone to Patrick, who chucked a shopping bag at Carrie, caught Jo's hand in his and kissed her fingers.

'That was fantastic!' said Carrie, wide-eyed and dress-less. 'We should make a wish list every year.'

'Agreed,' said Sarah, delving into her bra.

'Please tell me you're not getting your boobs out again, like the first time we met?' Jo smirked. 'Or the ping-pong balls?'

'Ta-dah!' Sarah pulled out a tiny pristine notebook with a miniature pen clipped to its side. 'My bag is so small I couldn't fit this in. Fire away with your new wishes!'

Carrie pulled an Abercrombie and Fitch T-shirt out of Patrick's bag. It didn't quite cover her bikini bottoms, but security ambled off, apparently satisfied. 'So my next wish, then . . .'

Jo tuned out of the conversation and gazed at Patrick as he joked with his daughter over the phone and thought she might actually burst with love. How could a face so familiar suddenly be so mesmerizing?

Her fingers found the Tiffany heart at her throat and she smiled a secret smile to herself at her earlier panic when she had thought it was an engagement ring. The necklace was perfect. There was plenty of time for their relationship to get to the next stage.

She blinked away the daydream and felt Patrick's hand tighten around hers.

'Jo, what do you want to put on the list?' Sarah was asking.

She grinned at her friends and then at Patrick. Maybe that was the wish for next year.

The Thank Yous

Thank you to my agent, Hannah Ferguson, who read this book a few years ago and fortunately liked it enough to take me on as her author. Thank you to Joanna Swainson for stepping into Hannah's shoes when Baby Nell came along in February. To the team at Transworld (awarded Publisher of the Year, no less), thank you as ever for your dedication and creativity in helping to bring my stories to life, especially to my editor Francesca Best, publicist Sarah Harwood and marketing executive Nicola Wright. A special note of thanks to my Writers' Workshop Self Edit course buddies, who cheered me on many moons ago with this book (and laughed at the funny bits): Debi Alper, Emma Darwin, Jackie Buxton, Britta Jensen, Jo Morgan, Ruth Stalker-Firth, Fiona Macleod, Isabel Rogers and Shell Bromley. Finally, thank you to my family, Mr B and the two Misses B, I love you lots.

Note from Cathy

Dear lovely readers

Just a quick note from me to say how much I cherish your company, comments and support. Writing books can be a bit of a lonely job at times, and so finding an email or a comment on social media from someone saying how much they have enjoyed one of my books can make such a difference to my day. So please do keep on getting in touch!

I am proud of all my books, but this one is a bit special in that it follows the story of not one but three women – complete strangers who meet at a funeral. The idea for it came to me when I overheard a conversation between two people who were mourning the loss of a friend. Life is short, they agreed, seize the day. So that is the theme of the book. We should make the most of every day, every moment, every opportunity that comes our way, because we never know what lies ahead or where life will take us.

And that's my heartfelt message to you – *carpe diem*, and I hope you enjoy reading *White Lies and Wishes* as much as I enjoyed writing it.

With love
Cathy xx

Cathy Bramley is the author of the best-selling romantic comedies *Ivy Lane*, *Appleby Farm*, *Wickham Hall* and *The Plumberry School of Comfort Food* (all four-part serialized novels) and *Conditional Love*. She lives in a Nottinghamshire village with her family and a dog.

Her recent career as a full-time writer of light-hearted romantic fiction has come as somewhat of a lovely surprise after spending the last eighteen years running her own marketing agency. However, she has always been an avid reader, hiding her book under the duvet and reading by torchlight. Luckily her husband has now bought her a Kindle with a light, so that's the end of that palaver.

Cathy loves to hear from her readers. You can get in touch via her website: www.CathyBramley.co.uk,

Facebook page: facebook.com/CathyBramleyAuthor or on

Twitter: twitter.com/CathyBramley

Q & A with Cathy Bramley

White Lies and Wishes is about three women who, one day, throw caution to the wind and decide to make a bucket list for that year. What's on your bucket list?

I LOVE this question! I'm always saying or sometimes just thinking 'that's one for the bucket list' and half of the time I forget all about it. But these are the ones currently taking up too much of my daydreams: I'd like to own a cape. A big swishy one like Demelza wears in *Poldark*. I'd like to go to a proper Regency ball and learn all the dances and get dressed up in all the requisite finery. There was one at Chatsworth House recently and I was so sad to have missed it (my husband, on the other hand, was most relieved). I'd like to live by the sea for a while, perhaps rent a house for six months and take long walks on the beach. Finally, did you know that Hotel Chocolat has a real hotel in Saint Lucia? It's the most gorgeous, decadent retreat and a stay in one of their lodges is most definitely at the top of my bucket list.

Was there any real-life inspiration behind Jo, Sarah and Carrie?

Between you and I, there is a bit of me in all of them. Jo is in charge of a business and is acutely aware of her responsibility to her staff. I used to run my own company and when things were tough, I felt very worried not only for my own livelihood but for those of my team too. Sarah is struggling to cope with a career and motherhood. I took very little maternity leave when my children were small and spent a lot of the time feeling guilty. It was also quite difficult to keep up with breastfeeding when I spent the day apart from them. There is an incident in this book which is taken straight from my own personal experience on that front! Carrie is probably the least like me; for a start, I can't arrange flowers to save my life! But I have had hypnotherapy and struggled to relax in the chair just like Carrie does.

Describe a typical writing day for you.

My day begins as follows: school run, dog walk, breakfast, more coffee, thick socks on . . . and then I'm ready to work! I usually will spend seven hours at my desk, punctuated by sneaky peeks at Twitter and Facebook and trips to the kettle. I start by reading through yesterday's writing and then make a few bullet points about what today's words should convey. I plot quite extensively before I begin writing a book. Sometimes I stick to my plan, sometimes I don't, but I need the plan before I can begin. My chapters are around 3000 words each and an excellent day means starting and finishing a whole chapter. But I don't beat myself up if this doesn't happen; some days I write faster than others. Arguments are super-fast to write! My daughters arrive home around four thirty, starving, which is usually a good time to stop writing and have a think about what I'm going to tackle tomorrow.

Female friendship is at the heart of this novel. How do your characters help each other develop throughout the novel?

Jo, Carrie and Sarah have such an inauspicious meeting – all outside at a funeral, doing things they'd rather not be seen doing. This throws them together and I thought it would be fun to see how a friendship could grow out of an awkward situation. They start off with such low expectations of each other: Carrie is convinced neither of them will like her; Jo thinks she's wasting her time; Sarah is intrigued by the other two and initially the most reluctant to make a wish. But gradually they form a support network for each other, at first offering advice but then later, seeking each other out for help and eventually wanting to extend the friendship circle by bringing Abi into it too. They are all happier people for having each other as friends by the end of the book.

Did you always know you wanted to be a writer?

Reading has always been an important part of my life, I can't imagine not having a book on the go – it just wouldn't happen. Actually writing one myself didn't occur to me until I was in my mid-forties, but when I did, I fell in love with it. I hadn't been planning a career change but after writing three novels I decided to give up my marketing business and write full-time.

At first, Carrie is shy and self-conscious. How does she change throughout the novel?

Carrie begins to contrast her life with that of Jo and Sarah and realizes how much more she could be achieving. Once she identifies what has been holding her back and that she has been comfort eating for years, she is able to begin taking control of her life. This grows her confidence and she starts to plan a brighter, fuller future for herself.

What authors and books have had a strong influence on your writing?

I can't really distinguish between authors I love and those who influence me, I guess it's probably one and the same. There are authors whose books I will automatically buy without even reading the blurb, like Lucy Diamond, Jenny Colgan, Miranda Dickinson, Rachael Lucas, Jill Mansell, Katie Fforde and Diane Chamberlain. However, my number one is still Marian Keyes, whose characterization and wit can make me laugh days after I've finished the book.

White Lies and Wishes deals with lots of issues modern women experience, including motherhood and work-life balance. How hard do you think it is to seize the day while living a busy life?

Incredibly hard! Sometimes it's enough just to get to the end of the day without a stiff drink (and/or a little cry!). But at the same time, I think we all make time for the things we really want to do and similarly make excuses for not doing the things we'd rather avoid.

What advice would you give a budding novelist?

Write the best book you can and then go on a reputable course or guided retreat to learn how to critique and improve your work. Some people prefer to go on courses first before starting to write, so whichever works for you, I guess. But think of that first draft as just you telling yourself the story. Once you've done that, it's time to re-tell it for the readers – this can be the tricky part!

White Lies and Wishes is about finding your own happy ending, no matter what your life looks like. What does happiness look like to you?

A family Christmas; baking the perfect Victoria sponge; date night with my husband; a hug from my daughters; a country walk on a crisp, sunny winter's morning; a glass of Champagne on publication day!

Or the irresistibly charming

The Lemon Tree Café

Rosie Featherstone loves her high-flying job at a social media firm. So what if she isn't married and settled like her sister? A relationship would only get in the way of this workaholic's hectic schedule!

So when she unexpectedly finds herself at a loose end for a month, Rosie keeps busy by helping her Italian Nonna serve espressos and biscotti at the Lemon Tree Café, a little slice of Italy nestled in the rolling hills of Derbyshire.

Worryingly though, the café's fortunes seem to have taken a turn for the worse since Rosie last went home. But with Nonna blind to the truth and angry at the idea of anyone interfering, the two are soon at loggerheads.

However, just when Rosie decides it's time to head back to reality, an old acquaintance suddenly reappears, and the prospect of life at the Lemon Tree Café begins to seem more appetizing . . .

Part One (A Cup of Ambition) is published as an ebook in March 2017 and is available for pre-order now!

To be followed by:
Part Two: A Storm in a Teacup
Part Three: Tea and Sympathy
Part Four: A Fresh Brew